She was standing naked . . .

The moonlight that had dominated this strange night flooded through Tesia's window and lit one side of her smooth young body. The image that struck John's awed eyes was of one smooth cheek, one shoulder, one round, pale breast, one gleaming hip and thigh.

"You too," she said. Her voice was hushed, neither brazen nor shy. John responded without thinking, and in another moment he was naked too.

They looked at each other happily. Then the several paces and the moonlight between them vanished, and they held each other, pressing their bodies and their mouths together, feeling the amazing touch of skin—and love . . .

THE WHITMARSH CHRONICLES, VOLUME II
A GENERATION UNTAMED

VOLUME II

The Whitmarsh Chronicles

A GENERATION UNTAMED

J. T. RICHARDS

A JOVE BOOK

Requests for permission to make copies of any part
of the work should be mailed to: Permissions,
Jove Publications, Inc., 200 Madison Avenue,
New York, NY 10016

First Jove edition published October 1981

First printing

Printed in the United States of America

Jove books are published by Jove Publications, Inc.,
200 Madison Avenue, New York, NY 10016

By J. T. Richards
from Jove

THE WHITMARSH CHRONICLES

VOLUME I: A GENERATION APART
VOLUME II: A GENERATION UNTAMED

To Suzanne

A GENERATION UNTAMED

Chapter One

No one paid him any notice.

What was there to notice? A tall kid, wearing a dirt-streaked, ill-fitting suit that was torn at the shoulder, a suit dug out of a dustbin. Carrying a carpetbag. Looking nonchalant, and a little lost.

Just another tramp, drifting into a hobo jungle. It was 1876, hundredth year of America's independence and fourth year of America's worst depression, and the country was full of tramps.

Still, there were a few things about him that were not run-of-the-mill. A closer look at the suit, for instance, would have shown that it was not a dustbin prize. It was dirty, yes, and torn, but the dirt was surface dirt, newly acquired, and the lining that showed at the torn shoulder was still white. The damage might have been done in the same mishap that had left fading bruises on his face. The fabric and the cut of the suit were of good quality and recent make.

The same could be said of the wearer. He was younger than he seemed at first glance. And his body was deceptive. It was tall and big-boned, giving an impression of strength. The suit that was too big for him hid his gangly thinness.

It was his face that showed his youth—and his quality. The jawline was strong, but the smooth, bruised skin had never been scraped by a razor. The features were fine— nose straight and thin, an angular, full-lipped mouth, a wide smooth forehead, hair that was dark and curled over his ears, eyes of a clear dark blue. But there was as yet no character to the face; the bone and muscle of his emerging strength was still covered with the padding of childhood.

The boy, in fact, was barely fifteen. His name was John Whitmarsh. Young John, he had been called at home, to distinguish him from his father who had the same name. But now his father was dead. They had called it suicide, but everyone knew who killed him, and why. It had happened just a week ago. He was the only John Whitmarsh now.

He did not know much about tramps, or being a tramp. He had read occasional items in the newspaper his father had published, and in the union journals that piled up around his father's office. He had formed in his mind romantic notions of unshaven men sitting around a comradely fire, cooking beans and coffee, playing the banjo and the mouth harp and singing songs of the road.

The camp he found was larger than he had imagined, and more crowded. There were thirty-five or forty people in all, John estimated. They were mostly men, but he saw some women too, and a few children. The camp was in a hollow below the railroad embankment, out of sight of the tracks. There were a dozen lean-tos scattered about, and a couple of makeshift shacks assembled from scavenged and improvised materials. The central shelter—around which the camp seemed to have sprung up—was an old boxcar, the litter of some long-forgotten wreck. It lay on its back, rusting underpinnings toward the sky, and its sides were battered.

A few men sat playing cards in the shade by the doorway of the inverted car. Another man sat cross-legged, hunched over a dog-eared newspaper which John recognized as a recent copy of his father's *Independence*. Some people were hanging wash on a line, and a woman tended a stew over a fire. It was a hot afternoon, and the atmosphere in the camp was listless.

John went over and squatted down at the edge of a small

group by the boxcar who were watching the card game. He slid his bag under him for a seat, and leaned his back against the weathered splintery wood of the car. Nobody paid much attention to him, and he was glad. He felt like a rube, and he wanted to blend in as unobtrusively as possible.

They were playing poker. The dealer was a beefy man, with a ruddy complexion, white hair to his shoulders, and a white mustache. His face was stubbled with a three-day growth of beard, but his mustache was neatly trimmed and trained upward at the corners. He wore a green velvet vest over his shirt-sleeves, adding a note of elegance to his dusty attire.

The dealer won the hand, and raked in the few coins that lay in the dirt. Then he turned suddenly and winked at John. "Now here's a lad that looks to know his way about," he said. His voice was a singsong caress, thickly Irish. "A travelin' lad by the cut o' him, with such a fine carpetbag and all. And a lad with a bit o' pocket money to be wagerin' on a game o' chance, if I be any judge. What d'ye say, young fellow?"

"I don't know," John mumbled, uncomfortable at having been singled out.

"Ah, t'be sure," boomed the Irishman. "It's much too uncertain a proposition to be gamblin' with strangers, for a fine young lad of sound intelligence, discretion, and the common sense he was born with. A game o' skill, perhaps?"

As he talked, he riffled through the cards. Three cards sprang from the deck, and fell face upward on the ground. They were the three of spades, the seven of clubs, and the jack of diamonds. The Irishman's fingers made a couple of passes over the cards. Then he scooped up the two black cards in one motion and threw them face down together, one on top of the other.

"Those two, me lad, ye need pay no mind, for they've nothin' to say t'ye. But this gentleman . . ." he flicked the jack of diamonds into the air, and then caught it, and held it out for John to see ". . . ah, now, this gentleman is the jack o' diamonds, the jack o' dreams, aye, he's the one to follow, for he'll lead ye to the pot o' gold at the end o' the rainbow just as sure as ever an Irish leprechaun.''

He threw the jack onto the ground, face up. Next to it he placed the three of spades and the seven of clubs, placing them so that each card slightly overlapped the card next to it. Then he flicked the jack so that all three cards tipped over.

''And it's spyin' is the name o' the game,'' he cooed. ''A simple game it is, a lovely game, and it's called Follow the Jack, it's called Jack to Win, it's called Sweet Mother o' God Smile on Your Eyes, Jack for the Jack . . .''

As his voice spun its silk his hands moved constantly over the cards, rearranging the order in which they lay. Every few moments he would turn over the jack of diamonds and display it to the onlookers. His hands flashed with a fluid speed, but each time he turned up the jack, it was where John thought it would be.

One of the poker players, a chinless, fortyish man in patched overalls, took a quarter from his pocket. ''He ain't so good,'' he whispered confidentially to John. ''I seen him do this. Watch.''

The Irishman placed the cards with a flourish. The chinless man tossed his quarter on the ground, and tapped a card confidently. John felt sure he was right. He would have picked the same card. The Irishman flicked the card over. It was the jack.

''There she be, jack for the jack,'' said the Irishman, sliding a quarter across the dirt to match the one that had been wagered. ''Ye win some, ye lose some.'' His eye caught John's, and twinkled. ''They say the hand is quicker than the eye, but is it now, is it? What about you, lad? Can ye follow Red Jack's trail? Can ye pick the jack, follow the jack, here he is, there he goes, here he comes again, follow him *now*?''

John's hands were already in his pocket, though he had not yet made up his mind to play. But his heart was pumping, and he slapped a quarter down and pointed to the center card.

"Begorra and ye've got me!"

"Give it up, Callahan," the chinless man laughed.

Callahan shot him a reproachful look. "Sure and a man needs time to get his fingers warm, Mr. Stebbins." His hands played over the cards again, and now his speed picked up. John fingered the cash in his trousers pocket. He had eleven dollars and thirty-five cents. Eleven sixty, with what he had just won. He would leave the ten dollar bill in his pocket and play with the rest. John felt a little sorry for Callahan. But after all, the man had asked him to play.

John bent over the cards. Concentrating fiercely, he no longer even heard the melodious brogue that floated over the Irishman's spread. It was a dollar a play soon, and the money in his hand multiplied to four dollars, then six. Then he started to lose, won again, lost again, and at last his stake shrank down to a single dollar. And then he lost that.

John was stunned. It had been so easy at first. Maybe he had been concentrating better in the beginning. He had only his ten dollars left now, and he was not going to risk that. Not on a game that had suddenly turned so baffling.

Stebbins was playing again, and John followed the game intently. Stebbins lost a couple, then won two in a row. He turned and grinned at John, sharing the relish of winning. John felt his excitement returning. And then, his eyes trained on the jack, he saw something that sent hot prickles the length of his body.

There was a tiny indentation near the corner of the card.

John looked sharply at Callahan. He did not seem to have noticed. He was spreading the cards around with the same crooning patter as before. John held his breath until the cards stopped moving and Stebbins made his play. With the dent on the back to follow, the cards might as well have been face up to anyone who knew the secret.

Stebbins chose wrong. He had not seen it.

John kept his hands in his pockets through another round, though part of him was screaming at himself to make his play before the dealer found the flaw. At the same time another voice in him told him it was wrong to take this kind of unfair advantage.

Heck, he told himself. *I didn't put it there.*

Again he knew beyond guessing where the jack lay. Stebbins threw five dollars down and made his choice. *Wrong*, John breathed. Callahan flipped over the three.

"Well, I'll be go to hell," Stebbins cursed, perplexed. "Cleans me. Son of a bitch," he muttered, shaking his head, and walked away.

"What about it, friends? Anybody else with a quick eye and a love o' wealth?" A crowd of about a dozen men had gathered by this time. The Irishman looked over at John again, his eyes merry. "Now what about you, me boyo? Sure and ye've got the feel for it back now. What d'ye say, lad?"

He went back into his routine again, weaving the cards one past the other, back and forth. John's eyes followed the dent like a mouse caught in the hypnotic pull of a snake's eyes. His hand went to his pocket and curled around the ten-dollar bill that nested in the bottom of it. He was thrilled and terrified.

The cards stopped.

Callahan looked straight into John's eyes, challenging. John gripped the bill. There would not likely be another chance. He drew the ten from his pocket and slapped it hard on the ground. The dent was in the center card.

"That one!"

The Irishman turned it over. It was the three of spades.

"Ah, 'tis a strange and a magical game, me boy," said Callahan, picking up John's ten dollar bill and pocketing it, along with the cards. "Like the game o' life itself."

John felt as if he had been kicked in the stomach. There was some laughter from the small crowd of onlookers. People started to drift away.

"Young John, is it?"

He whirled around, startled to hear his own name in this strange place. Behind him stood Walter Koch, a printer who had worked for his father at the *Independence*. John felt a rush of relief at the familiar face. But at the same time he was ashamed to have made a fool of himself in front of someone who knew him.

Callahan nodded in Koch's direction and turned to walk away.

"It is a pleasure to see you again, Ned," said Koch.

Callahan stopped and looked again.

"Walter!" he cried. "Faith, and it's me hardly knowin' ye after such a long time!"

"Four years," Koch said. "We spent a week traveling together through Illinois. Back at the start of the hard times . . . times you made much pleasanter, as I remember, with your unique gifts and delightful company."

John was amazed at the dignity and old world courtliness that marked this exchange in the middle of a hobo jungle. But Ned Callahan still had John's money in his pocket.

"This gentleman is Walter Koch," the Irishman announced. "A journeyman printer by trade, a son of Germany by birth, and a child of Israel by heritage. And a credit to all three. Well, and how've ye been keepin' your lovely self, Walter? Findin' any work at all?"

Koch nodded. "Until a week ago I was employed by a newspaper called the *Independence*."

"Ye don't say," Callahan exclaimed with interest. "That Whitmarsh fellow. And was it Franklin B. Gowen of the Reading had him killed, Walter, like they say?"

Koch nodded, glancing over at John.

"Ah." Callahan shook his head. "A fine man he was, John Whitmarsh, and his murder a tragedy for workingmen everywhere. My condolences, Walter. A loss to you, I'm sure."

John looked about him and saw the effect of his father's name on the tramps who were gathered, and his heart swelled with pride and grief. He began to cry. Walter Koch put an arm on his shoulder.

"A keener loss to some," he said very softly. "This is young John Whitmarsh."

Callahan looked from Koch to John, and then back to Koch again. "Is it, now?" He slipped his hand into his pocket, and drew it out again with the money he had won from John.

"A word of advice, lad," he said as he put the cash into the boy's hand and squeezed the hand closed. "Put the change in your pocket, but take the bills and pin them to your undergarments with a safety pin. That way they can't be stolen so easy . . . and they're a step further from temptation when ye come up against an unscrupulous rogue such as meself."

John took the money unwillingly. He felt more of a fool having it given back to him than he had in losing it.

"Sure, and we pulled a switch on ye, lad," said Callahan. "Would ye like to know where that red divil disappeared to?"

Faces around him grinned. Callahan reached an empty hand up to the side of John's head, circled his ear, and drew it back with the jack of diamonds between his fingers. The onlookers roared with laughter. John flushed with shame and anger.

"I should tell you something else about this young man," Walter Koch said. "He had the courage to stand up to Mr. Franklin Gowen, right in front of his own gun thugs and his Coal and Iron police, and accuse him of being the murdering scum that he is. And it is my guess that his was the hand that set the torch to the *Independence* building, cremating that great newspaper rather than seeing it fall into the hands of Gowen."

The laughter stopped. John listened, along with Callahan and the assembled tramps, while Walter Koch told the story. It was all true: how his father had been found hanged in the cell where Gowen had had him imprisoned on a patently false charge; how the authorities, under Gowen's direction, had called it suicide; how John had stood up in church at the funeral and denounced Gowen as a murderer, had escaped, and had later returned to smash the presses and burn the building of the *Independence* to keep it from passing into Franklin Gowen's control. It was true, it was what he had done, and still it sounded to John as if Koch was talking about someone else. He had never conceived of being the subject of a story told among strangers, and he listened, fascinated.

Chapter Two

He slept that night with a roof over his head, or rather a floor over his head, sleeping in the inverted boxcar. Walter Koch lay nearby, and beyond him Stebbins, stirring in his sleep and snoring in short, hiccupy bursts. On the far side the Irishman Ned Callahan slept deeply, trumpeting.

It was the first night John had spent in a four-walled shelter since he had left home nearly a week ago. It was the first night he had spent with human beings who knew his name and cared something about him. Walter Koch had made him at home here in this hobo jungle. In a way, that helped. But of course it was nothing like a home, and in another way it only sharpened his loneliness for the things he had lost.

But there was nothing to go back to. The house in Painter's Falls would be closed now, and his mother and sister and brother on their way to New York. Franklin Gowen did not want reminders of the martyred John Whitmarsh around to stir up trouble among the miners and workingmen of the Schuylkill Valley. So he was sending the Whitmarsh family to New York City. Helping them. "You'll want to get away from all these memories, Nancy," he had told the grieving widow. "It'll be too painful, staying here in Painter's Falls." Gowen had bought the house, to help them, just as he had bought the *Independence* to help them. He had promised to help them find housing and work and schooling in New York City.

Well, he hadn't got the *Independence*. And he hadn't got John.

It began to rain, a steady rain that rattled hollowly against the boxcar, and John was glad to be inside. Images of his father filled his mind as he drifted off to sleep.

It was a few days before Christmas, five years earlier. It had been snowing hard since the morning before; then this day, with thirteen inches of snow on the ground, the mercury had shot up into the forties. The sudden warmth had softened the dry white powder into good packing snow, and the children of Painter's Falls—the ones who did not have to work in the mines—celebrated it with a vengeance. They flung snowballs at each other. They divided into sides, built snow forts, and huddled behind them, raining hard-packed bombs of snow into the enemy stronghold.

Just before suppertime, Fannie and John built a snowman out in front of the kitchen window, while little Jamie toddled around squealing with delight.

The children were all in bed at eight o'clock when a loud knocking sounded at the door. John, half asleep, started upright in bed and listened. He heard the door opening, and a woman's voice: "Mr. Whitmarsh, there's been a cave-in at the mine!"

That was first. Only after that did he hear the sound of the alarm bell.

Crews of miners worked all night in shifts, trying to free the trapped men. There were seven of them. Water from the melting snow had triggered a flood, causing a cave-in at the tunnel where they were working.

Young John had sneaked out of his bedroom window and followed his father to the mine. His father went down the mine shaft to talk to the trapped miners. John waited in the dirty snow of the mine yard, at the edge of the anxious group of wives and miners keeping vigil.

"Nobody hurt, there's a wonder," he heard a woman near him say.

"Not yet," cautioned another voice, grim with worry.

"Don't even be talkin' like that!" reproved the first sharply. "Hail Mary, full of grace," she began reciting rapidly, "blessed be the fruit of thy womb . . ."

After a while another shift of diggers went down into the mine, and the shift that had been working came up. John's father came up with them, and John edged to the back of the crowd to avoid being seen. But his father went over to talk to the foreman. Then a little while later he went back down into the mine.

The people waiting clustered around the rescuers who had come up.

"How are they, then?"

"They're all right, they're all right."

"Praise God!"

"Is it the tunnel Jimmy was talkin' about last week?"

"Aye. Support timbers rotted away. It's like porridge."

"That tunnel ought've been closed. It's a shame!"

"Aye, we wanted to do that. The boss said no. Said fix it up. Fix it up! Small chance o' that."

"But they're all right, still. You can hear 'em?"

"Sure. Faith, they're singin'."

"Singin', are they?" There was laughter, relieved and proud.

" 'Eight hours,' they was singin' when we come up. P'rhaps when this is over we'll have a talk to the boss about them eight hours."

John knew the song. His father sang it sometimes.

It was a campaign song for an eight-hour workday. His father said Congress had passed it into law, but the mine owners didn't pay it any mind. John wondered how that could be, if it was law.

Hurrah, hurrah for labor, for it shall arise in might, It has filled the world with plenty, it shall fill the world with light . . .

*　　*　　*

John realized that he was singing it out loud. But some of the people standing near him heard, and picked it up.

> We want to feel the sunshine, and we want to smell the flowers,
> We are sure that God has willed it, and we mean to have eight hours!
> We are summoning our forces from the shipyard, mine, and mill—
> Eight hours for work, eight hours for sleep, eight hours for what we will . . .

Then the woman who was standing next to John gave a wail of anguish, and buried her face in her hands. The singing stopped. Everybody was tense suddenly, fearful. John had not heard anything. Everybody stared toward the entrance of the mine shaft. There was hardly any breathing.

The lift came up, and the rescue crew stepped out. John's father was with them. Their heads were bent. The woman next to John began to wail again, a high hopeless sound that cut through him to the soles of his feet.

His father talked to a few of the women. Then he saw John. He came over and stood looking down at him, but he did not scold. Instead he put an arm around his son's shoulder, and drew him close. John could smell the coal fumes on his father's coat.

"Let's go home," said his father.

Daylight was beginning, the leaden sky almost indistinguishable from the soot-stained snow. John's father put out his lantern as they walked back along the road.

"How come they couldn't fix it, Daddy?"

"What?"

"The tunnel. A man said the wood was rotten. He said the boss told them to fix it, and then he said small chance of that."

His father sighed. They walked along in silence for a few minutes, and for a while John thought he was not going to get an answer. Finally his father spoke.

"It's the system, John. The damned, vicious system.

These men don't get paid for the time they work. They get paid by the load of coal. That tunnel was so deep inside the mine that by the time they got to it, if they had stopped to rebuild the supports properly, they would never have gotten enough coal out of the ground to earn the day's pay they needed to feed their families."

"But that's not fair," John protested.

They did not speak again until they were nearly home. For a while, John could still hear the wailing of the women in front of the mine.

At the bottom of the hill below their house, his father suddenly and unexpectedly broke the silence.

"They spend their whole blasted lives working just to stay alive," he said. "Finally, they couldn't even get a decent shake on that. Poor bastards!"

It was the first time he had ever heard his father swear in front of him. It made him feel like a man.

John noticed something glinting in the wet morning grass outside the boxcar. It was a pair of glasses. He picked them up and wiped them on his sleeve.

"Mr. Stebbins," he said, "look. I found these."

"Let's see." Stebbis held them away from his face and squinted through the lenses. "Why, I b'lieve these must be Joe Grogan's. Ned?"

"Ho."

"Ain't these Joe's?"

Callahan took them and examined the thick glass. "Sure, and they must be. Who else would be wearin' lamps like these?"

"Say, Joe's left, ain't he? Didn't he head off yesterday mornin'?"

"I believe you're right," Callahan chuckled. "Now, there's a sorry picture for ye—Joe Grogan at large without his glasses! How d'ye suppose he ever made it out o' here?"

"Joe won a bottle of gin off'n a feller t'other evenin'. By the time he pulled out of here, he was blind with 'em or without 'em. He wouldn't of knowed the difference till he sobered up.'' Stebbins stood up, picked up his hat, and stuck the glasses in his overalls pocket. ''Best take 'em to him,'' he said, and strolled off.

John looked after him, surprised. ''Does he know where to find him?''

''Let me see, now,'' Callahan said. ''Seems to me Joe Grogan had been talkin' Ohio. It's a lovely place for trampin', Ohio.''

''Ohio? Gosh, that's a whole state . . .''

''Oh, he'll find him,'' Callahan assured him. ''There's tramps all over the land that know our Mr. Grogan. And if he's not in Ohio, there's bound to be someone knows where he's headed.''

''But . . . it could take him a long time . . .''

''Faith now, what's time to Delbert Stebbins? He's got no appointments he'll be after havin' to keep.''

''And it's true, Joe Grogan's lost without those glasses,'' said Koch with a smile.

''D'ye know Grogan, then?'' Callahan asked Koch.

''I spent two nights with him in jail, back in '74,'' Koch replied, chuckling at the memory. ''Poor Joe—I'm surprised he's kept his head this long, much less his glasses. Do you know that man lost his shoes in a six-by-eight cell? When it came time to let us out . . .''

Callahan roared with laughter.

John was amazed. There was so much for him to take in all at once. Sensitive, scholarly Walter Koch in jail—and laughing about it! Stebbins wandering off into nowhere without a second thought to find a friend and return his glasses, when all he knew was that the man might be somewhere in Ohio. And nobody else surprised in the slightest. It was all so wonderful. Why did men work their short lives away underground, when there was life like this to be lived?

''So, what will you be doing, Ned?''

''Ah, ye know me, Walter, livin' off the fat o' the land. And there's always folks willin' to part with a bit o' money for some illusion or other.''

John grinned. ''Like me, you mean.''

"Aye, lad," Callahan laughed, "that's the sort o' thing. When Stebbins . . . Faith, now, what am I goin' to do without old Stebbins? I'll be after needin' an apprentice now, won't I?"

"You'll remember, Ned," Koch warned, "that young John and I are traveling together, looking for work in the newspaper business."

"Ah, yes, of course," cooed Callahan. "I'd not be leadin' such a fine young lad down the daisy path into a life o' chicanery and deceit, would I now? Still, while we're all on the road, lookin' for opportunity of a decent sort to knock, well then . . ."

Koch looked at John, smiling. John nodded.

"Well, if he wants to, why not? It will be part of his education."

"Sure and it will," said Callahan with enthusiasm. "Well then, young John, we'd best begin with teachin' ye the ways o' subtlety. 'Tis a lesson ye surely need, after the way we nearly had to tear that poor jack to ribbons before ye noticed there was ought amiss!"

John's mouth opened in amazement. Callahan threw back his head and laughed, and even Walter Koch allowed himself a chuckle.

"Ah, ye thought ye were the sharp-eyed wonder, did ye, Johnny me boy? Well, there's plenty others thinks the same way. And they're fair game for thee and me now—eh, partner?"

Chapter Three

Fannie and Jamie were in the dray with the driver, waiting to go to the station. Nancy went back into the house to make one last tour, and Franklin Gowen followed her.

Nancy was afraid it would happen in the bedroom she had shared with John. She could not avoid passing through it, but she bustled through quickly, prattling the whole time, although she had been silent up until then. Her elbows flapped as she walked, and jutted out from her sides as if she were trying to turn her soft, plump body into something angular and bristling. Gowen, for whatever reason, left her alone.

It was after, in the boys' bedroom, that he took her.

She was neither unprepared nor ready for it. Franklin Gowen had not said, in so many words, that being his mistress was a part of accepting his help in starting a new life in New York; and so she had chosen not to think about it, although it was an unmistakable part of his understanding with her. Perhaps it was best not to think about it. It meant, among other things, that she did not have to think about Gowen wanting her because she was John Whitmarsh's wife.

And she did not have to think about her own sexuality; nor could she have. Nancy Ryan Whitmarsh had lived the last fifteen years of her life in a continuum of sexual arousal, sexual passion, sexual fulfillment, from the first time John Whitmarsh's smooth, aristocratic fingers had cupped her slim girl's buttocks to the last time, now a month past, that he had taken those solid, hefty cheeks in his broad and powerful hands and drawn them close to him as he entered her. She did not know that she had a sexuality of her own. It had always been theirs, a shared entity, for John as well as for her. And for all that Nancy knew or could imagine, there was no other sexuality than that which was theirs, which had enveloped them both.

Franklin Gowen directed her, not gently, down onto Jamie's bed, and uncovered her. Nancy felt remote—too remote to be shocked, or protesting, or afraid, or even embarrassed.

Gowen, however, did seem embarrassed at the sight of her round, white thighs glistening faintly with perspiration, the soft, limp hair the color of darkened flax at their center. He looked at the bunched black skirt and finally the bare mattress ticking. He turned away.

Nancy made no move to cover herself, neither by pulling her skirts back down nor by placing her hands over her sex. Her hands stayed at her sides. Franklin Gowen, his back to her, was taking off his coat and vest, and unbuttoning his trousers. He did not drop his trousers, though. He held them together with one hand when he turned around and walked toward her, shielding his private parts from her view. Nancy did not seem to care.

But she did.

Out of her remoteness, there began to swell an intense fascination. She was looking shamelessly at Gowen's stubby but powerful fingers, decked out with a heavy gold ring and a hard, glittering diamond, holding together the two unbuttoned flaps of his fly.

There was now more moisture between her thighs than just the perspiration from heavy black skirts and July weather. And pressure, coming from the center, that made her want to relax her stiff, locked knees and let her thighs spread apart just a little, just enough to make her feel less constricted.

The remoteness was gradually but inexorably becoming something else. Something entering her, like a foreign object, that she had never known as part of herself. Her sexuality.

She never did see Franklin Gowen's penis. He lay down between her legs before he uncovered himself. It felt different from John's, as he pushed and poked, directing the head of his penis with the sides of his fingers. But in another moment, she had stopped thinking about the difference, and was aware only of the urgency of her own reactions. Her hands still lay flat at her sides. But she twisted her pelvis to try and better line up her vaginal entrance with the angle of his butting penis, and when he finally penetrated between the outer folds of skin, she tightened her fingers into fists, and thrust hard, up into the pain that went with his entry and beyond it, to force penetration past the point of constriction, and to take his whole penis as deep into her as it would go.

She had never intended to put her arms around him; and she did not even notice that she had done it. She was not hugging him. She grabbed his waist, at the top of his buttocks, and squeezed as tightly as she could, pressing his pelvis against hers.

Her stomach was uncomfortable, with the lump of her rolled-up skirts pressing against it, and the hardness of Gowen's watch fob. Above that, he might as well not have existed. She could not feel his chest through her bulky clothes; he was up on his elbows, keeping his weight off her and his head raised above hers. Their faces were nowhere near each other. Nancy's was averted. She lay with her cheek pressed to the pillow. Her eyes were closed. Her mouth was open and stiff, except when she bit her lower lip.

But below her waist, she was alive, a different person. Her sex throbbed and burned with a sensation that was all its own, that belonged to and answered to no other part of her body, and certainly not to Gowen, though it was his job to fuel it and feed it.

She lunged at Gowen; she clutched at him. She thrust and rolled her hips and rubbed against him, moving in whatever way was necessary to make the pleasure keep building. Gowen was thrusting, too, but his movements were too leaden, too mechanical for Nancy, and she went beyond them; she overrode all his attempts to control. She pinioned his stout waist in her strong Irish hands, and bent him to her pace and her pleasure.

They both achieved orgasm at the same time, but that was just luck. Luck for Gowen. He rolled off her immediately, and sat on the other side of the bed with his back to her, buttoning himself up again. Nancy rolled over on her side, facing away from him. She felt the damp, bunched-up skirts pressing against her side, and smoothed them down to cover herself. She felt limp, and sad, and alone. And in her sadness, she thought, for the first time: *This man killed my husband.*

They did not speak at all during the ride to the station. Nancy did not look at Gowen, but she knew that he was glowering. She knew that she had overstepped the bounds that Gowen expected from a mistress, and she suspected that he would not want her anymore.

She guessed that was a good thing. She did not think she could let him touch her again, although she wondered how she and the children would get along. She had the address of the flat Gowen had arranged for them. She had the eight hundred dollars that Gowen had given her for the house and the printing press, and what little money John had saved: perhaps a thousand dollars in all. And she had the names of businessmen who Gowen had told her would help her find work, though she had doubts as to how much good that would do her now.

When they reached the station, Gowen did not get down from the brougham. They watched the driver unload the dray and carry the baggage to the train platform. Nancy thought that she should say something to him, but she did not know what. She waited for him to say something to her. Finally, they parted without either of them saying a word.

Chapter Four

They tramped the summer away, moving randomly through Pennsylvania, Ohio, Indiana, Illinois. Sometimes they worked, painting a fence, mending a barn. John and Koch continued to look for printers' jobs, but there were few to be found, and never two together. After a while John admitted to himself that he was just as glad.

He loved life on the road. He loved the freedom, and the constant newness of it. Home one day was a hayloft, the next the mossy bank of a creek. And the people he met—there was something to learn from everybody. A fellow from Texas taught him a little Spanish. In Indiana they met a man who had been president of a small bank, till the depression and a couple of larger banks had squeezed him into bankruptcy. He explained "Social Darwinism" to John, the economic survival-of-the-fittest philosophy that was the conscience of the industrial age. Another tramp showed him how to play the banjo.

From Ned Callahan he learned many things. He learned to shuffle a deck of cards with one hand and keep all four aces on the top. He learned how to eat well in a good restaurant and leave without paying the bill. He learned how to fast-talk a crowd, how to work the three-card monte game, how to hop on a moving freight. And he learned what a joyful thing life could be if a man looked for the joy in it.

Walter Koch kept an eye on John's traditional schooling. He talked history and philosophy as they stood in a soup kitchen line in Chicago, or lay down at night in a hay field outside of Altoona. When he could get hold of books he passed them along to John, and John read Plato and Dickens and Fenimore Cooper through flying cinders as they traveled on top of boxcars.

And Koch understood his moods, his sudden sadness or homesickness. He was John's only link to his past and his family. He became a father to him. Both men, Koch and Callahan, filled separate needs in the boy. For laughter and the gift of survival, John drew upon the Irishman; for patience and sensitivity and the tuning of his soul, he turned to Walter Koch.

Finally the warm weather was gone.

"There's them as opts for a small tweak o' the nose o' the law, just enough to warrant ninety days in a warm cozy cell to last out the winter," Callahan observed. "But for meself, I prefer the open air of the sunny South, where a man can earn a fair and decent livin' hoodwinkin' honest, hardworkin' citizens."

"Yes," said Koch, "and where the railroad bulls will make short work of a tramp when the spirit moves them."

"Aye, there's that," Callahan said, his eyes darkening. But then they twinkled again. "Sure, and there's hazards on the road wherever ye wander."

"Besides which," Koch added, "I seem to remember you've a fondness for the Southern racetracks."

"Ah, they've _lovely_ racetracks, Walter darlin'."

"And the girls?" John asked.

"Will ye listen to this one now! Surely he's the age for it, and so handsome he'll be beatin' them off with a stick." John grinned. "Well now, as to the ladies, me boy, ye'll nivver see fairer. Southern belles they are, and the very heat o' the equator sizzlin' their blood beneath that dainty powder."

And so they moved South.

"What d'ye think?"
John sat up. He had been sleeping in the sun, and

everything was brightness and blurred silhouette when he first opened his eyes. Then they adjusted, and he made out Callahan. Callahan was standing with a wagon, and there was a horse hitched to it.

"Where'd you get that?"

"I had a bit o' luck at poker last night."

"Terrific!"

Walter Koch was less enthusiastic. "What on earth are we going to do with a horse and wagon? That nag doesn't look fit to travel very far." The horse was swaybacked, heavy-footed, with long yellow teeth and one cloudy eye. The wagon looked in slightly better shape.

"Sure, and it's not much we'll be askin' o' the poor beast. Just up to Nashville. I've the makin's of an idea. But before we take our leave o' Memphis, we've a little job o' scavengin' to do."

Koch looked at him suspiciously. "Scavenging? For what?"

"Soap, Walter. Soap."

It was February, and they were gradually beginning to work their way north after a winter of traveling through the Deep South. It was sunny and springlike weather now. In Pennsylvania this weather would not come for two more months. That made it even more enjoyable—the warmth and the good fresh smells, plus the feeling that you were getting a bonus; getting something for nothing.

Late in the afternoon they camped about five miles outside of Nashville. Callahan sent Koch ahead into town so that he would already be there when they arrived the next day.

"You're to be my man in the crowd, Walter."

"What do I do?"

"There's nothin' to it," Callahan cooed. "When I start sellin', you start the buyin'."

"And what are we selling?"

"Soap, Walter. Soap."

Grumbling, Koch headed into Nashville. Callahan turned to John. "Roll up your sleeves, lad. Time to get to work."

"Okay. What do we do?"

"You will begin by takin' off that axle casin' there on the hub o' that wheel. I shall occupy meself with supervisin'."

John removed the casing. "Ugh—look at that grease!"

"It's more than lookin' at it ye've got in store, me boyo."

It took John till dusk, with sand and a soft rag, to finish cleaning the thick black grease from the trap of the axle casing.

"I'll inspect it in the mornin' by God's sweet daylight," said Callahan. He lay down by the campfire and closed his eyes.

In the morning, Callahan found a couple of spots John had missed, and set him back to work again. When he had finally finished, and the grease trap was clean, gleaming metal, he came over to where Callahan was sitting stirring something in the cookpot over the fire.

"What's that?" John asked, sniffing.

"It ain't your lunch, Johnny boy."

"Smells like soap."

"Ye've a nose as keen as your wit."

"All that soap we picked up in Memphis?"

"That's me boy."

It was liquid now, white and bubbling. Callahan used his hat as a potholder and carried the pot over to the wagon. He had rigged up a large square frame in the flat bed of the wagon. He poured the white liquid into the frame.

"We'll leave that to cool. And now . . ." He reached under the seat and produced a still-wrapped bar of Grandpa's Tar Soap, a heavy-duty black industrial soap. It too was melted over the fire. But this time the sticky black result was poured into the shining grease trap of the axle casing. John watched, bemused.

"Now ye can put it back on the wagon."

"Will it work?"

Callahan beamed. "It'll work just fine."

John replaced the axle casing. Callahan sharpened his

penknife and cut the solidified white soap into neat one-inch cubes. Then they hitched the horse to the wagon and drove on into Nashville.

Callahan pulled up the wagon in a vacant lot on a street corner that was close enough to the marketplace to draw a good crowd, but far enough from the police station for comfort.

"All right, Johnny," he said. "Take out your banjo and do your stuff."

John had mastered four songs: "Turkey in the Straw," "Old Zip Coon," "Weevily Wheat," and "Rosin the Bow." He sang and played them all, and between songs Callahan started barking up a crowd.

People began to gather around. John saw Walter Koch in the crowd, but he knew enough not to pay any attention to him. He saw a pretty girl nearby. She was dark-haired, slim, about seventeen. He played to her. She watched him demurely but admiringly, and she moved a little closer to the wagon as he played.

Callahan began his pitch as John finished.

"Now friends, we've come here for to entertain ye, and we've come for to help ye as well. I bring with me to your lovely city the most amazin' discovery in the history o' man's civilizin' battle against the dirt and grime o' the ages . . . Doctor Callahan's Incredible Soap Cubes!"

"Yeah, what does an Irishman know about gittin' clean?" a voice jeered from the crowd.

"Bejabbers, and when an Irishman decides to get clean, it *takes* a miracle to do the job," Callahan shot back, and the crowd rocked with laughter. "And 'tis just such a miracle that I bring to the people o' Nashville this fine day. As sure as Saint Paddy drove the snakes out of Ireland, just one o' these Doc Callahan's cubes in the family washtub . . ."

He had placed the soap cubes in a tin box. He took one out and held it up between thumb and forefinger, and the crowd pressed forward with curiosity and amusement.

The girl had arrived at the side of the wagon. As

Callahan talked on, John slid over to where she was standing. "Hello," he said.

Her eyes dropped away, then came back up to his more boldly. "My name's Connie," she said. "You surely do play nice."

"Thanks. My name's John."

"I'm delighted to make your acquaintance." She held out a soft white hand. John took it, realizing as he did how brown and rough his own had grown. The touch of her hand completed an electric circuit in him that began with the contact of her wide green eyes.

"I'm delighted to make yours," he said, grinning foolishly.

"John! Johnny lad!" He turned to see Callahan holding out a bucket toward him, with a look of amusement on his face. "My young comrade is sellin' somethin' of his own, it appears. Now then, lad, if ye'll fetch us a bucket o' water from yonder pump . . ."

John glanced back over his shoulder at Connie, and ran to fill the bucket.

"Now, I'd not expect ye to take my word," Callahan went on. " 'Tis a skeptical age, and seein' is believin' —and it's believers we'll be makin' of ye, nothin' less. Ah, here's the lad. Fine, pure Nashville water." He scooped out a handful and drank it, smacking his lips with satisfaction. "And there's your first miracle, an Irishman drinkin' water," he said with a wink to the crowd. "But it's to prove the point of its purity. But now for the proof o' this washtub phenomenon . . . does anyone have a handkerchief? A clean, white handkerchief?"

He took one from a stout lady who was standing in front of him, and held it up to show the crowd. "As fine and dainty a bit o' linen as ye'd care to see. I shudder to think o' the test we must put it to! Now John—would ye mind slippin' down and removin' the axle casin' off o' one o' them wheels."

John dropped down to the wheel where Connie was standing. She stepped back holding her skirts as he crouched down, and he could see her foot and a glimpse of white

ankle. As his hand closed on the axle casing he heard a
loud alarmed coughing from Callahan.

Oh, my God . . . "Uh, this one's kinda stuck," John
muttered, and moved quickly to the front wheel to pull off
the casing they had prepared. He handed it up to Callahan,
who shot him a heavy look.

Callahan displayed the grease trap to the audience with a
look of distaste. "Have ye ever seen such vile filth?" he
sang out. There was a gasp of dismay from the lady in
front of him. "Fear not, madam, if our little experiment
should fail it's me'll buy a dozen white hankies—watch
this!"

And he plunged the lace-trimmed linen into the grease
trap.

It came out dripping and black. "Oh no!" wailed the
stout woman, and there were mutterings of angry sympathy from the people around her.

"Now, now, friends, remember my guarantee. But first
be lettin' me finish me little experiment. As ye observe, I
now drop one single Doctor Callahan's Incredible Soap
Cube into this pure water from which I meself have drunk
only seconds previously . . . and we shall see the effect it
has on this foul, greasy handkerchief!"

He thrust the blackened handkerchief into the pail of
water, swirled it around a half dozen times, and brought it
out again. It was completely clean. A gasp went up.

"Yes, friends, seein' *is* believin'. And today, for just
fifty cents the cube, two for a dollar, while they last, a
lucky few will be able to purchase . . ."

"I'll take two!" It was Walter Koch stepping forward
with a greenback dollar bill in his hand. A moment later
people were pushing and shoving around the wagon, clam-
oring to buy the wonder cleanser.

To his dismay, John saw that Connie was among them.
He started to warn her, but he felt a hand tug at his elbow.
He turned around. It was Koch, shaking his head imper-
ceptibly.

*   *   *

"And now where to?" asked Koch.

"Across town to the racetrack," said Callahan, "where we'll sell the horse and the wagon. Where else can ye find such a group o' such poor judges o' horseflesh?"

By the end of the day they had almost a hundred and fifty dollars. They went to the barbershop. Callahan and Koch had a haircut and a shave, John had a haircut. They bought new clothes, and John had his father's suit cleaned and mended. They ate a huge dinner at a fine restaurant, and paid for it. ("Always pay, lad, when ye've got the money, and tip handsomely. They'll think the world o' ye, and it sets 'em up for the next time when ye're broke and have to work a scam.") They slept that night in a suite in Nashville's best hotel.

"Pretty girl, that one this afternoon," said Koch as they bedded down. John and Walter Koch shared one bedroom of the suite, and Callahan took the other. Callahan had a woman with him. They could hear laughter through the two closed doors.

"Yeah," John said. He made his voice noncommittal. But he could still remember the feeling when she had touched his hand. Girls as an attraction were a new concept to John, and the experience had left him confused and excited.

Koch, as usual, understood. "It is one of life's great mysteries, the importance those wonderful creatures suddenly assume. For years, they seem to be nothing more than a nuisance. Then suddenly one day you look into a pair of eyes—big, soft eyes—and it turns everything upside down. Isn't it so?"

John lay on his back in the darkness, with his arms tucked behind his head. With the lights off it was easier to talk about it.

"Yeah," he said. "It was funny . . . I never had a girl look at me like that before . . . ."

Walter Koch laughed softly. "You will, young John." There was love and nostalgia in his voice. "It will happen to you more and more. You are a handsome boy, and the girls like that. And you are a decent boy, and sometimes they like that and sometimes they don't. But you would be better not to change. It is not so satisfying."

"How do you mean?"

"Oh . . . for instance, that girl this afternoon . . . the pretty one . . ."

"Connie?"

"Connie, yes. It would have been nice to go walking with her, yes? To kiss her, perhaps?"

"I don't know . . ." In fact, he had hardly thought of anything else.

"But you did not do it. I wonder why—because you were bashful? But not only that. Because we had cheated her. Not such a terrible thing, I hope, and the stakes were small. But after that . . ."

John giggled. "Yeah, I couldn't just turn around and . . ."

"Ned could have."

"What do you mean?"

"Ned could have done it. Sold a bill of goods to a dainty little lady, and romanced her right afterward with his blarney." As if to underline, there was a peal of feminine laughter from across the way, and John felt it tug at his groin. Walter Koch chuckled wryly in the darkness. "I'm not saying anything against Ned. He's my friend, and he's provided well for us. But it is another part of life on the road, young John. It's another side of the sharper's life. And you know, you really can't play Ned's games with those nice young maidens who take a shine to you—and there will be plenty, I promise you. It's a different thing with the grass widows who know which side of the tree the moss grows on."

John did not say anything.

"Well, good night, young John."

"Good night, Walter."

"Walter?" he said, a few minutes later.

"Yes?"

"I haven't forgotten my father. And I haven't forgotten the things he fought for. I know it's not Commodore Vanderbilt we're hoodwinking with Ned's tricks."

"No," said Koch. "I didn't suppose you had, young John."

Soon Koch was breathing deeply. John was nowhere near sleep. He lay in bed looking up at the ceiling, thinking about Connie. Walter was right, of course. If a man was honorable, he couldn't go taking advantage of innocent girls like Connie. Anyway, you didn't really want to, not with a girl like that. You wanted to protect her, and be near her, but not . . .

Squeals and muffled giggles penetrated again from Callahan's room. Callahan had offered to set John up with a woman too, but John had turned him down. He had been embarrassed and scared, so he had said he wasn't interested. Callahan had laughed. Now John cursed himself for his lack of courage. The female sounds drove right through him, and his penis was hard and throbbing, standing erect beneath the sheet and comforter like a tent pole.

With a woman like that, there would be no guilt. That was a whole different thing from a girl like Connie . . .

He was feeling hot. He kicked off the covers and sat up in bed. He slept without a nightshirt. His penis was dancing with painful stiffness. Suddenly the doorlatch clicked and a faint beam of light fell across the room and onto John's bed. He grabbed his erection in panic and hid it between his thighs.

"Are ye awake then, Johnny?"

"Yeah." His voice was a ragged whisper, forced casualness.

"Come in and join us, lad. We've a bottle to share."

"I, uh . . . I was just getting ready to fall asleep . . ."

"Ah, come on now, Johnny!" Callahan was merry and cajoling. "The night's young for a young fellow like yourself."

"Well . . . okay. Let me get my pants on."

"That's a good idea, John. Get 'em on and come on over."

Callahan was fully dressed, in pants and shirt, vest and necktie. His feet were bare, but he was wearing his hat.

His cheeks and nose glowed with a cherry light, and his eyes were glistening with fun.

The woman wore a sheet wrapped about her like a cloak. As far as John could tell, that was all she had on. What seemed as if they must be all of her clothes were strewn around the room. Her drawers, bright red silk trimmed with lace and bows, were draped around the lamp chimney, casting the room in a reddish light. The woman was not pretty, but she was nice looking. She had a round, rabbity face, with large and slightly protruding front teeth, and happy eyes. Her neck came softly out to meet her chin in what was not quite a double chin, but was a long way from lean. Her hair had been up in a plump ring on top of her head, but most of the pins had been removed, and it now tumbled in loose resin-colored corkscrew locks down around the white bedsheet that she held at her shoulders.

"Allow me to introduce Miss Vanity Fair," said Callahan grandly.

"Vennie, silly," she giggled. "Vennie Ferris." She smiled at John. "It's short for Venelia, but I don't like Venelia. What do y'all think, honey? You think it's pretty?"

"Sure."

"I don't. I like Vennie. I think it suits me." She went into another fit of giggles, and Callahan joined her, his laughter low and chuckling. John laughed too, though he was not sure why. He was very nervous.

"Ain't he silly?" she said to John. She was about thirty, he guessed. She crossed her legs, and he could see one of them bare, all the way up to the knee and a little beyond. "Oh, he makes me laugh!" She saw John looking at her exposed leg, and she smiled delightedly. "I like your friend," she said to Callahan.

"Well, he's a likable young man!"

"And a friendly young man!" She giggled, and John, mortified, realized that her eyes were fixed on the fly on his trousers, which was jutting unmistakably out. He shoved his hands in his pockets and tried to hold himself back. Vennie squealed with laughter.

"Oh! Bejeezus," Callahan exclaimed, "I do believe

this bottle o' whiskey has breathed its last. If ye'll excuse me, I'll just see what I can turn up with a little bit o' foragin' downstairs.''

Before John could think of anything to say, Callahan was out the door. John looked back to the woman sitting on the bed. She was smiling at him expectantly.

"Come on over here, honey," she said. There was still a lilt of laughter in her voice, but there was sex in it now too. "Come on over. An' let go that thing—y'all don't want to choke it to death now, do you? Come on . . .''

John did not think his brain had sent any signal to his legs, but they began moving, and he found himself standing in front of her. She looked up at him, and slowly spread the bedsheet away from her body.

Everything was there. It was as he had always imagined it—breasts, belly, triangle of hair, thighs—but infinitely more powerful in the reality.

"Go ahead, honey," Vennie said encouragingly, "have a good look.''

He could not have torn his eyes away. Her breasts were large, with a heavy roundness at the bottom as if they were full of water. They sagged slightly to the sides, pushing out pinkish brown nipples as big as the end joints of thumbs. Her body was sturdy and solid, wide-hipped, tight-skinned, bulging in a fleshy shelf from the navel down to the limp cornsilk hair where her belly and thighs came together. Her thighs were slightly parted, but the low point of the pubic triangle disappeared in tantalizing shadow.

She had begun unbuttoning his pants. His body, still refusing any authority from his brain, remained motionless.

"Oh my, honey," she said in a pleased voice. "Y'all most surely are friendly!''

His pants dropped around his ankles. She kissed the end of his penis, and then slid her lips over it. The sensation was stunning—warm, and moist, and of a startling smoothness. A moan wrenched from his throat. She heard it and chuckled, and the chuckle vibrated him like a lightning rod. Her hands clasped his buttocks, her fingers nestling into the crease, and she pulled him deeper into her mouth.

A desperate wave began to build inside him, pulling at his knees and chest and belly, and he tried to twist and squirm, but she held him fast. Suddenly it all whirled together at his loins, his hips bucked, and he felt himself twitching and spurting, as his voice cracked in short, gasping cries and the woman held him tight, with her face pressed close against his belly.

After a while she leaned back on her elbows. "Some gals won't do that," she said. "Some gals won't do that at all. I won't do it, most of the time. But y'all are nice. First time, huh?"

John's head nodded. Vennie smiled.

"First time. That's nice. That's what your friend said. A virgin. Well, now, that's nice. Makes it kinda special."

"I . . . that was really . . ."

"Sure honey, I know. But say now, that ain't the whole thing. Y'all are still a virgin. We ain't done yet, not by a mile. That was just warm-up." She reached out and took hold of him with her hand. "I don't think we'll have to wait too long at all," she said.

She pulled him over to the bed. He stumbled over the shackles of his trousers around his ankles, and kicked them away. Vennie was cooing softly, as she guided him down on top of her, between her plump thighs. He was fully engorged again, and he butted at her with a wild, blind urgency.

"Now, now, honey," she said, "slow down. It ain't goin' anywheres."

She found him with her fingers and guided him to the right spot. He thrust again, and suddenly there was no resistance, and he glided in.

The next day they went back to the racetrack, where Callahan fell under the spell of a four-year-old chestnut gelding.

" 'Tis the configuration," he said. "Ye can always tell by the configuration. He's the shoulders and withers of Ten Broeck, or I'm a Welshman!"

That evening, with their money gone but their spirits

high, they headed for the railroad yards to leave Nashville on a boxcar. They hid out of sight until a train began to roll out of the yard, and then they raced to intercept it. They were fifteen feet from the train when their way was blocked by two burly railroad bulls. One had a length of pipe in his hand. The other had a revolver.

"Hold it right there," drawled the one with the revolver. "You're under arrest for vagrancy."

"Vagrancy, is it!" chuckled Callahan under his breath. "And us rich men this very mornin'!"

"Yeah, that's right," said John, out of breath and still too exhilarated to be really afraid. "If they could have seen us last night at the Regency Hotel . . ."

"Shut up, kid," growled the other man. "Don't give us none a yore bullshit."

He brought the lead pipe up sharply into John's chest. John staggered backward a couple of steps, but he kept his footing.

"Leave the boy alone," said Walter Koch. "He hasn't done anything."

"Oh, leave the boy alone, eh?" jeered the guard, mocking Koch with a nasal, mincing voice. "He hasn't done anything, eh? Trespassing on railroad property? Vagrancy? Leave the boy alone . . . leave the boy alone . . ."

With each sentence he gave John another hard poke in the chest or stomach with the lead pipe. John did not cry out, though he was afraid one of his ribs might have been cracked, and the last blow caught him in the pit of his stomach and made him want to retch.

Koch stepped between John and the detective.

"That's enough," he said. "That's not necessary. You don't have to do that."

The railroad bull leered at Koch, his eyes blazing.

"Y'all tryin' to start somethin' with me, old man?"

Koch shook his head.

"Y'all tryin to start somethin' with me, hey? Y'all tryin' to . . . Yankee scum!"

And without warning, he brought the lead pipe around

in a short, vicious arc, swinging with both arms, to the side of Walter Koch's skull.

John heard the awful crunching sound, and closed his eyes in the same moment. He did not see the impact, but he felt something splatter across his face and chest.

He dropped to the ground in a sitting position. He did not open his eyes. But a droplet trickled down his cheek to his chin, and hung there. He could feel it every inch of the way. It left an itchy trail behind it. He knew it was blood. Not his blood.

He could not lift his hand to wipe it away.

He opened his eyes and his mouth at the same time. In that instant, he saw Koch's lifeless body lying twisted on the ground, one side of the gentle face gone, less than a foot away from him. Then his eyes clouded over, and everything came out of him.

He could not move. He sat still, covered with vomit, and blood, and hair, and pieces of skull—just as if he were the one who had been killed.

But he was still alive, and he was dragged roughly to his feet by the railroad detectives, tossed in the back of a wagon, and driven to jail.

He spent the night in a cell with Callahan and a half dozen other tramps. John was still in a state of shock. He swung between silence, bitter weeping, and passionate demands for justice. He would speak up in court tomorrow, he would see that the judge got those detectives punished for what they'd done.

But the older tramps shook their heads. "No, Johnny," Callahan said sorrowfully. "The judge knows all about it. 'Tis not so uncommon as ye might think. 'One tramp less,' that's the way they size it up, and no tears shed by the 'decent' folk."

In the morning they were brought before a justice. Neither John nor Callahan spoke. Callahan was sentenced to ninety days at hard labor in the Nashville Penitentiary for vagrancy. John, because of his youth, was ordered to leave town and never set foot in Nashville again.

He was taken to the edge of town and dropped off on

the road. He had his carpetbag, but his banjo was gone. He wore the same foul, stinking clothes in which he had been arrested. He had no idea where he was going, or what he was going to do.

He began to think about his father, and Pennsylvania. There was still no clear idea in his mind of what he was going to do, but he sensed that it was time that he started growing up. He picked up his bag and began to walk.

Chapter Five

Nancy Whitmarsh had become the mistress of a gambler. His name was Heywood Catlett. Nancy liked him because he was free and easy, high-spirited and fun. With him she became free and easy too. She lived in the present, doing and thinking things that she had never dared with her husband. John's thoughts had been serious and important. She had loved him completely, but she had been intimidated too, by his mind and his sense of purpose. This intimidation had become a more or less unconscious thing over the years, so that it came to seem the way she really was.

But now Nancy became high-spirited. She had a new glow in her cheeks, and a new sparkle in her eyes. She had learned a new way of laughing, and she was pleasurably aware of the way it made her large bosom heave in the open-bodiced dress that Catlett had bought her for their evening casino forays. She was having fun. She felt young again, and looked younger too, less than her thirty-five years. Her new life was more exciting, more thrilling, than she could ever have imagined life to be.

Catlett was in his mid-forties. He was an immense, powerfully built man who had been a professional prize-fighter when he was younger. Now he was a full-time gambler; but though he had put on thirty pounds over his fighting weight, he was still a man to be reckoned with when he used his fists. He worked as a bouncer when he was down on his luck and needed a bankroll. And when his luck was running high he was an ebullient figure, generous with his money and his laughter, a well-known and popular character on the New York gambling scene.

Until she met Catlett, Nancy had not been with a man since she had come to New York seven months before. Sometimes in the middle of the night Jamie would have a nightmare and come and crawl in bed with her. Nancy would put her arm around him and comfort him until he went back to sleep. She liked that, just having a warm body to cuddle up to. But it was no substitute for a man. Nancy was not a woman who thrived on being alone.

Nancy, Fannie, and Jamie lived in a tenement on North Moore Street. It was clean, and not too overcrowded. Her apartment even had two tiny bedrooms—one for her, and one for the children. It was the apartment that Franklin Gowen had arranged for her. And her job, too, as an assistant in a photographer's studio, had come through one of Gowen's references. But she had never heard from Gowen, or seen him, since he had put them on the train in Painter's Falls.

She met Catlett at work when he came in to sit for a photographic portrait. He was looking his best, in a fine broadcloth suit, a bowler hat, and a huge diamond stick-pin. He caught her looking at him with admiration, and he grinned. She blushed and looked away, busying herself with cleaning photographic plates. When he came back to pick up the finished portrait, he invited her to go to Henderson's with him.

"Henderson's?" She had heard of the place. "Isn't that a gambling casino?"

He laughed, loudly and good-naturedly, at the shock in her voice. "You're from out of town, aren't you?"

"Yes," she said, a bit defensively. "But I've lived in New York City for seven months."

"Not long enough to know your way around. You'll need a gentleman to show you the sights. Starting with Henderson's. Tonight. And don't worry—everyone in New York gambles. Even the high-toned ladies."

"Really, Mr. Catlett, it's impossible! I don't even have anything to wear. I . . ."

"Don't worry about that. Where do you live?"

"At 18 North Moore Street. But you can't come there! I have children . . . That is, I'm a widow . . ."

He laughed again. "I'm sure you are," he said. "Meet me in front of your building then. Tonight. At nine o'clock, sharp."

"I don't know . . ." Nancy began helplessly. Catlett grinned, turned on his heel, and strode out.

Before she left work that afternoon Nancy received a package. It was from Heywood Catlett. Her employer, a dour German, would never have countenanced her stopping to open it on the job. He made it clear, in fact, that he strongly disapproved of such a breach of employee decorum as receiving a package at work at all.

Jobs were hard to come by, and Nancy was properly chastised. She was furious that this stranger, this gambler, should have jeopardized her position so brazenly. And she was thrilled to the point where she could hardly concentrate on the plates she was treating. She carried the package home with her and took it straight to her own room to open it.

It was a ready-made dress. It was not really expensive, but to Nancy it was opulent beyond anything she had ever dreamed of owning—and daring beyond anything she had dreamed of wearing. The dress was a deep wine color, a heavy velvet lined in satin, and cut so low in the front that it made her dizzy. She put it on and then took it off quickly. She could not possibly wear it, or go out with this man. She did notice that it fit her perfectly. She reflected that this Haywood Catlett seemed to have a good—and no doubt experienced—eye for women's figures.

She went back into the kitchen, where Fannie was cooking supper. She poured herself a glass of wine and went and sat at the kitchen table. Jamie came and sat down across from her.

"Have you done your homework?" she asked him.

Jamie nodded.

"Mummy has to go out tonight," she said.

Jamie looked up, indignant. "How come?" he demanded.

"An . . . an appointment." She looked up at Fannie. Fannie was smiling.

"Hush up, Jamie," said Fannie. "Eat your supper."

After that there was no more conversation, and at the stroke of nine Nancy was out in front of her building, wearing her new dress and the largest, heaviest shawl she could find, as much to hide under as to protect her from the cold. Catlett was waiting for her in a hansom.

They went to Henderson's establishment at 5 West Twenty-fourth Street, off Madison Square. The splendor of it took Nancy's breath away—the immense ballroom, turned into a casino, with its colorful clicking roulette wheels and green felt tablecloths, its faro and poker tables with nimble-fingered dealers and more money crossing the table at a single turn of the cards or spin of the wheel than she had ever seen. And the sumptuous banquet table, and the flowing champagne, and the expensive dress, some elegant and some flash, of the men and women there. Her new gown, she now realized, was really quite modest and conservative in comparison with some of the others.

But it was Catlett himself who most took her breath away. She could scarcely take her eyes off him. His face was large, red, and powerful. There was a shiny scar above his left eyebrow, and a huge handlebar mustache that drooped down to his wide jawline. His nose was flat and crooked from having been broken, but that only added to the rugged grandeur of his appearance. His eyes twinkled with humor, but Nancy could see ferocity in them too. It both scared and excited her. Just looking at him made Nancy tingle all over, and she knew that he was what had been missing from her life.

Catlett took Nancy over to introduce her to a man who stood by the bar.

"Mrs. Whitmarsh, this is Bill Henderson, the proprietor of this here establishment. Henderson, meet Mrs. Whitmarsh. Mrs. Whitmarsh is my personal guest."

"Delighted, Mrs. Whitmarsh."

Henderson was as big as Catlett; a little fleshier, but as powerful. He had a presence that was even more commanding than Catlett's; and it seemed to Nancy that Catlett, when he talked to Henderson, puffed himself up and adopted a posture of manufactured self-importance that was strangely at odds with his naturally self-confident bearing. Henderson, for his part, might have been just a little condescending to Catlett.

They moved away, but Heywood Catlett kept his eye on Henderson until he saw him call an assistant over, nod in their direction, and say a few words.

Catlett told Nancy, "I wanted to make sure he knew you were with me. Now you'll be able to gamble on the square."

"What?" Nancy exclaimed. "Aren't the gambling games here honest?"

"Not so loud!" Catlett flashed her a warning stare, and she looked apologetic. He patted her arm reassuringly. "Honest? Not bloody likely. He's in this for the money, ain't he, just like everybody else? But he won't cheat a friend, Henderson won't. He's square that way. I can gamble here all I want without having the tables turned against me. Well, the fact is, I'm pretty well known all over town. Everybody gives Heywood Catlett a fair play. And you don't have to worry about a thing neither, as long as you're with me."

"Oh, I couldn't gamble!"

"Maybe you need to get used to the place first. Here, this'll help."

He took two glasses of champagne off the tray of a passing waiter, and handed one to Nancy. She accepted it, took a tentative sip, and then drained the glass. Catlett laughed, tossed his off as well, and commandeered two more glasses.

"I fought Henderson back in '56," he said.

"Oh? Was Mr. Henderson a prizefighter too?"

"Was he?" Catlett chuckled ironically at her ignorance. "He was only the heavyweight champion! He beat Yankee Sullivan in twenty-six rounds, then he whipped Heenan for the championship. I fought him six months before he fought Sullivan. I went forty-five rounds with him, and I'll tell you he knew he'd been in a fight. I damn near whipped him, too." Catlett made a fist and looked down at his splayed knuckles approvingly. "And I sure as hell could've taken those plugs, Heenan and Sullivan. It was the purse from the Heenan fight that got Henderson his start. Bought his first casino down on Broadway with the money." Catlett struck his open left palm hard with his right fist. Then he laughed, and looked down at Nancy. "I've got a room upstairs," he said.

The champagne had gone to Nancy's head. Her eyes met Catlett's, and she could not disguise the desire in them. Her body tingled and glowed as she felt the squeeze of his powerful hand about her waist, and he led her out of the gambling room, away from the glittering chandeliers, away from the dizzying excitement of millionaires and roulette wheels and impossible sums of money drifting across tables like milkweed seeds in the wind.

The money was too vast to be real to Nancy. The male smell of Catlett was much realer, and made her even dizzier. So was the heat that she could feel from his body as they mounted the back steps, and she moved closer to him, walking as close as their clothing and the motion of their hips would permit. Catlett took the steps with a swift, impatient stride, so that Nancy had to scurry to keep up with him; but he could not have gone too fast for her.

*   *   *

He took her all at once. She felt her body engulfed by him. In one motion he went from being a provocative, thrilling intruder to the center of her universe. He mashed her body, and she pressed closer to be mashed more. Her face was buried in his shoulder. When she opened her mouth to cry out she found it filled with his flesh, and she closed her teeth on it, hard and passionately. He gave a grunt of pleasure, and bit her in return, in the hollow where her shoulder and her neck came together. It might have been painful; she could not tell. She was beyond distinguishing between pleasure and pain. It was all sensation. It was all him.

Nancy was beginning a rapid rush toward orgasm that started on a plateau of sensation that made her body tremble, and ended at a peak somewhere between feeling and numbness. And then that exploded, and she floated around, and came back to another explosion, this time together with his climax.

Nancy felt as if a warm, fecund, earthly paradise had suddenly opened up and let her in. She felt completely at home in it. She did not mind Catlett's brusqueness afterward, or the fact that he would not look at her. That was natural enough in a man, just as it was natural that he would dress and go back downstairs to the game without her, leaving her to get dressed by herself and find her way back down alone.

That was all right. It was not what John Whitmarsh would have done, but this man was not John Whitmarsh, not in the least. And that was all right, too. She said good-bye to John Whitmarsh, and then turned to the mirror and fixed her hair, and refastened her buttons and stays. She made the bed, too, before she left the room.

Catlett was playing faro, and winning. Nancy went over and stood near him, watching with interest as he concentrated on the game. She did not understand how the game was played, but she could feel the tension, and she could sense Catlett's concentration and suppressed excitement as he followed the turn of the cards.

At first Nancy just watched Catlett. She looked at the curve of his neck as he bent forward over the table, the command in his gesture as he pushed forward a stack of chips with his bulging knuckles, the corners of his mouth curling under his handlebar mustache. She could already feel a proprietary affection growing within her for those little gestures. It was funny about men; how a man could make love to a woman and seem so overwhelming, and then reveal himself afterward in such subtle and vulnerable little details, when he wasn't even looking at her.

After a while, she began to get interested in the game, too, and she began to follow a bit of what was going on. Catlett was not playing for big money, and he took a break after a while to show her around. He pointed out some of the well-known people who were there that night: the financier, Jim Fisk; the retail magnate, Alexander T. Stewart; Police Inspector Alexander Williams.

Catlett gave Nancy a handful of chips and showed her how to play roulette. That was easy, once he had explained it, and fun. Fun to watch the little ivory ball bounce and spin around, to listen to the click of the ball and the singsong of the croupier, to hold a trembling breath and wonder where the little ball would stop. It was exciting when she won, and fun even when she lost, just to have watched that little pearl of ivory do its dance, and to have had the suspense of guessing and waiting.

That evening she won more than she lost. She giggled with delight when she presented Catlett with her little stack of winnings, and she felt a thrill in her belly that was nearly as strong as the one he had given her upstairs. Catlett tried to make her keep her winning chips and cash them in, but she would not do it. It was his money, Nancy told him. Perhaps she knew intuitively that it would ensure his interest. In any event, he called on her again, and soon she became his regular mistress.

Nancy left her job soon after that. Catlett was supporting her. He wanted to move her into a larger flat, in one of the new apartment buildings uptown around Eighteenth

Street and Irving Place, but Nancy's conservatism resisted that. Catlett was generous. But he was a gambler, and who knew how long his flush days would last?

She did not know where Catlett lived. She knew that he was married, although he never talked about it. He could not be spending a great deal of time at home. He never came to Nancy's home, either. He had never seen her children, and they had never met him. When she stayed with him, it was always in his room upstairs at Henderson's.

Often, now, she was out late, almost all night. The children did not ask her about it, and she did not encourage questions. But on the nights when she was at home, Jamie stopped crawling into her bed in the middle of the night.

When Catlett was playing seriously, she did not see him. And that was just as well. She had gone with him once to Henderson's when he was gambling seriously, and he had ignored her completely. She amused herself for a while playing roulette, but she could not concentrate or enjoy herself when he was nearby, gambling for such terrifying stakes. The game lasted all night. Catlett's fortunes rose, and fell, and rose again.

In the morning they were still playing. When it grew light and the streets were safe, Nancy left alone and went home.

She did not see Catlett for about a week after that. She spent the time at home with her children. She felt guilty for having neglected them, and she tried to do things with them as a family—taking them out for walks and sightseeing, playing games with them, cooking dinners, talking to them. But she would lose interest quickly in the games; or the children would, which made Nancy irritable. And she had never been a very good cook; the meals Fannie fixed were better. Fannie had quietly taken over the running of the house in her mother's absence, and the care of her little brother too. She never complained or showed any resentment when Nancy reappeared to assert her motherly duties, but Nancy had the feeling that her daughter was only standing politely aside and waiting patiently to step back in again when her mother's enthusiasm waned. Nancy told Fannie that she could go back to school again now, if she wanted to, but Fannie preferred not to.

Jamie went out to school every day. But he did not talk about it, and was evasive when asked about his homework. Nancy could have questioned him more about it. But it was easier not to. Fannie was right, Nancy knew; she was not the center of the household anymore. She was like an adolescent, irresponsible, but with the wonderful independence of an adult. Her world was bound up in Catlett, and the excitement of the city and her new life. She did not want to press Jamie on his schooling, or on any other subject that might end up requiring her attention. And Jamie seemed to be doing fine. He was healthy, and he grew more beautiful every day.

One night, Nancy went alone to a place she had heard of, but never been to before. It was a brownstone in the Thirties, a quiet neighborhood. The driver of the hansom knew the address, and was not surprised to be taking an unescorted lady there. It was a gambling casino for women, one of several that had opened in the city in the past few years. These establishments were respectable, and enough protection money was paid regularly to the police to ensure that there would never, never be a raid. They provided a place for ladies to come alone and gamble without fear of damaging their reputations.

The casino was nowhere near as lush as Henderson's or Chamberlin's. It was more like a Fifth Avenue drawing room; and many of the ladies who came there to gamble had stepped out of just such drawing rooms. There was an atmosphere of grace and tranquility. The hostess, a tall, plain, aristocratic woman in her forties, greeted her guests, and found each one a place at the table of her choice. The dealers and croupiers were all female, mostly demure and serious-looking girls who might as easily have been sales clerks at Lord and Taylor.

Nancy took a glass of wine and a small tea sandwich, and moved quietly around the room observing for a time before she started playing. She suspected that the house was cheating against the players a little more here than they did at the men's casinos: at least, the ladies seemed to be losing more regularly. No one seemed to mind. Perhaps they expected to lose; or perhaps the money they were wagering did not mean very much to them. Nancy watched closely, and felt that her tutelage with Catlett gave her an edge.

She began to play roulette. She bought fifty dollars' worth of chips, and she played them, slowly and cautiously. She felt very alone suddenly without Catlett to fall back on it she lost her whole stake. She would have to bet carefully.

She picked up three five-dollar chips and held them in her hand. She weighed them, let one drop, then another. She placed a single chip on a four-number bet, and her fingers grew cold and numb as she pulled them away, leaving her bet on the table. The wheel spun around, the ball did its clicking dance, while her heart pounded. She lost, and she felt like crying. She did not know if she could bring herself to do it again.

But she did. She played red, and lost. Red again, and another loss. Red was due. She played red again, and won.

She was seized with an exhilaration like nothing she had ever felt before on winning a bet. She was still a long way from breaking even. But she had the chips from her first solo win in her hand, and she was on her way. Would the wheel take one more red, or was it time to switch?

Nancy had only intended to stay for a couple of hours. But she was still there at two in the morning. She ended up by losing the entire fifty dollars she had come with, but she could see what she had done wrong. She had made mistakes, but she was excited rather than depressed. She would not make those same mistakes next time. She knew she could beat the wheel.

Chapter Six

The locomotive hissed a peevish breath of steam and heaved backward, its gears, wheels, and rods flailing in a jerky motion. Behind it waited a line of freight cars, loaded with pig iron and coal. Moving slowly, but with better grace now that it had achieved motion, the engine closed the gap with the lead car.

John Whitmarsh stood poised above the heavy steel coupling, the pin raised in his hands like a sword, ready to strike. He felt the familiar thrill of terror in the instant before the engine was supposed to slow down—but the engineer's timing was right, and the locomotive slowed as he hit the air brakes and eased in toward the freight cars.

John braced himself against the shift in momentum. He timed the last yards, counting beats, and then as the metal members of car and engine closed together he slammed the pin down into its slot, secured it, and jumped clear.

The engine throbbed on the side track while voices yelled instructions above the din and doors slammed shut; then, at a signal, it sighed another heavy cloud of steam, shuddered, and began to roll forward, with eleven heavy-laden freight cars in tow. John watched as it swung out through the Pittsburgh freight yard, headed for Chicago.

He made his way across the yard to the main building. His shift was through. He had been at it since six that morning, and he had put in his twelve hours. For that he had earned a dollar fifty. He had been assigned to four days of work this week, and he had six dollars coming to him. Today was payday.

As he picked his way through the cinder-strewn grid of rails and ties, he pulled at his fingers, one at a time, cracking the knuckles. It was a routine he had fallen into, a kind of good luck ritual. Each time he came off a shift he went through it, half consciously, stretching each finger until he felt the knuckle pop and the tension ease. It reminded him that they were all still there. With each pop he counted his blessings, all the way to ten.

Not many railroad brakemen had ten good fingers. The saying was, you could tell how long a fellow had been working on the 'road by counting his fingers. John had only held this job for a little more than four months—time enough to lose one, certainly, but John's reflexes were sharp, and he had been lucky.

The job of brakeman was the lowest tier on the railroad ladder. It paid the least, and the dangers were the fiercest. A leg could go in a second, sliced off between wheel and track if a man stumbled while darting between cars to unhook a coupling. Mashed fingers and hands were the rule rather than the exception, especially in the winter months when bitter cold sapped feeling and coordination from them, as the men went gloveless about their work. And if a brakeman's concentration wandered at the wrong moment, he could be flung to his death from the top of a train as he rushed from car to car spinning the brake wheels, or he could be smashed like an insect against the stone facing of a low bridge.

Dozens of brakemen died each year in Pennsylvania alone. John had been told this by some of the veterans, and at first he had thought they were exaggerating. But since he had signed on in February with the Pittsburgh, Fort Wayne, and Chicago, he had heard of four deaths.

One of them was a man he had worked alongside.

The man's name was Vito Gasparo. He was a squat, red-faced Italian. He had the sort of face that ought to have been jolly, but his was not. He took John out drinking a few weeks after John started on the job.

"It ain't all accidents, Johnny." Gasparo was deeply depressed. A close friend of his had been killed a few days before. Gasparo stared down moodily into a thick tumbler full of dark red wine. John nursed a beer. "Nosir. You gonna fin' out. Some of dese guys, you know, dey jus' get so all of a sudden dey don' care no more. You know, dey gotta wife, bambini dey can't-a feed, dey can't-a buy clo's, dey can't-a stan' go home after a while. Hey, den one day you watchin' dose ties go by jus' under you nose, you gotta da fingers so col' an' da han's so col' it make-a you cry, an' den all of a sudden, it get so easy to jus' let go . . ."

Vito Gasparo had been killed a month ago falling from a train around a horseshoe curve near Lima, Ohio. The conductor said he had lost his grip on the handholds climbing up to the roof. It made John feel sick when he heard it.

Still, it was a job, and in the summer of 1877 jobs were hard to come by. John was satisfied just to be working. The horror of Walter Koch's murder just a few months back was still fresh and raw upon him, and he worked as much to keep his mind occupied as for the wages. The more dangerous the job, and the more concentration it required, the better it suited him. And he could live on a dollar and a half a day.

It was the men with families he felt sorry for. He did not see how they could manage.

Then too, John Whitmarsh knew that he was not trapped on the railroad, as most of the other men were. He had some schooling. He came from what was called a "good background"—his uncle on his father's side, after all, was an English lord, and his father's name was still highly respected, at least in some quarters. He could almost certainly use that name to get a job on a newspaper, if he chose to. But he chose not to.

He was doing his father's work, all the same. He preached union to anyone who would listen. Hardly anyone would.

Union talk could get a man fired, and there were not many who were willing to risk their jobs talking to a kid. John would not let himself get discouraged. He had read his father's editorials, and listened to people like his uncles and Walter Koch as they talked with his father about the injustices of the system, and what the workingman could do. John had learned their arguments well. He made sense, and there were plenty of people who agreed with him. But they avoided him, or made fun of him, and called him "the Communist Kid." And his dispatcher called him in and told him to quit being such a goddamned fool or he'd find himself without a job.

John kept talking. He was impatient with what he saw as the cowardice of his fellow workers. It was hard for him to appreciate what an exceptional background he had really had. He had grown up in a nest of men of extraordinary bravery. His father, his Uncle Mike, Walter Koch—all dead, all killed by different weapons of the system they had fought against. And his Uncle Tim was under a sentence of death as the reputed "King of the Molly Maguires." John had gown up surrounded by this tradition of courage, and he was still short of his sixteenth birthday. He could not easily understand the fear most men felt of losing their jobs and seeing their families starve. To him, it was a matter of clear principle. It did not occur to him that it was only because he was just a boy and not taken seriously that he had not been roughed up or fired for his union agitating.

John stood on the platform outside the paymaster's office and slit open his wage envelope. He counted the money and read the narrow printed slip of paper. He swore, and stormed back inside.

"What is this?" he demanded. He had the money and the printed slip in his clenched fist, and he shook it under the bars of the paymaster's cage.

"Did you read?"

"Yes, I read it! Ten percent pay cut . . . what the hell for?"

"Says on the slip." The paymaster, a hound-faced man with thick, bottle-end glasses, picked a slip off a pile of them on his desk and read: " 'Owing to the serious nature of the economic condition, all railroad employees earning more than one dollar per day will receive a ten percent cut in pay, effective immediately.' Hard times, sonny."

"Yeah, but hard times for who? You don't see Scott and Layng and Gowen starving!"

"I don't see 'em at all. Now get on out of here, before you make trouble for yourself."

"Listen, mister, it's not me making trouble! I don't see how they can . . . I mean, God, there's men who've got to try to feed a family on this! You can't just take ten percent out of 'em; they've got nothing left!" He was screaming. The paymaster jerked his head angrily, and a couple of men came around and took John by the arms and shoulders and hauled him roughly to the door. "Let go of me, you bastards!" he swore. They shoved him through the door. He staggered, lost his balance, and fell off the platform, landing hard on his shoulder in the dirt below.

Some men standing in the yard laughed. John turned his fury on them. "All right, laugh, you idiots! If you think this is funny, wait'll you see the next cut, and the one after that! Where the hell do you think this is going to stop?"

He picked himself up and stalked out of the railroad yard. His shoulder ached, and his insides burned with bitterness and hatred. If he had a gun, he thought, he would go back and shoot them all. He'd start with the paymaster, and then the two bastards who had thrown him out, and then those fools who stood around and laughed. They deserved everything they got, he thought. They deserved to be slaves.

He walked along scowling, nursing his bitterness. For a while he enjoyed it. It was intoxicating, and it buoyed him up. It gave him strength. He felt that if anyone crossed him, he could obliterate them.

But nobody crossed him, or even noticed him. After a

bit the fun went out of it. The bitterness went flat, like a beer nursed too long.

He had a little room above a shop about ten blocks from the Pittsburgh yard, but he did not feel like going back to it yet. There was a bar on Eleventh Street where the trainmen hung out. John did not suppose there would be many people there tonight, with the new wage cut. But he decided to go around and see.

To his surprise, Emil's Tavern was crowded. He heard laughter from inside before he even reached the door. The bar was packed, and noisy. John found a place to squeeze in, and ordered a mug of beer. Next to him a fireman was telling a story of a near-disaster he had had with some worn-out equipment. He was telling it as a funny story, and the men who were listening to him were laughing. John watched them in the mirror behind the bar, and felt the bitterness in his stomach again. It was not the hate-filled, murderous feeling he had had before, but contempt, and a feeling of not belonging. He was an outsider. He would never understand or be a part of these people who could laugh and get drunk while they were being robbed of their money and their dignity.

He finished his beer and left the tavern. There was still some daylight left, and some boys were playing baseball in an empty lot across the street. He leaned against a lamp-post and watched them, wishing he were playing with them.

"Hey, John!"

He turned at the sound of the voice and saw Joe Kovalchik calling to him from up the street. Kovalchik was a switch-man, a second generation Pole who was one of the few friends John had made since he had been working on the Pittsburgh. Kovalchik was twenty years old, but several inches shorter than John. He had sharp features dominated by a beaklike nose, and hair cut close to his skull. It gave him the look of a hawk; and that likeness was heightened now as his eyes darted cautiously around. He took John's arm and started him toward the middle of the street.

"You goin'?"

"Where?"

"Ain't you heard? Why, there's a meetin' tonight! Over in Allegheny City. Talkin' about gettin' up a union!"

"No! Who's behind it?"

"I don't know. There's been talk the last couple of days. Since word started gettin' out about this new pay cut. Where you been?"

"I had a layover in Fort Wayne. Just got back in town tonight. I can't believe this! I didn't think any of these guys would ever have the nerve."

"Well," said Joe, unsmiling, "the squeeze is gettin' pretty tight. You comin'?"

"Are you kidding? Let's go!"

Dietrich's Hall in Allegheny City, just across the river from Pittsburgh, was a large, bare room, one narrow flight of stairs above the street. And up those stairs, on that early June night, trooped firemen, brakemen, switchmen, conductors, and other railroad workers. There were even a few engineers in attendance, although the engineers had their own brotherhood and generally considered themselves a class above the rest.

The few dozen men who assembled in Dietrich's Hall on June 2, 1877, had two things in common: dissatisfaction and courage. If the first had been the only criterion, the old German social hall could not have held a fraction of the desperate workers who would have flocked there.

But more than dissatisfaction was needed. No matter how bad a worker's lot became, he was haunted by the fear that it could get even worse. If he rocked the boat, he would be thrown overboard. Employers had boasted openly of "hunting union members down like mad dogs." Every man in the hall that night knew that he was risking his job just by being there. There were bound to be management spies and Pinkerton detectives in the crowd, taking names.

In spite of it, the atmosphere was lively, even boisterous. There was a strain of manic high spirits offsetting the grimness of the situation, a kind of gallows humor. Speakers strode to the lectern to say their piece, buffeted along by hoots and cheers and shouts. Factions developed, roughly divisible as radical, conservative, and middle-of-the-road; but in fact the confusion was so great that no clear lines could be drawn at all. Resolutions, charges, and lists of demands resounded from the floor and through the smoke-thickened air.

At the height of the confusion a young man walked up to the speaker's stand. John Whitmarsh, standing near the door, had noticed him early. He had been sitting quietly in a chair tilted back against the wall in a corner, a small smile playing on his full, cherubic lips. He seemed to John to be the only completely calm person in the room. John had pegged him for a Pinkerton man at first, but then decided he had been wrong. A detective would have made some effort to blend in with the crowd.

This man now stood at the lectern, leaning on it slightly, with his hands wrapped around its edges. He had an athlete's build, and a college man's rakish deportment. He wore a jet-black Thibet suit, with a dark cravat knotted beneath a fresh-looking collar. The striking features of his face were those round lips, a straight, broad nose, a deeply cleft chin on a firm jaw, and eyes the color of blue sky seen through frosted glass.

"My name's Robert Ammon," he announced in a voice that carried above the noise in the room. "And if we're here to talk about organizing, we'd better start getting things organized."

Chapter Seven

It was late when the meeting broke with a solemn oath of secrecy. John had listened to Ammon with an excitement that bordered on awe. Now he joined the group of men who clustered around Ammon, talking urgently and asking questions. John stayed quietly on the fringes. Gradually the group grew smaller as people drifted away. Then Ammon looked over and noticed John.

"What's your name, kid?"

"John Whitmarsh."

The Grand Organizer nodded. "I thought so. I've heard of you."

John colored with pleasure. "You have?"

"Sure. 'The Communist Kid,' right? You've been raising some hell." He put out his hand. "I'm pleased to meet you."

"Likewise," said John. They shook hands, and John's excitement came spilling out of him. "Mr. Ammon, you were great in there, really great. I mean, these people listened to you! God, you could just feel it changing in there tonight. They went from being scared of their shadows to feeling like they could lick the world. I'm sure glad to meet you, Mr. Ammon, and look, if there's anything I can do . . ."

"Slow down," said Ammon, laughing. "There's plenty you can do. And my name's Bob."

"Bob," John agreed happily. "Okay."

"Well, little brother," the new Chief Officer said, putting an arm on his shoulder, "don't you have a home to go to?"

John shrugged. "Sure."

"You live with your family?"

"No. I've got a room."

"Well, come along, walk with me a bit."

John fell in beside him. It was wonderful to be at the center of things like this, and to be on familiar terms with Ammon. Ammon was a great man. But he was young, too, certainly not more than twenty-five. And he had good breeding, and education. He was somebody John felt he could talk to. There would be some common ground.

They walked along the river and up onto the bridge that led back to Pittsburgh from Allegheny City. Halfway across Ammon stopped, and they leaned on the railing and looked out over the water. It was a heavy night, moonless and overcast, but the orange spitting fires of the factories' night furnaces lit the banks of the river. A string of coal barges drifted noiselessly under the bridge, visible only by their running lights.

"Where are you from, John?"

"Painter's Falls."

"Your folks still live there?"

John told Ammon his story.

"That's why your name rang a bell," Ammon responded warmly. "The *Independence*, sure! I remember reading about that. And the paper burned down, didn't it, after your father was killed?"

"Yeah."

Ammon looked at him shrewdly. "Did you have anything to do with that?"

John scuffed his feet, and did not answer.

"You're right. That sort of thing doesn't bear talking about, even among friends," Ammon said. "Sure, I remember that business. I thought a lot of your father, from what I'd heard of him."

"Thanks." John felt a hard lump in his throat. He was

glad that it was dark. Ammon guessed his mood and shifted the conversation.

"I was just back from the West then."

"The West? Where?"

"All over. California, Arizona, Texas . . . up in the wilderness, too, the Rockies . . . and a stint as an Indian scout . . ."

"An Indian scout!"

"That was the work I'd just wound up when I came back East. I was with the Seventh Cavalry."

"No kidding!"

"Yes. I was at Western University here in Pittsburgh, but I got myself expelled—I'd run up a pile of gambling debts, and they'd gotten too steep to ask my father to settle them for me. So a friend of mine and I decided to organize a festival to raise the money—shows and dancings, that sort of thing." He laughed. "The thing turned into a saturnalia, and several young women were compromised. One of them was the daughter of the dean, and that ended my university career. My father put it to me that I should head out West—as far as possible from the scene of my follies. So I got out to St. Louis and signed on with an outfit taking a supply train up into the Rocky Mountains to a company of fur trappers."

John listened, fascinated. Ammon told his story with careless drama, his lips twisted in a mild, self-mocking smile. John was not inclined to doubt a word of it.

"That was as fabulous and as miserable a year as I have ever spent. I was the youngest in the party, and they made something of a pet of me. I signed on as a blacksmith's assistant, but the mountain men taught me shooting and trapping, and how to recognize Indian signs, and to tell one tribe from another.

"It was fine in the fall, but winter in those Rockies is the coldest thing you ever want to feel. I got frostbite clear through. We got caught in one blizzard and couldn't make it back to camp. The only way I kept from freezing was I killed a grizzly bear and slit open its stomach, and crawled in there for warmth till the storm broke.

"We spent time that spring among the Crow Indians. They'd never seen anyone quite like me—white, blond, and beardless. They took me to their bosom—especially the chief's daughter, a lovely little squaw named Deep Water. She made me a shirt and a pair of moccasins. And then she came to my tent at night in nothing but a buffalo robe, and slipped in with me, stark naked! I was scared. But I figured I better give her what she came for, or she'd kick up a rumpus and I might wind up with no more hair on my head than I had on my chin . . .

"We got out of there all right, but I was afraid I might not be so welcome in Crow country by the time next year rolled around, so I quit the company and went down to Texas, where I punched cattle for a couple of years—say, could I tell you stories about that!—and then I wound up in Arizona. A rich man there hired me to guide an expedition looking for a lost diamond mine. But he didn't know where it was, and I didn't know where it was, so it stayed lost. Then Major Devereaux sent to me, asking if I'd come and scout for the cavalry. He'd heard stories of my familiarity with the Indians. So I spent some time with the army. I left just a few months before Little Big Horn. Damn shame . . ."

John's eyes were wide. "Gosh, you've done about everything!"

"Not yet, John. I'll tell you, this fight we're getting into now, this'll beat it all! Do you know who runs this country? Who owns this country? I'll tell you who, the railroads. That's right. Mr. Tom Scott, president of the Pennsylvania Railroad, delivered the U.S. presidential election to Rutherford B. Hayes. No question about it—took it right away from Tilden. That's how it works. It's no democracy. He could have given it to you if he'd wanted to. That's how powerful those fellows are."

They were walking again. They left the bridge and walked up the hill. They passed the end of John's street, but he did not say anything about it. He wanted all of this night that he could get.

"The railroads in this country right now are probably the greatest single power the world has ever known," Ammon declared. They were alone, walking through the dark streets. "But the railroads are only a power as long as they run! And who makes them run? Does Tom Scott? Does Franklin Gowen?"

"We do!" John blurted.

"Right on the button, John. The men who work the railroads. We work together to keep the trains moving. And if we work together, why, we can stop them moving too."

They had reached Adams Street. Robert Ammon pointed to a house where a lantern glowed from a hook on the porch. There was a white picket fence around a small yard, and what looked like roses climbing a trellis by the porch.

"Here's where I live. Come on in for a drink."

"I probably ought to get going . . ."

"Come on, one drink."

They went in through the gate and climbed the steps to the porch. Ammon's voice rose as he described the military precision and discipline the trainmen would need to pull off a strike successfully. Suddenly the door opened and a woman was standing there, holding a lamp.

"Robert," she said, half sharp, half pleading. "Please! You'll wake the baby."

She was young and very pretty, but her face looked tired. She wore a dressing gown over her nightclothes, and her hair was braided into a rope on top of her head. Her lips were pursed, and pockets at their corners twitched.

"I'm sorry, sweetheart," said Ammon soothingly, dropping his voice to a whisper. "Say, could you bring us a couple of bottles of beer from the pantry?"

John saw a flash of resentment cross her face. But at that moment from somewhere inside a baby started to cry.

"Now look! You'll have to get it yourself," she said, and disappeared.

"Sit yourself down, John," said Ammon easily. "I'll be right back."

"Uh, maybe I should . . ."

"No, no." Ammon patted him on the arm, and went inside.

John felt like an intruder. It had not occurred to him that Bob Ammon would be married. He sat uncomfortably on the porch swing. He could hear the crying of the baby inside the house. After a bit the crying stopped. Ammon returned with two bottles of beer. The glass was cold and wet from having been sitting on ice.

"To the Trainmen's Union," Ammon toasted.

"To the Trainmen's Union."

The beer was good and cold. It picked them up. Ammon went down off the porch and urinated against the rosebushes. Then he stood out in the yard and looked at the sky. The clouds were beginning to break up, and they could see a few stars, but it was still very black.

"All that power, John," Ammon said. "It's in the railroads themselves. It's not in the men who sit at the desks, not in Scott and Vanderbilt, Cassatt and Gowen. They've got the power right now because they run the railroads. They call the shots." He came back over to the steps, and leaned on the railing, with his foot on the bottom stair. "But when we get ourselves organized—really *organized*—then *we'll* be able to call the shots. The people who work the railroads will run the railroads. And then, by God, John, *we'll* be the ones running this country!"

He slammed his fist hard against the wooden porch railing. Inside, the baby started crying again.

Chapter Eight

John Whitmarsh went up to the jail in Pottsville to say good-bye to his Uncle Tim. Tim Ryan was to die in a few days as a convicted Molly Maguire terrorist.

"I wrote to Governor Hartranft," Tim said. "I delivered the miner's vote to the man when he won the election. 'Tim,' he says, 'if there's ever anythin' I can do for ye . . .' I wrote to the governor suggestin' that this might be the time to show his appreciation." Tim looked over at his nephew and gave a little shrug. "But of course there's another election comin' up . . ."

Tim Ryan was shockingly thin. His prison clothes hung like bed sheets from his body. Even his beard seemed too large for him now, and his face sagged under it. The bags beneath his eyes extended well down his cheeks. But he did not act depressed, or seem to be feeling sorry for himself. The gentleness that had always seemed so incongruous in so robust a man as his uncle was still there, but now it fit more plausibly on the shrunken frame. Tim Ryan seemed, if not cheerful, at least at peace with himself.

"I'm working on the Pittsburgh," John told him. "A brakeman."

"That's rough work, young John. You take care, now."

"We're forming a union. I think it's going to work."

Tim looked at him with concern. "You mixed up in it, are ye, young John?"

"Up to my ears," John said proudly.

"I can see a lot of yer father in ye. More and more. I

don't suppose it'll have much effect to caution ye, but be careful, lad. They'll hurt ye. They might even try to kill ye, if ye're bothersome enough."

"I'm not afraid."

"No, I suppose ye're not. But consider, young John, it don't do any good to be killed, if nobody knows who ye are."

A few minutes later it was time to go. John hugged his uncle, and then left quickly, crying.

On the 21st of June, 1877, Tim Ryan and nine other convicted "Molly Maguires" were hanged in three separate ceremonies at dawn in three Pennsylvania towns. There had been rumors of an eleventh-hour rescue attempt, but armed militia patrolled the streets of Pottsville and Wilkes Barre and Mauch Chunk, and the men were hanged without interference.

It was a Saturday morning, and the weather was good over most of the Northeast. Comfortable citizens relaxed in their shirt-sleeves, enjoyed their breakfasts, did a little gardening, and read the morning papers. They read the item about the executions in eastern Pennsylvania and felt more secure, knowing that the terrorists were dead, and they could be safe in their beds at night once again.

Hardly anyone would have believed that in less than a month troops would be massed in the streets again, fighting pitched battles with thousands of Americans; that blood would flow and men would die, and the country would be embroiled in what some would be calling a revolution.

Chapter Nine

The day the Great Strike hit Pittsburgh, John Whitmarsh was sleeping late. He had lost his job two weeks earlier, on the 5th of July. He was surprised it had taken so long. Bob Ammon had been fired back on the 24th of June, and others in the Trainmen's Union had begun to get the axe within days after that first meeting at Dietrich's Hall. Pinkerton detectives and informers had done their work, funneling a steady stream of names into the hands of management. When it was known that a man was in the union, he was fired. Unionism was a contagious germ, and the men who ran the railroads were taking no chances of an epidemic.

The wholesale firings had their effect. Men feared for their jobs, and those who had lost their jobs feared even greater reprisals. The Molly Maguire hangings were fresh in everyone's mind. The men split into factions, or simply stayed away from union meetings.

Ammon called a strike for June 27. Word was spread all along the line. But then at a meeting at Dietrich's Hall on the eve of the strike, a lot of voices were raised in favor of canceling it. The men were scared. The meeting degenerated into a shouting match. The executive committee stood firm on the strike. But when the meeting broke up, dissidents went out on night trains and dropped off along sleepy stationhouses and spread the word among the skeleton night crews that the strike was off. By the time morning came around, nobody knew what was going on. The strike fizzled.

Ammon retrenched. He held meetings of his inner circle to plot a new strategy. They usually met around a table at the back of Emil's Tavern, and Ammon was willing to stay and talk as late as anyone else would stay. John always went, and almost always stuck it out to the end. Occasionally he would stop back at Ammon's house on Adams Street for a nightcap, but not often. John felt uncomfortable there, and he had the feeling that Bob Ammon did too. Domestic life was something that Ammon seemed not to have quite come to grips with. It was apparent from Mrs. Ammon's tired, resentful eyes that she felt his detachment too.

The plan they developed at the strategy meetings was to hold off any overt action until fall. They would spend the summer organizing and solidifying the power base of the Trainmen's Union.

"Panic comes from people not knowing what's going to happen," Ammon said. "By September we'll have every trainman in this country knowing just what we expect of him, and just what we're going to accomplish. We've got to take it slow, and build a solid confidence from the ground up. If we let management make fools of us one more time, we're finished. We've got to make them respect us. We've got to show them that we're united, and that we're more than a match for them in tactics and sophistication and strength. And resolution. So we'll take things slow and deliberate, and when we're ready, we'll strike, and we'll close the country down. And when I sit down to bargain with Tom Scott, we'll sit down as equals!"

On July 18, Bob Ammon left Pittsburgh to travel the lines. John went with him to the old Outer Depot. As they walked down the platform the telegraph operator came running out.

"Hey, Ammon," he said. "Hear about Martinsburg?"

"No, what?"

"Just came in over the wires an hour ago. Strike on the B & O."

"When?"

"Happened yesterday. And that's not all. They called in the militia, and some fellow got shot. Killed." The operator was looking nervously around. He saw the dispatcher watching them from his window. "Well, anyway, that's it," he said. He turned and hurried back to his office.

"Doesn't look good to be seen talking to me," Ammon said as they walked on.

"Only if you've got a job," said John.

"That's right. See what I've done for you? You've got nothing to worry about anymore. No job, nothing to lose."

"Say, what about this strike in Martinsburg?"

"Well," said Ammon, "I don't like it. It's premature. We don't want little strikes here and there, separate. They're too easy to put down. That's what I've got to hammer home on this trip. We've got to keep discipline, and act as a united power."

"What do you think'll come of this one?"

Ammon shook his head. "Nothing," he said.

The stationmaster came out of his office and confronted them. "What are you doing here, Ammon?"

Ammon reached in his pocket and pulled out a ticket. "Bought and paid for, Mr. Kruger," he said with a cheerful smile. "Just going for a little ride on the railroad."

"Hey, John!"

John heard the voice calling him through the end of his dream. He tried to stay asleep, incorporating the voice into the dream. But like it or not, he was awake.

"Hey, John!" The shout came again, from below his window.

"All right, hold your horses," he grumbled. He sat up in bed, disentangling himself from the rope of sheet that twisted around his body. It was hot already, although it was not much past nine. He got up, scratching, and stumbled to the window. Joe Kovalchik was standing down below in the street.

"Well, what the hell is it?" John complained. "I'm an

honest unemployed union man, I've got a right to sleep late.''

"Sleep, hell," Kovalchik yelled. "They're strikin'!"

"What?"

"Down to the Pennsy roundhouse. They ain't lettin' anythin' move!"

"Hang on!" said John. He dressed in less than thirty seconds, and raced down the stairs to join Joe Kovalchik on the street.

"What about Ammon? Is he back?"

"No, I don't think so."

They started running toward the yard. A lot of people were in the streets, all headed in the same direction. When they got there, they found a crowd of more than a hundred people gathered, with more arriving at every minute.

A lot of the crowd was made up of young men and boys, about the ages of John and Joe Kovalchik. They hung around in small groups, lounging about with nervous energy disguised as nonchalance, suddenly darting off in a pack to another corner of the railroad yard with no apparent object or purpose in mind. John asked a few of them what was going on, but nobody he talked to seemed to have any clear idea.

They found Bellows Chaney by the main switch. Chaney was a fireman, and a member of Ammon's inner circle.

"No freights are going out," Chaney told them. "Passenger travel hasn't been affected, not yet."

"How'd it start?"

"The doubleheader order. When it went into effect this morning, Gus Harris climbed down out of his cab."

The day before, an order had come down from Superintendent Pitcairn making all eastbound freights doubleheaders. A doubleheader was a train pulled by two locomotives. That meant that one train, with a single crew, could haul twice as many cars. But it meant twice the work for that single crew, at no more pay. And it meant that a lot of men would be laid off.

"Good for Gus! Then what happened?"

"The whole crew walked out with him. So then they

tried to raise another crew, but the boys in the shed told them to go to hell.''

"Damn!" said Joe excitedly, slapping his hands together. John felt prickles standing out on his skin.

"So they canned about thirty of the boys right there on the spot. Then the dispatcher got a yard crew to take her out. That got things stirred up good. There was some cursing and yelling, and a few stones started flying, and then Ray Stackpole slipped in there and cut the engine loose. Then a few of us went in and convinced the yard crew that they ought to give it up and throw in with us. That's about the last real try anyone's made to move a train out of here.''

"Where's Ammon?" John asked.

"We got a wire out to Canton. We had some job getting it out. The superintendant's got orders out not to let the strikers use the telegraph wire. We got it out, though, and I guess Bob'll be back tomorrow. He'd better. This thing could get out of hand.''

Ammon's absence worried John, too. It gave him an uneasy feeling about the strike. He knew Ammon was not ready for it to happen yet. Ammon's timetable was the fall, and he had said repeatedly that any premature action might do the cause a lot of damage. Listening to Ammon, John had come to see the importance of organization, strategy, and timing. Today's action was a careless match dropped into powder.

By late afternoon there were abandoned freight cars for miles in every direction, stretching out from the city like the legs of a monstrous, gray-glittering spider. As each new train came in, it was absorbed, and its crew bled out into the ranks of the strikers.

The crowds were becoming enormous. As John and Joe moved through the switchyard they saw very few familiar faces, and John guessed that most were not railroad men at all.

"Lots of folks don't like the Pennsylvania Railroad much," John observed.

"Hey, that's the truth," said Joe. "Folks seem to be havin' a good time, though."

Spirits were high. The crowds massed around the Twenty-eighth Street crossing that Thursday afternoon might have been on their way to a baseball game or a town picnic. Small groups rushed from one place to another, jabbering excitedly. There was a lot of hollering, and plenty of laughter. John saw several people with food, and more with bottles. A photographer had set up his camera on the roof of a shed and was taking pictures. People going by would stop and pose for him. Other sightseers crowded up onto the same shed roof, and it collapsed under their weight.

All through the day the numbers grew, diminished a little, grew some more, but always the spirit of expectancy animated the crowd, the spirit that keeps a crowd a living thing in the sureness that the event is still continuing, and that something is going to happen.

A dozen times that afternoon John checked at the passenger depot to see if Ammon had come in. No one had seen him. John worked his way up into a pitch of worry and resentment. Ammon had no right to be away at a time like this. No matter that the committee had sent him off on union business. He ought to be here when they needed him. John and Chaney had issued a call for a meeting at nine o'clock. Ammon had to be there. He was the only man who could keep things under control. And every time John checked and Ammon had not yet arrived, John fretted more.

At about six he went to Ammon's house. He knew there was no hope of finding him there. If Bob Ammon had somehow returned without being seen at the depot, he would certainly not have gone home. Still, the errand gave John something to do, it gave him an outlet for his nervous energy. And so he hurried to Adams Street and walked up the flagstone path and knocked on the door.

Mrs. Ammon answered quickly. She had the baby in her arms. She seemed surprised to see John.

"Hello Mrs. Ammon. Is . . . ."

"No, he's not," she snapped. John was taken aback. He always felt uncomfortable with Mrs. Ammon. He felt that she resented him and the other union men who occasionally came back to the house with her husband. Bob Ammon spent most of his time away from here, and preferred to conduct his business in taverns, though he was not an immoderate drinker. Ammon only rarely brought friends or associates home, and at home there was a change in him. He became forced. He tried to be lively and jolly with his wife, but she would not enter into the same spirit with him. He would then resort to a soothing manner that had patronizing tones to it that even John found embarrassing. Ammon would only relax and be himself again when she retreated, sometimes angrily, to her room or to the kitchen, and left the men to drink their drinks and talk their politics on the front porch.

John could understand why Bob Ammon spent so little time at home. It was not a congenial place.

"I'm sorry," said John. "It's just that there's a lot going on, and I was hoping I might find him here."

"With anything going on, this is the last place you'd find him . You ought to know that."

"Yes, ma'am." John ducked his head in a curt bow and turned to go.

"Hold on a second."

It was not said sharply, but with a conciliatory softness. To his surprise John saw an apologetic smile on her face. He did not remember ever having seen her smile. "Don't mind me. I'm not all bad. I just bark sometimes."

The smile changed her face remarkably. John saw that she was prettier, and younger, than he had thought. When she smiled, a soft light came on in her eyes, which were really more green than gray, and the light washed away the shadows beneath them. Her hair was the pale color of new corn. Her face was very thin. When it was sullen it looked creased and older; but John could see now that the skin was unlined, although it clung too tightly to the bones of her face, creating angles that caught the shadows. Her skin was pale, and finely pitted, as if she had been ill.

"I'm sorry," she said, "I don't know your name."

"John Whitmarsh, ma'am."

"I ought to have known it. I've seen you often enough. Mine is Deborah Ammon. I guess you knew that." In fact, Bob Ammon had never introduced them, or mentioned his wife's first name.

"Will you come in? I've made some lemonade."

John was anxious to get back down to the yards. He was afraid that something important might happen while he was gone. But there was something about standing here on this front porch with this fragile, slender woman holding her baby on her hip that took him back to summer evenings a half dozen years ago, when his mother held Jamie like that. The poignancy of that family scene struck him now as it never had then.

"All right," he said. "Thank you. For just a minute, though."

John followed her through the front hall and a sitting room and into the kitchen. It was a small, neat room, with counters and cupboards on two sides and a wooden table in the middle. A door in one corner led off into a pantry, and through a screen door in the back he could see a glimpse of yard.

"Do you mind holding him a minute? I'll get some glasses." She held the baby out to him. John took possession of the boy hesitantly. The baby looked doubtful, and his little face began to pucker. John bounced him up and down in a sitting position, holding him in his hands. He remembered that Jamie had liked that. The baby broke into a beaming smile. There were two tiny teeth poking through the lower gum.

"He doesn't usually take to people like that," Deborah Ammon said. "You're a great success." She got two glasses and a stone pitcher of lemonade, and filled the glasses. The baby was cooing and pulling at John's nose. "You look like you've been around babies."

"I've got a kid brother. He's six or seven now. I used to take care of him sometimes."

"Do you live with your family?"

"No. My father's dead. My mother lives in New York now, with my brother and sister."

"So you've gone off on your own?"

"Yes."

The baby was beginning to fidget with a tired restlessness in John's arms. Deborah Ammon took him back. "I'll just put him down for a nap," she said.

When she came back they sat at the kitchen table, and he told her his story. The sun was low now, so that it streamed brightly through the window at Deborah Ammon's shoulder to light her hair in a golden cloud. It caught the edges of her jaw and cheekbones too, lining them with brilliance, so that the light against which John squinted appeared to be coming from her face, and not from the sun itself.

"It must have been a strange life, living on the road—not having a home anywhere."

He thought about it. "I'd never been away from home. Just up to Philadelphia. My father came from England. He'd seen a lot of the world before he settled down, where I'd spent all my life in Painter's Falls. So I loved the moving around."

"But it must have been terrifying. Weren't you ever scared?"

"I guess so. Before I left, mostly. That was the worst. You imagine everything, but then things actually happening aren't ever as bad as the imagining. Of course, when they killed Walter—that was worse than anything. I couldn't ever imagine anything as horrible as that."

She shuddered, remembering the story he had told her. "How old are you, John?"

"Sixteen," he said, surprising himself with his honesty.

"Sixteen! That's so young . . ." She said it in a voice that was half motherly concern, and half the thrilled awe of a girl his own age; a girl he might impress, might kiss. Perhaps it was this combination of motherliness and attractiveness that made him want to talk to her. She was the first person in the past year, beside Ned Callahan, to whom he had confessed his true age.

"I've changed a lot," John said. "I've grown up a lot."

"How?"

He was not prepared for the question, and he remained quiet for a few moments, considering it. He thought about the agonies of missing his family in the first aftershock of death and separation. It would happen at night, mostly, but sometimes unexpectedly in the middle of the day, in the middle of doing something. Digging a drainage ditch for a woman in Youngstown, Ohio, in return for a meal and a hayloft to sleep the night in, he had caught a glimpse of her through the window, ironing. It had brought the memory of his mother in the same pose, at the same task. Walking across a field he heard a bird call, and he had thought of just such a bird singing near his father's office, and had looked for his father to come striding up to him with a bundle of inky proofs under his arm. He could have accepted such a miracle without astonishment, and his disappointment was bitter when it did not happen.

Growing up involved more than getting over those pangs of homesickness. As a boy on the road, he had spent a lot of time around older people, and he had kept his mouth shut and his observations keen. He had learned how to be grown up through careful study, and had stored the information away. He had been content to remain a boy during his time with Koch and Callahan. But since Walter Koch's death he had been truly on his own, with no link remaining to his past. It seemed to him that then he had put his boyhood behind him for good.

He explained this as best he could to Deborah Ammon, and she seemed to understand.

"I grew up fast too," she said, "the way girls try to grow up fast. I got married. I was seventeen, and I couldn't wait to grow up. But you're right about one thing—it's never like what you imagine it will be."

She gave a wry little smile, and John felt a surge of sympathy. "I'm sorry," he said. Then he was horrified by his presumption. She was Robert Ammon's wife, the wife of the man he idolized.

But she reached across the table and covered his hand with her soft hand, and her eyes met his gratefully. She could not, he realized, be more than twenty. She was perishably beautiful, and terribly sad. It struck John for the first time that this woman had been someone else before she became Mrs. Robert Ammon. And perhaps she still was that someone else.

As a child he had believed in the inevitability of things. If people were married, they stayed married. If they died, it was expected. If miners died in a cave-in or a tunnel fire, it was awful, and he vaguely understood the vicious unfairness of it. But still, it must have been expected. There was an aura that surrounded the victims of disaster. Whatever befell them must have been inevitable.

It was not until death became personal, exploding around him like mortar shells on a battlefield, that he began to question this view. And that questioning became an important part of his maturing.

Now he knew there were always many possibilities. And there were many possibilities before John now, as he sat at this kitchen table with this pale lovely girl's soft hand on his hand, and her green eyes on his eyes. But those many choices quickly narrowed down to one.

"I'd better be going. There's a meeting."

Disappointment traced across her face. But it was a face used to disappointment, and it absorbed it well. She nodded and withdrew her hand, trailing her fingertips regretfully along the back of John's hand.

They got up from the table and walked back toward the front door. Just inside the door she stopped, in the shadows at the foot of the stairs.

"I haven't sat and talked to someone in a long time. You're very nice. Thank you." She put a hand on his shoulder and, standing on tiptoes, reached up and kissed him on the lips.

"Oh, there's the baby crying," she said breathlessly as their lips came apart. She ran up the stairs, but at the landing she turned. "Good-bye, John. I hope you'll come again." Then she vanished upstairs.

John had not heard the baby. He opened the door and went out. As he crossed the yard he glanced with a sudden guilty feeling to see if any of the neighbors were watching. Nobody was. Relieved, he hurried through the gate and down the street.

Perhaps there weren't so many possibilities, after all. Perhaps it only seemed that way at the beginning. The closer you got to the situation or the more you understood the person, the narrower the possible choices came to be.

The Trainmen's Union met that night in a borrowed hall on Eleventh Street. Bellows Chaney and John Whitmarsh took charge in the absence of Ammon.

"We've got the public with us," Chaney yelled, standing on a chair at the front of the room. The place was a jostling mass of trainmen, many of them not union men, but bolder now. "The people of Pittsburgh hate the railroad as much as we do. There's not a man in this city who hasn't been bled or made to feel small by those bastards. Now we've got to use that solidarity that they've made for us. We can keep this whole goddamn railroad system tied up in knots if we keep our wits about us. So no violence!"

"Like hell!" shouted a voice from the back of the room, and a cheer went up around him. Chaney waved for silence.

"I mean it!" he said. "No violence! We're railroad men, we're not hoodlums—all we want is a fair load of work at fair pay, and the right to be treated like men! Just let 'em know that's what we want, and we mean to do no work till we get it. Then, we'll go back and run their goddamn railroad for them, and we'll bring our families home a loaf of bread and a hunk of bacon every day, and maybe a piece of red meat every now and then, too!"

"Blood or bread!" somebody called out.

"Make mine bread," another voice responded.

"Yeah, well, we'll need something to wash it down with, too!"

A barrel-chested man in shirt-sleeves with a bandana knotted around his neck stood up on another chair. He waved his arms for quiet, pushing out with his palms against the sound,

"Listen, they're makin' the choice for us," he said. "They've called out the troops!"

"Oh, yeah?" a voice said sarcastically. "The Duquesne Grays and the Fourteenth. Prime lot o' good that's gonna do 'em. Them's Pittsburgh boys!"

"Sure," yelled another. "My brother Mike's with the Fourteenth, and so's Bill Caroselli. Them boys ain't gonna fight for the railroad!"

"Hell, I'm with the fuckin' Grays, and I'm here, ain't I?"

There was more shouting and confusion. The barrel-chested man flailed out again for quiet. "Yeah," he shouted. "Well, that must be what Tom Scott figgers too, 'cause he's got the governor to send in the Philadelphia troops, too!"

That set off a new chorus of angry shouts.

"Philadelphia!"

"What do they want to do, start another damn war?"

"We'll send those bastards back to Philly in a hurry!"

"Yeah, one way or another!"

"If they want a fight," shouted the barrel-chested man, "I say, let 'em have it! There's plenty of guns at the Armory, and I don't believe we'd have much damn trouble gettin' 'em!"

"No!" It was Chaney, huge and thundering. He carried two hundred and forty pounds evenly packaged over six feet four inches, and he commanded attention. His straw-colored mustache bristled over teeth the size and color of old piano keys. "What are we trying to do, start a revolution?"

"Damn right!"

"Then you're a damn fool, because you don't fight a revolution against no fuggin' railroad. You strike a rail-road! Because I'll tell you one thing, if we strike, and keep our heads, we can win! But if we get guns and try to shoot it out with them, we're gonna have to fight the railroad and the whole goddamn United States Army! And let me tell you, if we do that, we're gonna lose, and lose a lot!''

The air in the hall was thick with smoke and sweat and excitement. John felt the electricity lacing his stomach.

"Listen,'' he yelled, "if we stick together, we've won! If we know what we want, we'll get it! Because we're not a mob, we're a union! We've got the organization, and we've got the strength, and we've got the will! This isn't something that's just happening here. It's happening all over, up and down the trunk lines, everywhere Bob Ammon's been, sowing the seeds! We've got a chance now, and we can't let it fall apart with shooting and rioting and wrecking! We've got to spell out what we want, and show the railroad that we've got the strength and the will to get it!''

By the time the long evening had ended, a list of demands had been hammered out and a delegation appointed to present them to the officials of the railroad. The demands included the rescinding of the doubleheader order, a rollback of the recent pay cuts, and the reinstating of all men fired on account of the strike. John Whitmarsh and Bellows Chaney were delegated, along with several others.

It was after midnight when John and Joe and Bellows Chaney left the hall and walked back toward the Twenty-eighth Street crossing. It was an hour that normally found Pittsburgh quiet and empty, except perhaps for a cop strolling on his beat, and the subdued nighttime sounds of the graveyard shift at the freight yard.

Tonight was different. Tonight there were more than a thousand men jammed into the Pennsylvania yards, waiting. Most were not sure what they were waiting for; but they would know when it came.

Chapter Ten

A number of bars were still open. They would stay that way as long as they could, to capitalize on the booming business. They knew that if the situation kept building, the authorities would close them down soon enough.

John, Joe, and Bellows found one of those bars: the Sea Horse, a once-elegant saloon whose polish had faded as the neighborhood had changed. The fancy customers had moved elsewhere, and it was now a workingman's tavern. Its long, ornate bar of polished cherry was pockmarked with gouges, glass rings, and cigar burns, and dust dimmed the glitter of the chandeliers. Sawdust lay in clumps on the floor like seaweed floating in dirty water.

The bar was crowded, though not as packed as it must have been a few hours previous. They found a space at the bar. John ordered a beer.

"No, let me buy you a real drink," said Chaney. "Barman, bring us over a bottle of whiskey!"

The bartender set three glasses in front of them. He took a whiskey bottle off the shelf and marked the level of liquor in it with a grease-crayon line on the side of the bottle. John, with his Callahan-trained eye, noticed that he had tipped the bottle slightly before he made the mark, so that the crayon line was higher than the actual whiskey line. John fixed an eye on it, and challenged the bartender.

"Hey, brother, you wouldn't be flimflamming an old bunco artist, would you?"

Chaney stood next to John, and looked down at the man behind the bar. "And a union man, at that!" he added.

The bartender looked them over, then smiled, shrugged, and rubbed out the line. He replaced it with one an inch lower. "That's on the house," he said. "Up the union!"

Joe poured three drinks. Chaney raised his glass in a toast: "Up the union!" As they drank, cheers rang the length of the bar.

"You boys trainmen?"

"We're here to tell ya!"

"All right, boys!"

"Hear, hear!"

"Up the union!"

A large, stocky man came over and shook their hands. He wore his hair close-cropped, except for a lock on top which was parted in the middle. A soft hat was crumpled in the pocket of his corduroy jacket.

"I'm a millman, boys, y'know," he said, "and we're with you all the way. It ain't just the railroads, it's the scummin' monopolies! It's them rich bastards who don't give a damn how a man lives or if he lives at all, so long as they can find a body to keep the damn machines running. My name's Hatt, Preston Hatt, and I'm proud to meet you. Let me buy you a drink."

The whiskey tasted better than John expected. In fact, it tasted good. But it burned going down, and left him choking and gasping for breath. Preston Hatt laughed and clapped an arm around his shoulders, knocking the wind out of him again.

"Hey, you're all right, you know? You railroad boys, you got the right idea. Now, over at my mill, there's been talk of a new pay cut next month. But we don't know what we're doin', see? It's just the same everywhere. I got an uncle in Cincinnati, works in a see-gar factory. You know what he gets for pay? Cigars!"

"What do you mean?" asked John.

"I mean cigars! Poor son of a bitch don't get no money, they just give him a box o' cigars at the end of the week.

He's gotta go around the saloons and try to sell 'em, 'less
he wants his wife and kids to eat tobacco."

"Talk about your surplus value theories," said Chaney.

"Damn right," said Hatt. "I've known some God-fearin'
men who turned into sodden drunks tryin' to make a livin'
that way in Cincy. Cigars! Shit!" He took the half-smoked
cigar from his mouth, its end still glowing with red-white
ash, crumpled it in his hand, and flung it on the floor.
Then his mood rocked upward again, and he threw an arm
around John and another around Joe Kovalchik and hugged
them. "But you railroad boys, you're all right! You showed
us we can stand up to 'em if we've got the stuff! Barman!
Another bottle over here!"

An hour later they were still at the bar. The second
bottle was two-thirds empty by now. Hatt slumped on the
next stool, his head cradled in his arms, snoring.

Joe Kovalchik came back from the bathroom, buttoning
his fly. A coonskin cap that was too large for him settled
down around his ears.

"Jesus bloody Christ, Joe, where'd you get that thing?"
Chaney demanded.

"What? Oh, this?" His eyes rolled upward. "I found it
in the gents. It's an old family heirloom."

"Whose family?"

"My family!" Kovalchik was drunkenly indignant.
"B'longed to my gran'father when he fought his way
'crost Kentucky with Dan'l Boone."

"Your grandfather lived in Poland," John pointed out.
"They didn't have any coonskin caps in Poland."

"Dan'l Boone could of gone to Poland," said Joe
defensively.

Preston Hatt sat up suddenly, his eyes serene and clear.
"I wasn't sleepin'," he announced. "Jes' closed my eyes
a minute. Why isn't nobody drinkin'? Hello, Bellows."
He smiled brightly, liking the sound of that. He poured
another drink from the bottle, humming "HelloBellows-
helloBellowshelloBellows . . ." He set the bottle down,
and, still humming, his head drifted down into his arms
again, and snores rumbled up from his sleeve.

"Could of been my mother's side," Joe observed. His two friends looked at him blankly. They had forgotten what he was talking about.

"Well, anyway," he said cheerfully, "I found it an' I'm gonna keep it."

"Good idea," Chaney agreed. "Well, let's drink up, boys. We got a call to make in the morning, and we might as well get some sleep."

Vice-president Alexander Cassatt of the Pennsylvania Railroad was having his breakfast in his suite at the Monongahela Hotel when a message was brought to him that a delegation from the Trainmen's Union was waiting outside. Vice-president Cassatt had ordered his eggs medium boiled, but the white of the egg whose shell he had just sheared with his knife was runny. He stared down at the thick, cloudy liquid with distaste.

"We do not recognize any such body," he replied coldly. "Further, we do not propose to deal with anyone while our property is being threatened by a mob of criminal malcontents. When the men are back on the job and the trains are running, then we will consider whether the men have grievances that have any merit. But these are hard times, as the men well know. We are all being called on to make some sacrifice."

He pushed his breakfast tray toward the waiter.

"Take this back," he snapped, "and bring me an egg that is properly prepared!"

Friday passed as Thursday had. No freights moved out of Pittsburgh, although passenger trains continued to run. Two thousand freight cars stood idle now. Beneath the July sun it began to be obvious which ones contained meat and other perishables. But the strikers would touch nothing; and they would not let anything be touched. And the huge crowds, sometimes more than three thousand Pittsburghers, stood with them.

The excitement that day was the return of Robert Ammon.

His train pulled into Allegheny City just after four in the afternoon. Bellows Chaney had gotten his wire, and he, John, and Joe were there to meet him at the station, along with a crowd of some forty railroad men.

Ammon's clothes were rumpled and he looked tired, but his eyes were shining.

"A few months early, boys, but we've got our strike! They won't talk to us? Wait a few days, till the stink in those cars gets a little stronger. Wait a few weeks, till the stockholders see that the Trainmen's Union means business; that we'll starve if we have to to get a decent living, but we won't starve to give them an extra penny a share! We'll wait a few months if we have to, and we'll live on bread and water if we have to. We've waited longer, and we've lived on worse! Let me read you something . . ."

He pulled a telegram from his pocket and unfolded it. He swept a shock of hair off his forehead with his hand, and looked around.

"A friend of mine sent me this from New York. You'll notice it's a long telegram. My friend says the telegraph operator sent it for free, as a gesture of solidarity with the Trainmen's Union." The men cheered and whistled their approval.

"It's part of the text of a sermon by the Reverend Henry Ward Beecher . . . the noted chaplain of capitalism."

"The noted adulterer!" came a shout from the crowd.

"The very same. Now it is the Reverend Beecher's opinion that . . ." he paused, and cocked his head at the yellow telegraph form ". . . that the working class *is* oppressed!"

There was applause from the crowd. It was derisive applause, mixed with hooting and laughter, as the men awaited the expected twist.

" '*But*' . . . he goes on to say . . . '*But* . . . God has intended the great to be great and the little to be little.' "

Hoots and jeers exploded from the crowd. Joe Kovalchik crouched on the platform, scrunched into a ball. "Look at me, Lord, I'm little!"

"The Reverend goes on . . . 'The trade union, originated under the European system, destroys liberty . . . I do not say that a dollar a day is enough to support a workingman . . .' " Ammon paused and looked up. His face and his mood had grown grim, and the shift in his tone of voice infected the men around him. " '. . . Not enough to support a man and five children if he insists on smoking and drinking beer . . . But the man who cannot live on bread and water is not fit to live! A family may live on good bread and water in the morning, water and bread at midday, and good water and bread at night!' "

There was an angry, shuffling silence on the railroad platform. Then Bellows Chaney said, "God damn it, we'll strike till those rich bastards crawl!"

The Philadelphia troops marched in crisp formation up from Union Station, the black stems of their rifles glittering on their shoulders. They were dressed in the different colors of their various units. Red and black, gray, gold, blue—like a magician's shuffle of a new deck of cards, they snapped along up the middle of Penn Avenue. Men, women, and children lined the sidewalks and filled the windows along the way, as if at a parade. But they cursed instead of cheering, and they waved fists not flags.

Hugh M. Fife, sheriff of Allegheny County, walked warily among the troops. With him were a dozen specially appointed deputies. In their hands they carried warrants for the arrest of the men whom the officials of the Pennsylvania Railroad considered to be the ringleaders of the insurrection.

There were twelve thousand people at the Twenty-eighth Street crossing. Two thousand, including a number of strikers, were massed along the tracks. Ten thousand more packed the hillside above.

They were men and women, boys and girls. They were railroad men, businessmen, Pittsburgh militiamen who had put down their rifles and joined the strikers. They were housewives and clerics, shopgirls and prostitutes, professional men, pickpockets, millmen, clerks, artists, and tramps. Everyone in Pittsburgh who could be there was there, cheering on the strikers and waiting to see what would happen.

The column of soldiers halted at an officer's command. Sheriff Fife walked forward and stood ten yards from the solid wall of strikers and their supporters jammed across the tracks. The paper fluttered slightly in his hand, although there was no breeze.

"I've got a bunch of warrants here," he called out, "by the power vested in me by the County of Allegheny . . ."

He began to read off names, spacing them out to try and outwait the shouts of defiance that exploded from the crowd at each name he read. John Whitmarsh, watching from the hillside, strained to hear.

"Robert Ammon . . . Augustus Harris . . . Bellows Chaney . . ." There were a few more names that John could not hear; then ". . . John Whitmarsh . . ."

He drummed an excited tattoo on his thigh. Joe dug him in the ribs.

"That ices it, John. You're a dangerous man."

By this time the sheriff had given up and retreated under a barrage of catcalls mixed with a few hurled stones and lumps of coal. General Brinton, the commander of the Philadelphia troops, strode forward.

"I know nothing of your grievances," he shouted, "and it's not my business to know. I've got my orders, and my orders are to clear these tracks. I don't want anybody to get hurt. But anyone who's heard of me knows I carry out my orders, and heaven help the man who gets in my way!"

A boy near John picked up a large round stone, and flung it. It arced through the air and landed a few feet from General Brinton's polished boot. John grabbed the boy roughly by the collar and shook him.

"Cut it out! Do you want to get us killed?"

But the air was suddenly full of flying objects—stones, bricks, coal, clods of earth, anything that could be thrown.

"Hold your fire, men," the general cautioned, and the orders echoed from officers down the line. "Fix bayonets! All right, move this mob out of here!"

The Philadelphians moved forward behind their tines of sharpened steel. For a moment the crowd stood firm, and voices yelled, "Don't fall back! Stick it to 'em!" The front line of soldiers slowed; then, spurred on by orders, fear, or the heavy lash of the hail of flying brickbats, they charged. Pointed blades pierced through clothing and flesh. Men and women screamed in panic and pain. People in front, dodging and squirming, tried to retreat, but legs became entangled, people fell, and others fell on top of them.

The troops, faced with this immobilized mass of hysteria, and with the shocking reality of Pennsylvanian blood on their bayonets, fell back. Seven men lay bleeding in the cinders. Two at least were dead. Another grappled helplessly with some part of himself that kept slipping out through a slice in his stomach.

The throwing from the hillside had stopped with the charge, and the noise had sucked in to a massive gasp, and then silence. Now the throwing started again. And as it did, the noise from the crowd swelled, growing from shocked cries to a deafening, threatening fury.

From somewhere to his right, over the din of the crowd and his own screaming, John heard a sharp explosion. It might have been a firecracker, or a pistol.

Oh, God, he thought. Whatever curse he was screaming fell back in his throat.

From the troops below there came a series of shots. They began distinctly, separately, almost like a school counting exercise: first one, then one-two, then one-two-three.

And then the whole colunn was firing. Puffs of smoke and little darts of flame popped out all along the line. Bullets whined up into the crowded hillside. A well-dressed man a few yards from John turned to run, then straightened abruptly as a bullet caught him between the shoulder blades. He bent backward and fell, his fingers scrabbling at the air.

Joe turned to John, and his face was bloodless beneath the coonskin cap. "Oh, hell, John," he said, trembling. "Let's get out of here!"

All around them people were screaming and running. Hysterical mothers snatched up children they normally could hardly have lifted and ran up the hill carrying them.

Pistols and muskets had appeared in the crowd, as men took cover behind sheds, boxcars, and hillocks, or dropped flat to return a round of fire before retreating. Many were Pittsburgh militiamen, fighting on the side of the strikers. The shouts and yells and screams of terror rose and blended with the heavy static of gunfire into one terrible nightmare as Philadelphia battled Pittsburgh over the property rights of the Pennsylvania railroad.

John saw a little girl no more than four or five years old standing stock still, wide-eyed and staring, frightened beyond tears.

"Where's your mama?" he asked her.

"I don't know," she whimpered.

"That's okay. Don't worry. We'll find her."

He reached out to take her hand. At that moment someone he did not see crashed into him, catching him off balance and knocking him several feet through the air. He picked himself up, stunned and winded, and looked around for the girl. In the instant that he saw her, a bullet ripped through her leg at the knee, spinning her to the ground. At least two people trampled her in their flight before John could reach her.

She was unconscious when he picked her up. He knelt, cradling her in his lap, and bandaged his handkerchief tightly about the shattered knee. The handkerchief was soaked through with blood before he finished tying the knot.

At last the shooting stopped. John stood up, holding the small body to his chest. Bodies were strewn along the hillside. Some stirred now, and cautiously began to pick themselves up. Others twisted and moaned. Some did not move at all.

"Hey, is there a doctor around here?" John called out. "Is anyone here a doctor?"

Nobody answered him; John hardly expected that anyone would. Nobody even looked his way. People began to move off, on their own or helped by others. Some remained where they were, staring at the devastation with disbelief.

Below, the Philadelphia troops were being assembled by their officers and withdrawn in the direction of the Twenty-sixth Street roundhouse. Some onlookers screamed and cursed at them. Others simply stood, mutely, watching them go.

John, carrying the little girl in his arms, walked down the hill. He had torn a sleeve from his shirt and bound it around her leg as a tourniquet, and the bleeding was beginning to slack off. He looked around for Joe, or Bellows Chaney, but he did not see either of them.

He turned up Butler Street and headed for the City Hospital. People streamed past him. Anger was beginning to saturate the shock of the mob's mood again, and John dimly heard the beginning of threats of vengeance. The little girl had stopped whimpering now, and was breathing softly through her open mouth. A bubble of blood had appeared in one nostril. He prayed that she had not had a lung crushed when she was trampled.

There was no twitch, nothing perceptible; but he was aware of the precise moment when she died.

Chapter Eleven

Robert Ammon was across the river in Allegheny City when the massacre took place. He had commandeered the telegraph office, and was using it as the field headquarters of his operation to coordinate the strike around the country. He was sending wires to every town he had been to that spring and summer of organizing. And wires were pouring in.

Baltimore was paralyzed. B & O trainmen had struck on Friday, in the aftermath of the Martinsburg walkout. There were some reports of skirmishes between troops and mobs; of shooting, and of casualties.

The strike was spreading east and west. From Albany and Buffalo, Lexington and Louisville, Detroit, Galveston, Kansas City, Omaha, as far west as San Francisco, word clattered in over the telegraph wire. St. Louis was a virtual workers' commune.

The telegraph key stopped clacking for a moment. But to Ammon, pacing the floor, his head filled with ideas and excitement, the sound continued like an echo in his ears. The door flew open, and Bill Shears, a young switchman, burst in.

"Bob," he cried, "come out here! Listen!"

He followed Shears outside, and stood and listened. From across the river, over on the Pittsburgh side, he heard the clacking, and he knew what it was.

"Good Christ."

"It's been goin' on five minutes!"

All around them people stood still, listening. The gunfire did not stop. With it drifted the sound of screaming.

Ammon shook his head. "It's war, then," he said softly. The day's date popped into his head. July 21, 1877. He wondered fleetingly if it would be a date schoolchildren would memorize a hundred years from now.

The gunfire still crackled from across the river. The strikers in the yard were looking at him.

"Arm yourselves," Ammon said. "If you've got guns at home, get them. If you don't, avail yourselves of what you can from gun shops. From the police. From the Armory. Matthews, take your crew and dig trenches along the east end of the yard. Hewatt, you and your people dig in along Strawberry Lane. Waldner, get your yard crews up to the second floor of the engine shop where you can control both directions. Shears, you get a patrol together and keep people off the streets. If they send troops into Allegheny City, we'll be ready for them!"

Across the river in war-torn Pittsburgh, two boys jumped from a boxcar and disappeared into the crowd at the Twenty-sixth Street yard. A moment later dark smoke seeped through the half-open door. Then fingers of flame poked out and spread themselves along the edge of the doorjamb. There was a whooshing sound, and suddenly the boxcar was consumed by fire.

The mob nearby gave a roar of excitement. A group of burly men heaved at the car behind it, pushing it into the burning car. The burning car began to roll. Another man raced ahead and threw a switch. The two cars rolled in through the open door of a train shed.

"Look at 'er go!"

"Hey, that's the spirit! Burn 'em!"

"Anything belongs to the railroad, up it goes!"

The shed was in flames now. Rioters soaked sticks of wood in coal oil, lit them, and ran through the standing cars. Soon the night sky above Pittsburgh was as bright as midsummer at noon, and many times hotter.

Bells clanged, and fire engines drawn by snorting,

blinkered horses forced their way slowly through the hostile crowd. But as the first stream of water began to play against a blazing machine shop, a rioter grabbed an axe from an engine and slammed it through the hose. The arc of water disintegrated, and the building burned.

Mayor William McCarthy hurried through the hotel lobby and was shown to the suite where Alexander Cassatt directed emergency operations for his railroad. The room was full of dark-suited men, most with their faces pressed to the windows, flickering in the dancing red light of the holocaust outside.

"Mister Cassatt!"

"Mayor McCarthy."

Neither man proffered a hand. McCarthy, big and sweating, stared at the Pennsylvania vice-president's cool, skulllike face with unconcealed dislike. His look was mirrored in Cassatt's pale eyes.

"Mister Cassatt, something's got to be done out there!"

"Mayor McCarthy, I have been standing here for the past hour watching my company's property engulfed in flames and torn apart by your constituents, whole companies of Pennsylvania militia driven to tenuous sanctuary in buildings already being put to the torch by these communist mobs . . . and now you tell me something has to be done. I do not completely understand what qualifications brought you to your high office, but I presume penetrating insight was not one of them. I am aware that something has to be done. My question is, what do you propose to do? Have you no police?"

"The answer is no, we damn well don't have any police force to deal with a situation like this! And the reason we don't is the same reason we've got this situation—because the Pennsylvania Raiload has bled this city dry, along with these men who work for you! We've had to cut back on our police force because we damn well don't have the money to pay them anymore!"

"Mayor McCarthy, kindly lower your voice!"

"The hell! My voice ain't the problem! Now my question is, are you ready to talk with these men and settle some of their legitimate grievances? I don't know how much good it'll do, because damn few of these people out there are railroad men. Most of the strikers, far as I can tell, are trying to protect your damn property. What these people out there have in common is, they hate your goddamned railroad! You people made this situation by caring for nothing but squeezing every last drop of profit out of Pittsburgh and your employees. Now why don't you think of some goddamn thing to say to them to cool them off!''

Cassatt's voice was as white and colorless as his parchment face. "There seems little point, Mr. Mayor. As you point out, this mob outside has little to do with the railroad. Any concessions we might make would hardly affect them; and in any case, to make concessions in the face of mob violence would be madness. It would establish a precedent that could well destroy the whole structure of American democracy. The Pennsylvania Railroad will not do that.

"Besides," he added, his eyes drifting toward the window, "it would appear we would have very little to gain by such an action. We seem to have so little left to lose."

"The city of Pittsburgh has a great deal left to lose," growled the mayor.

"Does it?" Cassatt said blandly. "Good day, Mayor McCarthy."

By dawn the fire had spread from Millvale Station all the way to Twentieth Street. Only railroad property burned. The mob helped firemen keep neighboring buildings drenched, but not a drop of water was allowed to fall on anything that belonged to the Pennsylvania.

Looting had begun in the early hours of the morning. Men, women, and children labored by firelight, tossing barrels and boxes and crates from cars not yet consumed by flames. They came with carts and wagons, wheelbarrows, gunny sacks. A brawny woman with sleeping babies tucked under each arm rolled a barrel of flour triumphantly away with her feet. A boy running with a sack full of eggs tripped over a fire hose; he picked himself up, emptied the gooey mess onto the street, and rushed back with his dripping sack for more. Two women pulled at a cheap dress like competing shoppers at a bargain sale. Periodic roars of delight signaled the discovery of a carload of whiskey, wine, or beer. All through the night they streamed to and from the freight cars; and the dancing light flickered red and yellow on a frenzied parade of parasols, blankets, calico and lace, bacon, lard, flour, eggs, pillows, tools, pots and pans, shoes, and Bibles.

John Whitmarsh had walked for hours with the dead girl's body in his arms. He did not know what to do with her. There was no clue to tell him to whom she belonged. There were no parents whose hearts to break with the news that their baby girl was dead. There were only the Philadelphia troops, who had killed her.

He felt hemmed in by death. He had lived fourteen years with death only a hearsay thing; in the past twelve months, it had happened all around him. His father, murdered in a jail cell. His Uncle Mike, his cousin Timmy. Walter Koch, struck dead at his feet, and his Uncle Tim, hanged—the gentlest of souls, both of them. And now today, the bodies of men and women littering the streets of Pittsburgh, and an unknown child whose heart had stopped beating while pressed against his own.

He had to get to Ammon. Too much had happened too fast. He had lost all sense of what it was about.

Inside the Twenty-sixth Street roundhouse the Philadelphia troops waited. They sat quietly, or sprawled against their packs, away from the windows. Here and there small knots of them talked in voices hushed with fear.

Gordon Reid, big and soft and bespectacled, stood in a doorway that looked out onto a quiet alley and smoked a cigarette. He was a Harvard graduate, married to a Pittsburgh girl, and the father of two young children. He owned a small printing shop in Bryn Mawr. Two days ago he had been in his shop, jacket off, shirt-sleeves rolled up to the elbow, skin smudged with ink. But he was a lieutenant in the Weccacoe Legion, and yesterday he had been called to arms. Now he was in a roundhouse in Pittsburgh, pinned down by a furious mob, twenty blocks from the house where six months ago he had sat down to a Christmas dinner with his wife's family.

Out of the darkness of the alley a figure suddenly appeared. Lieutenant Reid snatched up his rifle.

"Who goes there!" he snapped, and then shrank back as a young man deposited in his arms the blood-caked body of a small child.

"This belongs to you," the voice rasped, and then the young man was gone. The lieutenant looked down, appalled, at the small stiff corpse in his arms.

Chapter Twelve

The roundhouse where the troops were quartered had been an early target of the torches, but for some reason it was slow to burn. Finally the rioters discovered a boxcar filled with coke which they drenched with petroleum oil, put to the match, and sent careening against the roundhouse. Within moments flames were racing up the western wall like ivy.

At a few minutes past six, as dawn was adding its redness to the glow of burning Pittsburgh, the Philadelphia troops marched out of the blazing roundhouse at port arms, with Gatling guns in tow. The mob fell back.

In close-packed, orderly formation they marched up to Thirty-third and turned onto Pennsylvania Avenue. The mob surged after them. There was shouting and heckling and stones were thrown, but no shots were fired.

John had left the scene at the roundhouse sometime earlier, after he had turned over the girl's body to the Philadelphia officer. He had gone across town to Joe Kovalchik's room, but his landlady had not seen Joe since the previous day. He wanted to find Bellows Chaney, too, but he had no idea where Chaney lived.

He was at the corner of Butler Street, on his way toward the bridge to Allegheny City, when he heard the sounds of the troops and the mob advancing in his direction. The street around him suddenly was full, as advance groups of rioters raced out of side streets, and citizens poured out of buildings along the way.

Then across the street, in the midst of the darting, swirling crowd, he saw a tall figure in a long white linen coat. A breechloader was on his shoulder, a black cartridge box slung from his waist. On his head perched a coonskin cap.

It was Chaney.

"Bellows!" he yelled. "Hey, Bellows! Chaney!"

Chaney's head seemed to turn slightly, but whether in response to his shout or not John couldn't tell. The whole street was now a roar of sound.

"Bellows! Where's Joe?"

The troops were between them now, skirmish lines flung out to keep the crowds back. There was no chance that Chaney could hear him. Chaney stood there, massive and stone-faced, as the mob eddied around him, flowing along with the quick-marching troops. Then slowly, deliberately, he raised the rifle, sighted into the troop formation, and fired. A soldier at the edge of the column dropped.

"Bellows!" John screamed again, and darted out into the street to get to him.

"God damn it, get back you fucker!" snarled a soldier, and swung the butt of his rifle hard into John's face. The light shattered into a million tiny pieces, and he blacked out.

He came to a moment later, feeling a strong hand

pulling him back by the collar. His mouth was full of blood and loose teeth. He coughed and spat.

"Bellows," he said thickly. "That you?"

"Take it easy, honey."

He turned his head at the voice and saw a young Negro woman in her mid-twenties. She was slim, handsome, with an angular face, dark full lips, and black hair curling from beneath a kerchief wrapped about her head. The arm that pulled him away from the trampling feet was smooth, black, and sinewy.

She helped him up and leaned him against a wall.

"You look like hell," she said thoughtfully. She took the kerchief from her head and mopped at the blood that flowed from his cheek and mouth and nose.

"Lost a coupla teeth," she observed. "Well, they're back teeth. You'll be pretty enough if you don't laugh too wide. Once this cheek gets healed up." She touched his nose, and he winced. "Nose broke too. Look, honey, next time don't lead with your face. God, you got blood all over your shirt too—what's left of it. What'd you do with your sleeve?"

John gagged on blood in his throat, and turned his head to spit it out. The woman tore a piece of her kerchief off with her teeth. She wadded it up and tucked it into John's mouth.

"Here," she said. "Bite down on this for a while. That'll stop the bleeding. You got a gun?"

"No," he mumbled through the cloth. He shook his head.

"Here." She reached into a pocket of her apron and produced an army model Colt. It was shiny and unscarred, like something from a gunshop display case. "You know how to use this?"

John stared at it in surprise. He shrugged his shoulders. "I guess so . . . but . . ."

"Don't worry. I got plenty." She tugged at her apron and he saw three pistols tucked into the waistband of her skirt. Another sagged in the other pocket of her apron. She placed the Colt in his hand, and added to it a box of bullets.

"Next time don't use your face," she said, and smiled. "It's too pretty for these scum!"

Then she was gone, hurrying up the street after the retreating troops.

John shoved the pistol in his shirt, and pocketed the bullets. He ran after the pursuing mob, looking for Bellows Chaney.

He caught sight of him once, a long way away. Chaney was still a dot of lethal calm in the middle of the hysteria, looming tall above the crowd in his white coat, firing methodically into the troops who were now returning the fire. Others in the crowd were firing now, too, some from the sidewalk, some from roofs and windows. Chaney still wore Joe Kovalchik's coonskin cap.

The rear company of Philadelphians halted and swung their Gatling guns onto the crowd. As people dove and scattered, they opened fire, spraying the sidewalk and buildings with deadly bursts. Chaney took casual cover behind a lamppost, and continued his dispassionate sniping. After a moment the company of soldiers reformed and hurried after the rest of the column. More than a dozen men lay dead or dying on the sidewalks.

Chaney was unhit, as far as John could tell from where he stood. The last he saw of him, Bellows Chaney was still moving relentlessly after the troops, shadowing them with death.

John finally gave up hope of reaching him. Joe was dead. He knew that now. That was why Chaney now wore Joe's cap, and that was what had turned the pacifist giant into an avenging angel.

John made his way slowly toward the river. To his left the thunder of the running battle in the streets retreated, but hardly diminished. To his right, and before him, fires blazed. Death and ashes stank in the air. Behind him, the sun had just cleared the building tops.

When he reached the river he went down to the water and washed some of the blood off himself. His mouth had stopped bleeding. He took out the wadded piece of cloth and threw it into the river. His nose had stopped bleeding, too, although it was very sore and swelled out into his line of vision.

He climbed back up to the bridge and was about to cross when a man approached him nervously. The man was tall and pudgy and wore glasses. He was wearing a topcoat buttoned up to the chin, and he wore a bowler hat.

"Excuse me," the man said. "Are you a railroader?"

"Yes."

"Do you know a man over there named Ammon?"

"Yes, I do." There was something familiar about him, although John was sure he did not know the man. It was more like a face remembered from a dream.

"Look," the man was saying, "I don't know what to do. They say this man Ammon has Allegheny City all dug in and ready for war. We don't want that. All we want to do is to give up and go home."

"Who are you, anyway?"

"I'm . . ." He looked appealingly at John, as if asking for lenient judgment. "My name's Reid. Gordon Reid. It's my misfortune to be a company commander in the Weccacoe Legion. But look—I don't want any part of this. Neither do my men! We don't like killing workingmen, we don't like killing Pennsylvanians, and we don't care to die for the Pennsylvania Railroad. All we want to do is get out of here, give up and go home."

"Where are your men?"

"Over there." He pointed to a warehouse across the street.

John remembered where he had seen that face. At the door of the roundhouse in the middle of the night.

"All right," he said. "I'll take you to Ammon. There better not be any funny business. You in uniform under that thing?"

Lieutenant Reid nodded, and unbuttoned the top few buttons to reveal his tunic. It was smudged on the front with blood.

"All right," John said.

*   *   *

The column of troops marched stiffly through the yard
of the Pittsburgh, Fort Wayne & Chicago. Hundreds of
strikers watched. Most were armed.

On the steps of the administration building Robert Ammon
waited, tall and proud. John Whitmarsh stood at his side.
The company halted, stacked arms, and stood at attention.
Its young commander walked solemnly forward until he
stood in front of Ammon. He snapped a crisp salute.
Ammon returned it gravely.

Lieutenant Reid unbuckled the long, glistening gold-
trimmed sword from about his waist. He laid it across his
open palms and held it out to Ammon.

"Sir," he said, "we are in your hands."

The yard exploded with cheering. A huge grin broke
over Ammon's face, and he stepped off the porch and
embraced Gordon Reid. The strikers swarmed through the
troops, laughing and pumping hands and slapping backs.
John suddenly felt dizzy with relief and joy. He leapt
down into the crowd and started grabbing hands and shoulders, hugging, squeezing, kissing, and whooping with
delight.

A passenger train pulled out, eastbound, with Reid's
company waving from its windows and the strikers shouting farewells. John Whitmarsh and Bob Ammon stood in
the dispatcher's office, watching through the window.

"We're going to win. John, we're going to win!" Ammon
exulted. He grinned and gestured around the office.

"I'm running the railroad now, had you heard? The
whole shebang. Management tried to close it down, tried
to stop passenger service. Wanted to get the public down
on us. So we took it over. Running on schedule, too,
which is a damn sight better than they ever did. The press
is calling me 'Boss Ammon.' How do you like that?"

He turned and walked back through the office, and sat at
the big desk.

"There's something I want you to do for me, John," he
said. "This thing's not a strike anymore, it's a revolution.

Somebody's got to step out and take control. And that might as well be me.

"Go to Chicago. That's the big place now, with all the railroads coming together. Size up the situation. Talk to the leaders there. Find Philip Van Patten and Albert Parsons. They head up the Workingmen's Party; they're the big men. Talk to them, let them know what we're doing here. Get them to report to me.

"And keep an eye on them. They're a bit extreme, those Chicago boys. Anarchists, Marxists. They get a little crazy sometimes. They may be hard to control. Keep an eye on them, and report back to me."

Ammon sprang up out of his chair again, and paced the room. His whole body trembled with energy and excitement, and his eyes blazed like torches.

"God damn, John," he breathed, "we're going to win. We're going to win!"

Chapter Thirteen

William Henderson left the Young Democrats' clubhouse on Center Street, and stepped out into the bright sunlight and sudden warmth of a perfect July afternoon. Henderson could not have felt better. He had seen his doctor that morning for his annual checkup, and been told that he had the health and stamina of a man half his forty-two years. The Young Democrats would support his hand-picked slate for Congress, plus the city and state offices, in the fall. And with Tammany in a shambles, that meant the nominations—and the elections—were assured right down the line. And that meant that by the next congressional elections, he would be ready to move in himself. He could start thinking, then, about selling his casinos and moving on to the next stage in his life: politician and gentleman.

His gait was sprightly, and he swung his silver-headed walking stick. His only regret on this perfect afternoon was that he had not gone to Saratoga for the season's opening, the week before. Now this morning's papers carried news of the railroad strike hitting the New York Central. Workers had shut down the yards at West Albany. There might be an odd passenger train running still, but all in all, there was no harm in postponing Saratoga for a few days.

This railroad strike had driven the Tweed trial right off the front page of the *Times*. That was too bad; Henderson loved seeing it there in the right-hand column where it had been for so long that it had come to seem like a regular feature. But now the *Times* contained nothing but rioting and insurrection. Pittsburgh in flames . . . Baltimore . . . a local militia company in Reading turning their guns on the Philadelphia militia, and announcing: "If you fire at the crowd, we'll fire at you." It got even crazier: "Communism in the West" . . . Adjutant General Townsend cutting short his Fire Island vacation and returning to the capital in case the West Albany situation should get out of hand. And more of the same today: "A SERIOUS TIME IN CHICAGO—CITY IN POSSESSION OF COMMUNISTS . . ."

He was stopped at the curb by a girl in her early teens. She was pretty, with a fresh, smooth complexion, and a body that combined youthful awkwardness with a womanly softness; her bosom was startlingly full for such a slim young girl. Her eyes were dark, clear, and compelling. They hinted at an awareness beyond her years, and probably beyond her experience. There was something familiar about her, but he could not quite place what it was.

"Mr. Henderson . . .?" asked the girl.

"The same." Henderson smiled down at her. She was remarkably pretty, whoever she was, as warm and appealing as the July afternoon. And he was in a good mood. "But you have the advantage of me, my dear. What can I do for you?"

"It's not much of an advantage that you don't know me," said the girl. "Because I really want to get to know you. I'd like us to be friends. My name is Fannie Whitmarsh."

Whitmarsh . . . that was Catlett's mistress's name. Yes, of course. That was why she looked familiar: she must be the Whitmarsh woman's daughter. Could she have been sent as a spy of some sort, by Catlett? For what? There wasn't anything of value that Catlett could learn by spying on him.

"My mother and Mr. Catlett don't know anything about this," said Fannie. "My mother doesn't even know that I know anything about Mr. Catlett, or you."

Henderson offered her his arm. "Well, then, dear, why don't we take a ride in the park on this beautiful summer day, and get acquainted?"

Henderson had been a saloonkeeper and casino proprietor for ten years, during which time he had seen a lot and done a lot. He had taken girls in their teens into his bed before, and he had had virgins before, too. He was not inclined to be gentle with them. If they wanted to take their chances lifting their skirts for Bill Henderson, they'd get what Bill Henderson chose to give them.

But he felt a protective instinct toward Fannie Whitmarsh. He didn't know why. Maybe it was because she didn't seem to expect it, or ask for it.

There was a screen in his room for her to undress behind, but she did not use it. Perhaps she did not know she was supposed to. She stripped to her shift right in the middle of his room. Then she sat down on his bed, and took the shift off too.

She might have been trying to look exotic and alluring. She might have been trying to look bored and professional; or she might have been unsure of the effect that she wanted to create, and so trying to do both at the same time.

She was neither. Whatever she was, Henderson had never seen it before. And the image of her whirled in his mind until he almost forgot who he was, and how he expected a woman to bend to his will and his desires. He stood and looked at her.

She was younger than he had thought, and yet even more sensual. Her breasts were large, and almost perfectly round. They would elongate more at the tips, in a couple of years. She had almost no nipples. Her dark pubic hair was sparse, new, and impossibly fluffy. Her thighs were just beginning to get round, and her hips were thin and straight. Henderson crossed over to her in three steps, and enfolded her in his arms. She shivered, and clutched his sleeve.

He kissed her hair, her forehead, and the tip of her ear over and over again before he lifted her face to kiss her mouth. She was confused at first by his tongue, but quickly understood and made a place for it—in much the same way that, minutes later, she would receive his penis.

"What do you want?" Henderson asked her later, as she lay with her head on his chest. "I like you. Do you want to get away from home? Do you want me to set you up in an apartment and take care of you, like Catlett does with your mother?"

"No," she said. "I like you, too. I don't want to move away from home. And I don't want you to take care of me. I want you to teach me how to take care of myself."

Henderson was glad that she liked him. "Sure," he said. "What would you like me to teach you first?"

"Well," she said, "you could start by teaching me how to mark a faro deck."

Chapter Fourteen

Albert Parsons bought a copy of the *Chicago Times* on his way to work. This was an extravagance that he did not normally commit. His job was in the composing room of that paper, where there were copies of the *Times* lying around to be had for the taking. It was a fifteen-minute walk to the *Times* offices; it seemed unnecessary to pay money to get the news a quarter of an hour sooner.

But this morning he could not wait. History was crackling through Chicago, and Albert Parsons was at the center of it. The great social revolution was at hand, or so it seemed on that warm July morning as the sun rose over grimy Chicago rooftops and caught the fresh-inked headlines of the newspaper he held in his hands:

UNREST IN MARKET SQUARE
10,000 WORKERS HEAR PROVOCATIVE SPEECHES

Yesterday evening Parsons had spoken at a rally in Market Square, in front of thousands of cheering workers. They had cheered him as he climbed up on top of a wagon to address them, before he had opened his mouth. It had caught him by surprise. He had not thought he was so widely known. He was a leader of the Workingmen's Party of the United States, but very few of these whistling, shouting people were W.P.U.S. It made the hairs stand up on his neck, and his throat go numb; and if he had had to begin speaking right away, he would not have been able to. But the cheering went on.

It was not Albert Parsons they were cheering, he realized, but themselves. Because the revolution belonged to all the working classes, and there were no leaders of a revolution. There were visible crystals, like himself, to focus and direct it; but a revolution was not individuals, but a collective will, a tide of history flooding through fertile ground.

The crowd spread out through Market Square. He could not begin to see how many there were. It was dark, and beyond the faces nearest him, it was a moving, flickering sea of torchlight. The man who had spoken before him in German, August Spies, smiled wryly at him. Parsons raised his arms and waved for quiet. The cheering redoubled. Finally it began to quiet down.

"Do you feel it?" he shouted. "Do you hear it? Do you see it? The Grand Army of Starvation is on the march! Look around you. Here we are, and this time we will not be denied!"

The *Times* reporter who had covered the rally began his story with a grudging admission that it had been peaceful, both in conduct and in the tenor of the speeches. He hedged and temporized, and used phrases like "on the surface," and "apparently respectable workingmen," who, although avowedly socialist, "counseled (at least openly) moderation, and deprecated any resort to violence." The reporter wrote carefully, with one eye on the Market Square rally and the other on his employers. And gradually it was the second eye that took focus.

"But beneath the surface," Parsons read, "boiled a most frightening and dangerous lava of violence. For if the lips of the speakers dripped peace and moderation, the hands in their pockets were balled into fists, or clenched around pistols. The mob that roiled and festered in Market Square was laced with powder, and the speeches, especially that of Albert Parsons, came chillingly close to lighting the fuse."

Parsons felt sick. He knew who owned the newspapers, and what their politics and economics were. But he still had an idealistic view of the newspaper business, a view he had sustained through fifteen years, even owning his own paper for a time in Texas. He could not understand the deliberate distortion of truth. His friend Spies mocked him about this weakness. But Parsons still believed in his heart that people were essentially honest, and needed only to be shown the truth to embrace it.

"Look out, boyo!"

He jumped back as a police wagon went clattering by, hurrying somewhere. In the back of the wagon were two rows of stolid-faced, blue-uniformed officers.

The sidewalk in front of the *Times* building was crowded with people waiting for the latest bulletins from the East. It reminded Parsons of the Civil War days, when townspeople had flocked to the newspaper offices to wait for war news and lists of the wounded and killed. Now a rumor was buzzing through the crowd that President Hayes had ordered out the regulars, and some were saying that General Sheridan was marching with 20,000 men on the city of Pittsburgh. Someone had heard that foreign agents, veterans of the Paris Commune, had been filtering into Chicago for the past week, and that the city was on the verge of falling into the hands of the communists. Nobody had any real information, and everybody was talking. Parsons made his way through and into the building.

Bobby Bowden, the day janitor, saw him in the hallway. "Hello, Parsons, seen your name in the paper?"

"Yes, I did."

"Seen the editorial?"

Parsons shook his head.

"They got you in the editorial too."

"No, I didn't see that."

"Better have a look 'fore you go upstairs."

The train, slowed to a walking pace, rolled through the endless outskirts of Chicago. Already John Whitmarsh had begun to see evidence of the strike here. Freights stood idle on the tracks, and here and there knots of men gathered near them. As John's train came closer to the Great Central Depot, more and more tracks converged. As the tracks increased, so did the excitement.

The inside of the station was huge and intimidating. John walked through it quickly. Outside he found a policeman and asked directions to the *Chicago Times*. The policeman was courteous. He addressed John as "sir," and stepped out into the street to outline the route in the air with sweeping gestures of his truncheon.

It was noon, and getting hot. John felt himself sweating as he walked. He wore his suit, his father's suit that his mother had given him when he left home. He was beginning to fill it out better now. But it was heavy for this weather, and it made him sweat.

A squad of soldiers marched by at the next intersection. They carried muskets at their shoulders, and marched with imprecise, serious steps, like spear carriers in an amateur theatrical. They were Illinois National Guardsmen. People stopped and stared as they marched by, and some of the people applauded.

In a few more blocks he came to the *Chicago Times*. He made his way through the crowd that was massed in front of the building for the news bulletins, and went inside. He was curious, and a little afraid, to meet Albert Parsons. He had never seen an anarchist before.

The man at the desk was sharp and officious. He directed John to the composing room on the second floor. John walked down the hall in the direction he had been shown, and found the stairs. The stairs were wooden and well-worn, and dust seeped up through the dry wood. The air was heavy with the tangy smell of ink and newsprint that he remembered so well from his father's *Independence*.

The foreman came over to John when he entered the composing room, and looked at him suspiciously.

"What's your business?"

"I'm looking for someone. Albert Parsons. I was told I might find him here."

"Albert Parsons? What do you want with him?"

"I've got a message for him. It'll just take a moment."

"A message, is it? What kind of goddamned message?"

"I beg your pardon, sir," said John stiffly. The foreman's hostility unsettled him. "I didn't want to cause any inconvenience. Maybe I'd better come back later. When . . ."

"Voss! Kenny!" Two men came over. "Throw this communist sonofabitch out of here!" The foreman was red-faced with anger. "You goddamn communist agitators ain't gonna use the *Chicago Times* for your goddamn meetings!"

Voss and Kenny each grabbed one of John's arms.

"But I . . . I" John stammered. "I just wanted to . . ."

"Parsons is fired!" the foreman shouted. "And you can tell him and the rest of your anarchist friends if any one of you shows up here again I'll toss 'em through the window!"

John jerked his arms free angrily. "Look here, I don't know what you're so heated up about, but all I came up here for was to . . ."

He froze. The foreman had jerked a pistol from his pocket and was pointing it at John's face. "I've a mind to blow your brains out! Now get him out of here!"

John did not resist as the two men dragged him roughly down the stairs and flung him through a side door. His suitcase came open and his few possessions were scattered. Passersby looked at him, startled, and then hurried on.

Two plainclothes policemen came to get Albert Parsons in the office of the *Arbeiter-Zeitung*, the German language workingman's newspaper. He was in the office of his friend August Spies. The policemen had grim faces and carried guns under their coats.

"Mayor Heath wants to see you."

"What . . . now?"

"Right now."

"Just a minute," Spies bridled, coming out from behind his desk. "You haff no right to burst in here like this!"

One of the policemen looked threateningly toward him.

"No, it's all right," said Parsons. "I'll talk to the mayor."

The two plainclothes policemen took Albert Parsons through the streets to City Hall. There were troops in the streets, nervous-looking National Guardsmen, and squads of police who looked sure of themselves and ready for action. They saw roving bands of strikers, too, but there were no confrontations.

At City Hall the plainclothesmen took Parsons to a room that was crowded with uniformed officers. Superintendent of Police Hickey was at a desk at the far end of the room, talking with reporters. When the plainclothes police brought Parsons over to the desk, the reporters swarmed about him.

"Hey, it's Parsons!"

"Hello, Parsons, what've they got you on?"

"Mr. Parsons! Where were you arrested?"

"What's the charge?"

"Hold it, boys, I'm not under arrest. I'm just here to speak to the mayor."

Superintendent Hickey turned on him. "I'll tell you who you're here to see and who you're not," he growled. "And meanwhile, you'll be keepin' your mouth shut!" He spoke to the plainclothesmen, and they took Parsons to a side door and up some stairs to another room. They left him there alone and told him to wait. A uniformed policeman was stationed outside the door.

The room had a long table in it, and several dozen chairs. On the walls were lithographs of the city. Boxes of paper were stacked in one corner. There was nothing on the table but a few ashtrays, and there were two spittoons near the wall. At one end of the room was an American flag, flanked by framed, hand-colored photographs of Mayor Heath and President Hayes. After a while the door opened and about thirty men came in. Superintendent Hickey was among them, and there were a few other uniformed police. The rest were businessmen from the Board of Trade, and city officials. They wore expensive suits and expressions of hatred. Parsons was surprised and a little scared by the hatred on their faces.

"Sit down," Superintendent Hickey ordered him curtly. Hickey took the chair opposite Parsons, and the other men sat or stood around the room. Some stood behind Albert Parsons, where he could not see them.

"All right, now, Parsons, what the hell are you doin' here?" Hickey demanded.

"I understood the mayor wanted to see me."

"No!" The policeman's hand smashed on the table. "What are you doin' here? In Chicago? Why've you come here?"

"I have lived here since 1873."

"Doin' what?"

"I am a member of the Typographical Union, and have been working as a printer . . ."

"*And* labor agitatin'! *And* preachin' anarchism! *And* solicitin' workers to unlawful strike!"

"No, sir. I've never advocated anarchy or illegal strikes. My role, for whatever importance it has, has been to try to get people to the polls, to organize . . ."

"Do you hold a job, Parsons?"

"I did, until this morning." There was some laughter.

"American?"

"I was born in Alabama and raised in Texas, sir. My family came to this country in 1632, and served with distinction in the American Revolution."

"All right, bedad, don't get clever with me!" snapped Superintendent Hickey, whose own strong brogue suggested that he was not himself a native-born citizen. "Just answer the questions!"

"Yes," said Parsons, "I am an American."

They questioned him for a long time: Where had he come from? Why had he come to Chicago? Didn't he know better than to incite the workingmen of Chicago to insurrection? If he didn't like this country, why didn't he go back to Europe?

Parsons answered them patiently and quietly. He was feeling very tired, and his voice was hoarse. He made himself remain detached, and not rise to the baiting, as he answered the same questions over and over.

A man came in with a message which he handed to Hickey. Hickey read it, scowling.

"You can forget your rally tonight, Parsons. There's not goin' to be any rally. I've orders here from the mayor to shut it down."

"But you can't do that," Parsons protested. "We have the constitutional right to peaceful assembly."

"Peaceful," the superintendent snorted. "You just try holdin' it, bucko, and see how peaceful it'll be!"

"God damn it, what're we pussyfootin' around for," a man demanded. "Let's string the socialist bastard up!"

"Lynch him!"

"Lock him up and throw away the key!"

It occurred to Albert Parsons for a moment that they might do it. He was relieved when a few minutes later Superintendent Hickey escorted him out of the room. Hickey gripped him tightly by the arm, and steered him through a doorway off the end of the hall, which led into a dim stairwell.

"Get out of town, Parsons," Hickey advised him. His face was very close. "I wouldn't give two cents for your chances of stayin' alive in Chicago."

Parsons asked him what he meant.

"Why, those Board of Trade men in there. They're likely to have you shot down in the street, or strung up to a lamppost. You heard 'em."

"Can I count on your protection, Superintendent?"

"You can count on my ass, Parsons! Now get out of here, and watch your step. Tell your communist pals no meetin' tonight. No rally! Anything that happens, you're responsible! And remember, I'll have you watched every moment of the day, and if you fart I'll know about it. We don't like communist agitators here in Chicago, Parsons!"

The door slammed, and the sound echoed up and down the empty stairwell. There was no other sound, and nobody was about. Albert Parsons felt his knees begin to tremble violently, and he sat down on the stairs. Tears ran down his face.

He was more than American, he was *passionately* American. He knew his country's history, and the part his family had played in it from its earliest period. He knew what America had become, and what it ought to be. He had made one mistake in his life that he regretted: running away from his Texas home to fight for the slave-holding South in the Civil War. After the war, he had become a worker for Negro rights, and in the process had earned the contempt and hatred of many of his former comrades-in-arms.

Parsons sat in the stairwell for a while, and then he got up and went down the stairs and through a door that led into the main lobby of the City Hall. Parsons walked across the lobby, feeling thoroughly alone and at the same time under the most intense scrutiny, although no one appeared to be watching him.

Why do they want to do this to me? he wondered. And then he shook his head impatiently at the self-pity. What had they really done to him, so far, after all?

August Spies was waiting for him outside. "You vass in there an awful long time, Albert. Are you all right?"

"I'm all right. Listen, they're going to ban the rally."

"They can't do that!"

"Hickey told me to call it off. The order comes from the mayor." Parsons shrugged his shoulders. "Why do they think I can control it? Even if I wanted to."

"What are you going to do?"

"I'm tired. I'm going home."

"Vill you be at the rally?"

"Of course."

"Mr. Parsons?"

Albert Parsons turned and saw a young man who had been hanging back during his conversation with August Spies. He wore a bulky tweed suit and carried a suitcase.

"This young fellow comes from Pittsburgh," said Spies. "From the Trainmen's Union. His name iss Vitmore."

"Whitmarsh," John corrected. "John Whitmarsh."

"Mr. Whitmarsh." Parsons held out his hand. "Pleased to meet you."

"How do you do, sir. I'm just in on the train this morning. Robert Ammon sent me to . . . to get things coordinated."

"Good! Come along with me, then, and tell me what's been going on back there. Do you have a place to stay?"

"No, sir."

"That's fine. You'll stay with us. Tell me now, what's been happening?"

Chapter Fifteen

He went home with Albert Parsons and met Tesia. Tesia was the daughter of Russian immigrants. She had come to America with her parents at the age of three. Her father had died when she was thirteen, from a lingering infection that he got working in the meat packing plants. Her mother died a year later, from no specific cause. Since then she had been living with the Parsons. She was sixteen.

John first saw her in the doorway at the top of the stairs. There were four flights of stairs to climb to the apartment that Albert Parsons shared with his wife, Lucy, and the girl. Tesia heard their footsteps on the stairs and opened the door.

She had black hair that she wore in a long braid, loosely coiled at the back of her neck. Her skin was olive-tinted, and her dark eyes had an almost oriental slant. Her nose was wide, and so was her mouth, with thick lips that stretched far back over strong white teeth in a welcoming smile.

"Hello, Mr. Parsons. Mrs. Parsons, he's home," she called, turning away from the door to the inside. From behind the door they could hear her loud whisper: ". . . and he has a boy with him!"

A moment later they were inside an apartment that made John feel at home the moment he stood in it. It was not that it was like anyplace he had ever lived. It was more as though there had been a room like this somewhere in his mind. The wallpaper was faded but warm, a reddish-brown color. Most of it was covered with bookcases filled to overflowing with used-looking books: books packed in vertically, more piled horizontally on top of them, many propped open as if they had been put aside in the midst of reading and expected to be taken up again soon. There were paintings and drawings on the walls, and beautiful American Indian blankets and wall hangings. A rolltop desk nestled near the window under a clutter of papers and books. The sofa and chairs looked worn and lumpy, but comfortable. A bedroom was visible through one doorway, and another led to a tiny kitchen.

"Hello, Tesia," said Parsons. "This 'boy' is Mr. Whitmarsh, one of the leaders of the strike council in Pittsburgh."

"How do you do, Mr. Whitmarsh." She was not at all abashed. She seemed rather to be holding back laughter.

"How do you do," said John maturely.

Lucy Parsons came out of the kitchen. She was Spanish Indian, with copper skin and strong, handsome features. Albert Parsons made the introductions.

"I'm very pleased to meet you, Mr. Whitmarsh," Lucy Parsons said, and then turned with concern to her husband. "Albert, what happened today?"

"Well, my dear," he said, placing his hands on her plump hips, "let me see . . . I was fired from my job, I was black-listed in the trade. I was arrested and interrogated for several hours by the police and a delegation of leading citizens. I have been threatened with hanging, marked for assassination, and warned to leave town." He furrowed his brow in a burlesque of deep thought, and then brightened. "Aside from that, I would have to say things look pretty good."

Dinner was a spicy southwestern *chile con carne*, the cooking aroma of which had been part of the sensation of homecoming John had felt on his arrival. The *chile* was hot enough to make John's eyes water, but there was beer to cool it off with, and the *chile* stayed warm in the stomach and sent an electric rush up through the nervous system and into the brain.

The impressions John had received so far from Albert Parsons made it hard to maintain the suspicious preconceptions he had brought with him. He had come primed by Bob Ammon to find a power-mad egoist, but Parsons did not seem to be like that. Nor was he a wild-eyed bombthrower, nor a tubercular foreigner. On the contrary, he was an attractive, kind-spoken man of about twenty-nine, with chiseled, elegant features. His face was gentle, and inclined to smile. He had black hair that was thick and wavy, and a luxurious black mustache that curled up at the ends into a second smile. Thick eyebrows arched devilishly over black velvet eyes, giving him a rakish look.

But it was his earnestness that gave him his power. His sense of justice was a pure thing. There was no muddling of ego, no self-interest filtering through. For Parsons, the goal was what mattered, and the goal was economic equality, the eradication of privilege, and a chance for the workingman to share in the better life. His activism was a matter of conscience shaped by circumstance. To see him in his home with his wife was to understand that he saw himself as a human being, not a hero.

Parsons consulted his watch as they finished dinner. "Time to head out," he said. "You'll be coming, Mr. Whitmarsh?"

"I sure will."

"I'm coming too," said Tesia.

Parsons looked doubtful. "I don't think so, Tesia. It might get unruly out there tonight."

"Oh, Mr. Parsons!"

He relented, looking at John. "Would you mind looking after her?"

John shrugged. "All right," he said. His eyes met Tesia's, and hers were laughing. He felt his color coming up. "I don't mind."

It had grown cooler as the afternoon wore away. By evening the wind was whipping in gusts, and there was the flat smell of rain on it. Littered trash rattled in the gutters and then leapt into the air in short bursts of flight.

As Albert Parsons lead John and Tesia along Madison Street, a group of men and boys broke out of a side street and turned toward them, running hard. Close behind them was a squad of uniformed police brandishing nightsticks. A boy paused in his flight, grabbed up a garbage can, and flung it in the path of the police. It cut the legs out from under two of the officers and they went down in a heap. Swearing, one of the fallen policemen picked himself up, drew his pistol, and fired. The running pack scattered. No one fell. The runners disappeared along several streets, and the police abandoned the chase.

All this had passed within a few feet of where John's group stood flattened in a doorway. Now they hurried on toward Market Square. It was getting dark, not yet night-dark, but thick and shadowy. The violence they had just seen gave the twilight an ominous feel.

A huge crowd was already gathered in Market Square, with more arriving. A man was standing on a makeshift speaker's platform, a haywagon, making a speech. John could not make out the words from where he was standing.

"Are you sure you ought to make an appearance?" Tesia asked Parsons. "After what the police said to you this afternoon?"

"Oh, you can't take the police too seriously," Parsons answered with a laugh. "It's mostly bluster. The police know they have no right to interfere with honest workingmen exercising their right of free speech. And even if they should try, what then? Look at the numbers of people here. Besides, I've got to make my speech. Van Patten and I are the only orators we've got who speak English." But he took John by the arm and drew him aside. "You know, Mr. Whitmarsh, I *am* worried about Tesia being here. This business could turn ugly. Do you think you could do me a favor by getting her home after a bit? I'd be very much obliged."

"Of course," John said. He was not happy with the request. But he knew Parsons was right. Things could get out of hand in a moment, without any warning. And if this turned into another Pittsburgh, it would be no place for a teenage girl to be.

In fact, when John and Tesia left the rally three-quarters of an hour later and walked back along Madison, there had been no sign of violence. The crowd had been vocal but orderly, listening and responding to speeches which were mostly in German. They had stayed long enough to hear Parsons speak. John had been unexpectedly moved and impressed. Parsons at home was disarmingly quiet and modest. But on a speaker's platform he was transformed. From the moment he mounted the wagon there was a swell in the cheering, as if there was a chemical interaction between him and the crowd. They loved him; and he radiated that love back to them as strength and belief. He hit out with clean, cutting strokes at "the monopolies and wage tyrants," and singled out for scorn the newspapers who abdicated their responsibilities of fairness to shill for the money interests. He told the people that they were more important than money and profits, and that the mechanical wonders of the industrial revolution could be and must be turned to the workers's advantage. "The new machinery is not our damnation but our hope. If it is used properly, it means work for everyone and profit for everyone, and a chance for the worker to earn his living and still have time to spend with his family. It means the era of the eight-hour day is at hand!"

The square rocked with sound when Parsons finished. John applauded and shouted until his throat hurt and his hands were numb. When the cheering died down and another speaker began in German, he looked at Tesia.

"Want to go?"

"All right," she said. They made their way back through the crowd, which had now packed in densely for a long way behind them. Eventually it thinned out and they were alone, walking along the street. They could still hear the new speaker faintly in the distance.

"I have never liked German," Tesia said. "It always sounded like a made-up language to me. Like people inventing nonsense syllables."

"Well, what about Russian? Russian doesn't make much sense either."

"Oh, but it does! Russian is simple."

"Sure—I bet where you come from even the little kids can speak it."

"That's right," she laughed, delighted. "Shall I teach you some Russian?"

"I suppose if a little Russian kid can learn it, I can."

"All right." She danced along ahead of him, skipping sideways to face him as she began the lesson. Pointing to herself, she said: "Girl—*dyévotchka*."

"*Davochka*."

"No, you accent the first syllable—like this." She showed him, drawing the syllable in the air with her hand: "*Dyévotchka*."

"*Dyévotchka*."

"That's it!" She clapped her hands. "Now, boy— *malchik*."

"*Malchik*."

"Very good. Now . . ." she smiled mischievously. "*Potselooy*."

"*Potselooy*?"

"Why, Mr. Whitmarsh? What can you be thinking of? Why, we hardly know each other!"

He looked at her nonplussed, and she burst out laughing. John started laughing too.

"What does it mean?"

"Mr. Whitmarsh—you are too wicked! I shall certainly not tell you such a thing."

"*Potselooy*?" he said, taking a step toward her, and she danced away, pealing with sparkling, healthy laughter. John watched her with happy surprise, and began to look at her more closely. At first he had not thought that she was exceptional looking. But now he saw she was utterly beautiful. He had broken through to something true about her, and now that he had seen it it was his.

At the corner of Madison and Halstead they came upon the Academy of Music. It was a modern building, constructed, like so much of the city, since the Great Fire of six years earlier. The Academy of Music was a handsome two-story structure with an ornate, brightly painted facade. A sign leaned against the lamppost in front: "Performance this evening at 9:00 P.M. The Lydia Thompson Company. An Evening of Satirical Sketches and Song."

"Lydia Thompson," Tesia exclaimed. "Oh, she's wonderful. Have you seen one of her shows?"

"No. I've never been to a show."

"Never been to a show? I don't believe it!"

"Well, I haven't," said John, a bit defensively.

"Wouldn't you like to?"

John hesitated.

"I know a way to get in," Tesia said. She looked at him coaxingly, challengingly.

John felt that he was losing control of the situation. He was supposed to be protecting this girl and seeing her safely home. He was supposed to be in charge. And now she was calling the tune. But to say no might look as though he lacked the nerve. You could not turn down a dare from a girl. And besides, he had never seen a show.

"All right," he said.

Tesia led him past the arched doorway of the Academy of Music. Next door to the theater was a furniture store, and beyond that was an alley. At the end of the alley was a high wooden fence.

"Up here," she said.

"You can't get up there."

"Can't I?" She pulled a packing crate against the fence. Standing on it, she reached up and took hold of the fence; and with remarkable agility and scarcely any struggle she hoisted herself to the top. From there it was an easy climb to the roof of the furniture store. When she had gained the roof, she turned and looked triumphantly down at John.

"And you? Can you make it?"

"Of course I can!" He clambered up, less smoothly than he would have liked but with no real difficulty. Tesia gave him her hand to help him up to the roof, and he took it. They crossed the roof in the darkness. The Academy of Music rose another full story above them. Tesia pointed to a window.

"See?" she said. "It's always open."

"All right," said John. "You go first, I'll boost you up." He made a stirrup of his hands and she stepped into it, and he lifted her up until she could perch on the windowsill and swing her legs through. Then he climbed after her.

"Where does this go?" he asked, and he hauled himself over the sill.

"It's the ladies' lounge."

"*What*?"

"Come on, silly!" She pulled him inside.

An old woman in a dark attendant's uniform sat on a chair in the mirrored powder room. She nodded pleasantly as Tesia led John through.

"Good evening, Mrs. Beckwith," said Tesia politely.

"Good evening, dear. You've brought a young man."

"Yes. This is Mr. Whitmarsh."

"How do you do, Mr. Whitmarsh." She received him with a gracious formality, like a duchess in her drawing room.

"Hello," John mumbled.

"Speak up, young man, I don't hear so well."

"How do you do, Mrs. Beckwith."

"Very well, thank you." That dispensed with, she turned

to Tesia again. "You haven't seen this show yet, have you dear?"

"No. Is it good?"

"Quite good. Miss Thompson's shows are always merry and lively. The girls are very pretty, although their costumes are rather scantier than I should have thought in the best taste. But this is 1877, and one cannot ask fashions to stand still, especially in the theater. All in all, I think you'll enjoy it. The tunes are quite catchy."

"It sounds marvelous. We'd better be going in." To John she said: "Wait just a moment." She went to the door and peered about to be sure the coast was clear. John stood awkwardly in front of the aristocratic Mrs. Beckwith. He could not think of anything to say to her, but fortunately she did not seem to expect further conversation.

After a moment Tesia signaled from the doorway. "All right. Good-bye, Mrs. Beckwith."

"Good-bye, dear. Enjoy the show."

John said good-bye and quickly followed Tesia out.

"Who is she?"

"She's a very nice old lady. She lets me sneak in, and we talk about the shows. She used to be rich once."

"What happened?"

"Her husband was a banker. He lost everything when his bank failed in '74. He killed himself."

"That's too bad."

"Yes. She said it terrified him to be without money. I suppose it is hard, for rich people."

"It's hard for poor people too."

"Yes."

They found seats in the balcony. The stage was brightly lit in pastel colors, with painted scenery to look like a garden of flowers. Chorus girls in brief floral costumes sat and stood among the flowers, showing long, shapely legs encased in gaily colored stockings. A young man pushed a girl in a swing that hung down from what looked like a real tree limb. The branch and the swing were roped with flowers. The girl wore country clothes and a wide bonnet with a long ribbon that trailed after her as she swung way out above the orchestra. They were all singing a song about being in love in a garden in the springtime.

"Lydia Thompson's shows are called 'leg shows.' Isn't it fun?"

John nodded, entranced. Tesia looked at him and smiled. After a moment, her hand crept over his.

When they left the theater they were both in high spirits. They sang bits of the songs that they could remember, and told each other what their favorite parts had been.

"I go all the time," Tesia said. "Whenever I can. I just love it. I mean to be an actress someday."

"In a 'leg show'?"

"Oh, no. I would be a serious actress. Once I saw Helena Modjeska in *Camille*. Oh," she sighed, putting the back of one hand to her temple and staggering as if in a faint. John reached out instinctively to catch her, and she giggled with delight. "See? Wouldn't I be good?"

The idea of being an actor struck John as a strange one. But the romance and make-believe appealed to him too. His life had been heavily real for a long time.

The streets were empty. John and Tesia walked along happily, absorbed in the discovery of each other. A streetlamp spilled a pool of yellow light in front of a florist's shop, and they stood in the light and looked at their reflections in the window glass, and saw themselves surrounded with flowers.

John wondered later that the emptiness of the streets had not struck him. Years afterward, when he thought back on Chicago, and Tesia, he asked himself whether he ought not to have sensed the shock and fear and anger that must have crowded through those empty streets that night. He had looked in that florist's window and seen himself and Tesia garlanded for a wedding, or bedecked like the lyrical couple in Lydia Thompson's show.

Later, when he remembered it, of course, the flowers came to mean something very different.

Chapter Sixteen

Albert Parsons's face was pale with worry as he opened the door.

"You're all right. Thank God. What happened?"

Even before he answered, John knew that Parsons's concern was over something more than just staying out late.

"We . . . we stopped to see a show," he said. He felt humiliated. Tesia gripped his arm tightly.

"A show?" Parsons seemed scarcely to understand the words. "You weren't in it, then."

"In what?"

"The police fired on the rally." It was Lucy Parsons, speaking from the sofa. "People were killed. We've been crazy worrying. Albert was just going out to look for you."

"Oh, Mrs. Parsons!" Tesia burst into tears and ran to the couch. "It was my fault, it was all my idea. Oh, I'm so sorry!"

"It's all right, honey," Lucy said, stroking her hair as the girl sobbed against her bosom.

"Mr. Parsons, I'm sorry, I take full responsibility," John began, but Parsons cut him off.

"Hell, don't apologize. As long as you two are safe." He allowed himself a smile. "I felt I could trust you to keep our Tesia safe from harm, and you haven't disappointed me."

"I've got tea made," said Lucy. "Unless you'd like something stronger, Mr. Whitmarsh?"

"Tea would be fine," said John.

"With a little something in it," Parsons added.

They drank tea laced with brandy, and John asked about the trouble.

"It was godawful," Parsons said. He was exhausted, and his Texas drawl showed more clearly through his weariness. "The rally was peaceful. We had our W.P.U.S. marshals in the crowd, making sure it stayed that way. Then the police came, at a double-trot from behind. A brigade of 'em. They just charged right in, cracking skulls, and the crowd panicked. People started running, and there was nowhere to go. Van Patten was on the speaker's stand. He tried to keep order. He kept shouting 'keep calm, hold your ground, keep calm,' and the peelers drove the people right through that haywagon of a speaker's stand and they trampled it to matchsticks. Van Patten was knocked about pretty badly."

"Philip Van Patten? The Workingmen's Party secretary? How bad is he hurt?"

"He's all right. He's cut and bruised some, but there are people worse off." For the first time John noticed a large purple swelling along Albert Parsons's right temple. "In the middle of all this another group of workers came on the scene. A parade, it was. With flags and fifes and drums. The police opened fire. The music stopped, and the marchers turned and ran. They hadn't come to fight, so . . . Some people stood and fought the police, but they didn't have guns; the police just butchered them. After the shooting started it broke up pretty fast." Parsons took a long drink of his tea and brandy, and then looked up at John with eyes that were still tinged with shock. "I don't know how many were killed," he said. He shook his head, and let out his breath in a ragged sigh. "I ought to be out there now . . . helping . . ."

"No," said Lucy firmly. "Don't do that to yourself, Albert. That is not what they need you for."

"She's right," John said. "Mr. Parsons, I heard you

speak tonight. You've got a way of lifting people up and making them feel that this is their struggle, that they're right at the heart of it. When people listen to you they don't feel like they're listening to a speaker or a leader— they're hearing a voice that's coming out of their own guts, a voice that tells everything they feel. If you just go out there and lay your head on the block and get it chopped off, you're robbing them of that voice.''

Albert Parsons nodded thoughtfully, and then stood up. He put his hands in his pockets and walked over to the window. The rain that had been threatening on the early evening breezes was falling heavily now, exploding on the windowsill and spattering on Parsons's hands and sleeves.

"This rain will cool things off a bit," Parsons said. "But what happens tomorrow?"

Behind him no one spoke. Already the rain seemed to be letting up a little.

Rutherford B. Hayes, President of the United States by the frailest of mandates, slumped in a padded leather chair and stared out the window at the darkness. He had not slept in his bed in three nights, and he was not likely to do so tonight. Out there, the country that had been stitched together with railroads over roughly the span of his own lifetime was threatening to unravel along those seams here in the fourth month of his presidency.

He heard the carpeted rustle of approaching footsteps through the open door. He straightened in his chair and turned back facing his desk. Secretary of War McCrary was announced.

"Yes, of course, send him in," the President directed.

A moment later the Secretary strode into the room. The Secretary never walked; he strode. His crisp hair and whiskers were never mussed, his collars were never wilted even in the hottest days of these Washington summers. The Secretary had not slept much more than he had, Hayes knew, over this period of strike and riot. But exhaustion did not show on the Secretary. There might perhaps be a deeper tinge to the gray that lined his eyes and cheeks; otherwise, no change.

"More telegrams from Chicago, Mr. President." The Secretary snapped through the yellow forms in his hand one at a time, like a dealer at poker. "From the mayor . . . from Governor Cullom . . . from General Drum . . ."

Hayes held out a hand and took the telegrams. He glanced through them perfunctorily, knowing what they would say. He had been reading telegrams like them for a week, since the confrontations in West Virginia.

. . . it is impossible with any force at my command to execute the laws of the state . . .

. . . I call on you for troops to assist in quelling mobs . . . respectfully suggest that you prepare to call for volunteers . . .

. . . I call upon your Excellency for the assistance of the United States military to protect the law abiding people of the state . . .

"I wonder," President Hayes mused out loud, "whether these governors and mayors would be as quick to request our assistance if it were the property of the workers that was being threatened, and not that of the great corporations . . ."

"An amusing speculation," said Secretary McCrary. "Now, as to the situation at hand—General Drum informs us that he has six companies of regulars that can be moved at once from Rock Island . . ."

Hayes authorized the use of federal troops against the striking American workers. He was not pleased with himself for the decision, but he did not see any choice, any more than he had seen any choice in West Virginia or in Maryland. He was the President of the United States, whether the Democrats and Samuel J. Tilden liked it or not. He was the duly elected President under the Constitu-

tion, even if he had received a smaller popular vote than
his opponent.

As President of the United States, it was his duty to
uphold the Constitution and enforce the laws, and to protect the rights of Capital and of Property. It was not always
a pleasant duty, but it was not necessary for him to like it.
It was only necessary that he accept the realities of his
office, and conduct himself accordingly.

He stood up from his chair and rubbed his hands across
his face, massaging the inner corners of his hot, tired eyes
with his index fingers. He smoothed the rumpled creases
from his suit and left his office. It looked as though he
would make it to his own bed tonight, after all.

Whether he would be able to sleep or not was another
matter.

Chapter Seventeen

Lucy Parsons made John a bed on the sofa. The sheets
felt crisp and clean, and had a fresh-laundered smell. John
undressed to his underwear and slipped between them. He
lay for a while with his eyes open and his arms folded
beneath his head.

He felt strangely light, as if he were floating above all
the savage turmoil of the riot-torn week. His mind went
back to what he thought of now as his boyhood, that
period when he had lived at home in Painter's Falls with
his family, before his father's death. Then, step by step,
he tried to trace exactly how he had come to be here. His
life seemed to him to be made up of separate pieces, each

one unrelated to any of the others. And a new one had just begun. Like the others, this new break was clear and unmistakable. But it was not like the others, which had been violent ruptures brought about by death. Today, in the midst of so much violence and savagery, he had been lifted above it all. He had fallen in love.

It changed the way he looked at things. Everything now was in terms of Tesia. The struggle took on a deeper meaning now, because it was her future and their future together that he was fighting for. But it meant less, too, because it was no longer the most important thing in his life.

Without really feeling tired, he closed his eyes for a moment, and when he opened them again the rain had stopped completely and the clouds had blown away. The room seemed brighter, and when he shifted his position on the couch he could see that there was a moon. It was nearly round, with just an edge rubbed away. He drew in his knees and sat up on the couch, and stared back at the moon. His head filled with all the sentimental nonsense he remembered about moons and lovers. He smiled at himself, happy and uncritical at the romanticism he would have sneered at yesterday.

He could not stay in bed any longer, so he got up and went to the window. The city outside looked flat and clean, carrying the sweet-acid smell of the recent rainstorm, and swept by the pallid cleanness of moonlight. The moon had washed the sky, too, and erased the nearby stars with its brightness. Standing there, John Whitmarsh experienced one of those rare flashes of the soul in which the world seems manageable and eternity makes perfect sense. And in that moment he turned his head and saw Tesia, leaning on her elbows at the sill of her bedroom window.

She had not seen John, and he did not call to her. She was looking up, with her face cupped in both hands. She was not more than a dozen feet from him. It was very quiet, and when he stopped his breathing he could hear hers. She was smiling. He hoped she was thinking about him.

He watched her, trying to make her features into something neutral. It ought to have been easy, but he could not do it. Was it the face you fell in love with? There was not much difference between most faces, really, with their eyes and noses and mouths all shaped and patterned pretty much the same. But sooner or later one came along and it meant something much more than any of the others had ever meant, or ever would.

When he had first seen Tesia, he had not thought her the most beautiful girl he had ever seen. If he thought so now, it was not that her face had changed. So it had to be that his way of seeing had changed. Something about her had altered his vision, and what she was had now become his model of perfection.

Her head moved, and now she was looking at him. She did not seem surprised to see him, though he was sure she had not known that he was there. The smile widened, or deepened, on her face.

"It's so bright," she said. "It's like day."

"I couldn't sleep. It was shining in my face."

"I know. Neither could I."

In the distance they heard a low whistle, and the pulsing chug of a train as it wound its way past the breakwater.

"What was it like in Pittsburgh?"

"The fighting? It was pretty scary. Pretty awful. You couldn't believe it—armies in the streets, shooting . . . like war, I guess, only the other side wasn't soldiers, it was just people. And the fires—it looked for a while like the whole city was going to go."

"What do you think—is it going to happen here like that?"

"I don't know. Maybe it's already started."

From down the night-quiet street they heard a crisp, rustling sound. They were absorbed in each other and at first they did not pay any attention to it. But it came closer, and they looked down the street and saw a company of soldiers. The soldiers marched toward them and beneath them and passed them by, hard dusty men who marched with weary precision.

"Those weren't Guardsmen," John said. "That was regular army."

When the soldiers had passed, the street was the same as it had been before. The moon still shone with the same brightness. But the night seemed different, and for John the feeling of sureness and exhilaration was gone.

"John," Tesia called softly. He looked back at her. Her eyes were solemn with understanding, and she beckoned to him. "Come," she said.

Tesia's room was a tiny nook off the kitchen, a maid's room. She was waiting for him in the doorway. She took his hand and drew him inside.

"We can talk in here," she said. "It's far enough from their room so we won't wake them up by talking."

John sat on the edge of the bed. The passing of the federal troops beneath the window had shaken him in some way that he could not account for. It had broken in on his dream, and filled him with foreboding. Tesia searched his face, and seemed to understand the mood that was taking hold of him.

"I was waiting for you tonight," she said. "I thought I would die if you did not come to the window."

"Really? No . . . you didn't even see me for about five minutes. You were gazing off into space."

She giggled. "I knew you were looking at me. I thought I should look poetic. Did I?"

"You looked beautiful," John said earnestly.

"Did I?"

"Yes."

Tesia smiled, looking down at her twisting fingers. Then she raised her eyes again, and spoke almost in a whisper.

"*Potselooy.*"

"*Potselooy . . .*" He grinned, in spite of himself. "What does it mean?"

She touched his cheek with her fingertips in a gesture

that was half shy, half womanly. She drew their faces together, and her lips found his in the darkness.

"*Potselooy*," she said again when their mouths came apart.

He put his arms around her. The foreboding and despair were gone. All he could feel was the racing excitement of being here with her, alone in the dark, touching her. "*Potselooy* again."

Her nightdress was summer cotton, and he could feel her body beneath it.

"Close the door," she whispered.

The door was half open. He rose and crossed to it, and closed it quietly, twisting the knob so that the latch would not click. He had an erection, and it vaguely embarrassed him that she should see it, so he did his best to conceal it before he turned around again.

When he did turn, she had removed her cotton nightgown and was standing naked.

The moonlight that had dominated this strange night flooded through Tesia's window and lit one side of her smooth young body. The image that struck John's awed eyes was of one smooth cheek, one shoulder, one round, pale breast, one gleaming hip and thigh. There was a hollow inside the hip bone where the skin disappeared, and then it reappeared again in the gentle roundness of her belly, only as far around as the scallop of her navel. And below the navel it vanished again into shadow.

"You too," she said. Her voice was hushed, neither brazen nor shy. John responded without thinking, and in another moment he was naked too. He was still self-conscious about his erection, but he was not embarrassed by it anymore. It seemed like a good and a natural thing.

John and Tesia stood several paces apart and looked at each other happily. Then the several paces and the moonlight between them vanished, and they held each other, pressing their bodies and their mouths together, feeling the amazing touch of skin and love.

Chapter Eighteen

In their minds and their bodies John and Tesia were married that night.

When Lucy Parsons emerged robed and slippered from the bedroom in the morning to begin fixing breakfast, John was dressed and sitting in the open window with a steaming cup of coffee. Beyond him in the kitchen Tesia was breaking eggs into a bowl.

"Good morning, Mr. Whitmarsh. Did you sleep all right?"

"Fine, thank you."

The bedclothes had been neatly folded and set on the corner of the sofa. The expression on John's face as he rose politely to his feet was similarly neat and composed. But Lucy Parsons had no trouble reading the change that lay behind it.

She could see the same thing in Tesia. She could see it much more clearly in Tesia, who was like a daughter to her. There was an undefinable difference in the way she held her body, a womanly mystery in the smile with which she greeted Lucy as Lucy came into the kitchen.

This virginal border was one that everybody, almost everybody, crossed, sooner or later. These two were young, but it had been a happy crossing, you could see that. The boy had taken it as seriously as the girl, and that was good.

Lucy Parsons gave Tesia a kiss. " 'Morning, dear. You're up and about early."

"I thought I'd fix breakfast."

"Fine. I'll just give you a hand, now I'm up." She sniffed, and nodded approvingly. "Coffee smells good."

There was no holding of the girl's shoulders, no searching look into her eyes, no "are you all right?" It was obvious that she was all right. Lucy approved, but she kept her approval to herself. It was their morning. Lucy had had her own similar morning, not so long ago.

"I'll be going down to party headquarters right after breakfast," Albert Parsons said. Parsons looked bad. His face was sallow and unrested, and his body was tense. "We'll be calling another rally. We can't be intimidated. And we've got to get a sense of the way this thing is going."

"I'd like to come by, at some point," said John. "Talk to your people, and see if we can't get things coordinated between here and Pittsburgh."

"Good," Parsons agreed. "That's the important thing, all right. A national movement, that's where the power will come from. Get the reins here in one hand, get everyone channeling information here to W.P.U.S. headquarters, a central location, so everybody knows what everybody else is doing. We're working through our regional headquarters, but I'm anxious to set up communication with Mr. Ammon. By all accounts, he is the true power in Pittsburgh."

John nodded. He could see trouble coming. Ammon would not see the power structure the way Parsons had outlined it. Ammon's idea would be to have everyone reporting to him, in Pittsburgh. Still, John could see the logic in Parsons's assumption. The Workingmen's Party was, after all, a political force, established and organized. What Albert Parsons had outlined made sense. But Ammon would not see it that way.

"What time should I come by?"

Parsons consulted his watch. "About ten. That will give me a chance to clear away some tasks. I'll write out the directions for you."

"I'll show him the way," Tesia said.

John looked at her, and she gave him a quick, secret smile. John kept his expression straight, except for a flicker of his eyes. He did not want Albert Parsons to think of him as frivolous. He was going to have his work cut out for him at Workingmen's Party headquarters and he didn't want them thinking of him as a moonstruck boy.

It was a few minutes past eight when John and Tesia left the Parsons's apartment. It was bright and humid, with the sun drawing moisture up out of the puddles from last night's rain and hanging it thickly in the morning air. They hurried down the street, delighting in their anonymity.

The streets they walked along were prosaically quiet. A man stood outside of a fish market wearing a white apron, shaving ice into a container of the morning's catch. Three women gossiped in front of a greengrocer's. One of them bounced a baby on her hip, mechanically bouncing, although the baby was already fast asleep. There was a broken window in the tobacconist's shop on the corner, but it might as easily have been caused by boys playing ball (as some were on the next street) as by anything else.

Near the telegraph office on Archer Avenue they began to see signs of disturbance. Several stores had broken windows. A gun shop was boarded up. A delivery wagon belonging to the Crane Brothers Manufacturing Company lay half on the sidewalk, its wheels missing, its axles broken, and its sides staved in. They began to hear shouting in the distance, and shrill whistles. Once there was a series of sharp popping sounds that might have been gunfire. But it was some distance away.

"Gonna be trouble today, brother," said the clerk inside the telegraph office.

"Could be," John said. He took a telegraph form and printed a message to Bob Ammon.

Have met Parsons. Decent man. Will meet W.P.U.S. council today. They want central control. Will discuss. Chicago a powder keg. The new order is at hand. Returning Pittsburgh . . .

*   *   *

He paused, his pencil hanging uncertainly in the air above the yellow telegraph form. Tesia sat on a stool by the window, looking out at the street. Until the moment he had begun that line, John had not thought about the end of it. Now he looked at Tesia and thought that he could not leave her, not even for a little while. He would have to, though. Eventually. But not right away.

". . . soon," he wrote. He signed his name and handed the message to the clerk.

Tesia slipped her arm through his as they left the telegraph office.

"When did you say you were going back?" she asked. She smiled at the way his head snapped around in surprise, but her eyes were serious.

"I didn't say."

"You must have told him something."

"I just said soon."

They walked along, each mulling the problem separately. It seemed unfathomable.

"What *are* we going to do?" Tesia sighed.

"Could we get married?"

"Oh, yes!" she said, hugging his arm tightly and pressing her cheek against his sleeve. "But not yet. Not right away." But she was happy now, again.

"Why not now?"

"We're too young," she said, simply.

"I'm eighteen . . ."

She giggled. "Last night you said you were seventeen."

"Well, I'm almost eighteen."

"Well, I'm only sixteen. Anyway, you've got other things to think about now. We all do. Let's wait until this strike is won, first. Then we'll have time for nothing but each other."

"It could go on a long time, you know," John cautioned. "It could be this is more than a strike."

"I know. It doesn't matter. Whatever happens, I'm yours, John. We belong to each other now."

"I love you."

"And we will be married, won't we?"

"Yes! When?"

"Soon. I'll talk to Mr. and Mrs. Parsons. And you won't go back to Pittsburgh right away, will you?"

"No. I'll stay here as long as I can."

Deputy Superintendent of Police Joseph Dixon had had enough. If you coddled these howling animals, these communists and anarchists, they would kill you. There was one universal language these foreigners all understood, and if it had been used on them from the beginning, there would have been no riots, no strikes, and no disturbances.

Superintendent Hickey was a good man, but he had too much respect for authority. Mayor Heath was a dishrag. Mayor Heath had ordered police to keep the use of firearms and deadly force to a minimum, to avoid exciting the temper of the mob. That was a lot of shit. Dixon had seen from the first that conciliation was not the way you dealt with communist mobs. He had begun laying plans and assembling an arsenal at the first news of rioting from Pittsburgh. It was now or never, Dixon told himself grimly. The situation could brook no more delay.

Early on the morning of July 27, Deputy Superintendent Dixon met with his two superiors in the superintendent's office.

"Yer Honor," he said, addressing the mayor tersely, "I'll put it to ye the only way that's left: do ye want a city here tomorrow to be mayor of, or don't ye? Because that's yer goddamned choice!"

"Look here, Dixon," said the mayor, reddening, "I advise you to watch your tone!"

"Me goddamned tone! Jesus Christ," Dixon exploded, smacking the heels of his hands against his temples. "Mike, will ye tell him what I'm sayin'? I'm losin' men out there, Mr. Mayor! Me men are tough, they're good fighters, they can handle this scum, but ye can't send 'em out to play pussy wit' a bunch o' screamin' foreigners who're out to tear the city down! Will ye tell him, Mike?"

Hickey tugged uncomfortably at his mustache. "I think, Your Honor, that the time might be here when a real show of force might be in order."

Mayor Heath glared from one to the other. His eyes held the look of a man backed into a corner, and relieved to be there. The pressures on him had been mounting from all sides for the past three days. The issue had been forced. It was no longer his choice, or his responsibility.

"All right, Superintendent, do what you have to do. Use proper restraint." He left the room quickly.

"What've you got, Joe?" Hickey asked.

"I've requisitioned a hundred and twenty-five stands o' government arms that was stored in McCormick's Hall. They're bein' distributed to the specials we recruited. Captain Tobey has organized a battery wit' a pair o' six-pound guns, settin' 'em up on express wagons fer caissons. Tobey served wit' the artillery in the war, he knows his stuff. The military is prepared to move in on orders from yerself, and two mounted companies as well." He pointed to a map on the superintendent's wall that was heavily marked with pins and yarn. "The viaduct at Sixteenth and Halsted, that's where we can look fer the bastards to mob up again, where they was yesterday. We'll move in and obliterate 'em."

"Shoot to kill?"

"This ain't crowd control, Mike. This is war. No more firin' over heads, it makes 'em cocky. We crush the mob today, Mike, or they crush us tomorrow."

"Right. Make sure your men know what they're shootin' at."

"Anybody out there is fair game, Mike. There ain't no innocent bystanders. Anybody gets in the way gets what they deserve."

There was a wide stretch of open ground where the Sixteenth Street viaduct spilled out into Halsted Street. The dirt was still muddy from the rain, and strewn with debris. All morning crowds had been forming there. The viaduct spanned the tracks of several major railroad lines. Hundreds of cars and dozens of locomotives were stalled below, under the guard of an army of strikers. When passenger trains rolled by, the crowd massed about the viaduct pelted them with stones, though the strikers took no part in this.

Through the early morning, squads of police had been charging the mob, partially dispersing it, and then retiring as they threatened to be overwhelmed. Each time the mob reformed, it grew larger, bolder, and uglier.

John and Tesia heard the noise as they walked along Archer Avenue. They were headed toward the Workingmen's Party office, talking, and planning their future. They began to hear a swelling babble of sound, then a roar. Then there was gunfire. Then another roar went up, louder than before, and there was more gunfire. It came from the direction of Halsted Street.

"Let's go see," said Tesia.

"No. Come on."

"Oh John, please. We won't get too close."

"No!"

But she was already running toward the sound.

The streets leading to Halsted were full of people. Many were onlookers, and many more were streaming in to join the confrontation. As John and Tesia reached the open ground on Halsted Street they saw a company of police retreating toward them. The police were firing and retreating. The mob was surging after them, throwing stones and bottles and chunks of coal. Many in the mob had clubs of one sort or other, and some had pistols. The police were firing into the mob, and John saw a couple of men go down. He saw a young man in baker's whites clutch at his stomach where a bullet had smeared a red stain on his white apron. The police were rapidly running out of ammunition, and as they ran out, their retreat became less orderly. Now it was breaking down into panic.

Then there was a commotion from the rear of the ground where John and Tesia stood. There was shouting and pushing, and John and Tesia were carried forward, in the direction of the viaduct. People were running hard, and from behind now John could see a charging company of cavalry, and a large detachment of police dragging a battery of field guns.

"Tesia!" he shouted, and grabbed for her hand. The crowd of onlookers was stampeding now, and Tesia was being carried away from him. But he found her hand and gripped it tightly.

"Let's get out of here!"

She nodded mutely. Her eyes were wide with terror.

The mounted militia charged into them, swinging clubs. John lunged out of their path, shoving Tesia desperately into a doorway. A club caught him a glancing blow on the back of the head, and he went down. He heard Tesia's scream above the screams of panic, and he struggled up and motioned to her to stay where she was. He started toward her, and then from behind he heard the sickly sewing-machine sound of a Gatling gun. He smashed his way through the shrieking crowd and flung himself upon Tesia. He heard her grunt as his body hit hers and carried her down in the doorway with himself on top of her as a shield. The police and the military swept past them, driving the rioters back toward Twelfth.

John lay there covering her until the noise receded, holding her tightly. She trembled at first, and then stopped.

"All right," he said, "now!"

He jumped to his feet and held out a hand for her. Then he saw that there were two dark, white-rimmed holes opened below her left breast, and that her left side was drenched in blood. The front of his jacket and shirt and trousers were wet with her blood. Tesia's eyes were open, and she was dead.

"No!" he screamed. "No!" He screamed with all the force of his lungs, as if the volume could force the horror out, or change the truth.

Then he was running, still screaming, toward where the police and troops were battling the rioters. He picked up a bottle as he ran and flung it, then a brick. A pistol lay in the gutter, near the body of a bearded man in a crumpled hat and bloodsoaked overalls. John snatched it up and started firing. He saw a blue uniform bend and drop. Something hit him low on the thigh, something that seared red-hot for a moment, and then his thigh went numb. John kept firing. He armed himself again with a fallen rifle and charged in, blasting away with both hands. He saw the Gatling gun across the way. That now became his sole objective. Another bullet slammed into his shoulder, and he screamed with pain and fury and defiance. The soldier on the Gatling gun fell back, clutching at his side, with a look of shock on his face.

Behind John's charge, the tide of the battle was starting to turn again. John was not aware of any of this. He only saw the caisson with the automatic gun, and he blasted his way toward it until another bullet hit him, and then another, and he blacked out.

"*Je crois qu'il peut boire un peu de soupe maintenant.*"

John came slowly out of a dark, thickly wadded tunnel. It was slow, heavy going. There was a woman at the end of it. She was watching him as he came out, and then she turned to take a bowl of something from a man who brought it over to her.

"*C'est de la soupe,*" she said to John, lifting a steaming spoonful. "*C'est du consommé.*"

He was in a bed. He tried to sit up, but there were sharp pains in what seemed like every part of his body. Then he remembered about Tesia, and a pain infinitely more unbearable drove everything else away.

"*Non, non, jeune homme,*" the woman clucked soothingly. "Is all right. Is all over now."

John turned his face to the wall and wept. After a while, the woman left the soup on the chair by the bed and let him be.

The man spoke almost no English. The woman's English was not bad. She filled him in on what had happened.

"You were very wounded. *Très grave.* You fight like a madman, *comme un fou*, you make the police fall back. The people, they take courage. But you are too much hit. You fall, my husband Vincent he pull you away. He bring you here, *chez nous.*"

John had eaten the soup. They brought him some stew, and some bread and cheese, and a glass of wine. He ate them all dully, mechanically, begrudging his body the nourishment it craved.

"*Il a grand faim*," said the husband. "*C'est quatre jours.*"

The woman nodded. "Vincent say you are hungry. It is four days."

The riots, the strike, the revolution . . . whatever it was, it had collapsed. The railroads were running again. Capital was in full control.

It was over.

John could not stay in Chicago. The police were looking for him for his murderous assault. But it was another week before he was well enough to travel.

Chapter Nineteen

Within two years after the Whitmarsh family had arrived in New York from Painter's Falls, they had evolved a new structure that was tortured and secretive, based on a complex series of role reversals. They had lost the head of the family, and they had lost young John, his natural successor. They never heard from young John. They had no idea whether he was alive or dead.

And so there was no head of the family, and no center. Nancy did not provide it. Her life was with Heywood Catlett. Much of the time, she seemed to forget she had a family. The rest of the time, she was given to sudden and bewildering outbursts of affection, or anger, or tyranny—there was never any telling which it would be, or why.

She did not know what her children were doing. And so Jamie spent less and less time in school, and more and more time in the streets. He was nine years old—still too young to be accepted into any of the youth gangs that served as auxiliaries and apprentices to the vicious gangs that controlled the city's street crime. But he knew them. He knew the boys from the Little Dead Rabbits, the Little Forty Thieves, all of them; and they knew him. He learned how to ingratiate himself, through a mixture of charm and precocious toughness, and the older boys let him hang around, or run errands for them.

He came home at night. That was enough for Nancy. It let her assume that everything was all right during the day. When she demanded to know how he was doing in school, a shrug and "Sure, it's goin' all right, Ma," were enough to satisfy her. She thought that she was really grilling him, calling him to account, but she never pressed for details. She did not even notice that Jamie never brought home a report card. Jamie could always distract her with a smile, and make her reach out and hug him.

He was a beautiful child. His hair was straight and blond, his eyes a clear blue. His features were fine and aristocratic, but his little boy's round cheeks and soft eyelashes gave him an angelic look. Nancy thought that he must look the way his Uncle Roger, the Earl of Marley, had looked when he was little, and she told him so often.

Nancy took very little interest in Fannie. Jamie was her pet, when she turned her attention to her family at all. When she talked to Fannie, she was as likely as not to be cruel and cutting, or to impose strange, rigid, and arbitrary sets of rules and curfews on her. But she was rarely around to enforce them.

Fannie alone knew the overall picture. She knew about her mother and Heywood Catlett; she knew what Jamie was doing; but she never talked about it, to Nancy or to Jamie. Around the house, Fannie scarcey talked at all. But she took everything in. She came to know the bright glow on her mother's cheeks meant that Mr. Catlett had been making love to her. Or another glow, not quite as vibrant, but excited nonetheless, meant she had won at gambling. And Fannie came to see, as time passed, the glow from gambling became even more vibrant than the glow from lovemaking. She also knew the look of desperation that meant her mother had lost.

She could read Jamie's face, too: the bright, bubbling, youthful excitement over some new triumph in his life that always made his eyes a little harder and colder than they had been before. She would have liked to stop Jamie's life in the street, but she did not know how. And she did not want to usurp the place at home that was her mother's, even though her mother did not fill it.

Fannie had a secret, too. While she was nominally subject to Nancy's authority at home, her lover held sway over her mother's lover in the world outside. She had no ambition to use this against her mother. Nancy never had to know. But for Fannie Whitmarsh, reaching for the top was the only way. Because of her mother's lead, Fannie chose a gambler; but she chose the best, the most powerful, the king. It was the only way to get control of things, and to be able to bring happiness to the people she loved.

She loved her mother, and so her relationship with Bill Henderson would stay a secret. Haywood Catlett was second-rate. But he made Nancy happy and Fannie would do nothing to undermine that. Fannie did not look for happiness for herself. But in fact she found it—along with power—as a surprising dividend of her relationship with Henderson.

Fannie sat in the parlor of Bill Henderson's private rooms on East Twenty-third Street, in front of a card table.

She wore her shift and robe, and her eyes were tired but still bright. Her smooth forehead was pinched with concentration. She raised her right hand a foot above and a little to the right of her left hand, and a deck of blue-backed playing cards seemed for an instant to be strung out between them on an invisible thread. Then, with a whirring sound, all fifty-two cards snapped back into place in her left hand.

"Good," said Henderson. "Real flash. Now deal me five poker hands. Put the aces in the third hand."

Fannie started dealing, her hands nimbly skimming the cards across the surface of the table into five piles.

But as the fourth ace sailed toward its destination, Henderson's right hand darted out and caught it. In a single motion, he ripped the card in half with his fingers and threw it down, both halves face up, on the table.

'You're dead," he said. "Four men have just seen you rig that hand, and only one of them was your partner. Not good odds, little pigeon."

"What did I do wrong?" Fannie asked.

"Everything. Your hands still aren't fast enough. I could see you pull every ace."

"Yes, but you're an expert. And you were expecting it."

"Not even another good dealer should be able to spot a good dealer. Not even if he knows that he—or she—is doing it. That's how good you have to get. But that just takes time. You'll get it—you've got good hands. It's your eyes I'm worried about."

"My eyes?"

"Deal again. Set up the aces in one hand. Don't tell me which."

Fannie took a new deck, and shuffled it. Henderson's eyes were fixed on hers, and she knew it, and blushed. She caught herself, and concentrated on keeping a poker face. She did not return his gaze. She dealt out five hands, quickly. He did not take his eyes from hers throughout the process. Then he hooked a fingernail under the fourth hand, and flipped it over. He did not look down. He held the four aces, and the queen of hearts, face up for a moment, then turned them back down.

"How did you know?"

"You're still too honest for this business. Every time you throw a crooked card, your eyes glaze over, just for an instant. You flinch."

Fannie blinked back tears. Henderson put his hand over hers.

"You've got to learn how to be an actress. You've got to never let anyone know what you're thinking. Now, cheating is a very small part of gambling. You learn it so you'll know what it is, and as a hand-eye exercise. But that's not to say you'll never use it, and when you do, you've got to make sure you'll get away with it. And you've got to make sure your eyes don't give you away, no matter what you're doing. If you'll flinch when you're dealing an ace off the bottom, you'll flinch when you're raising on a busted flush."

He sat back in his chair, and looked at her. It was meant to be a calculating, appraising look, but where she was concerned, he could not follow his own advice. All the tenderness he felt for her showed through.

"You've got to learn to flirt," he said brusquely.

"How do you mean?"

"Flirt. You've got to learn how to look a man straight in the eye across the poker table, or the faro table, and promise him everything with those brown eyes of yours, while you're trying to get him to raise into you. You've got to play the men as much as you play the cards. You can't come up to every man the way you did to me."

"I could never come up to any other man the way I did to you."

Her words pierced right through to Henderson's core. They were not the effusive protestations of a fifteen-year-old puppy love; they were the honest words of a woman who meant exactly what she said.

"Are you sure you want to do this?" Henderson said.

"Yes," she said. "I'm sure."

"It's not right for you. I could loan you some money

. . . you could finish school and get yourself a little store . . . marry some nice merchant. . . . Do you know what's going to become of you, little pigeon? I don't want to see you get hard."

"I won't," she said. "Just as hard as I have to, that's all. Don't worry."

She fanned out a deck of cards in her hand and peeped coquettishly over the top at him. He smiled back at her. She came around the table, and sat down on his lap. Her body was tiny next to his, but warm. She put her arms around his neck, and kissed him.

"Let's go to bed," she said. "Then I'll practice some more before I go."

She made love to him with her mouth, which she had just learned to do. She understood how it worked—she instinctively found her way to the kind of pacing and strokes that he liked best. Henderson stroked her smooth shoulders, and looked down at her. He smiled deeply, and decided that he was glad he was as old as he was.

Nancy was in a deep sleep when the letter came to her. She had been out gambling at the casino on Thirty-fourth Street, and she had gotten back just a few hours before. There would be no waking her before the afternoon. Fannie held the letter in her hand, and looked at the envelope bearing her mother's name. The handwriting was familiar even though she had never seen it before. Heywood Catlett. Fannie was seized with a feeling that was at once paralyzing and energizing, and she realized she was going to open it.

She had to know. She had to know everything that was going on in the family; she could not let anything pass by her awareness. There was nothing she could do with all this knowledge—not yet. But someday, someday, she would do something to help them all. Make them a family again. Find Johnny, and bring him home.

She opened the letter.

*   *   *

My dearest lady, it read. *My dear old girl, hey.*

I will be lyin low for the next few weeks, I wont be around the club. I have a red sattin nightgown for you when I see you next, and I promise not to tear it off you the first night. At least so say I. Ha ha. When you next see me at Hendersons, it will be Catletts and the chips will be on me. I have 2 highly placed police ltenants in my pocket now and Williams will be next. I know now how to get to the doughty Chief Inspector. Money talks in this town and Hendo has plenty of that, but brains are good currency if you know how to use them, and I have got the brains, hey kiddo. Watch for Feb 23. No dont watch. Stay away from the club on Feb 23 as there will be some very embarrassed patrons there that night.

Yr affectionate friend and soon to frolic together in the luxury suite at Catletts Madison Sq Casino, ha ha,

Heywood Catlett

Fannie's fingers trembled so badly that she could scarcely get the letter back into the envelope and reseal it. If her mother woke up in a distracted, benign mood, she would never notice. If she woke up rageful and suspicious, she would be as likely as not to accuse Fannie of spying on her even if Fannie had never touched the envelope.

February 23 was just three weeks away. She had to warn Henderson.

But that would be betraying her mother.

She loved Henderson as much as she would ever love any man, except for her brothers. And she trusted him as much as she would ever trust anyone outside her family.

More than that, she owed him. But her mother depended on Catlett. To tell Henderson would be to take everything from her mother. And her mother had so little.

Suddenly she wanted to be away from everyone. She left the letter on the table for her mother to find, and went down into the street.

She walked a long way, blindly, not caring which way

she was heading. She walked past City Hall, and all the way down to the tip of the city, at the Battery. She stood next to a weeping willow and watched ships go in and out, and her face was so stricken with sorrow, so frozen against the world, that no one even approached her as a prostitute.

A dozen times during the afternoon, she whirled around, determined to go to Henderson and tell him. And each time, her hand did not break contact with the rough bark of the willow. She stood for a moment, her arm outstretched, her body leaning away; then she coiled back once more against it.

She could not do it. She knew with more and more certainty as the afternoon wore on that she would not be able to do it, and her heart went dead. Tears clouded her vision, but her eyes looked inward, and she saw Bill Henderson clearly, touching her hand as he leaned over the card table beside her, smiling at her pleasure when a sumptuous meal was brought in for them, lying asleep and peaceful on the pillow next to her.

She was trapped. She could not go to Henderson, and she did not want to go home, either. She wanted to run away somewhere, to wander the world by herself, maybe somehow to find Johnny. She wanted to run and throw herself off the end of New York City, into the icy waters of the harbor. But as the day slipped away and the sun went down, she walked back uptown, back to North Moore Street, and as she entered the tenement building, she knew it meant that she would not go to Henderson, and she cried. She stood in the hallway and cried, because she did not want her mother to see her. Then she dried her face and pulled herself together before she went in.

"Where have you been?" Nancy demanded suspiciously.

"I . . . nowhere," Fannie said.

"You'll have to do better than that, young lady. I demand to know where you've been. You're coming to no good, I can tell you that. You're going to go to work, that's what you're going to do. Next week, you're going to work in a factory. That's where you belong, not out on the streets like the common slut that you are. Have you shopped for supper?''

''No. I'll cook something from what we have in the house.''

''You horrible, lazy girl!'' Fannie thought that Nancy was going to hit her, but her mother's mood changed abruptly to a mysterious smirk. ''Never mind. We shall be eating in style soon enough,'' she said.

Oh, my darling, Fannie thought, and turned away.

Nancy went out less often, over the next three weeks. She and Fanny were thrown together much more than they had been in a long time, and it was almost more than Fannie could bear.

For the first time in her life, she could not stand to be around her mother. The outbursts of rage and abuse had always been painful, but not that hard to take. She had always been glad to see her mother come home. Now, Nancy was eerily benevolent, and Fannie turned away from her.

She never went back to see Henderson. She did not trust herself to be near him—she knew that she would tell him everything. She rarely left the house at all, during those three weeks.

The first few days she cried, when there was nobody else around to see her. Then she somberly accepted her new life, whatever it was, and the likelihood that she would never see Bill Henderson again. On February 22, left alone for a while when Nancy went down to the liquor store, she cried again. She thought, with one last burst of passion, that she would go and warn him. But in truth, her tears flowed out of bitter resignation.

Bill Henderson visited his tailor on the morning of February 23, and picked up the new evening clothes that had been made for him. He visited his barber for a shave and hot towels late in the afternoon, and arrived at 5 West Twenty-fourth Street shortly after ten o'clock that evening.

Catlett was not present. That was no surprise to Henderson. He made a quick tour of the premises, greeting people, but with a sharp eye out for other missing faces among his regular work force. It was a matter of a few minutes' work to total them up. Those would be the fools who had thrown in their lot with Catlett, believing his coup would succeed.

Smiling affably, Henderson walked back to his office. On his way, a portly man stopped him, and held out his hand.

"Congressman Porter, this is a pleasure," Henderson said.

"Don't see you here these days much, Hendo," the congressman said. "I declare, I'm more likely to see you down at the Democratic clubhouse."

"Yes, well, that's where the real action takes place, isn't it?"

Congressman Porter chuckled. "I daresay it is, at that. Good place for a man of your ability, my boy. The way you took on Tweed—I don't mind saying, you have the guts of—"

"A professional gambler?"

The congressman laughed so heartily he broke into a fit of coughing, and Henderson had to take his drink out of his hand and pat him on the back.

"Thank you, old sport," the congressman said at last, when he could breathe regularly again. "Good to see you here tonight. Don't see you around much these days."

"I like to keep my face around the place often enough," Henderson said. "I want my regular patrons to know that Bill Henderson has everything under control."

A few moments later, one of his employees knocked twice at the door, and entered. Henderson was waiting for him, with a list of names.

"These go to Inspector Williams."

The man took the list, and looked over it.

"Catlett's name ain't on here."

"I'll take care of Catlett myself," Henderson said.

*   *   *

Heywood Catlett had lunch at Corey's on the Bowery the next day. The regulars all moved away from him when he came in, and he stood alone, a pariah, at the center of the bar. But no one left the room. All watched him, in silence.

The saloonkeeper hung back too, studiously wiping his hands on his apron, until Catlett slammed his huge fist down, rattling the heavy beer steins all up and down the bar.

"Bring me a schooner of beer, damn your ass, Corey, if you don't want me back there with you!" he boomed.

Corey shuffled over, still wiping his hands, averting his eyes. He drew a beer and placed it in front of Catlett. A young man near the door sidled out slowly; then, as soon as he was on the sidewalk, he started running up the street.

"I ain't finished, you know," Catlett boomed out. "I ain't finished in this town, and I'm here to tell it to you." He tilted the beer to his lips and drank it off at one draught, his Adam's apple bobbing like a prizefighter in the ring. "Gi' me another."

Corey drew him another.

"You bet your candy asses Heywood Catlett ain't finished, every cowardly one of you!" he roared. "I ain't in jail. I don't care how many gamblers got jugged in this town last night, they ain't got me, and I ain't afraid of no man in this town. No man, do you hear me?"

He turned threateningly to his right. All eyes dropped from his but no one backed further away. To his left, the same reaction. Then he raised his fist and took a couple of steps, and people moved back. Corey reached for the baseball bat he kept under the bar, but Catlett stopped, and smashed his fist into his palm. "Anyone here thinks I'm finished, want to back it up with his fists? Any o' you cowards man enough to take on Heywood Catlett?"

No one spoke.

"Heywood Catlett," he said again, rolling his name out roughly, as though he were a ringside announcer.

He walked over to the lunch table, next to the big potbellied stove across the room from the bar, took a plate, and began to fill it. He took two large slices of beef tongue, knockwurst and sauerkraut, rolls and butter, a hunk of cheese, and three hard-boiled eggs. Then he went back and added two more slices of tongue, and some corned beef. He was turning away from the table, with his plate in his hands, when the door of the saloon swung open, and Bill Henderson filled the doorway.

Catlett dropped his plate. The heavy china broke into three large pieces, and the food splattered in front of him.

"Hello, Catlett," Henderson said.

"Now, just a minute, Hendo." Catlett took a step backward. "I don't know what you've been hearin', but it ain't true. Not a word of it. You an' me are pals, Hendo. We go back a long way."

"Back to 1856," Henderson said. "Remember 1856, Catlett? The Broadway Athletic Club?"

"Sure, I remember, Hendo. You were lucky. One lucky punch." Catlett's bravado was coming back now, as he thought of that long-ago, 45-round fight, and he stood firm. "I could have taken you. I should have taken you easy, and then where would you be now, eh? I was a better man than you were. I should have been the one. I should have had everything you have."

"Can you take me now, Catlett?"

Henderson drew off his gloves, one after the other, and stuffed them in the pocket of his greatcoat. Then he took the coat off, and handed it to a nearby spectator. Catlett removed his overcoat, too, but no one would take it off his hands. He finally had to chuck it into a corner, and his suit coat after it.

Henderson was advancing on him, his shirt-sleeves rolled up, his fists cocked.

"You're not tough enough, Catlett," he said. "If you were tough enough, you would have beaten me last night. But you ain't. That's why I never counted on you for any real important jobs. And I'll tell you something, Catlett— that's why I let you hang around all these years, knowing how it was you felt about me. Because I was never afraid of you."

Catlett circled slowly, keeping his distance, measuring Henderson.

"You ain't fought in too long, Hendo," Catlett grunted. "I've been doing all your fighting for you."

"Yeah? Learned anything, Catlett?"

"I'll show you what I've learned!"

Catlett moved in, pushing out his left in heavy, powerful jabs, moving his feet in a lumbering shuffle. Henderson kept his guard up, parried. They were still evenly matched for size, these two huge men: still powerful, not as agile as they had been the first time; but if they could no longer move, they could still put all their weight behind a punch.

Catlett was the one who had been using his muscle over the years, for Henderson and for others. He had been one of a team of enforcers who had collected bad debts. He had taken out opponents with a cosh, or a wooden club. He knew how to step up behind a troublemaker in the casino, twist his arm up behind his back, and get him out fast. And if it was necessary, he could finish the man off outside with a rabbit punch, a thumb to the eye, a knee to the groin. Catlett knew all the tricks, and few men gave him much trouble.

But he seemed to have forgotten all that. In his mind, he was back in the boxing ring, not in the middle of Corey's Saloon on the Bowery, where there were no rules, no bell to end the round, no referee to warn against butting, kicking, biting, gouging, low blows. He was fighting Bill Henderson once again for a shot at Heenan, and the heavyweight championship of the world. For his big break.

Henderson led him along, sparred with him for a few minutes, and then let him have it. He showed Catlett an opening, and when Catlett came in off balance with a vicious roundhouse right, Henderson turned aside, took the punch high on the shoulder, stuck his feet between Catlett's legs, and gave him a vicious twist.

With a roar of surprise, Catlett stumbled and fell forward. Henderson swung both fists together heavily, like a club, and caught Catlett on the back of the head. Catlett crashed into the free lunch sideboard, and fell to the floor in a sliding mass of beef tongues, boiled potatoes, ham and sauerkraut and grease and gravy. Henderson dived after him and drove a knee into his ribs, then landed on top of him with both fists pummeling.

Word had spread up and down the Bowery, and a crowd was gathering inside Corey's. Several policemen were among the mob, but no one was inclined to break this one up. In the doorway, a group of boys collected, members of the local street gangs. Jamie Whitmarsh was among them. Jamie was streetwise. He knew what was going on. Big Bill Henderson, king of the casinos, was there to beat the shit out of a mug who had tried to cross him. Henderson had gotten wise, busted up the whole plot, blown the whistle on the guys who were in on the double-cross to the cops. Henderson had the cops in his back pocket. But he was saving the mug for himself. Jamie knew all about it; all, except how close it was to his own family.

Jamie was for Henderson. Go with the man on top; that was the way he figured it. Someday, he figured, he would be like Henderson. That was the way to go. Not like this mug Catlett, playing his cards wrong, getting caught at it, and getting beaten to a pulp.

The fight went on. Catlett was getting the worst of it, but he held on. It was no holds barred for both men, now. Catlett's jaw was broken. It had been broken on the first rush, but he hardly felt it. He had hurt Henderson, too, and he kept coming after him, blindly, doggedly. There was a cut around Henderson's left eye, and his face was swollen badly.

They had been fighting for over half an hour. It was worse than the 45-round battle, when both men had been in condition, and when they had been able to rest every three minutes. There was no rest now; it was grim, and neither one of them would give up. There was too much at stake. It was as if the issue of Henderson's empire had not been settled the night before.

Catlett caught Henderson with a right hand in the chest that shook his balance, and followed it with a head-down charge that bowled Henderson over. He fell backward against the potbellied stove, and rattled it on its stumpy claw-footed legs.

The door of the stove popped open, and three glowing coals fell out on the floor. They lay smoldering on the floor, but no one made a move to scoop them up.

Catlett came for Henderson again. The two of them fell to the floor, with Catlett on top, and a gasp went up from many in the room. Henderson had fallen right on the coals.

Jamie felt his whole body tighten, and his face screwed up with tension. He could see Henderson's mouth set in a wordless scream. The smell of burning cloth and flesh filled the bar, and Catlett pressed his advantage, sitting astride Henderson to hold him down, and beating him with his fists.

With a supreme effort, Henderson caught Catlett's wrists and forced them upward. He twisted sharply, and jolted Catlett's balance, and then he had rolled over and was up, the smoke still pouring from his back, and Catlett was down.

Henderson came in for the kill now. He smacked Catlett across one side of his jaw, then the other, rattling Catlett's head into dizziness and pain. Then he grabbed Catlett by the collar and dragged his face across the floor, closer, closer, closer to the still-glowing coals.

Catlett could smell the burning, feel the heat, see the red glow as he was moved toward it, quarter inch by quarter inch. His eyes went wide with fear, and he snapped his head back and forth, trying to pull away from Henderson's grip. But it was no use; and now the pain of his broken jaw was growing more intense, sapping his strength.

"*Aaaaaa!*" he cried out, and his cheek was pressed hard against the fiery coal.

Men at the bar turned away now. The smell of burning flesh assaulted them. They could not shut out the look of pain gone berserk in Catlett's eyes, nor the piercing desperation of his screams. But they could turn their backs and stop looking.

Jamie had slipped just inside the doorway by this time. His eyes never left the struggle. Catlett's screams stopped when he passed out.

Chapter Twenty

Fannie answered the knock at the door. She saw a tall, burly man, his clothes disheveled, torn and bloody, his face almost completely covered with bandages. He wavered unsteadily on his feet. Something awful was happening to the part of his face that Fannie could see. Then she realized that he was trying to smile.

"G'd evening, girlie," he said. " 'S yer mother at home?"

Fannie screamed, and tried to shut the door, but the man had interposed his bulk against the doorjamb, and blocked her.

"I know who that is," Jamie said scornfully. "That's the mug who got beat up by Big Bill Henderson down on the Bowery yest'dy. I seen it. Get out o' here, ya no-good bum."

Catlett raised his fist at Jamie, who backed off and made faces at him.

Nancy came into the room, and stopped as soon as she saw Catlett. She looked at his ruined face as if she were seeing the ruins of her own life, and tears welled up in her eyes.

"For God's sake, let him in, Fannie," she said. "Can't you see the man's hurt? And go out and get me some liniment and fresh bandages . . . and a bottle of whiskey for medicine."

"Did you really see the fight where that man got beaten so badly?" Fannie asked Jamie as they went for the liniment.

"Did I! It was Big Bill Henderson done it. He's the gent runs all the posh casinos in town—you've prob'ly never heard of him, but if you were a man, you'd know. He's the real goods—he can make you or kill you in this town. This mug tried to muscle in on Big Bill's territory, so Big Bill let him have it. What a fight, sis! Big Bill's back was on fire when he finished him off, and he's so tough, he never even felt it!"

"His . . . back was on fire? What do you mean?"

"He rolled through the fire while they was fightin'. You shoulda seen the smoke, just pourin' out of the back of his coat. But does that bother him? Not a bit of it! 'Drinks for the house,' he says."

Fannie could picture it. She knew Henderson's courage too well, and the drive that made him remain in control, no matter what the situation. She thought of his back, which she had rubbed often in the evenings when the muscles were taut and knotted. Her eyes filled with tears, but she turned her face away and Jamie did not notice.

"Say, what's that mug doin' in our house, anyway?"

"I don't know. And you shouldn't be hanging around places like that."

"Oh, sis, you don't know nothin'."

Heywood Catlett was in Nancy's bed resting when Fannie and Jamie returned, and that was where he stayed. He moved in with them.

Nancy and Fannie nursed him until he was better. It was hard for Fannie. She wanted to help her mother, but she could not change the dressings on Catlett's wounds without thinking of Henderson, whom she could not go near.

Fannie and Jamie hoped that Catlett would leave after he got better, but he stayed on. He became a permanent part of the household.

*   *   *

Jamie was more beautiful than ever, and he knew it. It was his body that bought him an occasional night away from the madness of home, in the arms of Joe St. George of the Little Dead Rabbits or Mike Weissberg of the Little Forty Thieves or a few others who appreciated a soft ass, a pliant mouth, and a willingness to please.

But Jamie gave out his favors sparingly, and he was willing to give no one man—or woman, had the situation arisen—rights to him. He was not about to become a punk for some gang lord, and he used his charm only when he needed to, and only for as long as he needed to. He knew that the youth gangs were only a stepping stone. They had no power, they had no experience, and they had no guts.

Jamie knew that for sure. He had been out one day with a bunch of boys from the Little Dead Rabbits gang. They were twelve and thirteen. He was ten. Billy Dwyer, the self-appointed ringleader, was just fourteen. They were out for money, and out to prove themselves.

They were in an alley, off Delancey Street. It was dusk, and they crouched unseen behind a bunch of barrels, waiting.

Eventually, an old Jewish peddler wandered into the alley, and they surrounded him. He was a short, skinny man who limped along with the aid of a walking stick, no taller than the tallest of the boys. When he saw that he was cut off from escape, he shrank back against a wall.

Billy Dwyer held a knife out at arm's length, its blade as close to the old man's face as it was to his own.

"Don't make a sound if you know what's good for you," he warned. His voice was changing, and it cracked in midsentence. The sudden boyish squeak shamed him, and he grew more menacing, jabbing the air with his knife just inches in front of the old man's face.

"Get away from me!" the peddler hissed, terrified.

"Come on, you old kike," the boy said, pitching his voice self-consciously low. "We ain't got all night. Give us your money."

"No!" the old man said suddenly. He raised his cane. It smacked Billy in the hand, and the knife was sent flying.

For an instant, all were frozen, the gang and the old man equally startled by the act, no one knowing quite what to do next.

"Now, go on! Get away from me, I say!" the old man quavered, still holding his cane up.

Someone threw a rock. The old man saw it coming, and waved at it with his cane like a racquet player, as if the cane could somehow go on saving him indefinitely. The rock hit him hard in the temple, and he went down.

He did not move.

Billy went over and touched him, turned him over, looked at him closely.

"Shit," he said, and crossed himself. "He's dead. Let's get out of here."

None of them had ever seen a dead man before, let alone had a hand in killing. Fears and superstitious dread combined to panic the whole gang, and they turned and took off running down the alley.

All but Jamie. He stood and looked at the body for a moment, satisfying himself that it was not going to move. Then he knelt down, and began to go through the dead man's pockets.

He worked thoroughly. He did not give a second thought to fear of the corpse, and no one had heard the commotion. He kept his eye on the entrance to the alley, and he ran his hands up and down the body of the dead peddler, looking for any secret cache of money or valuables.

A few of the gang members had crept back to the corner at the far end of the alley. They peered around it into the quiet darkness.

Then they heard the scurrying sound of small feet, and saw Jamie emerge from the shadows. On his face was a smile of boyish but calculated excitement.

"Well, I got it," he said. "Everything the old kike had on him. Six dollars and forty-three cents."

"What was it like?" asked a voice full of wonder.

"It was nothin'," said Jamie.

"Share," Billy Dwyer said.

"Damn right," Jamie said. "We did it together, didn't we?"

There was only the subtlest hint of sarcasm in his voice. It could easily have been missed.

He knew there was something wrong as soon as he walked into the tenement apartment. The sounds were coming from his mother's bedroom, but they were not the usual drunken rattlings that he was used to hearing from his mother and Catlett. And there was fear in the air.

He walked quietly to the bedroom door.

Catlett was in profile, the scarred, monstrous half of his face toward Jamie. Fannie was across the room, keeping a straight-backed chair between herself and Catlett. Her face was flushed and frightened; there was a red welt across her cheek, where Catlett had struck her.

She saw Jamie, and tried to signal him to flee, but he stayed where he was.

Catlett turned around. "Get outa here, kid," he said. "Me an' yer sister 'r jush havin' a little fun. Go on. Go rob an old lady."

"You leave my sister alone or I'll . . ."

"Yeah?" Catlett leered. "You'll what?" He swatted at Jamie with his open hand. Jamie ducked, but the blow still caught him on the side of the head and sent him to the floor, dazed.

Catlett turned back to Fannie. "Come on, girlie," he said, angry and cajoling. "Stop foolin' around an' gi' me what I want."

"Get away from me!" Fannie screamed. "Get away from my brother! Don't you hurt him like that!" The blow to Jamie had triggered something in Fannie, and she went on screaming hysterically. Catlett ground his teeth, and put his hand to his brow.

"Shut up, you . . ." he muttered. He lunged for her. She stuck the chair out at him, and his feet caught in it. Drunk as he was, his balance was unsteady, and he could not recover. He fell heavily, and Fannie ran past him. She took Jamie's hand and ran out into the hallway with him, and down the stairs.

Catlett followed them. They hid behind a pile of garbage and debris in the courtyard until he ran past them. Then they ran back upstairs, and locked the door.

They did not open it until Nancy returned home. But Catlett did not come back. He never came back.

It was just the three of them again.

Nancy stopped gambling. She had lost even that shred of hope that sustains a compulsive gambler. She stopped going out. Fannie picked up her own washing and ironing now, and delivered it. Jamie helped her. He was subdued these days, too, and spent most of his time at home.

Nancy took most of what Fannie made and spent it on liquor. Fannie tried to stop her at first, hiding the money, buying food as soon as she was paid, but it did not work. Nancy would not eat the food anyway. And when she was deprived of her gin, she began to shake, and twitch, and talk in a wild, incoherent fashion that terrified her children.

Fannie would relent. She could not bring herself to buy the liquor, or give her mother the money for it, but she would leave money where her mother could find it.

The time came when the alcohol would no longer keep Nancy's tremors at bay. Her body locked in a violent fit, and the bottle fell from her hand. She was trembling so wildly at first, her body flailing in such great arcs, that they could not get near her. Jamie wanted to run, but he stood his ground, close by Fannie, and held her hand. When Nancy was quieter, they got her into bed.

Her illness lasted three days. She was feverish. She had periods of calm, periods of convulsion. On the third day, she began to hallucinate.

"No, John . . ." they heard her say. "No, I don't want to go home . . . Mrs. Finkel will take care of me . . . she'll get me a job . . . won't you . . . Mrs. Finkel . . ."

And then! "Oh, Lord Gretton . . . the castle is lovely . . . just as I imagined it . . . of course John and I will be staying . . . John wants the children to have . . . oh, yes, Lady Gretton . . . lovely, lovely . . ."

She stood up from the bed, smiling, bowing, wavering unsteadily. Then her eyes went wide. She screamed, and ran across the room. Before Fannie or Jamie could stop her, she had dived out the window.

She was dead by the time they reached her broken body.

Chapter Twenty-one

Fannie and Jamie never went back to the tenement apartment. They spent that night, and the next several after it, sleeping on a hay barge docked at a Hudson River pier. The hay gave them some warmth, but nowhere near enough. They clutched each other tightly and shivered through the night.

Fannie and Jamie were not alone. The hay barges were a magnet for young orphans, and they joined a ragged community of dirty, helpless children who knew no other home. There was shelter of a sort at the docks, and food, too: bruised or partially rotted oranges and bananas off ships from South America and molasses that leaked out of poorly lidded barrels. The police chased them off occasionally, but mostly they were left alone. The barge children were too weak to be dangerous to anybody. And they died quickly enough.

For four days, Jamie and Fannie were inseparable. Jamie had nightmares each night, and Fannie held him. During the day, they said nothing and moved little, always staying close enough to reach out and touch each other. Then on the fifth day, Jamie wandered off.

He did not come back. There had been no change in his mood that Fannie had detected, but there must have been something that brought the period of shock and mourning to an end between one heartbeat and the next. Fannie waited for him for two more days and nights, but she knew in her heart that he had gone back to join his gang.

And she . . . what was she to do? She had no gang to take her in. She slept alone in the dusty hay, tossing fitfully, and dreaming that Johnny had come to find her. She woke, still not knowing what to do. A factory . . . selling her body . . . or turning to the one person outside her family who had cared for her, the man whom she thought she could never face again, because of her betrayal. Bill Henderson.

She knew the Twenty-third Street flat as if it were her own home. She knew how to get in without being seen, and when there would be no one there.

She was amazed to discover how much her soul felt at home in the parlor she had thought never to see again. Her ragged dress, the caked dirt on her face, her greasy, matted hair made her seem like an intruder. But she was home again.

Her clothes were still in the closet with the lace peignoir that she had worn for Henderson. And there was steaming hot water, and soap, and towels. She drew two baths, the first to wash the dirt off her body, the second to soak in, to open up her pores and luxuriate in the warmth and the steam and the soap bubbles. She stayed in the tub for a long time. Then she dried herself with a soft Turkish towel, and threw her old rags into the stove.

What should she wear? She picked up the peignoir and looked at it fondly, then shook her head. She must wear street clothes. She must not presume too much. She must be proper and circumspect. She was already presuming a great deal from a man to whom she owed much. She did not want to go too far.

But as she started to place the lacy garment back in the closet, she heard footsteps, and a key in the latch. She hurriedly wrapped the peignoir around herself, and tied the sash at her waist, as the door to the outer room opened.

She heard Henderson's voice, and a second voice. A woman's voice. Her heart sank, and she looked frantically about for a way out, for some forgotten secret passageway to suddenly catch her eye. Then the door to the bedroom was filled with a plump, striking blond woman in her thirties, and behind her, the massive figure of Bill Henderson.

Fannie shrank back against the wall. The blond woman stared at her for perhaps five seconds, then let go a peal of drunken laughter.

"Well, what do we have here, Hendo?" she said. "Not a burglar, that's for sure. Well, I like a little surprise as well as the next girl, but this . . . ! Listen, if you give me a little advance warning next time, I'll help you pick out someone who's more my type. Say, don't feel bad, though, honey. You're kind of a cute little thing, ain't you? What's your name?"

Henderson put his hand on her shoulder.

"Let's call it a night, shall we, Lily? I'll see you later. That's a good sport."

In a single motion, he turned her around, pressed a large banknote into her hand, laid his arm across her shoulder, and led her out into the front room. A few moments later, Fannie heard the door open and close. Then she came out into the parlor to meet him.

"I'm sorry if I spoiled your plans," she said.

"I didn't have any plans. Are you all right?"

"I think so . . . I mean, yes, I'm all right. I know I shouldn't have come. I just wanted . . ."

She stood about six feet from him, and did not move. One hand was at her throat, the other folded across her waist. She kept her head up, and looked straight at him. "I want to explain. There's something I have to tell you."

"You don't have to explain anything." He crossed over to her now, and wrapped his big arms around her. She rested against him, her cheek and both hands pressed against his chest.

"Are you hungry?" he asked. "I'll get some food sent in for you."

"I'd like a glass of brandy," she said.

"Brandy? Have you started drinking, little pigeon?"

"I'd like some now," she said.

He got a bottle and two glasses. He poured a small portion for her, a larger amount for himself. She drank hers in small sips. It burned her throat, but she had been expecting that, and she was able to swallow it without choking. And it did make her feel different inside, just as it was supposed to, just as she had hoped it would.

"I do have something to tell you," she said. He started to reply, but she held her hand up to silence him. She walked over to the sideboard, and took out a deck of cards. She returned and sat across from him.

"Watch my eyes," she said.

She shuffled and cut, and shuffled again. She dealt out five poker hands. Her fingers trembled, but they did what she wanted them to. She kept her eyes focused on his. When the last card was dealt, she put the remainder of the deck down, and nodded her head at the table.

Henderson hesitated for a moment, then reached for the second hand, and turned it over.

It was a pair of deuces.

Fannie scooped up the third hand, and laid it down face up. Four aces, and the queen of spades.

"Well, you've learned it," Henderson said. "And I'm sorry."

She tossed the cards aside, and laced her small white fingers between his broad, splayed knuckles. "Don't be," she said. "I had to."

Chapter Twenty-two

John Whitmarsh sat in a saloon in Dallas with a deck of cards. He moved them fluidly in one hand, cutting the deck into three sections and folding the sections into each other. Then he snapped the deck together again, set it on the table, and with a swift motion of his hand spread the cards in a rainbow arc.

"Pick one," he said.

The man sitting across the table was a stranger to John, met ten minutes earlier over a drink. Still, there was something naggingly familiar about this man. He was of medium height, with fierce thick black hair and whiskers which surged about his plump face with amiable energy. He was stout, but his girth suggested strength, not flabbiness. By his voice he was a Texan. By his dress he was a rancher. And by everything about his appearance he was a successful man.

He reached out and selected a card, cupping it in his broad palm and scooping it back to him. He tilted it upward with his thumb and glanced at its face.

"Okay."

"Slip it back in, then."

The man slid the card back across the smooth wood and into the deck. John swept the cards together and gave them two crisp shuffles. Then he set them neatly in the middle of the table.

"Just to be sure," he said, "we'll cut the cards." He

took out a large hunting knife, and with no hesitation sliced it cleanly through the deck, cutting the cards in half.

"Damn!" said the Texan. "That's some knife."

John grinned, and began to shuffle the two half decks. The bearded Texan watched him, highly entertained. John began laying the truncated cards out on the table, face down. When they were all down, he stared at them for a few moments with a frown of concentration on his face. Then he selected two halves and pushed them over to the other man.

"Turn them over."

"I will," the man said. He turned one, and then the other. They were both halves of the seven of clubs.

"I'll be damned!"

"Is that your card?"

"It sure is, friend. I don't believe it!"

"I know what you mean. I'm pretty thirsty myself."

The man laughed. "What're you drinking?"

"Mescal, thanks."

While his companion ordered the drinks, John studied him more closely. No, he decided, the man was no one that he knew. And John had a good head for faces. Perhaps this was what Walter Koch used to call *déjà vu*—a holdover memory from another life, if you believed that sort of thing.

But there was a will-o'-the-wisp quality to the responsive chord this man's face struck in John. It kept flickering and changing. One moment it would seem to center on the mouth, which had an unexpectedly refined line to it behind the wild bristle of whiskers. Then that would vanish and the haunting likeness would appear again in the dark eyes, and the thick black eyebrows with their rakish arch. It was as though there were another man, shy and elusive, concealed within this beefy, vigorous package.

"I know you!"

John showed his surprise.

"Sure," the man said with a little grin of triumph as he set a glass and bottle in front of John. "Been nagging at me the past ten minutes. I knew I'd seen you before." He paused a moment, and gestured at John with a bobbing motion of his thumb. "Hamlet, right?"

John nodded. "That's right."

He had been playing Hamlet. That was what had brought him to Dallas. For the past two years he had been an actor, traveling with a repertory company through the West and Southwest. He had hooked on with them quite by accident, and begun as a stagehand. He had moved quickly to playing bit parts, and finally to leading man.

Five years had passed since the illusion-shattering days of 1877, when America had seemed to teeter on the brink of a new era, only to collapse back again into its old ways. When John Whitmarsh had left Chicago he had been running from more than the police. He had run off to hide from everything that had brought him to that point. His whole life had been causes, from his earliest awareness of the earnest talks of his father and his uncles and their friends, back in the *Independence* office or in the house in Painter's Falls, Pennsylvania. He had been aware of the earnestness in their voices long before the words had meant anything to him. And after learning the words he had learned the ideas behind them.

The ideas were simple, really, once you were old enough to understand them. All men had a right to live with dignity and to earn a decent living for their labors. No man had a right to grind another man under his boot heel in pursuit of profit. These were the essential ideas that John had inherited from his father.

But perhaps he had not inherited his father's dedication. Or events had brought him along too fast. Perhaps he had been thrown into the swift part of the current before he was old enough to handle it, and the fight had been battered out of him by the rapids. All John knew was that when he had left Chicago amid the bitter ashes of the strike that had failed, he had gone looking for nobody and had taken nothing with him. No baggage and no causes. Nothing but the memory of a beautiful and innocent girl who had been shot and had died in his arms. He still carried her face with him, and it could still make him cry.

The rest, he was rid of. And in the years since Chicago he had kept on the move. He had ridden the rods and lived off card games and bunco tricks, as he had in the days with Callahan and Koch. He had shipped to the Orient and back on a merchant steamer. He had punched cattle in Wyoming.

But the theater suited him perfectly. He took a fierce pleasure in the traveling world of greasepaint and make-believe. He was a commanding presence, a powerful six foot two with curly black hair and piercing eyes, and a baritone voice that raised gooseflesh on the bare arms of women as far back as the second balcony. In San Francisco he was hailed by critics as a "raw talent," and in Denver his Hamlet was favorably compared with that of Maurice Barrymore.

But in Dallas, the company's director had disappeared with the box office receipts and a long-legged dance hall girl, and John was out of a job.

"That's a goddamn shame," John's companion reacted indignantly. "Took the whole kit and caboodle?"

"Every red cent."

"Which one was he? The king?"

"That's right. Claudius."

"Sniveling bastard. Piss-poor actor, too."

"That's the truth."

"All those things in your speech, he did 'em all: mouthing, sawing the air . . ."

John laughed. "If I'd known then what he was up to, I'd have gone ahead and killed him while he was at his prayers."

"His words rose up, his thoughts remained below."

"Hey, you know your *Hamlet* pretty well."

"Oh, I'm a great reader. Sometimes it takes Shakespeare to hold a man's mind together when he's spent a couple of weeks looking at nothing but the ass end of a herd of cows and listening to the wisdom of a bunch of cowboys."

"Yeah," John agreed, "I've spent some time punching cattle."

"Have you? Yeah, you don't look like an actor—no offense son, but you know what I mean. A lot of these actors have a kind of . . ." He made a weak gesture with his hand. "You play a mean Hamlet, though. I've seen a few of 'em, and I can tell you, yours stacks up."

"Thanks."

"So . . . what are you going to do?"

John shrugged. "Something generally turns up."

"Tell you what," said the Texan. "Show me a few more of your card tricks, and I'll buy you dinner."

"You've got yourself a deal, mister. We'll need a fresh deck, though."

"So we will." He turned and called over his shoulder to the bartender. "Frank. A deck of cards."

The bartender reached under the counter and flipped a sealed deck through the air. "Here you go, Mr. Parsons."

Then John knew why the face that he had never seen before had looked so familiar. Albert Parsons had told him about a brother in Texas, an older brother who had raised him. This Parsons had those same black eyes, and the same dramatic raven's-wing sweep to the brows. John concentrated on the eyes now. The rest fell away, and he was looking at Albert Parsons.

He slit open the wrapping and riffled through the cards, smelling their newness.

"Shall I read the cards for you?"

"You mean tell my fortune?"

"That sort of thing."

"Sure. You do that? Yeah, let's see how you do."

John handed him the cards. "You shuffle them, and then deal out two rows of ten, face down." While Parsons did that, John drained his glass and poured another. Chicago was coming back to him; and with Chicago, Tesia. But she was never far away, anyway. Sometimes he still talked to her.

He examined the twenty blue-patterned pasteboard rectangles in front of him. He began to talk, turning them over slowly, one by one, as he did.

"Your name is William H. Parsons. People call you Wild Bill."

Parsons was smiling, but his shrug showed that he was not yet impressed. "Easy enough to pick up," he said.

"Sure. Now, you're a rancher, but that's not the way you started out."

"No?"

"No. That came after the war. You were a cavalry officer—a Major General, right? And that's where the 'Wild Bill' moniker took hold. But before that, you were a newspaperman."

"Say, that's not bad."

"A newspaper editor and publisher. In Tyler, Texas. The Tyler . . ."

"*Telegraph*!"

"The Tyler *Telegraph*. And that's when you took charge of a little bit of a fellow who happened to be your baby brother, who later turned up as a Noted Anarchist in Chicago, Illinois."

Parsons's beard split into a wide grin. "Well, I'll be hanged," he said. "So you're a friend of the Noted Anarchist?"

"I knew him a short time. He made a great impression on me."

"Albert's a good boy. A blamed bull-headed young fool, mind you, but a good boy. Smart as a whip." Bill Parsons shook his head. "But dumb, too, if you know what I mean. Albert made a lot of enemies before he left these parts."

"So he told me."

"I'm not saying he's wrong, mind you. Oh, I reckon he's half-cocked with some of his notions, but they come out of a good heart, and a good head. Trouble with Albert is, he don't understand how to do business in the real world."

That, thought John, is probably the key to everything. And if you can't figure out how to deal with the real world, the best thing to do is to get the hell out of it.

"Now myself," Parsons was saying, "I'm more what

you'd call a Noted Pragmatist. I may not have Albert's brains, but I've got sixty thousand acres of fine grazing land and ten thousand head of cattle—speaking of which, here comes one of 'em now,'' he said, as the waiter arrived with a couple of thick steaks and set them down on the table. John had not eaten that day, and the smell brought a sudden fierce hunger.

"Well, what about you, son? You a Noted Anarchist too?"

John was cutting into his steak. "Not me," he said. "I'm an actor."

Chapter Twenty-three

In Texas terms, the Parsons ranch was not an especially big one. Its sixty thousand acres made a respectable spread, but it was not in a league with such legendary outfits as the XIT, which covered 3,050,000 acres of Panhandle land, or the JA Ranch, where Charles Goodnight ran one hundred thousand head of cattle on 1,335,000 acres.

But the Parsons land was rich, and varied. It straddled the Trinity River midway between Dallas and Houston. There were wooded hills on it, and grassland, and streams that elbowed down mountainsides and tumbled over cliffs in lacy, sparkling waterfalls. The ranch house stood on a beautiful piece of high ground overlooking a lake. Beyond the lake a green meadow sloped up into a stand of pines, from which deer would emerge under cover of the dawn mists and come down to drink, and then drift slowly back to the trees again as the mist line rose.

John Whitmarsh lived in the bunk house down the road, but he was always welcome at the main house. He spent considerable time there, talking to Bill Parsons and using his library. And he took to hanging around the kitchen, where Parsons's cook baked him little pies and special delicacies.

Her name was Minnie Montana. She was about twenty-three, a plainspoken, practical girl. She was not a beauty, but she had a kind of self-confident honesty that made physical beauty irrelevant after a while. Her face was flat and square jawed. Her nose was a straight, uncompromising line. It was not a face that looked over-used to smiling, but when she talked to John and parried his banter in the kitchen, her wide thin mouth tucked up at the edges, and her dark brown eyes sparkled with pleasure, and she looked almost pretty.

"Hello, Minnie. What've you got to feed a hungry cowboy?"

She sniffed. "We don't feed hungry cowboys here. Cowboys eat down the road."

"All right then, what've you got for a hungry Shakespearean actor?"

"I don't see no Shakespearean actor. All I see is a cowboy trackin' dirt into my kitchen."

He leaned over the counter and took a piece of the trout she was preparing, and popped it into his mouth.

"Ugh!" she exclaimed, disgust overcoming reprimand. "That's raw! How can you do that?"

"Raw fish. Big delicacy in the Orient, Minnie. Good for you, too. Try a piece."

"I will not! And you keep your hands off it too. This here is for dinner."

"I'm invited for dinner."

"Then you just wait till it's ready. Land, I never saw such an appetite! Wonder you ain't fat."

"Three days in the saddle, Minnie. Mending fences and eating hard tack and cold beef. I dreamed about you."

"Dreamed about my apple pie, I shouldn't wonder."

"Apple pie! Is that what I smell?"

Her lips twitched into a grin, and she pursed them to ‘
cover it up.

"There might be apple pie. But it's for dinner."

"Oh, but mightn't there be a little extra? A tart, maybe?
An *hors d'oeuvre* for the starving Shakespearean actor?"

"Oh, get on with your Shakespearean actor!" She pulled
a nicely browned pastry from the Dutch oven and set it on
a plate in front of him with a show of exasperation.
"There! Now maybe you'll leave me in peace."

"Being your slave, what should I do but tend
Upon the hours and times of your desire . . ."

"What?"

"I have no precious time at all to spend,
Nor services to do till you require.
Nor dare I chide . . ."

"Oh, get *along* with you! I swan, I never saw nobody
clutter up their head with gibberish the way you do, John
Whitmarsh. Shakespeare! I daresay it must be nice to have
nothin' to do all day but sit 'round readin' poetry . . ."

"Thanks for the pie, Minnie." He leaned over and
kissed her playfully on the cheek, and then danced out of
the kitchen followed by her cries of pretended outrage.

But after he was gone, Minnie stood a while and gazed
at the door where he had left. Her hand drifted up to the
cheek he had kissed, and her fingers stroked the spot
distractedly, leaving a floury trace.

He was a wild one, this John Whitmarsh. Not like any
cowboy she'd ever come across. Oh, she'd known bookish
cowboys before, and God knew she'd met plenty who
liked to flirt. As a rule, Minnie Montana didn't have much
time for either.

It wasn't quite the same with this one, though. He
wasn't really bookish, though he could quote all that Shakespeare and poetry and stuff till it made her head spin. But
he wasn't glum and quiet like the bookish ones. And he

was a flirt, but he wasn't crude and pawing like some of those cowboys could be. The fact was, he hardly seemed like a cowboy at all.

He'd been an actor, he said. Well, that might be, but he seemed to have put all that behind him. No, it was more than that. He seemed to have a quality that Minnie could only define to herself as "good breeding." That was it, she decided. John Whitmarsh came from a good family, somewhere back up the line. He had a solid streak of gentleman in him, you could tell. He might be footloose and wild now, but Minnie Montana had great respect for "good breeding." Cream always rose to the top.

He was good looking, too, with more charm than was good for him, though Minnie told herself those things weren't so important in a man. Still, he didn't seem conceited. High-spirited was more the word.

Minnie decided to marry him. She mulled the idea for a time, because there was something that seemed a bit wrong. She worried at it for a while, and tried to get at what it was. There seemed to be a great sadness in him somewhere, buried very deep, or a great emptiness; something lost, or unfulfilled, or both. That was as close as Minnie could come to figuring it out. But she wouldn't ask him questions about it, or pry too deep. That sort of thing was a man's private place, and as long as he didn't fill it up with drink, it was not a woman's business to poke around in it.

The rest—the wildness and the footloose spirit, and what she detected as a lack of ambition—those things Minnie Montana felt she could handle. So she decided to marry John Whitmarsh, and help him along. And someday they would own a spread just like Mr. Parsons's, and John would be a solid, important citizen.

Cream always rose to the top.

Chapter Twenty-four

Fannie took the night off on November 5, 1882. She could afford to. She had money in the bank now, a comfortable nest egg. She worked six nights a week at Miss Shaw's, the ladies' gambling casino on Thirty-fourth Street. Summers, she took off and worked the packets that steamed up and down the Hudson River between New York and Albany. And she worked Saratoga. Henderson had sold out his casinos in New York, but he kept his interest in the Grand Union Hotel in Saratoga, and Fannie always had a favored seat in the biggest games there.

She made big money in the summers, playing cards and playing the men who played the cards. She never had to sleep with them. She was too good a poker player for that. She just manipulated them at the tables, and whatever they thought there . . . well, it was part of the game. And if they followed her afterward, she knew how to get rid of them.

She did not make as much off the ladies, but she made as much as she needed to. And they never gave her any trouble.

So she took November 5 off. It was election night—and a victory celebration for newly elected Congressman Big Bill Henderson.

There was champagne and oysters and a brass band that played Irish jigs and reels. There were men smoking cigars a foot long, and beautiful women in evening clothes. As stylish and striking as any of them was Fannie Whitmarsh, wearing a maroon velvet gown that was demure, but showed off her dark hair and the deep warm tone of her complexion to their fullest advantage. She carried herself regally, she was clever and animated in conversation, but there was still a barely perceptible reserve wrapped around her that held her separate from everyone but Henderson.

He was the center of everything, the man whom other men crowded around for handshakes and backslapping, whom all the ladies had to dance at least a few steps with, who was making the deals and dispensing the favors and patronage even as the corks popped and the band played "Garryowen." But he made time to talk to her.

"Bill, I'm so proud and happy for you," she told him.

"I'm not so sure, little pigeon," he said, grinning and squeezing her. "Maybe I should have gone to Albany, where I could keep a closer eye on things. Well, Washington's not bad. And maybe next time, I'll run for mayor. Won't we have a city then, my sweet! But what about you? My offer still stands, you know. Anytime you want a club of your own, I'll set you up. And even if I'm off in Washington, the police aren't going to bother a protégé of Henderson's."

"No, Bill, not yet. Thank you. I just don't want it. Not now."

"Don't think you could handle it? Of course you could. You're as good as any man in this city."

"That's not it. I'm just not ready, Bill, not yet."

It was Jamie. He was living at home with her now, and going to school. As soon as she had gotten money and a decent place to live, she had found him and taken him off the streets. Their roles were reversed, now—she was the one who went out and made a living on the wrong side of the law, and he was a clean-faced, nicely dressed schoolboy.

She could ply her trade in anonymity. But if she became proprietress of a fancy gambling casino, she would become one of the most notorious women in New York. And she did not want Jamie to suffer from that.

* * *

Jamie had undergone a remarkable change in the years since his sister had taken him in hand. He had taken to school—not with a passion, because Jamie did nothing with passion—but with total acceptance. He did not try to drift back to the streets and to the gangs he had run with. For the first year Fannie had watched him closely, because she knew her brother too well to let herself be taken in by appearances. She made him do his homework, and quizzed him on it. But she soon gave up doing that, because it became apparent that he was going far beyond her in education. She became convinced of her brother's conversion, and allowed herself to fill with joy and pride, and to feel that whatever she had had to do had been worthwhile.

Jamie's grades were excellent. He discovered early that he could do well without working hard. He also found that by putting in a bit of work he could do extremely well, and he had no objection to working. He could have deceived Fannie when she sat him down to do his homework, and only pretended he was doing it. But that would have been empty cleverness, and not in his own interest. And Jamie Whitmarsh was especially precocious in developing an awareness of where his interests lay.

They did not lie with the Little Dead Rabbits. He saw some of the hoodlums from his street days from time to time, but now they seemed to be part of another world. Eugene Smith had been one of the leaders of the gang. Jamie had idolized him a few years earlier. Now Eugene Smith was eighteen and he pushed a wagon in the garment district.

"How's it goin', Jamie?"

"Fine."

"Whatcha doin'?"

"I'm in school."

"Yeah?" A knowing grin. Eugene smoked cigarettes, and could keep one dangling from the center of his mouth while he talked—a trick that Jamie still admired. "Say, we got a job lined up. Me an' Pepper, Carl, a coupla the others. Warehouse on Canal Street. Easy pickin's, and the stuff's a breeze to unload. It's all set up. What we need is a guy can get in through the second story window. Whaddya say? Want in?''

"No."

"Look, kid, there's nothin' to it. I'm talkin' 'bout a full share for ya, y'know. Coupla hundred, easy."

"I'm not interested, Eugene."

"Ya dumb little fuck! Whatsa matter wit' cha? What, you got somethin' goin'?"

"More than you do, Eugene."

"Yeah?" Eugene Smith stepped menacingly forward. He had four years and twenty-five pounds over Jamie, and he was tough. But Jamie stood his ground without a flinch. His eyes were cold and without fear. It unsettled Eugene. It broke an automatic chain of cause and effect. When he menaced a younger boy, he expected to see fear, just as when he dropped an egg he expected it to break. Now, he did not know how to react.

"Well, okay, kid. Another time."

Jamie just looked at him.

"Well, okay then. Take care of yourself, hey? See ya."

"So long, Eugene."

When school let out for the summer, Jamie got a job as a messenger boy for a Wall Street firm. Ever since he had lived in New York he had admired the fine office buildings and the fancy houses and carriages of the rich. But now, delivering messages, he began to get a glimpse inside them, and a look at the men who worked and rode and lived in them. He compared what they had to what people like Eugene and Pepper and Carl had, even after their flushest haul, and he discovered that there was no comparison. And he knew which world he wanted for himself.

And he knew he could have it, too. Because he was smart, and he was ambitious. And most of all, because he was one of them. He was not one of the gutter people, whatever his recent circumstances had been. He was a Whitmarsh, an aristocrat. Jamie did not remember his father well; but his mother had always talked about the aristocracy of the Whitmarsh family, and how one day, when they got pulled together, she would take Fannie and Jamie and go to England to see their Uncle Roger, the Earl of Marley. Jamie did not understand why, if they were aristocrats, they had come down so far in the world. But he knew it was somehow his father's fault, and he hated him for it. That hatred was the one strong emotion that Jamie Whitmarsh felt.

As a rule, he did not feel things strongly. That would have clouded his vision of self-interest. Jamie's self-interest was a pure thing. He understood better than most people that each human being is the center of his own universe, and that outer-directed passions—love, hate, jealousy, patriotism, religion, sex, loyalty—only create distracting illusions. Jamie had no such illusions. There were no mirrors to trick his view and reflect his center outward. And this enabled him to see things clearly and to make decisions soundly.

Wall Street in the hour before noon was the busiest place in the world. It was alive with frenetic activity from the street up to the tops of the new "sky scrapers," towering ten and eleven stories above the ground. The air itself was a fury of energy, as wires crisscrossed above the street. There were wires for the telegraph, wires for the telephone, wires for electricity; together, they wove a canopy of the technological wizardry of the new age.

There were people who felt that the price of these wonders came too high, and who decried the visual blot on the city that this cat's cradle of wires produced. But Jamie Whitmarsh was not one of these people. As he walked along Wall Street toward Broadway he looked up and admired the sight. He was like a medical student admiring the network of veins and arteries in a human body. These wires performed the same function in the life of modern business as veins did in the life of the body. Whether or not they were beautiful was a question that simply did not come up. Their beauty was in their function, and their function was sublime.

He went into the building at the address on the envelope
he carried. He rode the elevator to the tenth floor. He gave
the floor number to the operator in a crisp voice, and stood
stiffly in the back of the car without speaking. Most of the
messengers chatted with elevator operators and doormen
and other uniformed help. But the businessmen did not;
and that was the example toward which Jamie's inclination
took him. Jamie dressed well, too. He had spent all his
money on clothes since the time a year ago that he had
read in a self-improvement pamphlet that "clothes make
the man." He made a great effort not to be taken for a
messenger. He tried, by his attitude and appearance, to
convey the impression that he was a businessman-apparent.
On any other fifteen-year-old boy this would have probably seemed pretentious and overreaching. But Jamie, with
his golden good looks and air of cool command, managed
it effectively.

He entered the outer office. A young secretary was
behind the desk, working efficiently at a Remington type-
writer. Jamie walked up to her.

"I have some papers for Mr. Scoville to sign," he said
importantly.

"Oh yes . . ." She looked up, not placing him, but
feeling somehow as if she should. "I'm sorry, Mr. . . . ?"

"Whitmarsh."

Whitmarsh. Perhaps he was one of the junior clerks, or
one of the partners' relatives taken on as summer help.

"Mr. Scoville is in a meeting right now, Mr. Whitmarsh,
but perhaps . . . if you'll just have a seat a moment . . ."

"I hope he won't be long?"

"Oh, I shouldn't think so . . . let me just check."

She tapped on the door. A voice called out "Yes?"

"Ah, Mr. Scoville, Mr. Whitmarsh is here with some
papers."

Mr. Scoville sat behind an oak desk between two windows that looked out through a cross-hatching of wires at
the ornate tower of the Western Union building. He was a
sallow, nervous man, an odd note of pallor in his other-

wise dark and somber office. He seemed only slightly more substantial than the wraith of smoke that drifted from a cigar held by the man with whom he was talking. Jamie could not see the other man; only a cuff of excellent broadcloth, a white margin of shirt cuff, a hand, and a large cigar. The rest was concealed behind a high-backed leather chair.

"Whitmarsh?" Scoville asked.

"From Fiske and Hatch, sir," Jamie said, stepping past the secretary and into the office. "Contracts to be signed and returned."

"Contracts? Well, yes, all right, give them here."

As Jamie walked forward the envelope was plucked from his hand by the figure seated in the high-backed chair.

"Contracts, eh? Let's see what you have here."

Jamie looked around in surprise. The man in the chair was about fifty, with a round cherubic face which was made to seem more so by a hairline that had receded to a graying fringe at the sides and back, and cottony sideburns that bracketed his plump cheeks. The bright glass moons of a pince-nez straddled his chubby nose. Standing, he would be below-average height. He was impeccably dressed in a brown suit with a pale pinstripe, a matching waistcoat, and a maroon cravat held in place with a jeweled ivory pin. He wore several rings, including a large ruby on his right hand. There was an air of elegant assurance to him that dominated the room.

"Mmm . . . mm . . . hm-hm," he muttered to himself, occasionally emitting a scornful laugh as he flipped rapidly but methodically through the papers. Then he handed them back to Jamie, with an ironic smile, and nodded in the direction of Scoville. Jamie took them and gave them to the man at the desk.

"Really, Scoville," the man behind Jamie said with a dry laugh. Jamie felt the man's eyes on him, and began to feel uncomfortable. Scoville looked uncomfortable too, like a boy caught without his lessons prepared.

"Allow me to suggest, my dear Scoville, that you not commit yourself to anything contractual without consultation with your legal counsel. Of course," he added disinterestedly, "it need not necessarily be myself; any competent lawyer could point out to you the flaws in this—or have you consulted with a lawyer on this matter already?"

"No, Mr. DePuyster, I . . . of course, my own department has been over the papers, but of course that was simply a preliminary . . . I of course intended . . . ."

"Up to you completely, old man."

"No, er, I . . . what do you think?"

"What do *I* think? Why, *I* think that this golden-haired cherub might well have delivered Scoville and Company into the grasping hands of Fiske and Hatch, Bankers, if it hadn't been for the fortuitous circumstance of my being here in your office this morning."

Jamie's cheeks reddened, and he turned anxiously to DePuyster. "Please, sir," he said. "I'm only a messenger!"

Depuyster grinned. His mouth was a V, with the ends tucking up into his apple-red cheeks. " 'Course you are, lad. Though I daresay you contrived to give a different impression." His glance lingered a moment longer on Jamie, enjoying his confusion. Then he returned his attention to Scoville, who was staring uncomfortably at the papers in front of him.

"Suppose you give me those to take along with me, Mr. Scoville. I'll make some notations on 'em, and send 'em back later in the day."

"Yes," said Scoville gratefully. "Yes, of course."

"All right with you, my boy?" DePuyster asked Jamie with a thin ironic smile.

"Yes, sir," Jamie answered.

Jamie rode the elevator down with DePuyster. He was recovering his composure rapidly, and he selected an attitude that combined earnestness with respectfulness. DePuyster was a man to impress. And despite his bad start, Jamie was determined to take his best shot at it in the limited time he had.

His name was familiar to Jamie. Cleveland DePuyster, one of the city's most powerful lawyers and one of its bluest bloods. The DePuyster family was said to own vast real estate holdings in the city, as well as a magnificent estate up along the Hudson in Barrytown. Cleveland DePuyster was the senior partner in the law firm of DePuyster, Chase, and Schuyler. He was a director of the New York Central Railroad, and a member of countless other corporate boards. The DePuyster mansion on Fifth Avenue was one of the sacred temples of New York society, and Mrs. Cleveland DePuyster was one of its celebrated priestesses.

Fortune did not bring a man like Cleveland DePuyster around every day, Jamie realized. If he let him get away now, he would have no one to blame but himself.

The elevator door opened and Jamie stood aside to let the great man pass. Then he hurried after him.

"I'm awfully sorry if I made any trouble up there, Mr. DePuyster. I was told to bring those papers to Mr. Scoville and get them signed. I swear I had no idea . . ."

"No more should you, my boy. You're only a messenger." He paused, looking Jamie up and down. "Is that correct?"

"It is at present, sir."

"At present, eh?" The weary smile. "You have plans, then? Ambitions?"

"Yes, sir, I do."

"And what might those ambitions be?"

"To be a lawyer, Mr. DePuyster."

"A lawyer!" DePuyster chuckled. "Not much of an ambition, is it?"

"I think it a very fine ambition," Jamie said respectfully.

"Well, and so it is, so it is. What is your name, young man?"

"Jamie . . . James Whitmarsh, Mr. DePuyster."

"Ah, but they call you Jamie, do they? Well, stick to it. It suits you. You're a lovely boy, you know."

Jamie blushed. "You're good to say so, sir." He began

to see his opening. He allowed no trace of it to show on his face, but he could read the signs. He would just have to follow them, and make the most of the opportunity. He would not have to do very much. He would just have to avoid making any mistakes.

DePuyster tapped his ebony stick thoughtfully on the ground. He drew a heavy watch from his waistcoat pocket, clicked it open and consulted it, and then put it away again. Jamie held his breath.

"Well, Jamie . . . do you have time to tuck into a bite of lunch before you go on your way? I'd like to hear more about these ambitions of yours."

"Oh, thank you, sir," said Jamie. "Thank you very much!"

They lunched in one of the oak-paneled dining rooms at Delmonico's at 25 Broadway. It was the old Delmonico's, built in another era forty years before. It was smaller than the new, fashionable Delmonico's uptown on Madison Square, and less dazzling. But what Jamie felt when he walked inside was the wealth and power that had been absorbed into those walls over the years. There was an aroma to the place that had nothing to do with food. It smelled of schemes hatched, deals made, trusts plotted, markets cornered. Jamie's nostrils flared as he inhaled it, and it went straight to his brain like a drug. Delmonico's, with its quiet, sober atmosphere, was more sensual and exciting than any place he had ever been.

"So, you want to be a lawyer, do you, Jamie?" Cleveland DePuyster asked as Jamie sliced carefully into his cold squab.

"Yes, sir."

"What steered you onto this perilous path?"

"My father was a lawyer, sir. I've always thought it was the noblest thing a man could be."

"Noblest, eh?" DePuyster smiled. "Well, and who was this father of yours? Whitmarsh . . . did he practice in New York?"

"In Pennsylvania. He was an associate of Mr. Franklin Gowen. Before that we lived in England. My uncle is the Earl of Marley."

"Is he, now? And what became of your father?"

"He died of a fever. Mr. Gowen gave the eulogy at his funeral. They were very close."

"And your mother?"

"My father's death left her with very little money. She became ill, and . . ." Jamie's lips trembled, and he blinked his eyes very fast ". . . two months ago she passed away."

"Why, you poor little fellow," said DePuyster sympathetically. His plump hand reached out and patted Jamie's. "Who takes care of you, then?"

"I take care of myself," Jamie answered. "I'm seventeen, you know," he added, knowing from past experimentation that he could safely put on two years. "I live alone."

"That must get very lonely."

"Yes, sir. It does, sometimes."

"I know. I'm a summer bachelor myself. Wife and daughter away for the summer. Most of the staff with them, too." He smiled brightly. "Rattle around in the old house a bit, all by myself."

There was more to the lawyer's smile now than there had been earlier. It was not dry with irony, not wearily aloof as Jamie had seen it in Scoville's office. Something else had crept in, and Jamie, with his cool, passionless perception, had little trouble in identifying it as desire.

The hook was in. But the fish still had to be played carefully, or it could all just as easily be lost.

Artfully, over a dessert of two flavors of sherbet with wafered sugar bisquits, Jamie brought the conversation around to the law again.

"It's a demanding profession, you know," DePuyster observed.

"I know it is, sir. But I'm not afraid of hard work."

"Aren't you? Well! That sets you apart from a good nine-tenths of your generation. Did well in school, did you?"

"I was always at the head of my class. But now . . . with Mama gone . . . I'm afraid I may not be able to . . ." Jamie's voice grew thick with emotion, and he gazed down at the tablecloth. DePuyster stroked his hand again.

"Well, now," he said consolingly, "we'll have to think of something for you, won't we?"

Jamie looked up at him, eyes glistening with tears and hope. At that moment the waiter appeared with a silver coffee urn.

"Ah, coffee," DePuyster said. "Yes, indeed. Jamie?"

"Yes, please, sir." In his heart he cursed the waiter for breaking the flow.

"Cream and sugar, sir?" the waiter asked DePuyster.

"No, thank you. I prefer to drink it the way God made it."

"For you, sir?"

Jamie shook his head. He had never tasted coffee before. He raised the steaming brew to his lips. It smelled bitter. He sipped it. It scalded his tongue, and tasted even worse than it smelled. He swallowed it without a change of expression.

"If there were anything I could do for you, Mr. DePuyster, anything in your office . . . It would be such an opportunity for me, to read law, and to be around a great man like you . . ." He turned his widest eyes on DePuyster and spoke with throbbing sincerity. "I'd do anything."

Cleveland DePuyster leaned back in his chair, and dabbed at his lips with a napkin. Jamie waited. He felt his heart pounding with the tension. But he was reasonably sure he had won.

"You know," DePuyster said, "it just might be that there would be a position open for an office boy at the firm. It would be hard work, and not much pay, but for an enterprising young man with a real vocation for the law . . . would such a proposition interest you, Jamie?"

"Mr. DePuyster," Jamie replied solemnly, "there is nothing I wouldn't do for an opportunity like that."

"Well," said DePuyster approvingly. "Well, well, well."

"Mr. Dominy, this is Mr. Whitmarsh."

The young man stood up hurriedly from his desk. He was tall and thin, with moist black hair combed across his forehead. He was coolly handsome, with pale, slightly pimpled skin and eyes of a milky blue. He flicked them uncuriously over Jamie and looked back at his employer.

"Yes, Mr. DePuyster."

"He will be coming aboard with us as an office boy. He will be under your supervision. I expect you'll find plenty for him to do."

"I expect so, sir."

"Be good enough to show him around, and make him familiar with our layout here. I shall be in my office. Come and see me when you've been around, Mr. Whitmarsh."

"Yes, sir."

"And Mr. Dominy . . ."

"Sir?"

"Ask Mr. Rogers to step into my office for a moment."

"Right away, Mr. DePuyster."

Richard Dominy turned and started down the hall. "This way, Whitmarsh," he ordered, and Jamie followed him. Cleveland DePuyster stood in his office doorway and watched Jamie walk away, and noted the smooth grace of his body and the angelic shine of his golden hair. He felt a pang open deep inside him.

A few moments later there was a knock on his door. "Come in!" he barked.

"Dominy said you wished to see me, sir?"

"Yes, Mr. Rogers. I want you to run a check for me." He handed Rogers a slip of paper. "Go 'round to the British Consulate. Is there an Earl of Marley? Does he have any family in America? Check out these other points, too. Discretely, I need not add. I want the answers this afternoon."

*   *   *

It began to rain about three, and they left the office in DePuyster's brougham and rode up Broadway. The coachman sat on the outside, hunched under a large black umbrella. The compartment was closed. Jamie sat close to DePuyster and watched the rain beating against the windows. In the distance, over the tattoo of the rain, he could hear the strident clatter of the elevated train above Third Avenue.

They passed through Madison Square, practically deserted because of the sudden shower, though normally at this hour it would have been bustling with shoppers. A policeman stood stoically in his slicker, and two ladies hurried along sharing one umbrella, laughing with the mild hysteria of people making the best of disaster. The brougham proceeded north on Fifth Avenue.

They reached the DePuyster mansion at Fifth Avenue and Thirty-first Street. It was a stately brownstone, built before the Civil War. This part of Fifth Avenue was no longer the choice residential district of town, and the wealthy were now building their palaces up in the Fifties, beyond the reach of the masses. But an aura of glamor clung to the DePuyster mansion that no encroachment of trade and clubs on the neighborhood could take away.

The footman came around and opened the door, and sheltered them with the big black umbrella as they hurried through the gate in the chocolate-brown wall and up the steps to the front door. The door was opened by a butler, who made deferential remarks about the weather as he took their hats and coats.

"Ah, there was a call on the telephone, Mr. DePuyster," the butler said. "From Mr. Rogers, of your office."

"Oh, fine, fine, thank you, Tucker," DePuyster said. "Ring Mr. Rogers back and tell him to wait for my call."

"Very good, sir."

They walked up thickly carpeted stairs that felt like sponge underfoot. The bannister was heavy rich mahogany, gleaming and smooth. Expensive-looking prints lined the stair wall. Oil paintings in massive frames hung from the walls in the hallways, and Jamie was sure that if he had known painting at all he would have recognized them. He made a mental note to familiarize himself with art. It was an area in which a gentleman ought to be versed.

A rush of feeling came over Jamie that was not unlike the sexual excitement Cleveland DePuyster was experiencing as he hurried ahead through the halls of his mansion. Jamie was not awed or overwhelmed. But he was flooded with a sensation of belonging that was so keen that it nearly brought tears to his eyes. He felt as if he had come home.

DePuyster stopped at a door and opened it. Jamie looked at him, and then walked inside. A large, canopied four-poster bed stood against the back wall. To the left, a bay window protruded out over the garden. The gray rain still streaked down outside, and the wind brushed the leafy branch of a tree back and forth across the glass of the window.

DePuyster closed the door behind him. Jamie waited in the middle of the room. DePuyster walked over and stood looking out the window at the storm for a moment. Then he turned back to Jamie. There was a strange, suffering look on his face, a look of longing, almost of apology.

"I do get terribly lonely sometimes," he said.

Chapter Twenty-five

Cleveland DePuyster, wrapped in a satin robe and smoking a cigar, sat in his study with the door to the bedroom closed. He held the conical black receiver of the telephone to his ear. Rogers came on the line.

"Good evening, sir."

"Good evening, Rogers. What do you have for me?"

"I'm afraid it's not a great deal, sir. I did my best in such a short time, but . . ."

"Yes, yes, just let me hear what you have."

"Yes, sir." A pause, the crackling of paper over the wire. Rogers cleared his throat. "There is an Earl of Marley, titular name Lord Gretton, family name Whitmarsh. The current Earl, Roger Lord Gretton, is about fifty years of age. There was a younger brother who is believed to have emigrated to America. I'm afraid that's all the details I could get from the British Consulate."

"All right, good. What else?"

"No record of a Whitmarsh on the Philadelphia bar over the past twenty years. There was a Whitman, and a Whitmore. I was unable to contact Mr. Franklin Gowen, who has been traveling in the west since his dismissal from the presidency of the Reading Railroad."

"Mm. I see. And what else?"

"Young Mr. Whitmarsh has been employed as a messenger for six weeks. His supervisor spoke very highly of him. I was able to get his home address, an apartment on Bleecker Street. It is a clean and respectable building, but extremely modest. He lives there with a sister, a Miss Fannie Whitmarsh.''

''A sister?'' DePuyster frowned. ''You're sure?''

''Yes sir. She, ah . . .''

''Well? What is it?''

Rogers cleared his throat again. ''She appears to be a professional gambler, sir.''

There was a scratchy silence over the phone.

''I'm sure with a bit more time, sir, I could conduct a more thorough investigation. Shall I . . .''

''No. That will be sufficient, Rogers. That will be all.''

''Yes, sir.''

''And Rogers . . .''

''Sir?''

''You understand that this is to remain absolutely confidential?'' DePuyster's voice was smooth, but there was no mistaking the threat it carried.

''Yes, sir. Absolutely, sir. You may count on my discretion.''

DePuyster put the receiver back on its hook and sat quietly smoking his cigar. It had stopped raining, but the heavy overcast gave an early yellow-gray twilight to the August evening. DePuyster sat in the stillness of his study and listened to the dripping of rainwater from the gutters of his mansard roof, and sucked thoughtfully at his cigar.

The boy had not told him the truth about everything. That came as no surprise. What did surprise were the areas of falsehood. DePuyster had not believed for a moment the story about the Earl of Marley, for instance. And now that seemed to emerge as the likeliest element in Jamie's history. Lord Gretton. Family name, Whitmarsh.

Then there was the business about the father being a lawyer. Not in Philadelphia, apparently. Well, there were probably a half dozen ways of explaining that without giving total lie to Jamie's account.

The information that had most startled DePuyster was the revelation about the sister. A professional gambler. Why had he said he lived alone? *Well, no wonder*, he decided. *The boy wants to make something of himself, you can see that. A sister like that must be a painful baggage to him.*

DePuyster stood up and walked over to the heavy oak door that separated his study from his bedroom. He opened it quietly.

Jamie was asleep on the big bed. He was curled up like a child, his body a smooth pale curve on the dark coverlet. Jamie's back was to where DePuyster stood. One shoulder jutted up, and a hip too, almost like a woman's body. But it was not a woman's body, nor was it a man's. It was a body of androgynous sensuality; firm, unmuscled limbs, buttocks soft and round but without heaviness, skin smooth and elastic—the stunning sexual perfection of a boy who has passed childhood and held off maturity without stumbling into the awkward arms-legs-and-pimples angularity of adolescence.

DePuyster went over and stood by the bed. He could hear Jamie's even breathing. The light from the window behind him spilled over the boy's shoulder, catching a circle of smooth, downy cheek, and the pale lashes of one eye. His pink-lipped mouth was parted slightly, like a child's, as he slept.

There was nothing more Cleveland DePuyster wanted to know about this boy. No investigation could add anything of importance to what his fingers and his lips had already told him. There was a light happiness in his heart that answered any questions that might be raised.

He did not ask himself the one cold question that might have arisen out of Jamie's sister's profession: was he being set up for blackmail? He did not ask himself, but he was already planning something that ought to make blackmail unnecessary.

The darkness outside had deepened dramatically, so that the light that remained was the garish yellow of an electric bulb. Now there was thunder, the velvet rumble of thunder several miles away. Jamie sighed and rolled over. His penis was soft, innocent, and almost genderless on its pillow of cornsilk hair. DePuyster sat on the bed and took it lovingly in his fingers. Jamie opened his eyes and smiled.

"Would you like to live here, Jamie?"

Jamie's eyes widened.

"It's lonely for you, living alone. That's no life for a boy your age. There's a maid's room here where you could live. If you'd like to." DePuyster hesitated for a moment, looking for Jamie's reaction. "If . . . there's no one else you have to consider."

"There isn't," Jamie said.

"Well, then?"

"Mr. DePuyster, do you really mean it?"

DePuyster smiled, and lowered his lips to where his fingers were.

Jamie went back to the apartment on Bleecker Street in the evening, when he knew Fannie would be at work. He took only a few things. He took his best clothes, though he was confident he would soon have better. He took his gold watch. He went through his books and took the ones he thought would make the best impression.

He knew where Fannie hid her money. He had never taken any, not wanting to squander his knowledge until the need was there. He did not take any now.

He left the apartment, locked it, and slid the key under the door. He did not leave a note.

When Fannie came home from work in the early hours of morning she knew immediately that Jamie was gone. Not just out, but gone. She ran quickly through a series of emotions, seizing on them and tossing them aside like someone rummaging frantically through a drawer. Shock first. Then outrage at Jamie, then anger at herself for having let it happen, for not having seen it coming, for having let herself be taken in. Then tears, and asking herself hopelessly *why, why*? And finally guilt and worry.

She went to see Henderson. Henderson listened, scowling.

"That little bastard!"

"No, Bill!"

"I'm sorry, pigeon. But that's what he is, an ungrateful little bastard, and it makes me mad. I tell you right now, if anybody else treated you like that I'd break his legs for him."

"He's just a little boy, Bill. He's only fifteen."

"That kid's never been a little boy."

Fannie flared up. "I want to find him, Bill! I'm worried about him! I don't care what you think about him, I want to know that he's all right! I want him home!"

"All right, all right." Henderson's beefy face looked contrite. "I'm sorry, pigeon, I guess I was out of line. I know he's your brother, I know how you feel about him. It's just that—well, you know how I feel about you. What do you want me to do?"

"You know everybody. Ask around. Somebody's sure to have seen him." She laced her fingers through his and looked up at him. "Help me find my brother."

Henderson nodded. "All right," he said. His voice was gruff. "I'll have him on your doorstep in a week."

"No! Just find him . . . please? Make sure he's all right, and if he is, don't say anything to him, don't even let him know. Just find him for me, and tell me where he is."

Henderson reached out and put his arms around her, and hugged her gently to him. Huddled against his chest Fannie did not need to be strong anymore, and she allowed herself to cry. Henderson stroked her hair with those big hands that had pounded dozens of faces as a fighter and shaken thousands of hands as a politician, and still were capable of wondrous tenderness.

"Don't you worry, pigeon," he soothed. "We'll find your baby brother for you."

On a morning late in August Fannie Whitmarsh walked along Thirtieth Street with a fluttering in her stomach and a white piece of paper clutched tightly in her hand. It was a hot, perfect summer day. The sky was an unblemished blue, and the sun shone down to paint the leaves two shades of green, dark on the underside and yellow-bright above. The leaves in turn dappled the bluestone sidewalks, providing a cool, dancing shade in collaboration with the light breeze that stirred them.

Fannie had dressed carefully in deference to the address on the piece of paper, although she did not quite believe it. She wore an English tailored suit in a plain fawn color, trimmed with burgundy velvet at the lapels. She had done her hair up in a chignon on the back of her head, and pinned a simple hat to it, pancake-flat and lined with flowers. She carried a parasol, rolled up pencil-thin. She looked coolly elegant, and she knew it; but still she was nervous. She looked again at the paper, uncrumpling it and smoothing it out to read the words that were scrawled there in Henderson's bold hand.

Here it is, pigeon—he's living at 300 Fifth Avenue, corner of 31st. It happens to be the home of Mr. Cleveland DePuyster, of whom you will no doubt have heard. I'll say this for the kid—he knows how to land on his feet.

Yrs. affectionately,
Bill

It was not that it was impossible. Anything was possible. There were odds, but as Fannie well knew, the world was not bound by them in individual cases. She was a pragmatic person, and inclined to the belief that what was *was*; there was no point in astonishment. If a thing was as it appeared, there was certainly a logical explanation; and even if it were not, the truth would be more easily arrived at through calm. So she was willing to believe that Jamie *could* be living at the address Henderson's sources had come up with.

It just seemed so damned unlikely!

Fannie stood on the corner of Thirtieth Street and Fifth, and looked up across the avenue at the chocolate-brown mansion. She had probably passed it a hundred times and never paid it any special notice. Now it stood out as a looming presence, and everything around it faded to ether. She stared for a while, somehow expecting Jamie to appear at a window. He did not.

She was suddenly seized with indecision. Should she present herself at the front door, or at the servant's entrance? What tone should she take? What should she say? "I demand to see my brother, and I think you should know that he is only fifteen years of age!" Or: "Excuse me, but is my little brother Jamie employed here? Jamie Whitmarsh?" Would he come away with her willingly, if in fact he were here? How would they meet each other, after what he had done?

As she stood there, an elegant brougham drew up in front. A footman jumped down and came around and opened the door. At about the same moment the front entrance of the mansion opened. Two figures stepped out. They were both immaculately suited and hatted in business dress. One of them was Jamie.

Fannie stood rooted dumbly as they came down the walk and through the gate in the low wall. They disappeared into the brougham. The footman closed the door and remounted to his perch. The coachman flicked the reins, and the pair moved off smartly. As the brougham passed Thirtieth Street, Fannie could see Jamie inside. His hat was off, and his yellow hair shone in the window. He was laughing.

Fannie turned around and walked back down the street. When she passed a trash container, she crumpled the piece of paper again and threw it away.

Chapter Twenty-six

Henderson's time these days was taken up in trips back and forth to Washington, in meeting, in settling various scores on favors bought and sold. It was a couple of months before he could find the time to see Fannie again.

But she was on his mind. He wondered how she was taking the separation from Jamie. Henderson was not surprised that Jamie had abandoned Fannie. He had seen kids like Jamie before. Smart kids; ruthless kids. The ones who always tried to get every edge they could. And if they were smart enough, and lucky enough, they would get to the top. If not, they would be cut down. Hard. Henderson did not know which way it would go with Jamie.

He knew how Fannie felt about the boy. But he thought she was better off without him. Henderson did not like cool, smart kids like Jamie. He had gotten his start with his fists. He had made friends, and kept them. He had made enemies, and he knew enough to watch out for them. He had made his fortune in the gambling world, where a sucker was fair game. But Bill Henderson always kept his word, and his friends knew it.

Fannie was probably his best friend now. Even if she was a woman, she was squarer and tougher and better to talk to than any of the men he knew. They rarely had sex together anymore. It was the friendship that counted. Fannie had never asked him for anything . . . except how to handle a deck of cards, and, when Jamie disappeared, to find where he had gone. But she was always there. When he had those dark moments of the soul that even a simple, straightforward man has sometimes, and he needed someone, he could go to Fannie and sit with her, or lie with her. He could talk about nonsense until the dark mood passed, or he could talk about the darkness itself, though that was not his style.

So he came to see her now in his time of success and as soon as he sat down across from her in her parlor, he brushed away her insistence that she was "fine, Bill, just fine."

"No, you ain't," he said. "Don't try to flim—flam old Hendo, little pigeon. What is it—Jamie?"

Fannie sat in a rocker, her hands clasped over her waist. "Yes, I miss him," she said. "I know it's better for him this way, but I do miss him."

Henderson stared hard at her, and she bent her head down and gathered her legs up, as if she were about to roll herself into a ball. She looked more like a child than he could ever remember seeing her, even back when she had first become his mistress at the age of fifteen.

"That ain't it," he said. "You've got something else troubling you, and it's more than on your mind. Stand up and let me look at you.

"Bill, no," Fannie protested. "I'm not feeling well. I'd rather just sit and . . ." She tucked herself together even more tightly.

"It don't matter anyway," Henderson said. "I know you well enough. I can see what you look like sitting down. It's true, ain't it?"

"I don't know what you're talking about."

"Damn it, woman, do I have to say it out loud, in plain English? Are you . . . you're . . ."

Henderson paused, and made jerky gestures with his hands. Belligerent but confused, he appeared to be trying to punch the words out.

Fannie smiled, for an instant, through her fear. "I'm going to have a baby, Bill."

"Is it mine?"

"No, Bill, it's not."

She watched his face carefully. It was all concern, concern for her—but mixed with it, so subtle that no one but she could have seen it, was relief.

"You're sure?"

"I'm sure, Bill."

"Well, then, tell me whose it is. I'll see that the bastard marries you."

Fannie giggled, in spite of herself.

"What's so funny?"

"Nothing, Bill, really. I can't tell you who the father is. I don't want to marry him. I don't ever want to see him again."

"What are you going to do?"

"I'm going to have it."

"And then what?"

"I'm going to keep it with me!" she said with sudden passion. "I'm going to keep it, and raise it to be proud and strong and honest, like . . ."

Her voice trailed off, and she would not look at Henderson, though he was looking closely at her. "That's very important to me, Bill."

"All right, then, keep it you shall," Henderson said briskly. "But we're going to have to start making plans for taking care of you. Have you seen a doctor?"

"Of course."

"When is it due?"

"In five months."

"All right, then. You can go up to my place in Saratoga to have the baby. You should be away from New York. Just a bunch of prying eyes and wagging tongues, and no one to help you. Don't argue. And when the baby's born . . . you'll need a house in the country, and someone to look after it. Yonkers, maybe, or Teaneck. And one more thing. You should have your own place. You're ready for it."

She could look at him again now, and her eyes were fixed on him in unspoken and indescribable love. It was a tough, unsentimental, and unshakable love that she would feel forever. Her voice was tough and businesslike as she answered him. "Yes, you're right, Bill. I'm ready. And it'll be the biggest and best damn casino in New York."

"You're damn right it will! It'll make people forget Henderson's."

"Never. Nobody will ever forget Henderson's." And suddenly Fannie was crying. The tears were coming out of her eyes and rolling down her cheeks almost before she knew they were inside her. Henderson bent over and held her warmly but gingerly by the hands.

"Come on, little pigeon, don't cry. It's a happy time. Everything's going to be all right."

"No, let me, Bill." She held his hands tightly in hers, and sobbed quietly until the tears subsided by themselves. She was silent for a moment. Henderson offered her his pocket handkerchief, and she took it, mopped her face, and blew her nose.

"It's a business proposition, of course," Henderson said, and his voice was thicker and hoarser than he had intended it to be. "I'll loan you the capital to start, and I'll expect to be paid back. I've got a good location in mind, and we'll go over the details together. I know you've got ideas of your own."

"I've had the place all set up and furnished in my mind for years," Fannie said. "I know what it will cost, where everything will go, every detail."

"That's my pigeon!" Henderson laughed delightedly. "You'll be the queen. The queen of New York."

Chapter Twenty-seven

Jamie was working hard. The zeal of a religious convert possessed him. His god was his own self-interest. But suddenly opportunity was there in bottomless supply. And his appetite for opportunity was insatiable.

He read voraciously in DePuyster's law books. He read fast, and astounded the old man with his retention and comprehension. He asked endless questions. Often DePuyster did not know the answers, as it had been many years since he had read those books and concerned himself with such abstract points of law. At these times DePuyster would tell Jamie to "look it up for yourself—you'll learn things better that way than to have me feed you everything with a spoon." Jamie looked things up, and he learned.

DePuyster used his influence to get Jamie enrolled at Columbia University. Jamie would leave the house early in the morning and walk or be driven in DePuyster's carriage to the Columbia campus on Madison Avenue between Forty-ninth and Fiftieth. He would attend classes and lectures all morning, and then race downtown by the elevated train to work in DePuyster's office in the afternoon. In the evenings he would dine with the family, and then retire to his room to study. DePuyster still came to his room sometimes, but less and less as time wore on. The first flush of his infatuation began to wear off, his wife and daughter were back in residence, and . . . it was not that Jamie discouraged or rejected his advances, not at all, it was just that . . . Jamie was working and studying so hard, and

DePuyster began to feel as if he were intruding. But he was proud of Jamie, and fond of him. Eventually he came to think of him as a son.

Mrs. DePuyster quickly adopted Jamie too. She was a plain, powdery woman, with a mushroom nose and jowly cheeks. She had white hair which she wore curled tight in little sausage ringlets. Her eyebrows were white as well, which made them practically invisible, so that the blue pupils of her eyes made her appear startled. By nature she was shy, and preferred to be around no one except her own family. But her social prominence as *the* Mrs. DePuyster made that impossible. So she developed a cheerful vagueness, a birdlike flutter that was made fun of behind her back. She knew it, but she did not mind.

When she arrived back in New York with her daughter Cornelia, she had been upset by Jamie's presence. DePuyster had written her, of course, that he had taken in this bright young orphaned clerk. Mrs. DePuyster would not have dreamed of questioning his right to do so, or his motives. Still, in her shyness, she resented the intrusion.

Jamie went to work on her at once. There were few people who could resist Jamie at his most charming, and Mrs. DePuyster fell easy prey. One of the secrets to Jamie's charm was his ability to decipher people quickly, and address himself to them at their most receptive points. Mrs. DePuyster's grandfather had been English, he discovered, and she was strongly Anglophile. So Jamie told her how *English* the decor of the house was, and how much more *English* than American she seemed, and he emphasized his Marley connections, and even began to develop a hint of a British accent when they talked.

Cornelia, who was a year older than Jamie, accepted him too. But she embraced him after a fashion closer to her father's than her mother's. One evening in early December, a little after midnight, Cornelia got out of bed and put on her robe, and crept barefoot through the halls until she came to Jamie's room. A light was still burning behind the door.

Jamie was at his desk, reading Russell's *The Police*

Power of the State. He heard the door open behind him. He assumed it was DePuyster, and went on reading as if in his concentration he had heard nothing. After a few moments when nothing had happened—no plump hand on the back of his neck, no soft, cooing "Jamie?"—he became curious and turned around.

Cornelia was leaning against the closed door. She was smiling with anticipation, and she burst into giggles at his surprise.

"You're reading late."

"It's the best time for it. It's quiet. Not many interruptions."

"Like me, you mean. Don't you ever go to bed?"

"I don't need much sleep. It's a waste of time."

She giggled. "Bed isn't."

"So," said Jamie, a bit uneasy. "What brings you here?"

"You do. I came to see you."

"I'm glad. But it's kind of dangerous. Your father sometimes comes by at night. To talk business."

She caught her lower lip between her teeth and smiled. Her fingers started pulling at the ribbons of her robe. "He won't tonight," she said. "He and Mama went to the opera. They came home about an hour ago, and went straight to bed. He's snoring like an old puffing billy now."

She took off the robe. Her nightgown was a young girl's nightgown, formless and unprovocative. But the thought of what was so accessible beneath it intrigued Jamie. Still, the risk was too great. If DePuyster were to catch Jamie in bed with his daughter, this whole setup would be destroyed. The opportunity of a lifetime would be squandered. It was too big a gamble to take for the sake of satisfying his sexual curiosity.

"I'm sorry," he said. "But I daren't."

"What, Papa?"

"Yes."

"I told you . . ."

"I know. But he might wake up. Honest, Cornelia, we just can't risk it."

Cornelia DePuyster looked at him stubbornly. She had dark hair with red highlights, and it hung down her back in a long frizzy fall. Her eyes were dark. Her coloring was like her father's, and she had the same apple-red cheeks, except that hers were not fat. Her mouth was smoothly curved, and she smiled prettily. But now it had a willful set.

Suddenly she reached down, crossing her arms and taking hold of her nightgown. She snatched it up over her head, and threw it defiantly aside on the floor. She faced Jamie, arms folded beneath her small breasts. On her face was self-consciousness overcome by excited determination.

"Are you going to throw me out?"

"No."

"Well, then, what are you going to do?"

"I think I'd better put out the light."

He turned and extinguished the lamp on his desk. When he turned back again, she had crossed the room and was standing next to him while he still sat at his desk. She stood with her hips thrust forward. The thatch of her pubic hair, dark against the dim whiteness of her belly, hung just below his chin. He put his hands on the backs of her knees and ran them up along her thighs, and she shivered. She locked her hands in his hair and pulled his head against her. He was struck with the rubbery softness of her body, and the sharp clean smell of her pubic hair.

He undressed, and they lay down on the bed. He was not sure what you did with a girl, but he found that it came to him easily. He experimented, making mental notes of what brought the most response. He tested with his finger the route most familiar to him, and brought forth a loud, sobbing gasp, and a hand that came down and pushed, not insistently, at his wrist.

But when he entered her, he did so in the traditional way. His body performed long and well, because he did not allow it to become short-circuited by passion. He concentrated on technique. And when he finished at last,

Cornelia DePuyster held him tightly with her arms and legs and sobbed happily against his chest.

It was not until after the New Year, in January of 1888, that Jamie finally did something about his sister. He did not feel guilty about the way he had treated her. There was no question in his mind that he had done the right thing. It could not have been handled any differently. Fannie was emotional. She would certainly have made a scene, and she might have tried to prevent him from going with DePuyster. Still, it must have been hard on Fannie. And now that his position was more secure, he could afford at least to let her know that he was all right.

Jamie had graduated from office boy to junior clerk. He sat at a desk now near Richard Dominy, who watched Jamie's rise with coolness and distrust. A new office boy had been hired. His name was Billy Abbott. He was about the same age as Jamie, but no one, least of all Jamie Whitmarsh and Billy Abbott, would have thought of equating them.

At noon of a day that was gray and heavy and threatened snow, Jamie arrived at the office from his morning at Columbia. He sat down at his desk and wrote a note to Fannie. He had been composing the note in the elevated train, going over it in his head for phrasing and tone. Now he wrote quickly and surely. He told his sister that he was fine. He told her that she must not worry about him, and she must not try to find him. He was in a good situation, and it was important that he operate completely on his own for the time being. He would, he assured her, be in touch from time to time. She must not, he emphasized again, make any effort to find him, or she would ruin everything he had been building. He signed the letter, and sealed it in an envelope with a fifty dollar bill.

He waited until the office had emptied for lunch, and Richard Dominy was gone from his neighboring perch. Then he summoned Billy Abbott to his desk. There existed between them the old boy-new boy relationship of boarding school tradition. Jamie ordered his underling about with benevolent tyranny, and Billy responded with the fervent respect that the schoolboy accords the senior prefect but denies the masters.

"Billy," Jamie said, "I want you to deliver a letter for me."

"Yes, Mr. Whitmarsh." He held out his hand. Jamie withheld the letter, tapping it against his fingers.

"The letter is to be delivered to the address on the envelope. You are not to wait for a reply. Understand?"

"Yes, sir."

"Don't speak to anyone. Don't answer any questions. And especially, you're not to say who this comes from, or where you're employed. Have you got that straight?"

"Yes, sir. I won't say a thing."

Jamie held Billy Abbott in his most serious stare for another moment, and then handed him the letter.

"And report straight back to me," he said.

Jamie felt better about things now. It had begun to occur to him, belatedly enough, that Fannie might even call on the police eventually to find him. She might possibly have done so already. It was better to handle these things properly, after all. Now she would know not to worry. And the fifty dollars should help to smooth things over, too.

He worked through the lunch hour, as he often did. When Cleveland DePuyster returned to the office, Jamie brought in to him a list of precedents pertinent to a case on which DePuyster was working, and a detailed analysis of their application. DePuyster read them with approval, and pointed out three minor flaws in his young clerk's interpretations. Jamie listened respectfully, and then diplomatically corrected his employer in two of the cases. The third he accepted.

As Jamie left DePuyster's office, he saw Billy Abbott, red-cheeked and powdered with snow, coming through the outer door. Billy still had the envelope in his hand. Jamie moved quickly to intercept him in the cloakroom.

"I'm sorry, Mr. Whitmarsh, but she wasn't there. They said she moved out a couple of months ago. There wasn't any forwarding address." He looked nervously at Jamie.

Jamie frowned thoughtfully. "All right," he said, and took back the letter. "Get on about your work. And don't mention this to anyone!"

When Billy had gone, Jamie slit open the envelope. He removed the money and returned it to his pocketbook. Then he struck a match and set fire to the letter and envelope, setting it on the open windowsill, and watching it burn to a white ash and float away into the snow.

Chapter Twenty-eight

"Well, we did it," said Eric Iverson, the ramrod. "One more round, bartender."

"Did it?" jeered his trail boss. "Hell, Eric, we're gettin' so good at this, next time we'll sit home in our rocking chairs, put daguerrotypes of our handsome faces on those cowponies, and let them move the damn ol' herd up to Laramie."

"You gonna make another drive, John?"

John Whitmarsh did not answer right away. His fingers felt the pocked surface of the bar, the chipped rim of the glass. He was thinking about the drive. It had been a good one. No men lost. A few close calls. A flash flood in Kansas, where they had lost a cowboy named Slattery for several hours, until he and Eric had found him, miles down the swollen river, semiconscious and clinging to a log. The drive was so filled with danger that it kept everything else far, very far away, and made the boys John rode with into his family, the best fellows he knew or could imagine.

Eric did not press the question. This was his first drive as John Whitmarsh's ramrod, but he had learned quickly enough that his boss sometimes fell silent, and would stay silent until he was ready to talk.

John felt Eric's presence. He felt the presence of all of them, the Parsons men he had brought with him from Texas. He heard them around the bar, and heard their drunken shouting and hollering out in the street. Before the night was over, there would be a fight—a senseless fight, most likely—but the Parsons hands would come to each other's aid, and he would most likely be in it too, although he had walked away from fights before.

"I don't know," he said out loud. "Minnie won't want me to. And I won't have to, not much longer."

"Every cowboy's dream, hey, pard?"

Every cowboy's dream. Five years of driving cattle for Wild Bill Parsons, four years as foreman and trail boss. When John had married Minnie, Wild Bill had given him a dozen head of cattle as a wedding present, and registered John's brand with the local Cattlemen's Association, so no one would question his right to run cattle on the open range. When little Bob Whitmarsh was born, Wild Bill had given him a stud bull. John drove his own cattle north with Parsons's herd, and invested the money from their sale in more cattle. By this time, he had a good-sized herd. And after this drive, he would claim the bonus Wild Bill had promised him: five hundred acres of grazing land with water, even a stand of timber. His own spread.

"Hah. Who am I going to get to drive a herd up north for me? You slickers'd end up in Mexico without me to help you along. Same again, bartender, and leave the bottle."

"Bullshit. The only thing you do on a trail drive is to give the men a laugh on account of the way you sit a horse."

Same old stuff. He drank down the bad whiskey, and poured himself another glass. He wondered if men like Wild Bill Parsons drank too much because the only link they had left to the insults, the danger, the dust, the brawling and singing and searching, was the bottle of whiskey and the warmth that came with it.

"Tell me about it when you're rolling Bull Durham in a sandstorm and I'm sittin' at the Cattlemen's Exchange smokin' a big cigar."

An older cowboy sat down at the bar on the other side of him. He was short and thin, with bony hands. The deep creases in his weather-beaten face were unexpectedly soft, like the folds of a woman's body. "You Whitmarsh?" he asked.

John nodded.

"My name's Woodruff. Folks call me Woody."

"Woody it is, then."

"Talk is you used t'be a pretty good union man."

"Talk's cheap."

"Talk around here is, there's boys wantin' a cowboy's union."

"He ain't interested," Eric said. "He's gonna be management now."

"What d'you say, Whitmarsh?"

"Not interested," John muttered.

"Yeah, why should you be?" Woodruff said bitterly. "You've got someone who's handin' you your own spread and the protection of the Texas Cattlemen's Association. You know what it's like for the rest of us. The big ranchers won't even let us graze our own cows on open range. *Open range*—hah! Piss-poor wages, no job security—"

"And no solidarity, and not enough jobs to go around," John broke in angrily. "You know what happened in Texas in 1882, when they had that big strike up in the Panhandle. I was down in central Texas then, and I heard about it. Everybody heard about it. The minute the word got out that the Panhandle drovers were ready to organize, the big ranchers started scouting out scab cowboys. And the minute that cowboys all over the Southwest heard about it, every damn one of them was headin' for the Panhandle to scab—not to mention all the tenderfoot kids from the East who'd read about cowboys in dime novels and come out to Texas. And the minute the Panhandle ranchers had a new crew lined up, every one of those cowboys was out on their ass. *And* blacklisted. The Cattlemen's Association said they were to be treated just like rustlers.''

''That don't mean it can't be done,'' said Woodruff. ''Them Panhandle cowboys, they did it all wrong. But we've been talkin' to the Knights of Labor. We can't do it alone, I know that. And we can't do it if we don't organize right. But if we get together with the Knights, with the miners and railroad workers and all the other workingmen in the cattle states, and if we know what we're doin' —what d'ye say, Whitmarsh? You could help us, you know you could.''

''Not interested,'' John said again, and turned his back.

It was late when he got back to the Parsons Ranch, too late to call on Bill Parsons and make his report, so he went straight home. Home was the little house Parsons had given them the use of, when John and Minnie were married. It would not be home much longer, though. Pretty soon he would have his own house. His own land. His own ranch. Property. Real estate.

The house where they lived was a half mile downhill from the ranch house. That suited Minnie fine, she said— uphill in the morning when a body was still fresh and full of rest, downhill at night after a day of workin' 'round that kitchen, and often as not with a sleepy-headed child to carry. There was a pond near the house where little Bobby could sit with a fishing line or splash around in the shallows. It had been a nice place to live; for John, a nice place to come back to, because as a cowboy he was not home all that often. As a rancher he would be spending a lot more time at home.

Bobby would be long asleep by now. But Minnie was up. John could see a light burning. He took care of his horse, and then went in. Minnie was reading a book.

''Hello,'' he said.

''Well, John!''

She jumped up eagerly, but then stood and waited as

John came across the room to her, and she gave him her cheek to kiss. That was Minnie, John knew. The stronger she felt an emotion, the less likely she was to show it. Displaying emotion was like undressing, and she would do those things in front of no one, not even her husband.

John didn't mind. He could not help comparing her to Tesia sometimes, although he knew this was not fair to Minnie. He had never shown her much passion either. He had never been with Minnie the way he had been with Tesia. But he had been younger then, and a different person. He respected Minnie, he cared for her more than he had cared for any woman since Tesia died. It might even be that he loved her. She was the mother of his son. And if he wondered sometimes what he was doing married, the thought had nothing to do with Minnie.

He had never been passionate with her. He told himself that Minnie would only have been embarrassed by passion, and it was probably true. But it might have been true in part because Minnie told herself the same thing about him.

"Good drive?"

"Yep."

"Praise the Lord. Reckon you're starved."

"I'm a bit hungry, I guess."

"I've got some beef bourgignon. It's a kind of a French beef stew. I'll just heat it up."

While she busied about with the stew, he went in to look at Bobby. Bobby was asleep as he always slept, crossways on the bed. His pudgy little hand clutched his rag doll by the throat. He had kicked off the covers, and John drew them up again and kissed him on his dark curls.

When he came out again his eye fell on the book that Minnie had left on her chair.

"What are you reading?"

"Oh . . . cookbook."

"Ah." He had given her books to read—Dickens, Tolstoy, Shakespeare. Minnie never read them. They maintained a wry sparring about each other's reading habits. It was a subject that cut deeper than either would admit. To Minnie, novels and poetry and philosophy and such were foolishness, a waste of a body's time—what was the sense of a book, unless it told you something practical, like cooking? At the same time, she felt John's disappointment in her, though he tried not to show it, and it hurt.

The stew was excellent, and he told her so. She brightened up, and said, "Oh, get on, now!" John went outside and relieved himself and washed his face and hands in the rain barrel. Then he went into the bedroom and undressed to his long johns, and got into bed. Minnie cleaned up the kitchen for a while, and then she came to bed too.

"You'll be seein' Mr. Parsons about the land tomorrow?" she asked as she settled down, lying straight on her back.

"First thing. When I make my report."

There was a long silence. He listened to her breathing. He wondered if she could have fallen asleep already. He felt disappointed. He would not bother her in her sleep, but . . . he had been a long time on the trail.

"I surely will like that," she breathed. "A place of my own. My own house. My own furniture, and drapes, and rugs, and linens. My own kitchen stove and pots and pans, and a pantry full of good things, and when folks sit down to my cookin', they're sittin' down to Minnie Whitmarsh's table. Oh Lord, John . . ." To his shock he felt her hand grope and find his hand, and wrap itself around it. "And you out there in the corral, or up in your office. And Bobby growin' up, and maybe learnin' to be smart like his dad, growin' up to be a businessman or a lawyer even. And maybe another child, a little girl maybe, to help me 'round the house and learn all the things I know . . . I'm goin' on, ain't I?"

"No . . ."

"Sure I am. But . . . it's what you want too, ain't it? All them things? Real roots?"

"Sure I do," he said.

He turned over on his elbow, facing her, and he thought he saw the gleam of a tear in the corners of her upward-staring eyes. He tugged softly at the skirt of her long nightdress. Immediately she raised her hips to help him, not sighing or pretending she didn't notice, the way she sometimes did. John pulled the garment up across her belly, letting his hand trace up along her skin and pressing against her cleft, hair-tufted mound as he went. He watched her face, saw it stiffen, saw her pinch her lips together. Her hands clutched the bedclothes tightly against her chin. He rolled on top of her, and brought his fingers to his tongue to moisten her, but when he put them down between her thighs he discovered another surprise, that it was not needed.

Afterward she got up to wash herself, and John pretended to be asleep when she came back to bed. Finally he did fall asleep, and he dreamed about the house he would soon begin building. He saw the house going up, the skeletal framework. He saw himself on the inside, framing himself in; and the studs, instead of wood, were bars of steel.

John liked Wild Bill Parsons's house. It was a man's house, built by a man who had respect for good materials and good workmanship. It was simple and comfortable, and it reflected the pride of a man who had worked hard and made himself a success. Ever since John and Minnie had gotten married, and he had started thinking about a home of his own, he had used Wild Bill's place as a model. Nights alone on the trail, he had built and rebuilt it in his head, from the study lined with books and furnished with rich leather, to a light, bright nursery with big panes of glass in the windows, to the smokehouse on the sheltered side of the house, only a short dash from the kitchen.

But when he came to report to Parsons this time, just as he had done on every drive from the time he had become Wild Bill's trail boss, he suddenly felt awkward and out of place.

Like just another dumb cowboy, he thought. But he was going to be a rancher himself. Today. Parsons would give him the deed, and tomorrow he would start building. A ranch house. Corrals. Stables. He would be having Parsons over to his house for dinner. And Wild Bill surely knew how well Minnie could cook.

Parsons greeted him with a hearty handshake, brandy, and cigars. They sat in leather armchairs next to the great stone fireplace, unlike their meetings at the end of previous trail drives, where Parsons had sat behind his desk. John handed over the receipts and the bank draft for the sale of the cattle. Parsons gave him an envelope which contained a folded document that made John Whitmarsh, Esq., the owner of 500 acres of land west of the Trinity River.

Parsons made a little speech. He was awkward about it, even with his years of experience as a newspaperman and a business leader, but he seemed to feel it should be done. After that he poured the brandy and made a toast, and then it was easier for both of them. Wild Bill refilled their glasses a couple of times, and John told him stories about the drive. Wild Bill laughed over and over again at the stories, and slapped his knee. The more violent the stories, the more danger and difficulty and discomfort, the more he laughed; and John knew how to embellish a good story.

After an hour or so, they fell silent. John was ready to leave. But Parsons had something more to say. The silence was weighing more on him than it was on John.

John waited for a moment, but nothing seemed to be forthcoming. Finally, he stood up. "Well, Mr. Parsons—"

"Bill."

"Bill, I'd better be going on over to give Minnie the good news."

"Yes, you do that, John." A pause. "John—"

"What's that, Bill?"

"You know, you've been like a son to me in many ways, over the last few years."

"Thank you, Bill."

"My kid brother was like a son to me, too. . . . I damn near raised him."

"I know that, Bill."

"And . . . sometimes you wonder if it was something . . . if you went wrong, somehow . . . ."

His voice trailed off. John looked down at him, bewildered. He was going to say something, but Wild Bill Parsons spoke again, and his voice was filled with controlled emotion.

"I worried a lot about you, too, when I first met you. I knew what was inside you. That same kind of craziness. You didn't have your feet on the ground. An actor! And you were on the run . . . from a lot of things. You didn't know what you wanted, and you could have gone either way—my way, or Albert's. But you made the right choice. Minnie helped, I know that. But you did it, and I'm proud of you, John. A man's got to have his feet on the ground. Not like Albert. Not like Albert."

John looked at Wild Bill Parsons closely. And he could see that if Wild Bill had been a different man . . . a very different man . . . he would have been close to tears. But what was it all about?

"I don't understand, sir," he said.

Parsons looked at him blankly for a moment.

"You don't . . . oh, of course. You've been out on the trail, haven't you? You wouldn't have had much of a chance to read the papers."

"I'm afraid I haven't looked at a newspaper since I came to Texas, sir. There's so much to keep me occupied right where I am . . . and I guess I haven't wanted to know anything else."

"Oh . . ." Parsons looked up at John, studying his eyes. He looked as if he were regretting he had ever begun this conversation with John. But he went on speaking, in a weary, pained voice. "Then you didn't know . . . I suppose I should begin at the beginning. About a year and a half ago there was a riot in Chicago, at a place called Haymarket Square. You know it?"

"I didn't get to know Chicago very well."

"Doesn't matter. My brother was speaking at this rally, of course. And a bomb went off."

"Was he hurt?"

"No, he'd apparently left the scene sometime earlier. But some policemen were killed."

"Oh, God." John could see the scene; he could see a great deal that he thought he had put out of his mind. He clutched the white envelope in his hand tightly.

"The police opened fire on the crowd. God knows how many people they killed. Nobody ever knew who threw the bomb. But they arrested Albert, and seven others. Inciting to riot, conspiracy to murder . . ." Bill Parsons's heavy jaw worked bitterly. "They were tried and convicted. Sentenced to hang. The public wanted revenge, you see, they wanted blood. I wrote to Albert. His friends wanted him to appeal for clemency. He might have had it, if he'd asked; he had a lot of support too. But he wouldn't do it. Stubborn! He'd done no wrong, he said. He'd been convicted for his ideas." Parsons paused, looking past John. He seemed to be struggling with his thoughts. John waited in dread.

"I wrote him again at the end. I told him I was proud of him, of his heredity and his heroism. Last week they hanged him."

John did not know how long he had heard the words in his ears before Parsons actually said them, like an echo preceding the sound waves that should have given rise to it. Then why, if he had been expecting it all along, did the revelation hit him with such shocking force?

"I said he was hanged. November 11th."

There they were again. The same words. Albert Parsons hanged. Tesia, her white blouse soaked with her own blood. Albert Parsons's voice, raising the hair on the back of fifteen-year-old John's neck, thrilling the crowd who listened with its message of what men could be, if they would only work together. Albert Parsons, hanged. His father, hanged. Tim Ryan . . . Walter Koch . . . Tesia . . .

"Yes, sir, I heard. You must feel very sorry."

"It was inevitable," Parsons said gruffly. "A man has to look to the future, not the past. And you've got your future in your hands right there, John."

"Yes, sir."

"You look pretty shaken. That's how I felt when I first heard the news, too. Have another brandy."

"Thank you, no, sir."

"Bill."

"Bill. I should get over and take this deed to Minnie."

Minnie was standing at the stove when he came in. He closed the door behind him, but did not advance farther.

"I'm leaving, Minnie," he said. "I'm going away."

She did not answer. But she nodded to show that she had heard.

"Do you want to go with me?"

"The ranch?" she asked with almost no upward inflection in her voice.

He tapped the deed in his hand.

"Here. It's ours."

"Then I reckon I'll stay with it."

It was his turn to say something, but he did not. Nor did he come farther into the room. Finally, she spoke again.

"Are you going back to play-acting?"

"No."

"Going back East, then."

"I might."

"There's nothing there for you, you know. You might better head out West. California . . . open country . . . life's a lot simpler."

"I wish it were."

She let that pass. "Will I see you again?"

"You're my wife. Bobby's my son."

"I'll go ahead and build, John. I want my home. It'll be yours, too, if you can ever stand to have one."

"I'll send money."

"Don't. You'll need it more than I will."

Chapter Twenty-nine

By his nineteenth year Jamie Whitmarsh—James Whitmarsh now to all but the bosom of the DePuyster family, with whom he still lived—had been graduated with a law degree from Columbia University, and admitted to practice before the New York bar. This was accomplished almost entirely on merit. His record at the university had been exemplary. His performance at DePuyster, Chase, and Schuyler had been outstanding. He was a tireless worker, meticulous on detail, and original in approach to the most sophisticated legal problems.

There was no frivolous side to Jamie. He was not impulsive, and he never did anything "just for fun." He did not really understand what other people meant by that phrase. For Jamie something was only rewarding if it promised to do him some good, professionally or socially, or, as was often the case, both.

Just as there had never been much of a little boy in Jamie, now there was scarcely any discernible youth. He had no excesses, no vices. He never went out with young friends on the town. The friends that he did make and cultivate tended to be his elders and betters. He was helped in this by the fact that he had, two years earlier, finally established a correspondance with his Uncle Roger, the Earl of Marley, and verified his aristocratic credentials beyond dispute. He began to find himself a sought-after single man for dinner parties, particularly in households where there was a marriageable young daughter. James

Whitmarsh, everyone said, was a young man with a brilliant future.

But not everybody wished him well. Richard Dominy in particular hated him. Dominy was twenty-seven years old now, and he had not advanced as fast as he had hoped and expected. He had seen Jamie move from his underling at the firm to his equal, and lately he sensed that there was a general understanding that Jamie was going far beyond him. Choice assignments went to Jamie that ought by rights of seniority to have gone to Dominy. Most recently, Jamie had trespassed on a case that Dominy was actually preparing. In addition to his own work load, Jamie had prepared a brief on a water rights case that Dominy was handling, and had submitted it directly to Cleveland DePuyster behind Dominy's back.

Dominy had confronted Jamie, furious.

"You little sneak! You had no right to do that. That's my case!"

"I saw a better way of approaching it."

"How could you see a better way? You hadn't seen my work. You don't know what I was doing."

"I know the way you think. I knew this wouldn't have occurred to you."

"Then why not tell me?"

Jamie looked surprised. "Why should I? It was my idea."

"Look, you little bootlicker, I'm warning you. Watch your step. That was my case, and you'd better not try anything like that again!"

"It was the firm's case, Dominy. I will keep doing whatever is in the best interests of the firm." He smiled unpleasantly. "You are certainly welcome to do the same to my work, anytime you think you can improve on it."

They had never remotely been friends, and never could have been. Jamie had assessed Richard Dominy from the first as someone who could not be of help to him, and so Jamie had for the most part steered clear of him. There was no hostility on Jamie's part toward the older man, just a total lack of interest. For his part, Dominy had never had

any use for Jamie, whom he saw as a bloodless drudge.
Dominy liked to have a good time once he left the office.
He went around with a fast crowd of fellow Princeton
graduates. And it was through one of these friends that he
found his means of getting at Jamie.

From Billy Abbott, the former office boy at DePuyster,
Chase, and Schuyler, Richard Dominy had once learned
that James Whitmarsh had a sister. The boy had let it slip
inadvertently; and Dominy, recognizing the look of guilt
on his face, correctly surmised that Billy had revealed
something on which he had been sworn to secrecy. Dominy
had proceeded to use all the means at his disposal, which
ranged from bullying to blandishments to blackmail, to
wring the few remaining facts from the boy: that the
sister's name was Fannie Whitmarsh, that Jamie had tried
to communicate with her in utmost secrecy a few months
after he came with the firm, and that the sister had disappeared without a trace. When Dominy was satisfied that he
had pumped all the information out of Billy that was there,
he felt disappointed. It did not seem like anything of much
use. Still, he salted it away. Someday something might
turn up.

It was in the period when his hatred of Jamie burned at
its fiercest, in the weeks following Jamie's intrusion on his
water rights case, that the day arrived. A friend of Dominy's,
a young lawyer named Chester Davis, was describing
Divine's, the fabulous gambling casino on Thirty-third
Street. Divine's was a playground for only the highest
rollers. The doors were not open to young men earning a
living. The means to lose a thousand dollars at the turn of
a card without turning a lash, to drop twenty thousand at
the tables and walk out into the night with an untroubled
soul—these were the financial standards a sporting man
had to meet if he wanted to pass through the inner door at
Divine's.

None of the young men in Richard Dominy's crowd had
these credentials, so they listened avidly as Chester Davis
described beautifully furnished halls and rooms, frescoed
and gilded walls hung with masterpieces of modern and

ancient painting, electric lights draped with colored veils so that they seemed like balls of colored fire glowing softly in the air. He told them of a new automatic elevator that carried patrons who did not wish to walk up to the gaming rooms on the second floor, and of the faro banks where dealers dispensed cards from wrought silver boxes while wealthy gamblers stood and made small talk, holding handfuls of ivory chips worth many thousands of dollars.

Chester Davis had recently won a seat on the City Council, and was at Divine's as the guest of a Tammany chieftain who wanted his vote on an upcoming bill. As they were feasting on the magnificent midnight supper and drinking the imported champagne that was served (theoretically) free by the establishment, a slim and elegant young woman had passed through the room, speaking to most of the gentlemen, including Davis's patron, in a friendly and familiar tone.

"Who is she?" Davis had asked admiringly.

"Why, that's Fannie Divine," his patron had replied. "This is her place. She's a protege of Bill Henderson's, who used to have gambling in this town locked up before he went straight and got himself elected to Congress. Some say she's his mistress, too. Real name's Whitmarsh, I think. Fannie Whitmarsh."

Jamie broke into a cold sweat as he walked west along Thirty-third Street. His stomach was twitching convulsively. He stopped, rested his hand against the cool fluting of a lamppost, and closed his eyes, willing his nerves to quiet. *Whatever the facts turn out to be*, he told himself, *they can be dealt with best by staying calm*. But when he opened his eyes and went on, his stomach started jumping again.

Number 33 was an attractive brownstone. From the outside it looked much the same as the other brownstones that lined the quiet street. Ivy grew up its dark walls. A wide stone stairway led up from the sidewalk. At the top of the stairway was the one visible feature that set number 33 apart from its neighbors: a massive door of finely worked bronze. It showed, in bas-relief, scenes of repentant sinners being welcomed into heaven, as they laid their earthly treasures at the feet of the Virgin Mary. It was said to have come from a fifteenth-century palace in Venice.

Jamie paused before this door at the top of the stairs, and rebuked himself again for his nervousness. It was not likely to be her, he told himself. And even if it were—he had nothing to apologize for. The burden would be on her.

He rang the bell. A breeze stirred the air as he waited, chilling the slick dampness at the back of his neck. Suddenly a buzz sounded, and he jumped and looked wildly around, and then realized that the sound was coming from the door. He pushed at the handle, and the door swung open. He found himself standing in a small vestibule. It was painted—walls, door, and ceiling—a creamy white trimmed in gold, and beneath his feet was a thick carpet of the same colors. The space was brightly lit from above, but the source of the light could not be seen. It was cool in the vestibule, a good five degrees below the outside temperature.

A panel in the white inner door slid back, and a dark face filled the opening. Neutral, slitted eyes regarded Jamie.

"Can I he'p you, suh?"

"I am here to see Miss Divine."

"She expectin' you?"

"No. Uh, tell her that Mr. James . . . no, say that her brother is waiting to see her."

The white slitted eyes floated for a moment in the opening, and then the panel slid shut. A few moments later it opened again.

"All right, suh. If you'll just close the door."

"I beg your pardon?"

"That outside door. This one don't open less'n that one's closed."

Jamie looked at him blankly, and then realized that he was still holding the knob of the bronze door in his hand. He released it self-consciously, and the door swung shut with a heavy *chunk*. The inner door opened, and he stepped inside.

He was there on a mission of discovery, and, if the discovery bore out his worst fears, a mission of survival. At the same time, the thrill he felt at being inside these doors was not altogether negative. This was the latest and grandest in a succession of pleasure domes that held New York's interest for a season or two, a decade perhaps if the magic was right and the management was flawless. Divine's was now the unchallenged place, and the look and feel of it beyond the inside door more than lived up to all the awed whispers that described it.

But it was the wrong kind of place as far as a certain kind of propriety was concerned. In the circles in which Jamie moved, gambling establishments were considered disreputable and a blight on the community. Cleveland DePuyster was an ally and active supporter of the Reverend Dr. Charles Parkhurst, who led the moral battle for the crackdown on casinos. In their eyes there was no difference between the fashionable and the tawdry, the casinos of the rich and the gambling hells of the poor. It was all a sin against decency, and the palaces like Divine's that coated the pill with elegance and art and catered to the fashionable and the mighty were worse, if anything, because they lent a false patina of desirability to the decadent scene. So as Jamie Whitmarsh stood inside the parlor hall of Divine's, and looked upon the magnificence that was only hearsay to most people, the paradox of his being there struck him suddenly and almost made him smile: if the information with which Richard Dominy was threatening him was false, then he had no right to be here and would quickly be given the gate; but if Dominy was telling the truth, then Jamie's entree to this most exclusive of establishments was unquestioned . . . and he was a ruined man.

The house manager, a short, leather-faced man whose evening clothes suited his body like a circus costume, led Jamie down the hallway past a spiral staircase that led to the gambling rooms above. At the end of the hall was a door. Jamie stared at it as he approached with fascination and dread. *It's the lady and the tiger*, he thought, *but there's only one door, and the choice has already been made*. They reached the door and the manager knocked, two quick raps, and then two more. After a moment there was a short electric buzz, and the door swung open.

And there was Fannie. She was half reclining on a divan against the far wall of what seemed to be her office. She was wearing a maroon dress of watered silk flecked with forest green, and patterned with fine gold stitching. Her bosom was revealingly latticed with soft pale lace. Her hair was swept back in a loose dark wave that ended in ringlets at the back of her neck. Two men sat on chairs nearby, another at the desk. All three had cigars and a snifter of brandy. Jamie recognized one as the president of a leading bank, another as the playboy heir to an enormous manufacturing fortune. The man at the desk, a large flat-faced man with thinning hair and an inquiring expression, he did not recognize. They had been laughing, and Fannie's mouth was still twisted in wry response to something that had just been said. She looked up and saw Jamie standing in the doorway, and the smile stayed on her face, exactly as it was.

"If you gentlemen will excuse me a moment," she said. The banker and the playboy and the other man said of course, and got up and filed out, nodding curiously at the blond young man who stood aside as they passed him. When they were gone, Fannie made a motion with her index finger to the house manager, and he closed the door, leaving Fannie and Jamie alone.

"Well," she said, a little breathlessly because her voice would not work right. "Jamie! It's really you?"

"Yes."

"I can't believe it! I thought . . ." She shook her head with a little baffled laugh. "I thought it would be Johnny."

"No." Jamie groped from the obvious to the common-place, feeling off balance. "Have you seen him?"

"No! Have you?"

"No. No, only I thought . . . no, nothing."

"Jamie!" She smiled with pleasure, but it was a wary smile too. "I'm glad to see you. It's been . . . it's been five years, since . . . How have you been?"

"Fine. I've been fine. I've done very well."

"I can see that." She spoke with something of the old pride in him. She wanted to hug him. But something made her hold back. It would certainly make him uncomfortable. And besides, he was here because he wanted something from her, she knew that. What—money? Probably. It didn't matter. She was seeing him face to face for the first time in almost five years.

Jamie turned away and started walking around the office. There was a dark mahogany desk in the corner, with nothing on it but an ebony pen set. The walls were matched panels of white mahogany inlaid with mother-of-pearl. The floor was teakwood. There were paintings on the wall—a Millet, a Courbet, or a copy of a Courbet. In spite of some study, Jamie was still not confident with his knowledge of painting.

"I know you must have wondered what became of me," Jamie began. He was not looking at his sister. Instead, he studied a vase of Chinese porcelain as he talked. Fannie watched the yellow hair that curled at the back of his neck, and waited. "I tried to get in touch with you, you know. You'd moved."

"Did you?"

"Yes, I did!" He said this angrily, interpreting her remark as questioning his truthfulness, and using the chance to take the offensive. "I thought you might have been concerned. But I needn't have worried, you'd already skipped along!"

"I waited for five months after you disappeared, Jamie. Finally I gave up hope that you'd want to get in touch with me. I knew where you were."

"You did?" Jamie looked stunned.

"And I thought you preferred to be . . . unattached."

"How did you . . . did you spy on me?"

"Yes."

He had been ready to wither her denials with his out-rage. Now he was forced to shift to another tack. "Well— if you know where I am and what my position is, then you must be able to guess why I'm here."

Fannie shook her head. She felt the worst was coming, and she tried to fortify herself with irony.

"You missed me?"

"Fannie, let's not play games with each other," Jamie snapped with guilty irritation. "We've gone different ways with our lives. When I was a little boy you took care of me, and I'm grateful for that. It may not seem so, but I am. But I'm not a boy any longer—and you're not the person you were then, either. I had an opportunity to go in a direction that you with your gambling games and your cheap companions could never have helped me in. I took that opportunity and I've worked damned hard, and I've got a law degree, and I've made myself a life in the best kind of society. And now you come along and ruin it for me!"

"What have I done, Jamie?"

"What have you done? Do you know what happens to my career and my social standing if it gets about that the notorious Fannie Divine is my sister?"

"Why should it get about? I changed my name to protect you, darling. I haven't told anyone. And it was you who came to see me tonight. I've known where you were for five years, and I've never tried to approach you. I've just kept an eye on you from a distance, just making sure you were all right. I won't give you away."

"You won't have to!" He told Fannie about Richard Dominy.

"What does he want from you?"

"Nothing much," said Jamie bitterly. "He wants me to leave the firm."

"I see. That is serious, isn't it?"

"Fannie, you've got to help me!"

Fannie sat down behind her desk. She rested her elbows on it, and folded her hands to stop them from trembling.

Her face was white, but her voice was steady. "Can this Dominy be bought?"

"I don't know . . . yes, I suppose so. Anyone can be bought."

"Send him to me."

"You will? You'll take care of it?"

"Yes, I'll take care of it."

"You see how it is for me, don't you? I could have a partnership in a couple of years. You see how I can't . . ."

"I know." She could not look at him now. She pressed a button on the floor beneath the desk with her foot, and the door buzzed open. "I'll take care of it," she said.

The next night, at half past ten, Fannie sat alone in her office. There was a knock at the door, the signal knock of two quick paired raps. She pressed the button, and Richard Dominy was ushered in.

He looked less sinister than she had imagined. He was tall and almost handsome, but his attractiveness was spoiled by a lax, loutish quality. His hair was black, and his thick black eyebrows stood out against his whey-colored skin. He had a body that should have been thin, but had gone to fat, so that it squeezed at his trousers at the hips and buttocks, and hung out over his belt. Around his mouth, he wore a nervous sneer.

He was awed to be here, she knew. His hair and skin were slick with sweat like an overstrung racehorse.

"How do you do, Mr. Dominy?" She remained seated and did not raise her head, so that only her eyes looked up at him.

"Fine, thank you."

She let him stand in silence a moment. "I understand you have it in your power to cause some difficulties for Mr. James Whitmarsh?"

"I've no desire to do him ill, ma'am. I just want what's due me."

"Oh? And what is that?"

"Your brother is making inroads, you might say, on

territory that's justly mine. I have been with the firm of DePuyster, Chase, and Schuyler for a good many years. I've had certain expectations. Your brother comes along. He's a zealot. He's a prig. He's a bootlicker. He wangles a place in the DePuyster household, and becomes like an adopted son. The son the old man never had, if you know what I mean. Do you see the picture? And where does that leave poor Richard?'' He spread his hands laconically. He had not been asked to sit, so he stood, legs apart, doing his best to look casual, slightly humorous and slightly bored, in the sophisticated Princeton manner. "There was no son when I came on the scene. Nor, with Mr. DePuyster advancing in years, Mr. Chase a bachelor, and Mr. Schuyler no longer living, was there likely to be one—and certainly not one of an age that could pose any threat to me.''

Dominy's voice had grown stronger—he spoke without the nervous flutter as he warmed to his phrasemaking. "In short, Miss Divine, your brother—leaping full-blown, and with overblown ambition, from Mr. DePuyster's brow, as it were, has created an annoying obstacle in my road. I have no objection to fair competition. But I see no reason to sit idly by and see my career founder on the shoals of unnatural nepotism.''

"You've said a great deal, Mr. Dominy. What is it I can do for you?''

"Do for me? There's nothing you can do for me.'' He smiled, a close-lipped thumbnail slice below his nose. "You've already done enough, Miss Divine . . . just by being yourself.''

He was enjoying himself now. He had tested these fabled waters, and found that he could handle himself pretty well, after all. His superciliousness did not bother Fannie. She had dealt with cocky gamblers before. And she knew that there was no such thing as a sure thing.

"You want Mr. Whitmarsh to resign from the firm, then.''

"That's it!'' said Dominy with enthusiasm, as if she had made a clever discovery. She ignored his irony.

"Would you entertain a financial proposition instead?"

"I don't think that would work out."

"Shall we say twenty-five thousand dollars?"

She saw the money register in Dominy's eyes, and drive a spike into his resolve. But he shook his head.

"Mr. Dominy, I have a casino to run, and I know you must have important things to do. I suggest we skip all the stops in the middle. I am prepared to give you one hundred thousand dollars—tonight, in cash—if you will drop this matter."

The Princetonian *sang froid* froze on the young lawyer's face. His only movement was the struggling rise and fall of his Adam's apple in a dry swallow. Finally he nodded his head several times, and mouthed the word "yes," with no sound coming out.

"I shall require your assurance—written of course—that this will resolve the matter for good." She turned a piece of paper toward him on the desk, and handed him a pen. "Sign at the bottom," she said.

The paper read: "IN CONSIDERATION OF A SUBSTANTIAL PAYMENT OF MONEY, I PLEDGE TO MAKE NO FURTHER ASSAULT ON THE CHARACTER OF JAMES WHITMARSH."

"I can't sign this. It's incriminating."

"You can hardly expect me to give you such a sum of money without a receipt," said Fannie matter-of-factly. "It's the very fact of its incriminating nature that assures me that you will keep your word. I don't want to pay and pay."

Dominy nodded thoughtfully, and then his mouth curled into a smile of grudging admiration. He leaned over the desk. "You're quite a woman, Miss Whitmarsh," he said. His breath was rank. He signed the paper.

Fannie picked it up and looked at it. "You won't call me that again," she said.

"Of course." He grinned. "Sorry."

She folded the paper into three sections and put it in a drawer of her desk, which she locked with a key. "The safe is in that wall, behind the landscape," she said, pointing to the Millet, a dark scene of storm clouds gathering above a wheat field. "It is open. Inside you will find an envelope containing one hundred thousand dollars."

Dominy followed his instructions. When he found the envelope, he counted the money, his face dripping greed and awe. "All there," he said. "You keep a lot of money around."

"I sometimes lose," Fannie said. Dominy's face twisted into an involuntary grin as he stuffed the envelope into his jacket pocket. "Now," said Fannie, "I think you'd better leave as quickly and as quietly as possible. This door leads out through the garden. In the rear of the garden is a gate. The gate has been left unlocked. I think it goes without saying that I never want to see you again."

So that was what had driven Jamie back to her, she thought with distaste after Richard Dominy had left. This pompous, fat-assed weakling of a lawyer, with his womanish body and parasite's soul. *He scared my little Jamie and Jamie came running to me.*

Fannie was too much a realist, and too well schooled on the subject of her little brother, to be overly sad at the motive behind Jamie's reappearance, or the unrepentant, unloving face he had shown her. Jamie had never been much for emotions. He would always come to her if he needed something, and only then. Now that he had reestablished the pattern, he would do it again. It might not be the way most families got together . . . but then again, perhaps it was.

Anyway, she knew where Jamie was, and how he was; she had known since Bill Henderson had found him for her all those years ago. But when they had informed her last night that a young man claiming to be her brother was at the door, it was Johnny who had come first to her mind. She had not seen Johnny in fifteen years, nor heard from him in all that time. *Not since Papa was killed*, she thought. Her father had receded into a comfortable zone of memory, and her mother had too, now, almost. But Johnny was every day active and troublesome in her thoughts.

She had no way of knowing even if he was alive. She could not picture him in any specific job or way of life. But she thought of him constantly, and to Fannie that meant that he must be alive somewhere.

The signal knock came again at the door. Fannie opened it herself.

"They're bringing him around now, Fannie." It was the third man who had been with her the night before when Jamie had come. His name was Michael Christie, and he was a chief inspector on the New York City Police force.

"Thank you, Inspector Christie."

A moment later Richard Dominy, red-faced and sweating fear, was hustled into the office by two stout policemen.

"Apprehended this fellow climbin' over yer back fence, mum."

"No," Dominy pleaded. "The gate was locked!"

The officer jerked him sharply by the arm. "Ye don't know this miscreant rascal by any chance, do ye, mum?"

Fannie shook her head, bewildered. "No."

"Naw, I didn't think so." The officer reached into his uniform pocket and produced the envelope, which he handed to Fannie. "Had this on him, mum. There's a powerful lot o' money in there."

"Please," Richard Dominy begged. "Tell them who I am!"

Fannie examined the money. "Why . . . this is cash that I keep in my safe!" She turned in alarm toward the safe, exposed where the Millet painting was swung back on the wall.

"Just a moment, Miss Divine," Inspector Christie cautioned. "I wouldn't touch it yet. There might be fingerprints."

"Fingerprints?"

"It's a new device in detection. In use now in Brazil. We're just experimenting with it. If he's handled that safe, there'll be his fingerprints on it, just like a signature."

"Goodness!"

"But you told me to open it! You told me it was open!"

"If you'll swear out the complaint, Miss Divine, we can haul him down to the precinct and put him away."

"No!" Dominy screamed.

"Leave him alone with me for a moment, Inspector," said Fannie. "I'd like to have a talk with this young man."

"I don't know, Miss Divine . . ."

"I'll be perfectly safe—with you standing right outside."

"They're with you, aren't they?" Dominy wailed when they were alone. He was crying, his face scrunched up like a child's and very red around the nose. "You're going to ruin me!"

"Not if you're a good boy." Fannie thumbed through the bills in the stuffed envelope. There were twenty bills, each with a denomination of five thousand dollars. "You've been awfully stupid so far. But you will get smarter, won't you?"

When Richard Dominy left the brownstone at 33 West Thirty-third Street, he had in his pocket a five thousand-dollar bill. The next morning he resigned his position at DePuyster, Chase, and Schuyler. Three days later he had packed his belongings, given up his apartment, and was on a train heading south to Delaware, where his family operated a small hide and leather business.

Chapter Thirty

John took a room for two dollars a week in the tenement section of Homestead, down near the river, to the west of the plant. Behind him, the town rose up a grimy hill, on which the soot-gray frame houses and filth-littered streets were choked together. They had been laid out by the contractors who had built the town for Andrew Carnegie to conform in the easiest, cheapest way to the uneven topography of the hill.

The best houses were at the top. Even they were pressed together so tightly that the sun never touched the ground-floor rooms. But they had two stories, and two rooms to a floor; some of them had patches of scraggly gray grass in front, and a few of the very best had a single cold-water faucet.

The streets were of yellow mud, from which sharp stones jutted at crazy angles; even the main streets like Eighth Avenue, where the saloons were, remained unpaved and without a sewage system.

To the east of John's part of town, there were barren mud flats where the poorest workers, the Eastern European immigrants, lived. John walked through them. There were no streets at all there, and the buildings were shacks and lean-tos, hastily constructed out of the cheapest materials. Few of the immigrants spoke any English, and those that did had little to say to John, and could not understand why he came to talk to them. The union had no interest in unskilled Slavic laborers. In fact, John had to make sure that he did not go over to the Slavic shantytowns while he was on union hours.

But go there he did, and he told them that there would be a big strike at the Homestead steel mill soon, that it was unavoidable; and that everyone would be involved, not just the union.

The Slavs knew about Frick. They knew about his violent hatred of Eastern European immigrant workers, and the violent strong-arm tactics he had used on them, in other labor disputes.

They knew about the Amalgamated men, too. The Slavs kept to themselves, because of language and cultural barriers, and did not mingle with the other immigrants or the native-born Americans; but the union men kept to themselves, too. They did not play in Sunday baseball games with the non-union men, or drink in the same bars. They lived in the houses at the top of the hill, and were generally resented by the rest of the working families of Homestead.

In front of John's tenement building, stretching for over a mile around the bend of the Monongahela, was the Homestead steel mill. It covered six hundred acres, thirty-seven of which were taken up by the ugly low buildings with the tall smokestacks that turned the air thick and yellow, and blocked out the sun every day, the year round. The rest was the grounds, crisscrossed by railroad tracks, inhospitable to even a single blade of grass, open and unfenced all around, as if to demonstrate that there was, after all, no line between town and mill, that they were all one, and that there was no escape from the mill, not in the bedroom, not in the bars along Eighth Avenue, not up or down the Monongahela River, where the mills at Duquesne and Munhall loomed, or across the river at Braddock, where the J. Edgar Thomson works spewed out steel rails and thick, yellow smoke. The mill went on forever.

John reported to William Weihe, the president of the union, in Pittsburgh. His job was to recruit skilled laborers for the union, and to act as liaison between the different lodges of the union—the smelters, puddlers, heaters, and so on—eight in all, each with its own organization and officers. It was a cumbersome, archaic system, and John had little patience with it.

He was glad, at least, that Weihe was two hours of unpleasant train travel away in Pittsburgh. Weihe was a dull, unimaginative, conservative politician of a man who had been president of the union for ten years and had never, so far as John had been able to figure out, done anything to improve the lot of the iron and steel worker in western Pennsylvania. He would never have hired a man like John Whitmarsh—or John North, as he still called himself publicly—if it had not been desperately apparent, even to Weihe, that the union ranks needed to be expanded. Only four hundred of the several thousand workers at Homestead belonged to the Amalgamated Association of Iron and Steel Workers.

A confrontation was coming; even Weihe knew that. The three-year union-management contract, signed before Frick had become chairman and general manager of Carnegie Brothers, Inc., would be up in June. All around them, the union had been broken. The Duquesne plant was non-union since 1890, the Thomson plant since 1888.

John worked in the mill as a heater's helper. The floor of the blast furnace room sizzled like the top of a stove under his feet, and he wore shoes with thick wooden soles. He worked a twelve-hour shift, six days a week. His shirtsleeves cut off at the shoulders, his muscles knotted from the strain and tension, he stood next to the blasting heat from the ovens, snatched out billet after billet of hot steel, and passed them along to the rougher, whose job was to feed them into the roller that flattened it into steel plate. There was no lunch break. John snatched grimy handfuls of food from his lunchpail when he got the chance, while working.

It was a hard job, but there were worse, even among the skilled and semiskilled workers. The top fillers, who dumped the iron ore into the blast furnaces, worked in 128-degree heat. Each one could only work for a few minutes before the heat overcame him. Then he would be dragged out and revived, while another jumped in and took his place. The craneman worked alone, high up in the cab of his crane, for twelve hours. He could not even take a break to piss.

The mill ran all the time, and the shifts were from six o'clock to six o'clock. John worked the day shift for two weeks, then a double shift of twenty-four straight hours. After that, he was given a full day off, then went back to work on the night shift. It did not leave him much time for organizing, but he used all the time that was available to him, and worked tirelessly.

Hugh O'Donnell, the shop steward for the heater's lodge, worked alongside him. O'Donnell was John's age, a short, good-looking Irishman with dark bristling hair, a square face, and thick, squarish lips that could still, when he relaxed, curl back in an impish Hibernian grin. With his seniority and the union contract, O'Donnell had an eight-hour day and earned $144 a month, as compared to John's $98. O'Donnell was a lifelong Republican, and had no problem in accepting the exclusivity of the Amalgamated's philosophy, but within his limits he was a courageous man and a good organizer, and John liked him. After his first month in Homestead, John was invited by O'Donnell to move in and board with him and his wife, and he accepted.

O'Donnell lived on top of the hill, in one of the best houses in Homestead. He had a Brussels carpet on the parlor floor, a piano, and a number of books, including a full set of the Encyclopedia Britannica. Margaret O'Donnell, his wife, was a hospitable woman, glad to have company. She was in her late twenties, tall and large-boned, with an angular attractiveness. Her pale Irish skin easily picked up the soot-gray that hung in the air, and she fought it constantly, taking advantage of the running water tap in her house to scrub her face and hands, neck and arms, three times a day or more, so that she always had a polished look.

Her parents had come to Homestead from Pittsburgh fifteen years before, when the first steel mills had opened there, and she was eleven years old. Her younger sister, Nora, had been a baby when they moved, and had grown up in Homestead. She was seventeen now, softer and plumper than Margaret, with a pillowy bosom and dreamy eyes that could flash with anger in an instant, when she felt she was being belittled or ignored. She visited the O'Donnell household frequently, and even more frequently after John moved in.

John knew what she wanted, but he did not respond to any of her hints. He did not want to deal with the demands on his time that an affair would make, or the complications that this particular affair would create.

All his energies were absorbed by the town of Homestead, and the upcoming showdown. All his time away from the mill was taken up by talking and organizing: talking to the union members, recruiting new members, talking to the semiskilled and unskilled workers who could never join the Amalgamated, but whose help he knew they would need.

O'Donnell thought that he was wasting his time with them. "It's the union that matters, North," he would tell him. "And that's your job here—to organize it, not talk gibberish to a bunch of Hunkies."

"I'm organizing," John told him. "We're up to seven hundred members."

"I know you're a good organizer. But you've got to keep at it. That's where we'll win. The stronger the union, the better our bargaining position."

"We have no bargaining position. They're not going to bargain with us."

"They can't run the plant without us. That's why we have to stick together—the union men, the skilled workers. The Hunkies aren't going to help us. How are they going to go out on strike when they know another load'll get off the boat and take their jobs? They're not going to stick together. They don't even speak English."

John smiled. "You sound like 'Divine Right' Baer. When a reporter asked him about the suffering of the Slavic miners under the working conditions in his mines, he said: 'They don't suffer. They can't even speak English.' "

'It's not the same.'' O'Donnell brushed away the comparison quickly. "I'm talking about skilled workers. We're the ones that Frick needs, and he's going to have to bargain with us."

"You're wrong. Don't you see how much mechanization is changing things? The skilled workers can't stand alone anymore. The bosses don't need you as much. They don't need as many of you. They won't bargain with you."

"Damn it, North, we're reasonable men in the Amalgamated, not a bunch of anarcho-syndicalists. It's only May, and we've got till the end of June to work out an agreement. And look at the way the mill is going now— production's at an all-time high. They've got to recognize that. They can't say they're caught in an economic pinch."

"Stockpiling. They're going to lock us out."

"We'll make a deal."

"I have to go home," broke in seventeen-year-old Nora. "Will you walk me home, Mr. North? I'm afraid of the dark."

"Sure, I'd be glad to," said John.

"I'll go with you," O'Donnell said.

Nora pouted, and glared at him.

She walked close to John on the way home, but not too close, under the watchful eye of her brother-in-law.

"I bet you've lived a lot of places, haven't you, Mr. North?"

"I've traveled some, yes."

"Where?"

John shrugged uncomfortably. He did not want to talk about his past, and he was not up to inventing a story. "Different places. I lived in Pittsburgh before I came here."

That seemed to satisfy her. "I've never been in Pittsburgh but twice. Not counting when I was a baby. It was exciting. I'm going to go again sometime."

"There's nothing for a young girl in Pittsburgh," O'Donnell said roughly. "You'll stay here in Homestead and find a husband."

"I'll do what I please."

John could feel the anger rising between Nora and her brother-in-law. He could feel more, too—the musk, the electric restlessness in the air that emanated from her. It was a sexual urgency, an urgency for life, for freedom, and he was close enough to her for it to touch him. He pictured her without looking at her, and he thought about how long it had been since he had had a woman. But Nora's restlessness was not for him; it did not connect with his restlessness. She thought it was for him, and he could have reached out and tapped it, anytime he wanted to. But he was not interested.

They had arrived at her parents' house. She said good-night, glared again at Hugh O'Donnell, and went inside.

John and O'Donnell walked home together. John could feel electricity from O'Donnell, too, an electric charge of anger and suppressed violence. It was harder to be near than the innocent predatory sexuality of Nora; and yet John dealt every day with angry men, and he understood and sympathized with their anger. Now he was confused. He did not want to say anything, so they walked in silence until O'Donnell spoke, vehemently and bitterly.

"Pittsburgh! Do you know how many young girls run away from home in this town, and go to Pittsburgh?"

John did not answer. O'Donnell did not seem to be expecting one. After a short pause, he went on.

"A Homestead man goes to Pittsburgh, he don't dare go to a brothel, for fear he'll see his niece or his cousin or even his sister. That's what happens to 'em. That's what happens to 'em all. The fast life—excitement. That's all they come to . . . a bunch o' whores. Not that a Homestead man ever gets the time to go into Pittsburgh."

When they reached home, O'Donnell brought John into the parlor, and poured them each a glass of whiskey, his good Irish whiskey. Margaret O'Donnell stood in the doorway and watched.

"She wants to be a whore, your sister does," O'Donnell snarled at her over the shot glass.

"You don't know what you're talking about," Margaret answered.

"Oh, don't I? This is a working family, and we've always worked hard for our money and the few good things we have, and held our heads up. We've worked, I tell you! I'm a workingman, by God, and I'm a union man! They can't run this factory without us. You tell her I want no disgrace brought on the name of O'Donnell from her. Pittsburgh!"

"Her name's not O'Donnell. And you don't know what you're talking about." Margaret O'Donnell turned and left the room.

John wanted to leave, too. "Well, thanks for the whiskey, Hugh," he said. "I'm going to turn in. I start my double shift at six tomorrow morning."

"One more round," O'Donnell insisted, and poured John's glass full again.

"All right," John said.

"Pittsburgh," O'Donnell murmured. "I've spent seven years in Homestead, and I'll spend the rest of my life here." He tossed off the whiskey quickly, and poured himself another glass. "You can't help it . . . you become more and more a machine, and pleasures are few and far between. It drags you down, mentally and morally, just as it does physically. I worked the twelve-hour shift my first five years here. Twelve hours. You know what I mean."

He looked up at John again. "I never asked you anything about your life, North, and I don't intend to now. I've heard a few stories. I know you're a good organizer, though you've got some damn fool ideas. They may even be dangerous ideas, but all in all, you're all right. From what I hear, you've had a hell of a life. You've been in some tough places, and you've proved out. Maybe some of it's just stories, I don't know. But it makes a girl like Nora . . ."

"I'm not going to do anything to Nora," John interjected.

"She wants to leave," O'Donnell said. "She wants to escape, get out. *She wants to get away!* And you're going

to do that, too. It's an easy life, North. It's an easy life.
The girls can do it. They can get away. They can get
away.''

John knew what O'Donnell was talking about. It was
easier for him to be in Homestead because he knew he
would leave it. But that was what made it possible for him
to work as hard as he did, to organize for the union and
prepare for the troubles ahead as no one else could do.
That was what gave him the energy to sleep for four hours
after his twenty-four hour shift, then use his ''turn'' day
for organizing and proselytizing. That was what gave him
the mental discipline to be alone.

The next day, when John reported to the plant for work,
he saw that a new piece of construction had begun—a
fence, surrounding the plant.

It went up quickly. It was clearly a high-priority item on
Henry Clay Frick's agenda. Within two weeks, it was
complete: a fence twelve feet high, three miles long, made
of two-inch board. It started from where McClure Street
met the waterfront on the western edge of the plant, continued east, then south for half a mile to Eighth Avenue.
The drunks, and the workers leaving shift who had stopped
to wash the dust out of their throats, could look out the
saloon windows down the whole length of the street until it
ended at a new bend of the river, and see the incredible
structure going up.

John stopped at various saloons during the course of the
construction, and watched, and listened. Three strands of
barbed wire were stretched along the top of the fence.

''Figure they're electric?'' a man at the bar next to John
asked.

''I can't be sure,'' said John, squinting at them.

''Who wants to be the first one to try and find out?''

Then, along the length of the three miles of fence,
twenty-five feet apart and at about the height of a man's
shoulder, were drilled three inch holes. At strategic places
along the top of the fence, platforms were built and search-
lights were mounted on them. Behind the fence, pipes

were laid, to which hoses were attached that were capable of throwing water under high pressure.

"It's a fort," John said.

"Fort Frick," someone else tossed out, and that made the rounds, and stuck. Fort Frick. An awesome paramilitary emplacement where once had stood a factory that melded into the town so completely that one could forget there was a difference.

"Do you still think they'll bargain with us?" John asked Hugh O'Donnell.

Chapter Thirty-one

The job was a routine one. Renegotiate contracts with all the companies who bought steel plate from the corporation, in such a way that they would accept much smaller orders for as long as necessary, but still remain loyal customers. It was made easier by the knowledge that the presidents of all those companies understood how important it was, in terms of long-term cost effectiveness, to break the union. But the Carnegie Steel Corporation was the DePuyster firm's biggest client, and this was the most important assignment Jamie Whitmarsh had yet received since joining the firm.

Henry Clay Frick liked him. Jamie could tell that; he could always tell. By itself, it meant nothing. He still had to deliver. But if he delivered, he knew, Frick would appreciate it, and show his appreciation. So Jamie would give everything he had on this job.

And he knew, too, that the more he got involved in this

steel mill business, the more responsibility and authority Frick would end up giving him.

The chairman had taken Jamie to lunch in his club, when the young lawyer arrived in Pittsburgh. He had shown Jamie a statement drafted by Andrew Carnegie, then vacationing in Scotland: "There has been forced upon this Firm the question whether its Works are to be run 'Union' or 'Non-Union.' As the vast majority of our employees are Non-Union, the Firm has decided that the minority must give way to the majority. These works, then, will be necessarily Non-Union after the expiration of the present agreement. . . . This action is not taken in the spirit of hostility to labor organizations, but every man will see that the firm cannot run Union and Non-Union."

"You haven't released this statement," Jamie said.

"No."

"And you're not planning to."

"Oh? What makes you think that?"

"Well, first of all, it seems to me that you can destroy the union as effectively, or even more so, if you don't announce that you're planning to do that beforehand. You've certainly shown you could do that in the past, Mr. Frick."

"Go on."

"And, since Mr. Carnegie has made known his generally benevolent attitude toward the institution of labor unions in the past, it can hardly do us any harm to lull the union into a false sense of security by allowing them to think he still feels that way."

"Mr. Whitmarsh, I like the way your mind works." Frick leaned forward. "How are you in a courtroom, son?"

"I'm your man, sir. Who is it you want taken to court?"

"We'll know soon enough, Whitmarsh. I don't know how things are going to turn out. I talked to the union yesterday. They are a gang of thugs. There will not be any more negotiations."

"You have men to take the place of the strikers?"

"There are plenty of steelworkers looking for jobs. We're recruiting in Boston, Philadelphia, Cincinnati, as far away as St. Louis. We'll replace the Amalgamated men, all right. And I have written a letter, this morning, to the Pinkerton Detective Agency.''

He took a folded piece of paper out of his pocket, and handed it to Jamie. Jamie read:

> We will want 300 guards for service at our Homestead mills as a measure of precaution against interference with our plan to start operation of the works July 6, 1892.
>
> The only trouble we anticipate is that an attempt will be made to prevent such of our men with whom we will by that time have made satisfactory arrangements from going to work, and possibly some demonstration of violence upon the part of those whose places have been filled, or most likely by an element which usually is attracted to such scenes for the purpose of stirring up trouble.
>
> These guards should be assembled at Ashtabula, Ohio, not later than the morning of July 5, when they may be taken by train to McKee's Rocks, or some other point upon the Ohio River below Pittsburgh, where they can be transferred to boats and landed within the enclosure of our premises at Homestead. We think absolute secrecy essential in the movement of these men . . .

Jamie looked up from the letter. ''Three hundred men,'' he said. ''That's a navy.''

''As far as I am concerned, Mr. Whitmarsh,'' said Frick, ''free enterprise and organized labor in this country are in a state of war.''

Chapter Thirty-two

The first layoffs came on June 28. Without warning, the armor plate mill and the open-hearth department were shut down, and eight hundred men were put out of work. John Whitmarsh was among them; so was Hugh O'Donnell, who had been named chairman of a five-man Advisory Committee which had been set up after the meeting with Frick. The committee was supposed to take charge of future negotiations, but they knew what their real mandate was: to prepare for what now seemed the inevitable strike.

That night there was a huge demonstration by hundreds of laid-off workers—inside Fort Frick. The men chanted, and cursed, and strung up effigies of Frick and plant superintendent Potter from a telegraph pole.

Jamie, at Frick's Pittsburgh headquarters, was informed by telephone.

"Send someone in to cut them down," he said.

"Someone? One man?" John Potter asked. "I don't think that will—"

"One man," said Jamie. "And don't make him too menacing."

". . . a clerk from Potter's office. So the men grabbed one of the Fort Frick firehoses and turned it on him. Like to washed him clear to McClure Street."

John and O'Donnell were on Eighth Avenue again, listening to eyewitness reports as men popped excitedly into the saloon, not part of the demonstration themselves but unwilling to be too far away from it.

O'Donnell shook his head. "One clerk? Of course they drove him away. I have a feeling that's just what Frick wants. He's going to use it as an excuse to get tough. Maybe we should have stopped it."

"Frick'll get tough anyway," said John. "He doesn't need an excuse. And you can't stop those men now. They're too angry. They've lost their jobs."

"They'll lose more than that, if they're not careful."

"They aren't going to be careful! They don't have houses on the hill and encyclopedias, and they don't vote Republican. They don't have that much to lose. Listen to me, Hugh, I've seen labor lose battles before, and I know what it means to lose. But when men have to fight, then they have to. I don't know if it's wrong or right, and maybe that doesn't matter, any more than it matters if a thunderstorm is wrong or right. But even if we lose, one way or another, someday all these battles are going to mean something."

"Someday. That's easy for you to say. You don't . . ."

"I know, I don't have to live here after the union's crushed and the men all go back to work with a twenty percent pay cut and no safety regulations. So try to stop them! Tell them how right you are, and how smart the union is, and how any day now Frick is going to reopen negotiations with you and make a new offer. Tell them they're only hurting your cause by their demonstrations. And after you're through with that, go out on the road and try traveling and organizing with no home to call your own, if you think that's such an easy life. Go ahead—there's room for more."

He and O'Donnell stared at each other. John's muscles were knotted, and his fists were clenched. He moved up slightly on the balls of his feet. O'Donnell gripped the bar rail, and stared into his face.

John's tension ebbed, and so did O'Donnell's. They dropped their guard, and O'Donnell held up two fingers to the bartender for another round.

"There's going to be a fight here, John," he said.

John nodded.

"We're not a bunch of revolutionaries. We've always worked within the system. We believed Andrew Carnegie when he said he supported unionism."

"You see how far he supports it."

"What do you suppose Frick will do?"

John did not speak. He gestured with a nod over his shoulder toward the mill with its sight holes, its towers that looked like machine-gun emplacements, its wood and wire fence.

"There's only seven hundred men in the union, even with the new ones you've recruited."

"Seven hundred and fifty-two.

"It's not enough. The rest won't stand with us. It's a union matter, and they're not going to care. They won't be with us."

"They're all against Frick."

O'Donnell stared at his drink.

The next day, several hundred more men were laid off, and the same the day after. As July began, the mill was virtually closed down.

Crowds of men stood outside the walls daily, staring at it, wondering. Others went to the bars, or to the union halls. Few stayed home. There was too much tension in the air. What was going to happen? Walled off from their work . . . the mills shut down . . . what would be next?

Next came an announcement from Frick. The mills would reopen July 6. Any employee who would renegotiate his own, non-union contract would be welcomed back, at no cut in pay except for the skilled, former union employees.

Hugh O'Donnell called a meeting that night, in the Homestead Opera House. Three thousand men showed up. O'Donnell was an intelligent, forceful speaker, but it was the cause, not the speech, that turned the day. The entire Homestead work force, union and non-union, went out on strike.

By the next day, the firings were completed. The entire
work force was laid off, and the factory was shut up tight
as a drum.

O'Donnell circulated a statement to all the workingmen
of Homestead:

The Committee has, after mature deliberation, decided to organize their forces on a truly military basis.
The force of four thousand men has been divided into
three divisions or watches; each of these divisions is
to devote eight hours of the twenty-four to the task of
watching the plant. The Commanders of these divisions are to have as assistants eight Captains composed of one trusted man from each of the eight local
lodges. These Captains will report to the Division
Commanders, who in turn will receive the orders of
the Advisory Committee. During their hours of duty
these Captains will have personal charge of the most
important posts, i.e., the riverfront, the water gates
and pumps, the railway stations, and the main gates
of the plant. The girdle of pickets will file reports to
the main headquarters every half hour, and so complete and detailed is the plan of the campaign that in
ten minutes' time the Committee can communicate
with the men at any given point within a radius of
five miles. In addition to all this, there will be held in
reserve a force of 800 Slavs and Hungarians. The
brigade of foreigners will be under the command of
two Hungarians and two interpreters.

John read over the statement by the first rays of dawn as
he stood watch. He had command that day of a force of
men on the *Edna*, a small paddlewheel steamer that had
been set up as the first line of defense against a naval
attack. The men of the *Edna* were armed, and the boat
carried flares and steam whistles for sounding the alarm,
should it become necessary. Accompanied by several two-
man skiffs, also equipped with guns and flares, the steamer

cruised up and down the Monongahela, day and night, in front of the mill.

John knew every word of the document; he had helped to draft it. But reading it over still made him burn. Reading the words on paper, and on the bridge of a flagship of the working class, or walking through a town where every workingman was reading the same words, and preparing to organize for the attack, his spirit flamed with purpose. All the pain, all the fervor that had seethed in the hovels of the Eastern Europeans, that had hissed in the cauldrons of molten steel inside the plant, that had flared up as the arrogant fortifications arose with their message of force— all of it was inside John Whitmarsh now, and ready to be summoned in the event of any move by Henry Clay Frick and his Pinkerton forces.

Chapter Thirty-three

John and O'Donnell were on alternate watches for July 4, so they took turns with the family at the Independence Day picnic down near the skating rink off McClure Street. There was beer and fried chicken, and they set off some fireworks, but the mood was distracted. Nora tried desultorily to flirt with John, but she had given up on him by this time. Mostly she was sullen and withdrawn. John found it easier to admire her plump, voluptuous figure now that he had established his distance from her.

It was a sunny day, and with no smoke coming from the mill, the permanent yellow-gray cloud over the town of

Homestead had lifted slightly, and there were patches of
blue in the sky. No one was glad to see them.

"I wish there was a band," said Nora.

"Next year," John said.

"There'll be one for me next year," Nora said. "You
can be sure of that. I'll be where the loudest, brassiest
brass band in the world is playing, and I don't give a hoot
about the rest of you."

She folded her arms, cocked her head belligerently, and
waited for a response. None came.

"I wonder where we'll be next year," Margaret O'Donnell said softly, to herself.

Nora looked up in surprise. "You mean you're thinking
of going away too?"

Margaret shook her head, and would say nothing more.

At six o'clock, O'Donnell came off his watch, and John
went to relieve him.

"Sheriff McCleary sent a bunch of deputies from Pittsburgh to take over the mill today," O'Donnell told him.

"How many?"

"Eleven."

John chuckled. "The only qualification for office that
anyone ever figured out for McCleary is that his mustache
looks more like John L. Sullivan's than anyone else in
Pittsburgh," he said. "What was he trying to accomplish?"

"Keep Frick off his back, I guess," O'Donnell said.
"Not much else, that's for damn sure. Eleven unarmed
deputies. They had about a thousand damn men around
them, the minute they stepped off the train. 'I am here as
the sheriff of Allegheny County to put deputies into this
mill and protect the property of the company,' McCleary
says. 'No deputy will ever go in there alive,' our man tells
him. And that was that. We took them back to Pittsburgh
on the *Edna*."

"And the next move?"

"John, I'm scared, I don't mind telling you. We've got
a right to picket and defend our jobs against scab labor,

but I sure as hell didn't want it to go this far. We've been trying to reach Mr. Carnegie by telegram in Scotland. He's always been a friend of the workingman. We've kept hoping he'd step in and help save our union, and our jobs. But he hasn't replied to any of our telegrams.''

"No, I'm sure he hasn't."

"So the next move is up to Frick."

Hugh O'Donnell sat alone in the watchtower atop the Electric Light Works of Homestead, and waited. It was 4:00 A.M. on the morning of July 6, and he was nearly finished with his watch. He hated this part of his responsibility more than any other. Organizing, leading men, negotiating—that was one thing; even organizing men into a militarily prepared force. But this sitting alone, through the night, with nothing to do but think, was unnerving.

He peered into the grayness, but there was nothing to see. He looked at his watch. Another hour until his shift was up. And it would not be light enough to read for another hour. Nothing to do but sit and think. Think about the damn fool chances he was taking with his life.

That was when he heard the noise cut through the fog off the river. Gunshots: one, two, three, then several more, and close together. O'Donnell yanked down hard on the steam whistle, and blew a long, steady, moaning blast.

Everyone in town knew what the signal meant—a river invasion. And as lights went on in every house, the blast from the Electric Light Works was echoed by another one, from the *Edna*. O'Donnell raced downstairs, and found John waiting for him out in the street.

"Are the divisions assembling?" he asked.

"It's beyond that," John shouted in his ear. "Everyone in town is heading down for the landing. It's a free-for-all. It's all gone crazy!"

Even as he spoke, a man on horseback—a sentry who had been posted upriver—rode past them, and through the town, shouting, "The Pinkertons are coming! The Pinkertons are coming!"

John watched him go, and laughed out loud. "You see what I mean?" he said. "Come on!"

There were ten thousand people at the riverfront. Men, women, children: all of Homestead was there, milling about, shouting and cursing, as two barges, towed by a single tugboat, came out of the fog and beached in front of the mill.

There was no more Fort Frick. The Pinkertons never got out of their barges to man the observation towers, or the gunsights, or the water hoses. The two-inch boards were battered down by the weight of the crowd, and the mob swarmed onto the mill property, and gathered around the landing.

A uniformed Pinkerton captain came up on deck, and glared down at the crowd. He spoke with sharp, disdainful authority: "We are coming up that hill anyway, and we don't want any more trouble from you men."

"He's got guts," said O'Donnell. The Pinkerton captain turned away from the crowd, and walked along the length of the barge, to the stern. No one in the crowd made a move.

Several more Pinkertons came up from belowdecks now, and with the captain's help, began to lower a gangplank.

"Are they going to do it?" O'Donnell asked. "Are they going to just walk right through us?"

"No!" hissed John, his voice venting his own frustration at being so far away. They were pushing their way through the crowd, but still nowhere near the front of it.

The gangplank was down. A second Pinkerton officer came out, and behind him, a group of about forty agents. All were armed with 45-70 Winchester magazine-fed repeating rifles.

"We're taking over this plant," he called to the crowd.

"Don't step off that boat!" came a voice from the shore.

The Pinkerton officer turned in the direction of the voice, and stared coldly. Then he began to walk, slowly and deliberately, down the gangplank.

A man from the front of the crowd ran up and threw himself across the gangplank, blocking the way with his body. The Pinkerton officer kept walking, until he was directly in front of the man. Then without looking down, scarcely breaking stride, he drew back his left foot and kicked the striker hard, in the ribs.

The man groaned, and the crowd took a step forward. Slowly, the Pinkerton officer drew back his foot. He brought it up, heel first, and planted it on the striker's side. Then he pushed hard, and forward, trying to dislodge him.

The striker rolled over a half turn, and as he did, reached into the pocket of his baggy pants. The officer pulled back, but it was too late. A revolver was pointed at him, and the roar as it went off shook the waterfront. The Pinkerton officer went down, a bullet through his thigh.

Then hell broke loose. The full body of Pinkerton agents on deck began firing. Everyone who had guns in the crowd was firing back, a constant, raking barrage across the decks of the barges. Bodies fell on both sides. Within the first few minutes of shooting, three strikers were dead and thirty wounded. One Pinkerton agent had been killed, and five wounded, as they had the structure of the barge for protection. The strikers retreated, carrying their wounded, leaving the three dead bodies behind. One, lying in a clearing, became a target for fusillade after fusillade from the Pinkerton guns. John watched in horror, forcing himself not to throw up as the body kicked and jerked with each new impact, and chunks of flesh were thrown into the air.

He had little time for watching, though—only a few seconds, out of the corner of his eye, as he and O'Donnell ranged up and down the line of battle, leading the women and children and old people out of the line of fire.

The strikers were falling back, and throwing up barricades of scrap steel and pig iron. The Pinkertons were transferring their wounded to the tugboat. When they had finished, still under heavy fire, the tugboat pulled out, and went off down the river.

"Holy shit," said John. "They're just going to leave 'em stranded out there."

It was bright morning now: July 6. The sun was rising high in the sky, and the temperature was sweltering by ten o'clock. There were no Pinkertons to be seen. And all along the shore, the strikers were preparing for a siege, hauling a small cannon into position on the side of the hill, and gathering dynamite together. For half an hour, both sides were silent.

In the calm, the strikers were ready to look to their leaders. They were dug in; they had the Pinkertons trapped.

"It's time to negotiate with them," O'Donnell told a hastily gathered assembly.

"Let's blow them out of the water!" someone shouted.

"Yeah, what's to negotiate?"

"Men, I know how you feel!" John shouted over the noise. "But we're here to win the strike. That's all—to win the strike! Let's get these birds out of here, and get on with bringing our real enemy—Henry Clay Frick—to his knees!"

"They're too well fortified to attack, anyway," put in O'Donnell. "Let's talk to them first. John North and I are going to go out there and try."

The Pinkerton captain was in his mid-thirties, tall and steel-eyed, with the inevitable John L. Sullivan mustache.

"I am Captain Charles Nordrum of the Pinkerton Detective Agency," he said with cold, condescending bravado.

"Hugh O'Donnell and John North of the Homestead Advisory Committee for the Amalgamated Association of Iron and Steel Workers," said O'Donnell. "What are we going to do?"

"My orders are to secure this mill for its lawful owners, and for whatever honest workingmen need their right to work protected," said Nordrum.

"Oh, come off it, Nordrum," said O'Donnell impatiently. "I'm talking about right here, right now. We've got a hell of a mess on our hands, and it's your men who are going to be the big losers if we don't do something about it. I don't want to blow you out of the water, but there's plenty of men here that do. Now what do you propose? If you're willing to talk surrender, I think I can talk my men into no more bloodshed.''

Nordrum snorted at O'Donnell. ''I have no such authority to change my orders, and no plan to do so.''

John and O'Donnell looked at each other. ''This man is crazy,'' John said.

Nordrum stepped around O'Donnell, and addressed the mob.

''Men, we are Pinkerton detectives,'' he barked. ''We were sent here to take possession of this property and guard it for the Carnegie Steel Company. And if you men don't withdraw, we will mow every one of you down.''

With that, he turned on his heel and walked back into the barge, leaving John and O'Donnell openmouthed with astonishment.

''What the hell do you suppose he's thinking of?'' O'Donnell asked as they withdrew.

They found out soon enough. Almost immediately, a group of detectives burst out of the barge, firing as they came. It was a hopeless effort. The strikers were dug in and fortified now, and they returned the fire to devastating effect. Four Pinkertons fell on the first volley, and the others dived for cover and kept shooting. The battle went on for two hours, until the remaining detectives finally made it back to the safety of the barge.

It was not like Chicago, or Pittsburgh, or anything John had ever seen. In Pittsburgh, the violence had been directed against property, the railroad property. In Chicago, the violence had been directed against the strikers. But here he was seeing a war, an all-out war against a human enemy, and the overwhelming desire of the crowd was to fight back, to kill, to destroy the despised, brass-buttoned detectives from the Pinkerton Agency which had strong-armed so many labor protests.

He thought of Jimmy McKenna, the Pinkerton spy who had betrayed his father. One man, a man he had known, whose friendship had turned out to be bitter deceit. But this was not one man: this was the slouch hat with the bright, gaudy band, the brass buttons, the dark blue trousers with cavalry stripes. The enemy.

"Somebody wants to see you."

John followed the worker to the rear of the line of combat. The man waiting for him was William Weihe, his boss, the president of the union. Huge, round-faced, bland-eyed, Weihe looked down at John Whitmarsh.

"What is going on here?" he demanded. "It is your responsibility, sir, as an employee and representative in the field for the Amalgamated Association of Iron and Steel workers, to see that this mob degeneracy is brought under control."

"I don't think I'm working for the Amalgamated Association of Iron and Steel Workers anymore," said John.

"What do you mean?"

"I mean you can take your union and shove it up your ass. I'm going to stay here and do everything I can to help these goddamn mill workers."

Arms and ammunition were flooding in from Pittsburgh to the strikers. Men were coming in from Pittsburgh, and Braddock, and Duquesne, swelling out the army that was taking on the Pinkertons. The barge was surrounded by a flotilla of skiffs, carrying men who fired at it without letup, and others who hurled half-pound sticks of dynamite at it.

The barge was riddled with bullets; great holes had been blasted in it by the dynamite. Still it remained afloat. Strikers upriver poured hundreds of gallons of oil on the water, set fire to it, and let it drift downstream toward the barges, but the current carried it wide.

John Whitmarsh was just watching now, almost in a trance, as the orgy of violence continued. Midway through the afternoon, a Pinkerton detective struck a white flag out through one of the holes in the side of the barge. It was riddled with bullets.

Finally, Hugh O'Donnell appeared at his side.

"I know what you're feeling, John," he said. "I've been feeling it, too. But we've got to end this sometime. We really can't let them kill them all."

"No," said John. "You're right; we can't."

Chapter Thirty-four

John left Homestead three days later. He had been ordered to leave by William Weihe, and though he did not want to go, there seemed no alternative. He had quit the union, and if he had tried to withdraw his resignation, Weihe would have fired him.

He left with the numbers in his head. Forty strikers wounded, nine killed. Twenty Pinkertons wounded, seven killed. After all, the strikers had come out on the wrong end of the body count.

But they had not lost. Oh, no, they had not lost. The Pinkertons had surrendered. They had been marched up the hill, three hundred of them, to be locked into the town theater as a temporary detention center. But as they were halfway up the hill, the crowd had lost its head. Sticks, stones, the tips of umbrellas, fists, feet . . . they beat the detectives without mercy. Not a one escaped injury. One man's eye was poked out; others had cracked ribs, concussions. Those strike leaders, like John Whitmarsh and Hugh O'Donnell, who tried to stem the violence and protect the Pinkertons, were roughed up as well. And it was only some impassioned and persuasive talking by those same leaders that saved the hated enemy from being torched to death in the theater, or taken out and hung.

John said his farewells to Hugh O'Donnell. There was not much to say. John could not help but feel that O'Donnell had been right. He was leaving. He was not staying to finish up the job, or to live with the aftermath.

He sat down by himself near the window of the railway carriage, and looked out at the ugly, blasted landscape of Homestead. He tried to sort out his feelings, but they danced and flickered through his consciousness, and it was no use. They were like wisps: no sooner did he try to pin one down than it was gone. It was simple: he wanted more than anything else to be out of there. Then why did tears well up in his eyes as he looked up Amity Street at the cramped, dirty frame houses, or down to the sulphuric acid-saturated Monongahela River? And why, when he looked back at the silent, empty steel mill, did his jaw tighten, and his whole body grow tense?

Homestead was not, would never be his home. If he were looking for a home, this would not be it. He was leaving now, and he could no more have gotten out of the train and gone back into the town than the train could have derailed itself.

Just as the whistle blew, and the train began to pull out of the station, he heard someone coming down the aisle behind him, and he looked up to see Nora stopping beside his seat.

"Is this taken?" she asked.

He smiled at her. "No," he said. "Sit down. Please."

She was wearing traveling clothes, and carrying a carpetbag, which she pushed under the seat.

"You're leaving Homestead, aren't you? I heard Hugh saying you were. He was talking to Mr. Roberts of the union, and Mayor McLuckie."

"Oh? What else did he say?"

"He said you had a right to leave. He said Homestead wasn't your town, and you'd done more than anyone could have asked already. He said there never would have been a strike at all if it hadn't been for the work you did with the Hungarians and the nonskilled workers.''

John's ears burned. "He was wrong. It would have happened anyway. Those people had so much anger burning inside them.''

''I don't care,'' said Nora. She looked straight ahead, not at John and not out of the window.

''I'm leaving Homestead too,'' she said.

''What are you going to do?'' John asked.

She did not answer right away, but John had the impression she had heard the question, and was considering it, so he waited.

''My sister told me what Hugh said about me, and what he said I was going to do. She told me he said it right in front of you. I don't think that's right, to talk about someone like that. Especially in front of someone that's not even family.''

John was embarrassed. ''No,'' he muttered.

''What do you think?''

''I think . . . I'm sure you're right. It must have been very embarrassing for you.''

''No, I mean do you think I'd ever do anything like that?''

''Oh, certainly not,'' John said automatically, without pausing for an instant to consider what he really did think.

''I just want to get away. Nothing is more important than leaving Homestead—*nothing*. Don't you understand that? These people . . . they're all dead! There's nothing in their lives but that mill, that living death, every day, all their lives, and when they die they don't even know it. Do you understand what I'm saying?''

John found himself paying attention. Suddenly, he was very interested in what she was saying. He was remembering the day when he had seen someone die at Homestead, in a hot metal explosion: the awful, unchecked destructive power of molten steel, the helpless awareness that, with safety conditions what they were, there was no way out of the path of danger once something went awry. He remembered the mood of the plant after an accident—which was to say, the mood of the plant all the time, since no day ever came that was very long after an accident. Nora was wrong; the difference between life and death was the one thing these men did know.

"Yes, I think I understand," he said.

"I know you understand. You have to. You're different, just like I am. You couldn't stay in Homestead either."

"No, I couldn't stay."

"But I don't understand you. I don't understand why you came to Homestead at all. I don't understand why you spent all your time hanging around with those Hunkies who live like pigs. Or why you never want to have any fun."

"I like to have fun." But he knew what she meant. There was the fun you had with women, and the fun you had to get away from women to have. Nora was only talking about one kind. *I like both kinds*, he told himself. But he found himself wondering whether she might be right. Perhaps he never really did want to have fun.

"I want to have fun," she said. "And if that's wicked, then I want to be wicked. I don't care if I go to hell. And I don't care if I die before I'm twenty-five, just so long as I get to live first."

"Good for you!"

It just burst out of John, with a spirit that was very much like enthusiasm. It surprised her. It surprised him.

The train was nearing the Pittsburgh station. "Hey," she asked shyly, "you wouldn't feel like having a little fun with me when we get to town, would you? We won't be in Homestead anymore."

John looked at her. That was what he was going to do, all right. Get drunk. Get laid. Go to a whorehouse—take on two, maybe three ladies at the same time. Find a casino with a roulette wheel. No poker, that was too much like work. Pick a fight. Have fun.

But not with Nora. Not with little Nora from Homestead, Hugh O'Donnell's sister-in-law.

He shook his head. "No," he said. "No, not me. I wouldn't be much fun."

She looked at him pityingly. "No, I guess you wouldn't," she said.

John Whitmarsh kept in close touch with what happened at Homestead over the next several months. He read the newspapers. He got eyewitness reports, and secondhand reports, from people who were involved with the union.

He read about the furor that grew from the Homestead strike. Never had a labor dispute stirred so much interest and debate: in the press, in Congress, in bars and union halls, parlors and classrooms all across the country. Its repercussions were tremendous, and John was to think about them often for years to come, but through the summer and fall and winter of 1892, he concentrated on following what was happening to the town, and the men of the mill.

The strikers held firm, union and non-union alike. They were supported by contributions from workers all over the country, including a "Homestead day" in Chicago where 90,000 unionists assembled and $40,000 was raised for the Amalgamated strike fund. But the town of Homestead was taken over by the Pennsylvania state militia, under the command of General George R. Snowden, who wrote in an official report to headquarters: "Pennsylvanians can hardly appreciate the actual communism of these people. They believe the works are theirs quite as much as Carnegie's." And small boats came down the Monongahela weekly from Pittsburgh, bringing scabs and strikebreakers into the plant.

John knew that the scabs were all unskilled workers, many of them derelicts and alcoholics. They were kept inside Fort Frick as if in a giant concentration camp, night and day. Many had been virtually shanghaied, promised jobs but not told where they were being taken, and they defected and escaped from Fort Frick almost as fast as they were brought in. They made very little steel, and it was of inferior quality. John knew that they were no real threat; not right away, anyway.

More of a threat was the campaign of legal harassment that was being waged against the Amalgamated leaders. Hugh O'Donnell, Homestead Mayor John McLuckie, and the other members of the Advisory Committee were arrested, jailed, freed on bond, and then arrested again. On July 18, warrants were issued against Hugh O'Donnell, John McLuckie, "John North," and five others, for murder. Just as in Chicago six years earlier, none of those charged with murder had been seen carrying a weapon—they were all strike leaders. Like John, most of those charged had gone into hiding, but O'Donnell and McLuckie waited in Homestead for the warrants to be served. They were out on bail within a week, but the harassment did not stop there. O'Donnell was behind bars four or five more times during the course of the summer, on one charge after another—and finally, on September 30, for treason.

John remembered Haymarket, and prayed that none of the charges would be upheld. Ultimately, none of them were. But he knew how effectively lack of leadership would hamstring a long strike. And he knew how devastating it must be for his friend Hugh O'Donnell, conservative, patriotic American that he was. Murder and treason! ("I am still a Republican," O'Donnell said in an interview from the Allegheny County jail.)

It was going to be too much, John knew, and he was right. By November, the strike was over, the union defeated utterly. A victory for Frick and for Carnegie, John admitted bitterly to himself. Frick had even turned the attempt on his life by an anarchist named Alexander Berkman into a personal triumph.

But John did not know that another ambitious man would gain by the defeat of the union as well—a brilliant young lawyer whose name did not make the newspapers, but who was the legal strategist behind the courtroom destruction of the Homestead strike: his brother, Jamie.

Chapter Thirty-five

In the *New York Times*, Monday, July 2, 1894:

Newport, R.I.—The gala event of this weekend was the lawn party given by Mrs. August Van Lier at the family's summer residence, "Windward."

Among the guests was Mr. James Whitmarsh, who will wed the Van Liers's lovely debutante daughter, Miss Josephine Van Lier, in Newport later this month. Mr. Whitmarsh, who at the age of twenty-two was last week named to the presidency of the New York & New England Railroad Company, is a nephew of the Earl of Marley.

It would be difficult to overstate the satisfaction felt by the nephew of the Earl of Marley as he sat in his office high above Broadway that Monday morning and perused that item in the newspaper. There it was: a bringing together of the core elements of his ambition, set forth indelibly in the public record. It was a milestone, a checkpoint perfectly realized in the scheme of his life, and still too soon for the bittersweet realization that even perfection is the explosion of a moment and inextricably linked with time.

Even so, there would have been no need for Jamie to sit like Alexander in his tent and cry because there were no new worlds to conquer. He had yet to make his first million, and he had no intention of stopping at the first.

The New York & New England was far from being an industry giant. This was a stepping-stone post, and one where he did not expect to stay for more than a few years. But for his age, and from where he had come, he was more than on schedule.

And there was Josephine. This was, in the popular-novel phrase that had been taken up by Mrs. DePuyster, a "brilliant match." August Van Lier was a shipping baron. He had inherited a considerable fortune from his father, and had parlayed it into a phenomenal one. The dowry he was settling on his daughter included a splendid townhouse on Fifth Avenue, just a block north of the William Kissam Vanderbilt mansion. The house was even now under the frantic assault of an army of workmen and decorators, preparing it for the arrival of the newlyweds a few weeks hence. Jamie had stopped by to inspect the progress before taking the train up to Newport, so that he could make a report to his anxious bride-to-be.

"Oh, James, is it *ever* going to be finished?"

"Don't worry, dear. They'll pull it together. These things have a way of falling into place."

"Falling into place? Oh, you're *too* horrid really, you say that just to tease me! Nothing falls into place unless you watch them and make them do it, every little bit of it!"

He smiled at her. "Of course, you're right, my darling. You should be the railroad president, not I. You've the instincts for it. I'll keep an eye on things and make sure those devils keep hopping."

"Will you? Oh, it's *too* awful being stuck away up here when all I want is to be with you in New York, and watching over my house—*our* house," she corrected herself quickly, squeezing his arm and giving him the clean-toothed sparkling smile she knew she did so well.

Josephine Van Lier was the acknowledged star of the season's crop of beauties. Her hair was honey-colored, and her eyes were the startling deep gray of wet pebbles. Her jaw was squared and firm, almost masculine. Her mouth stretched wide over teeth that were even and large and abundant. She was a light around which other young people, men and women, gathered like moths; not a flame, but an electric bulb, glowing with a designed, scientific energy. And though she talked like a debutante, with many "oh's" and "*too*'s" and flirty pouts, she was not just any debutante. She was giving a performance in a limited run, and she would make her debutante an unforgettable heroine, a benchmark people would measure against for seasons to come.

Jamie admired her. He did not love her, in the most romantic sense of the word. He did not lose himself in her. No passion arose in him that ever threatened his judgment. But Jamie did not really believe that passion of that sort existed. As far as he was concerned, he was as in love as people got. And it did not hurt that Josephine would be of enormous value to him, financially, professionally, and socially.

So as Jamie sat that morning in his new leather-smelling office at 409 Broadway and read about himself in the society column of the *New York Times*, his cup was filled nearly to the brim. There were just two small cracks that kept it from running over.

The first was a letter, long awaited, that had arrived late last week from his Uncle Roger in England. It read, in part: "I congratulate you on your upcoming marriage. The young lady sounds admirable in every respect, and her family of the very finest. While I do not have the pleasure of a personal acquaintance with her father, I know that Mr. Van Lier is well known and regarded in shipping circles here.

"I deeply regret that previous engagements of an unavoidable nature make it impossible for me to attend this joyous occasion. I must, therefore, keep an absent but loving vigil, like your late father, who, from wherever he is watching, I know is very proud . . ."

That had been a bitter pill. The presence of Lord Gretton in his wedding party would have added a luster to the affair, and to Jamie personally, that could hardly have been measured. Still, there was an undeniable warmth to the tone of the letter, and Jamie gave it the maximum exposure he could without seeming ostentatious, by showing it to his future in-laws and to the DePuysters, and trusting from there on to word-of-mouth.

The other flaw in Jamie's happiness was the strike. It had begun as a strike of workers at the Pullman Car Company in Illinois several weeks earlier. It had seemed a particular irony to Jamie that Pullman should be on strike. George Pullman, like Andrew Carnegie, was well known as an idealistic and paternalistic employer. His concern for his workers had extended to the building of a model town, Pullman, Illinois, where the workers at his factory were housed. Now these same workers, caught in a temporary economic bind by the continuing depression and wage cutbacks, were demanding more money and shorter hours and all the usual things workingmen demanded when stirred up by agitators; and in addition they were bitterly denouncing the controlled community in which they claimed they were virtually forced to live, at rents that they said were higher than they would have paid for better housing in the nearby towns. Job preference was given of course to employees who lived in Pullman, the company acknowledged, and those who lived in Pullman were expected to buy their food and clothing at the company store. But the strikers' propaganda made it sound as if this were all some sort of diabolical plot against the workingman. Some workers, they claimed, wound up after deductions with paychecks as little as two cents.

Whatever its ironies and whatever its truths, the Pullman strike ought to have been beaten in a matter of days. But the Pullman strikers appealed to a new ogranization, the upstart American Railway Union and its president, Eugene V. Debs. Debs was a man in his late thirties, a knowledgeable veteran of labor struggles, who ought to have known better than to take on such an impossible challenge. In fact, he was said to have gone through a show of demurral; but like Caesar, the cries of his supporters and the voice of his own ambition had persuaded him to accept the crown and lead the strike. And now the American

Railway Union was refusing to work any railroad that pulled Pullman stock out of Chicago. And the strike was spreading. A.R.U. organizers were fanning out along the nation's trunk lines carrying Debs's fiery call to strike. Already the newspapers were terming it the greatest strike in the history of the United States of America.

In newspaper interviews, Debs took this stand:

"The Pullman Company must meet with its employees and do them justice. The employees will accept any reasonable proposition. Let them meet together and agree as far as they can. Any points that are still outstanding, let them submit to impartial and binding arbitration. The American Railway Union is making no demand for official recognition as a part of any settlement solution. Our only interest is in seeing these employees dealt with fairly and given what they deserve, and in insuring that the strikers be restored to their positions without prejudice.

"We have been deliberately and maliciously misrepresented by our enemies, but have borne it in the conviction that the truth will finally prevail. It has been asked: what sense is there in sympathetic strikes? Let the corporations answer. When one is assailed, all go to the rescue. Labor is simply following their example."

Jamie Whitmarsh held his new presidency on the strength of his reputation, earned during the Homestead strike, as "a young man who knows how to deal with the unions." As such, he would be the point man, the railroad executive who would be thrown out front to deal with the A.R.U. As yet, the strike had not reached into New York. But in Chicago, it seemed to have been virtually won. The railroads were at a standstill. And a story in the *Times* reported that Debs's agitators were on their way, or here already. Jamie's own sources backed this up. His colleagues and his stockholders would be watching closely to see how he handled himself. It was not an exaggeration to say that his entire future depended on his performance here.

The *Times* was also full of news of mob violence in

Chicago, rumors that President Cleveland was about to call out federal troops (against the urgent plea from Illinois Governor John Altgeld that he not do so), and denunciations of Eugene V. Debs.

PULLMAN STRIKE NO LONGER THE QUESTION, pronounced on editorial page headline.

The attempt of the American Railway Union to lay an embargo upon the railroad traffic of the United States involves an issue compared to which the controversy between the Pullman Car Company and its employees sinks into insignificance. It is no longer a question of boycotting Pullman cars or striking work on the railroads without justification and regardless of the consequences, but of rebellion against law and order and public authority. As Senator Davis of Minnesota bravely says in his reply to the request from Duluth that he support the demagogical resolution of Senator Kyle, "it is a usurpation of the power to regulate commerce among the several States, and it is verging dangerously close upon the overt act of levying war against the United States." The question now is simply this: are the laws to be upheld, the rights of the people maintained, and public authority vindicated? Or is popular government to be found impotent in the face of inexcusable action? In a contest like this, there is but one patriotic side.

"A good objective analysis of the situation," John Whitmarsh observed. He was sitting in the cab of an idle engine in the yard of Grand Central Station, sharing a jug of cold water and a lunch of bread, cheese, and hard salami with a steward of the local chapter of the Firemen's Union.

"That's what you have to love about the newspapers," agreed the fireman. "A real sense of objective journalism."

"Money can't buy public opinion."

"Heck, no! Not in a democracy."

"Any poor jerk can grow up to be president."

"Sure. Look at Cleveland."

John was still browsing through the paper. "Say, here's a cute one. DEBS A WRECK FROM LIQUOR."

"Yeah, ain't that a beaut? Story comes from a doc who treated him about five, six years ago. Not from the doc himself, actually, but from his assistant, who dug through the doc's files while the doc was on vacation. End of the story, it says the doc says Debs was completely cured and hasn't touched a drop in five years. Top of the story makes Debs out to be a screaming dipsomaniac."

"What a lot of crap," John said with disgust. "I know Gene Debs. He's clean as a whistle."

"Well, if you're going to read the *Times* . . ."

"Yeah. My father once wrote for the *Times*, back during the Civil War. When John Swinton was editor. I guess coming into New York now, it seems like a kind of alma mater."

"John Swinton—he's the only honest guy in the bunch. He's with the *Sun* now. That's the paper you want to read."

The fireman finished his lunch and left. John had been talking to him about bringing his people in with the A.R.U., and joining the strike. The fireman had been sympathetic, but had not gone along. The New York Central ran Wagner cars, anyway, not Pullman.

Left alone, John glanced through the sports news. The Brooklyns had beaten Pittsburgh, 4-2, despite two home runs by the Pittsburgh shortstop. The Detroit team had thrashed New York and its seven-thousand-dollar battery, Meacham and Caldwell. John popped the last of the cheese in his mouth and reached for the water jug. Then his eye fell on an item on the facing page, under the heading "News of Society."

"Well, look at that!" he exclaimed, and a slow grin of amazement spread across his face.

The secretary wore a worried, suspicious look as she came into the office. Before she closed the door she glanced again into the anteroom. She approached halfway across the room and stopped, leaning forward on her toes toward the desk, with her hands clasped hesitantly at her bosom.

"Yes," said Jamie, a little impatient, "what is it?"

"Sir . . . it's a Mr. Whitmarsh."

Jamie raised his eyebrows. "Mr. Whitmarsh? I don't know any Mr. Whitmarsh." he frowned thoughtfully. "Is he an Englishman?"

"Oh, no, sir. He's not at all. He's sort of . . . sort of rough looking, in a way . . ."

Jamie shrugged and shook his head.

"Mr. John Whitmarsh," the secretary added, having just remembered the first name.

Jamie shook his head again. "No," he said, and then: "Oh, my God!" His head jerked around, and at that moment the door swung open and there was a tall, rugged figure that he recognized instantly, filling the doorway.

"All right, Miss Fehlinger," he said, barely able to hear his own voice, "you may go now."

John crossed the room in three long strides. Jamie came around the desk. But they stood apart, separated by a few awkward feet. Neither seemed to know quite how to proceed. They had been fifteen and seven the last time they had seen each other. The ways they had touched then were no longer appropriate, with so many years in between.

"Jamie!"

"Johnny! I can't believe it!" His hands hung ridiculously at his sides. "Where did you come from? What have you been . . . here, let me get you a drink!" Jamie turned and rushed headlong across the room to the cupboard where he kept a few bottles for entertaining. "What can I pour you? I have Scotch whiskey, and a very good brandy. Or I could have Miss Fehlinger send out for something. Shall I do that?"

"No, no. Whiskey's fine."

"So—how are you?" Jamie spoke more heartily now that there was a safe distance between them. He filled two tumblers halfway up with whiskey, and brought one to his brother. He handed it over with a flourish. "Fifteen years!" he said, shaking his head. "Well, my God! Chin-chin!"

He raised his glass, and John brought his up to meet it. There was a wry, bemused smile on John's face that Jamie tried not to notice. They both drank. Jamie exhaled the whiskey fumes with an exaggerated shudder. "Ahh! Say, that does the trick. Well, Johnny! My God! Sit down, tell me about yourself."

"First, you tell me. How is everybody? Mama? Fannie?"

Jamie's face fell. "You don't know? Mama's dead."

"No," John said, with a slow, stunned shake of his head. "No, I didn't know." Jamie watched him with curious sympathy as he absorbed the news, twisting his drink around in his big, leathery hands. "When?" John asked at last.

"A long time ago." Jamie described when and how it had happened. He told it as a sad story. He told it well, with a disarming absence of self-pity. Still it was hard to look John in the eyes. Instead he focused mainly on those brown hands, workman's hands. He found it odd that his brother should have hands like that.

"And what about Fannie? Is she all right?"

"Oh, yes, she's all right."

"Are you in touch with her? Is she in New York? I'm dying to see her."

"Yes, she's here. Only, she's . . ."

"Well? What?"

"It's a bit awkward, Johnny. I'm afraid what she's doing isn't exactly respectable."

John drew back in mock alarm. "Not respectable! Good heavens! What is she? A Pinkerton agent?"

Jamie forced a laugh. "No, but just about as bad. Our sister's the gambling queen of New York. She's got a casino called Divine's, on West Thirty-third Street. It's an elegant place, she's really quite successful. But—well, you know. It's hardly . . ."

"Respectable."

Jamie squirmed under his brother's ironic tone. This was the person whom he had held in awe when he was a child. It was hard now to suddenly dispel that aura. He laughed, and tried to maintain a breezy give-and-take.

"Well, and what about you, Johnny? You don't look so very respectable yourself. You scared the very dickens out of Miss Fehlinger. I believe she thought you were an anarchist or something."

"Do I look like an anarchist?"

"No," said Jamie, laughing.

"No, I'm not. But I have a feeling you're not going to find me too respectable, just the same."

"Oh-oh," said Jamie, beginning to feel more uneasy. But he kept up the bantering tone. "Don't tell me. A publican? An undertaker?"

"No. Worse yet. I'm an organizer for the A.R.U."

Jamie did not quite stop grinning. "You're joking," he said.

"I'm not. I arrived in New York forty-eight hours ago, after meeting with Debs in Chicago."

"I heard there was an A.R.U. organizer in town," Jamie said. "But the name I heard was John Fowler."

"I've used different names in the past few years. John North . . . John Fowler . . . but it's all me, little brother. I mean to bring New York's trainmen into the strike. That may include yours too, Jamie, unless I can convince you to support our stand."

Jamie's face drained of blood. "Johnny, no. You can't do this to me."

"It's not me, Jamie. And it's not you. It's men's lives and families. You don't know how these men live, kid, what some of them have to . . ."

"Stop it!" Jamie brought both palms down hard against his desk, and started drumming excitedly with his fingers. "Don't read me that litany. The men get paid what their labor is worth, and if someone else will pay them more, they're free to move to another job. That's what free enterprise is all about—the right of an employer to hire whom he pleases under whatever terms he's willing to offer, and the right of a workingman to accept those terms if he chooses to, or look elsewhere if he doesn't.''

"You can't really believe that, Jamie. The major industrialist holds all the power. Enormous power. There's no even give-and-take—not unless the industrial workers band together and bargain their labor as a united package.''

"That's communistic claptrap! There's no honest reason for even give-and-take in business. Management takes all the risks. Management supplies the capital. Management provides the skill and imagination and brainpower that keep a business alive and competitive. If a man can do something no one else can do, he'll get paid for it. If he can't, he'll have to settle for the going rate—or be replaced by someone who can do the work just as well. You know, Johnny, there's something you've got to understand. These railroads are publicly owned. We can't just sit up in our offices throwing money around. We've got stockholders! We've got an obligation to a lot of little people—widow and orphans—whose dollars are invested with us, and that obligation is to run the railroads on as low an overhead as possible and return them the largest profit we possibly can.''

"And even if that were your only obligation—are you serving those widows and orphans well when you dehumanize your workers to the point where they rebel because they can't stand it anymore? How many millions of dollars do you suppose will be lost every day that this strike goes on? Half that much, a quarter that much would have been enough to satisfy the just demands of every railroad worker in this country! But your Railroad Managers Association would rather spend the money to starve a worker than to feed him.'' John was standing now, pacing the room.

"Oh, come on, Johnny! In the first place, it's a matter of precedent . . .''

"No!'' John exclaimed violently. "In the first place, it's a matter of humanity! You talk about people as if they were ciphers, Jamie! You can't dismiss people that way.

Look—you were pretty young when we all lived at home, before Papa was killed, and maybe you don't remember. But our cousin Timmy was killed in the breakers, when he was just twelve years old, because the mine operators didn't think it was important enough to put in safety reforms. A lot of men and boys we knew, friends of ours, died that same way. They died because in the company's judgment, it didn't make economic sense to keep them alive. They had nothing to say about it. And when people tried to have a say in it, people like our Uncle Tim and our Uncle Mike—you remember what happened to them, don't you, Jamie? They were murdered, because they stood up and said you can't treat people like that, you can't let them suffer and starve and die to save a few extra dollars of profit! Don't you remember any of that, Jamie? Don't you remember our father?''

''Sure, I remember him! He could have given us everything. Instead, he got himself killed tilting at goddamn windmills, being a hero for other people, and he left us with nothing. Mama wound up drunk and crazy, and Fannie and I wound up on the streets. Look, Johnny, I've fought my way back by myself; you weren't around, and nobody gave me anything! And now I'm on the brink, I could have it all, and here you come and all I can see is that everything I've worked for could go up just like that!''

Jamie glared at his older brother defiantly, and was disconcerted to see a look of understanding soften his face.

''I could really mess things up for you, couldn't I, kid?''

Jamie nodded glumly. ''You sure could.''

'' 'Boy wonder of the New York & New England brother of A.R.U. agitator.' They'd eat you alive.''

''Johnny, you don't know how hard I've worked to get here.''

''No, but I can guess. Look here, Jamie, we're on opposite sides of the fence, I don't know how you wound up with some of the ideas you've got. You're wrong, you're dead wrong about all that, and I hope I can change your mind. But all the same, I'm proud of you. Look at you! Hell, I can't believe you're wearing long pants yet, and here you are with your own railroad! No, kid, I don't want to pull it all down on you."

"I'm getting married, did you know that?"

"I read it in the *Times*. That's how I found you."

Jamie took a breath. "I . . . I wish I could invite you to the wedding, Johnny. But . . ."

"No, no. I don't think that would do at all. No, I'll keep a low profile and stay out of your way as much as I can."

"Will you steer clear of the union stuff? Till all this is over?"

"What? No, I can't do that. Any more than you could give all this up. But don't worry. I'm John Fowler to the world, and we'll keep the family connection out of this. Now, I imagine you'd be just as happy if I didn't stay around your office any longer than necessary."

"I . . ."

"That's all right. After all, I've got my reputation to think of, too. It wouldn't do it any good with the rank and file to be associated with you."

"Perhaps we could meet later," Jamie said, getting up from behind his desk and coming around, and then regretting it quickly as his confidence ebbed without that oak shield to protect him.

John stood too, towering over him, too close. "It hasn't been the reunion brothers dream about, has it? Look, why don't we meet at Fannie's?"

"At Fannie's?"

"Oh, come on. You could come in disguise."

"All right, look, I have a dinner engagement this evening, so let's say eleven o'clock. It's at Thirty-three West Thirty-third."

"I'll be there." John reached out and clasped Jamie's hand. It was the first time in their meeting that the brothers had touched. "Take care of yourself, kid."

After he had closed the door behind John, Jamie turned

and leaned his back against it. His hand was still wrapped around the smooth cool brass of the knob. He breathed slowly and methodically, quieting the jumping of his stomach.

From where he stood at the door he could see the whole room. Law books gleamed dark leatherbound wisdom from shelves that hollowed the far wall. Vaulted windows behind his desk looked out upon the warrens of wealth and power of the men who ruled the nation, men with whom he was now practically an equal. On the opposite wall were framed photographs, of Cleveland DePuyster, of the President of the United States, of New York City Mayor Big Bill Henderson, of various railroad magnates, and one of a piercing-eyed Henry Clay Frick that bore the signed message: "To James Whitmarsh, a true and remarkable friend of America and her system."

Yes, Jamie thought, *I will take care of myself.* It was what he had been doing, with instinct and skill and fierce determination, for most of his life, and so far he had done it about as well as it could be done, he calculated. He would manage now, too.

On reflection, he decided he had won the first round, though he had been caught badly off guard. He had gained more than he had given up. That was part of the secret. But it was not the whole secret. The real heart of success was to give nothing up.

He would work on that. Now he was prepared.

Chapter Thirty-six

It had been hot all day, and toward evening it seemed to become hotter still. Or perhaps it was just that darkness did not bring the anticipated relief from temperatures that had held the city trapped in the low nineties since midmorning.

In a tavern on Twenty-eighth Street, John Whitmarsh stood beneath the slowly whirling blades of a wooden ceiling fan and drank cool beer and talked strike and weather with a couple of men from the Central Labor Union of New York. They drank in shirt-sleeves, with dark sweat patches spreading out from their armpits beneath their unbuttoned vests, and soaking through the vests. The C.L.U. men asked John if it was hot enough for him, and assured him that their councils were in full sympathy with Debs and the Pullman strikers and the A.R.U. There was to be a big citywide rally at Cooper Union in a few days, to show solidarity and support. However, they did not see much chance of a sympathetic general strike in New York. Not at this time, the way things were now.

A little past ten John left the tavern and walked north through what felt like a dark oven to Thirty-third Street. Heat lightning danced above the trim brownstone rooftops, a dry silent flickering of colorless light without the answering rumble of thunder or the promise of rain. John came to number 33, and stood at the bottom of the steps looking up at the great bronze door, watching it change from dark gold to pale milk and back again, as another wash of lightning filled the sky.

He knew what would be behind that door—what inner doors and passwords and machinations of security he would find. He knew that he could get his name in to Fannie and gain admission that way. But that was not the way he wanted to come to her, not after so many years.

He glanced around. Another ripple of lightning outlined for him a wrought-iron gate that guarded an alley. He climbed it easily and dropped down on the far side. The alley led back to a walled garden. There was a door in the garden wall, but the door was locked, and the wall was too high and smooth to climb. But he found that by using the doorlatch as a toehold he could vault and grab hold of the top and pull himself up.

Twenty feet away from him were three windows that gave into a lighted room. The room was empty. On the floor above, an elderly man in evening clothes leaned against the sill of an open window with a glass of champagne in his hand. The windows on the next floor up were shuttered. Light shone through them. The man with the champagne glass exchanged it for another, a full one from a tray passed by a waiter. Someone presumably said something to him, because he laughed, called out something that John could not understand, and left the window.

A woman came into the empty room on the parlor floor. She paused for a moment at the door, talking to someone unseen, and then closed the door. She walked across the room to the spare, simple desk, pressing her hands to the small of her back and arching her body backward. She was an extremely handsome woman, bare-shouldered in a striking bead-embroidered gown of yellow tulle with one satin strap. John watched her fascinated for almost a full minute before he realized that he was looking at Fannie.

Shrouded in darkness and wonder, he watched her as she moved about the room. She was a greater shock than Jamie. Men grow to manhood by getting bigger, stronger, more defined. But a girl metamorphoses into a woman, and she is not the same creature. It was hardly Fannie at all—more like his mother, except that his mother had not been this beautiful, or this elegant. But as he leaned forward against a branch of the ailanthus tree that grew against the wall, he could recognize his sister by her face, slimmed and molded now, but still her, still Fannie.

It was a strange, haunting perspective, this watching from darkness, seeing without being seen. It was like being a spirit, dead and returned to earth, being among the living in a way that was never possible while actually walking among them. Fannie smiled at something as she tucked a loose curl back into the soft mass around her head with a hairpin, and John had the feeling that it was a smile, dreamy and vulnerable, that she allowed herself only while she was alone. He felt with a deep pang how much he had missed her.

Fannie turned and started to the door. John dropped from the wall and ran across to the window.

"Fannie!"

He climbed the garden steps, and saw her as she stopped and turned with a puzzled look on her face. "Fannie!" he called again.

She came toward the window, squinting into the darkness. "Who is it?"

John moved so that the light from the window fell on him. "It's me, Fannie. It's Johnny."

She caught the windowsill with her hands and stared at him. A look of joy and disbelief numbed her face, and a tear spilled from each eye, suddenly, as if squeezed from a dropper.

He reached out and put his hands on hers. "Well . . . are you going to invite me in?"

They sat in her office, chairs drawn up knee to knee, and Fannie, with wet cheeks and glistening eyes, asked question after question, hardly able to wait for the answers, and laughing at herself for her breathless assault. John answered as best he could, and asked questions of his own. Finally they just sat back and looked at each other, catching their breath, holding hands.

"I've seen Jamie," John said.

"Have you? I was going to ask." She giggled. "See, there are still things I haven't asked. Isn't he doing wonderfully, Johnny?"

"I'll say he is. But I'm afraid he and I are going to have our problems."

"Oh. Oh, yes."

"He's coming here tonight. I thought we should all be together. Although I guess it won't be just like old times."

"Jamie is coming here?"

"Is it that much of an occasion?"

She smiled. "He's a bit nervous about coming here. He doesn't feel it's the sort of place where he can afford to be seen."

"Not respectable?"

"Not entirely respectable."

"But don't you ever see each other?"

"Oh, yes. But not here. I have a house in Bronxville. A separate life. . . . I have a daughter, Johnny! I didn't tell you."

"You do? Fannie, that's great! How old is she? What's her name?"

"She's seven. Her name is Dolly. Oh, she's adorable. You'll love her. She doesn't know anything about all of this, by the way."

"All what?"

"Divine's. Fannie Divine. I'm a whole different person out there. Dolly goes to a nice school, has nice friends, she's growing up in a way even Jamie could be proud of. She thinks her mother's respectable."

"So do I."

"Aren't you going to ask me if I'm married?"

"I wasn't going to. But I will. Are you?"

"No."

"Never?"

"No."

"Do you mind?"

"A little. Not too much. We love each other, we're close friends. That's enough." She gave a rueful little smile and looked away. "Well, almost enough. But it can't be any other way." Almost challengingly: "I don't regret it, not a bit."

"Nor should you," said John. "I'd like to meet your daughter. I'd like to meet your friend, too, if I can. And I promise not to play the outraged brother and punch him in the nose."

Fannie started to laugh. "Oh, no, I wouldn't do that, Johnny!"

"He's that rough a customer, is he? Well, there, you see? It pays to be broad-minded."

Jamie arrived at half past eleven. Fannie had wine and champagne brought into her office, and food from her famous late supper. As they toasted their reunion, Jamie watched warily to get a sense of whether Fannie had told John how he had deserted her, or complained of his neglect. As far as he could tell, she had not. He could not have said why it was important to him. He would almost certainly have denied that there was any importance at all if he had been asked, or had even asked himself. But it did matter to him still what John thought of him, if only to a small part of him. The rest of him looked at that small part with pity and scorn.

At a quarter past twelve Jamie left, pleading an early meeting. He had felt like an outsider. There was an easy warmth between his brother and sister, and he was out of harmony with it. They had made an effort to include him, but between the two of them there was no effort, just an easy, lively flow of talk. They reminisced about a life he barely remembered, and a family he had never felt a part of. They steered clear of the one subject that had to be uppermost in their minds: the strike, and the struggle that was looming between him and John.

Chapter Thirty-seven

It was love at first sight between the seven-year-old girl in ribbons and ringlets, and the tall, broad-shouldered man with the tanned face, the huge hands, and the wild look of adventure in his eyes.

"This is your Uncle John, dearest," Dolly Whitmarsh heard her mother say. "My big brother, whom I haven't seen in years." And her heart sang. It was true, then—this wonderful, exciting, gigantic creature was hers, to love and climb on and hug and be picked up and carried by.

"Miss Wilcox!" she turned breathlessly and called to the sharp-faced woman who stood in the hallway behind her. "That Uncle John is *my* Uncle John!"

It was love at first sight for the big man, too. John saw Fannie in the little girl's eyes, and his mother, too. He saw a streak of his father, as well. But most of all, he saw Dolly, a new Whitmarsh, his newfound niece. Little and pretty and vulnerable, round-faced, and wide-eyed. Innocent and sheltered in her white ruffled pinafore, her white stockings and little pumps, her curly hair brushed back and tied with a ribbon, her face shiny. But she had backbone, too, like a real Whitmarsh. She stood up under the sharp, peremptory orders of her governess, Miss Wilcox, without flinching; and though she obeyed, like a well-brought-up little girl, John knew that her spirit was strong and unbowed. And she had love, a warm open heart and open arms, for her grizzle-faced new uncle from the West.

John spent his days in tireless negotiation and planning

sessions with the Central Labor Union and the New York City representatives of the American Federation of Labor. He communicated daily by telegram with Eugene Debs in Chicago, and would not duck any meeting, at any hour, with any New York labor leader who might help the cause.

But his heart was in Bronxville with his curly-haired enchantress, and he managed to get up there for at least a short visit every evening. He brought her a stuffed animal, and taught her how to play dominoes. He borrowed a banjo from a locomotive brakeman and played songs for her, as she clapped and sang along delightedly, and Miss Wilcox frowned severely in the background, and waited impatiently to send her off to bed.

Late at night, he would drop by to see Fannie at the casino. She had offered him a room upstairs, and he had taken it, the better to be able to spend time with her during those rare hours when they both had free time together. He loved to watch her in action, slipping in and out among the faro tables, the dice tables, the roulette wheels, talking and laughing with the men in white tie and tails, welcoming ladies in furs and men in tall silk opera hats, disappearing into the back room at an unseen signal and returning with the same unruffled smile, or dropping a word to one of the impeccably dressed, unassuming, but very large men who walked through Divine's. It all worked perfectly. There was never any trouble. And everyone had a good time.

He sat in Fannie's office, and they played two-handed poker for matchsticks. They both cheated on every hand, and soon they were laughing so hard they could no longer pick up the cards.

"You're very good, big brother," Fannie said.

"Not as good as you. You've got moves I've never seen before."

"I invented a lot of them. There's no cardsharp between here and Saratoga I can't beat."

"I believe it. And none on the Mississippi either. I'd better give you another drink, so I can slow you down to my level." He poured her a glass full of Madeira, and a shot of Fannie's bonded bourbon for himself.

"You're not going to drink me under the table like that," she teased.

"Oh, yes, I will. At least I should be able to outdrink you, if nothing else."

"Don't be so sure. You never had to . . . oh, this is terrible! I shouldn't be talking to my big brother like this. You'll be outraged."

"Go ahead—outrage me."

"Oh, well, then—you asked for it. You never had to drink three traveling salesmen under the table on a Hudson River packet boat after you've spent the evening demonstrating that a pair of artfully exposed bosoms will beat four aces."

John swallowed, then howled with laughter. "No," he said with a rueful grin after he had composed himself again. "But I do remember waking up alone one morning on a floor somewhere in Kansas City with only the top button of my trousers unbuttoned, and with nothing to show for it but an empty money belt, an empty bottle, and a queen of hearts stuck in my waistband."

"Good for her!" crowed Fannie. She lifted her glass in a toast. "Here's to sisters in crime—and the suckers like you who are born every minute."

"I'll drink to that," John said. "If a man has to have one weakness, it might as well be drinking, gambling, staying out to all hours of the night, and beautiful women."

"Sure you haven't left anything out?"

John thought for a moment. "Actually, I have. Wait a minute." He reached deep into his pocket, and brought out a small pouch. He opened it, and passed it over to Fannie. "Did you ever see this before?"

Fannie looked at it, and sniffed it. "No, and right up to this moment I can't say that I'm sorry. What is it? It smells a little like tobacco, and a little like tea."

"Well, you smoke it like tobacco," said John. "They grow it down in Texas and Mexico and all over the Southwest. It's called marijuana."

"Oh, I've heard of that!" Fannie said. "It's like opium, isn't it?"

* * *

"Jamie doesn't have fun like this very often, does he?" John asked dreamily.

"I'm afraid not," said Fannie. "Jamie's too grown up. He knows you can't carry on this way, and expect to have your nose to the grindstone bright and early the next morning."

John looked out the window. The air was light gray and getting lighter.

"It's a good thing I don't," he said. "Because I've got a hell of a day in front of me."

"What is happening with the strike, John?" Fannie asked.

"It's spreading all over the West and Midwest," John said. "It's been peaceful, so far. But yesterday the government sent federal troops into Chicago, and I don't know what's going to happen next. Did you see yesterday's *Times*?"

"No."

"They quote Debs—I've got it right here—'The first shot fired by the regular soldiers at the mobs here will be the signal for a civil war. I believe this as firmly as I believe in the ultimate success of our course. Bloodshed will follow, and ninety percent of the people of the U.S. will be arrayed against the other ten percent. And I would not care to be arrayed against the laboring people in the contest, or find myself out of the ranks of labor when the struggle ended. I do not say this as an alarmist, but calmly and thoughtfully.' "

Fannie listened to the tone of John's voice. "You think a lot of Debs, don't you, Johnny?"

"He's the greatest leader American labor has ever had."

"Do you think there will be violence?"

"I'm not afraid of violence. But I hope not. I think we can win without it. This moment has been coming closer and closer for the last two or three years. Homestead . . . Coeur D'Alene . . . Coal Creek . . . Cripple Creek . . . workingmen all over America are starting to realize they can join together and change their lives. In the general strike in New Orleans last year, even blacks and whites stood side by side. And right now there are a hundred different unions in Chicago alone who are ready to walk out if Pullman won't negotiate with the A.R.U. There are unions all over the country that have promised to join us, and if I can swing New York, that could be the key. Fannie, I tell you this could be different from anything that's gone before it. And Gene Debs is the difference.''

"But not the most important difference to you, is he, Johnny?"

He was blank for a moment; then he looked into her dark, searching eyes, and he understood. After all these years apart, nothing had changed. She still knew just what was in his heart, the same way she had known when they were children.

"No, you're right," he said. "Jamie is. Jamie's the difference for me."

Now the euphoric sense of well-being that the marijuana had given him was slipping away as quickly as the night, leaving other feelings in its wake. Feelings that were open and exposed to the probing glow of dawn: feelings of pain, and love, and emptiness, and confusion.

"I don't know Jamie anymore, Fannie," he confessed. "I look at him, and I remind myself that he's my little brother, and I try to conjure up images of Painter's Falls. But nothing comes. Nothing I can connect to the man in the expensive suits in that oak-paneled office downtown."

"You can't mix up a class struggle and family, Johnnie. Jamie's more than just an expensive suit."

"Is he? I wish I could see it. But I don't. In Painter's Falls—''

"Johnny, Johnny, Johnny! Painter's Falls was another lifetime. I don't even remember what Painter's Falls looks like anymore. We grew up in New York, Jamie and me. On the streets, in the slums. We had to fight for everything we got. Jamie did. And I did, too."

"But you didn't turn out cold and hard, the way he did."

"I'm in a tough, illegal business, Johnny—surely you've noticed. And I've been in it since I was a girl. You have to be hard to run a casino, hard and ruthless—especially if you're a woman. I'm not fighting for any causes except my own, and my daughter's.''

She spoke harshly, but then she permitted her face to soften just a little. ''Of course, I did send some money to the Homestead strike fund,'' she admitted almost sheepishly. ''In Papa's memory.''

''I don't imagine Jamie did that.''

''No . . . no, not at all. Jamie was . . . Jamie was Mr. Frick's lawyer during the Homestead strike.''

''*What*?''

''Oh, there I go,'' said Fannie. ''That's the last thing I should have told you.''

''Does Jamie know I was at Homestead?''

''I certainly haven't told him. Johnny, try to understand Jamie.''

''I'm sorry, dearest, but I'm afraid it's you who doesn't understand Jamie.''

''I understand how I feel! I understand seeing him grow up with nothing . . . *nothing* . . . and he was my baby. There was no one but me to take care of him. Mama couldn't . . . and he couldn't understand why. He was too little. And he was a boy. You wouldn't have understood either, Johnny. No man would have. You didn't understand Mama back in Painter's Falls. Don't pass judgment on Jamie, Johnny—please!''

John hugged her, and rocked her, and hugged her some more. She sobbed into his chest.

''And promise me, Johnny—promise me you won't do anything . . . I know you have to fight for your union, and that's only right. But don't do anything to Jamie . . . you know . . . *personally*. Don't do anything to hurt his life, or his marriage, or the happiness he wants for himself.''

''I promise,'' John told her. ''Give my love to Dolly. Tell her I'll be by and see her, and we'll play dominoes again.''

The violence happened in Chicago. From the 4th of July, when the troops entered the city, the mood turned ugly. For the better part of a week, mobs surged through the rail yards, overturning cars and setting fires. The troops called for reinforcements, and fought back. By the end of the week, the occupying force totaled 14,000 soldiers, state militia, and deputy marshals hired and paid by the railroads. Over thirty strikers had been killed, and fifty severely wounded.

In Trinidad, Colorado, in Raton, New Mexico, in Los Angeles and Sacramento and Oakland, and all through the West, violence flared up. In Indiana and Illinois, Nebraska, Iowa, Minnesota, Oklahoma, federal troops were mobilized against the strikers.

On the East Coast, things were still quiet. But how long could it last? Jamie Whitmarsh was not about to wait and find out. The lovely and petulant Miss Van Lier, his fiancée, was right: nothing falls into place unless you watch them and make them do it, every little bit of it. So on July 8, Jamie met secretly with Eugene Hines, Joseph Barr, and Christopher Miller, representing the Brotherhoods of Trainmen, Conductors, and Engineers in New York. These were the old lodges, the exclusive craft unions whose existence was being threatened by Debs's industrywide, all-inclusive membership policy.

They all had one thing in common: their hatred of Debs, and their desire to see his union smashed. But the railroad men were distrustful of James Whitmarsh, too. After all, he was Frick's man, the man who had destroyed the Amalgamated, a fine old craft union, at Homestead.

"Frick?" said Jamie with a casual laugh. "No, I wasn't working for Frick. I was working for Mr. Carnegie, and you know he's always been a friend of responsible labor unions. I only came in on the Homestead situation after things were totally out of hand, or you can bet that there would have been a different resolution of that dispute. And that, gentlemen, is what we are all after here, isn't it? A peaceful agreement between the responsible representatives of labor and capital in the railroad industry. Please, gentlemen—join me in a drink? Your choice from my bar

. . . or I can offer you some cold beer, my personal favorite."

Jamie and Miller each had a beer; Hines and Holland chose gin. Jamie had been practicing drinking beer over the previous two days, so that by now he was able to get it down with a look of enjoyment on his face.

"I want to work with you boys," he said. "I want to do what's fair for you, and the men in your brotherhoods. But if I'm going to be able to do that, I've got to be sure that there's going to be law and order in New York—no damned communism and anarchy."

"We're with you on that, Mr. Whitmarsh," said Miller. "And most of the labor leaders in New York'll back us up, or at least not oppose us. But you know, it's the mob that those outside agitators appeal to, and that could be a problem. This man Fowler, this A.R.U. man from Chicago, he's a real problem. He knows how to stir things up. He's been doin' a lot of talking, and he's got a lot of people listenin' to him."

"Fowler, eh? John Fowler . . . ?"

"That's the man."

Jamie pulled another bottle of beer out of the ice bucket, wiped it off with a towel, and opened it. He paced slowly around his desk. When he was behind it, he put the bottle on the table and brought his open palm down hard on the oak surface.

He leaned forward over his desk, and the three trainmen leaned toward him, as he spoke in a hoarse, conspiratorial whisper:

"Gentlemen, if John Fowler were out of the picture, would it make a major difference in settling this matter?"

"Reckon it would."

"Then I think we can reach an understanding. I believe that I know how to get rid of this . . . John Fowler. And if that's what it takes to nip this insurrection in the bud, I'll do it."

Chapter Thirty-eight

Fannie was not at the casino on West Thirty-third Street, when John arrived there that evening. Robinson, the black butler who was Fannie's chef lieutenant but who never stepped out of his public role as the perfect servant, not even with John, met him with a message to call her.

She was fighting tears when John telephoned her in Bronxville from her office. "It's Dolly, Johnny."

John's heart sank. "Has she been hurt?"

"No . . . not the way you're thinking, anyway. I fired Miss Wilcox, her governess. I found that she'd been stealing from me. She left today. But before she left, she told Dolly all about me—all about what I do for a living. She told her I'm an evil woman, and God is going to send me to hell."

"How did Dolly take it?" John's voice was compassionate but calm.

"She was terribly upset. She ran to her room, and she won't talk to me."

"Well, Fannie, you know she had to find out someday."

"I know, I know. I was going to tell her. I would have told her soon, I really would have, Johnny! When I thought she was ready. But not yet! And to hear it like this . . . all those dreadful, cruel things that woman said . . ."

"Would you like me to come out and talk to her?"

"She's asleep now. I think she'll sleep through the night."

"Tomorrow, then. I'll come early in the morning and spend the day with her."

"Oh, Johnny—can you take the time?"

"Things are picking up their own momentum here. They'll roll right along without me. Of course I can."

John knocked at the door of Dolly's room in the morning. She had not come out for breakfast, and she did not answer the knock.

"Dolly, it's Uncle John."

"You can come in," she said in a small voice.

She threw her arms around his neck. She had been crying, and she cried more now, in John's arms.

"Uncle John, Uncle John," she sobbed. "I don't want to be wicked and go to hell."

"Dolly, Dolly," John crooned, rocking her, trying to get a sense of her pain.

"I want to run away."

"Would you like to run away with me?"

Curiosity made her stop crying for a moment. "What do you mean?"

"Oh, let's see. We could run away to the West and be cowboys together."

"Oh, you're being silly."

"That's not so silly. I used to be a cowboy."

"You did?"

"Sure did."

"What was it like?"

"Well, I'll tell you what. Why don't you get dressed, and I'll take you into New York with me. We'll spend the day there, and I'll take you to see some real cowboys who are friends of mine."

"There aren't any real cowboys in New York."

"There are this week. Buffalo Bill's Wild West Show is playing at Madison Square Garden. Now, you get dressed, and we'll go."

They went to the Central Park Zoo first. They walked around and looked at the animals, bears and elk and deer,

buffalo from the West like the ones, John told Dolly, that
Buffalo Bill used to hunt, and exotic creatures like mon-
keys that scampered around their cages and swung from
tree limbs. Dolly stayed very close to John, clinging tight
to his leg every time they stopped to look into a new cage.
But John could feel her little body getting less tense; and
she even began to laugh at the silly jokes he was making
about the zoo animals and the people they looked like.

Finally, they sat down on a park bench to rest.

"What did Miss Wilcox say about your mama?" John
asked casually.

He felt her stiffen again. "It's all right," he said gently.
"Just tell me about it. Things always seem worse than
they are when you don't talk about them."

"Honestly?"

"Honestly."

Dolly took a deep breath, and began talking. Her voice
trembled a little, but she spoke with surprising restraint
and calmness—a measure of the trust she had in her uncle.

"She said my mama was the wickedest lady in New
York, and she was going straight to hell, and everybody
knew about it and knew how wicked she was. She said
that what my mama did was wicked even if a man did it,
but it was even worse because she was a lady. She said no
lady should ever even think about doing the things that my
mama does. She says my mama does something that God
says in the Bible is wicked and evil, and anyone who does
it will go straight to hell, and that's why my mama would
never tell me what she did."

"Hmm. Did Miss Wilcox tell you what it was that your
mama does that's supposed to be so wicked?"

"*Grambling!*"

Dolly's eyes were wide with seriousness as she intoned
the word. John tried hard not to laugh, but failed. He
sputtered helplessly, as Dolly watched him with a look of
confusion in her serious dark eyes.

"I'm sorry, sweetheart," he finally said.

"It's not funny," Dolly scolded him, and he began to
laugh again.

"I know, sweetheart, I know. But it is, really. Nothing's ever so bad you shouldn't be able to laugh about it."

"Why?"

"Because laughing makes you feel good. And the world's a hard place, and whenever you can laugh and feel good, the world becomes a nicer place."

"Miss Wilcox didn't think so. She used to scold me a lot for laughing. She said it was in . . . a . . . propiut."

She struggled with the last word, fighting it one syllable at a time.

"What did you think of Miss Wilcox?"

"What do you mean?" Dolly's eyes showed panic.

"What did you think of her? It's all right. It's just you and me and the squirrels. You can tell me."

"I didn't like her," Dolly whispered. "I didn't like her at all. She was mean. And she kept telling me I was bad. I didn't think it was fair, but she always seemed so sure, and she kept telling me how God said she was right, so I guess she must have been."

"And what about your mother? What did you think of her? I mean before all this."

"Oh, my mama's nice!" Dolly burst out. "And she's beautiful, and she loves me. I just wish she could spend more time with me, and . . . and she wasn't wicked."

Dolly put her head on John's lap, and started to cry again, but the tears were different now. She was crying it out. John patted her shoulder.

"I think you should listen to your feelings, and not what some mean woman says to hurt you. You were right, you know. About Miss Wilcox. And about your mama."

"But Miss Wilcox said that God—"

"Miss Wilcox doesn't know anything about God. Anybody can say that God says something or other, but that doesn't make it true."

"But what about the grambling?"

"Do you know what *grambling* is, Dolly?"

"No."

John leaned back and crossed his legs. Dolly sat up beside him, and he put his arm around her. "See that squirrel?"

He pointed. The squirrel was about twenty feet from them, sitting up on his hind legs, his pointed nose sniffing the air first in one direction, then another. He was halfway between two trees. John swung his pointing finger over to the tree on the left. "I'll bet you he runs up that tree."

"I'll bet you he runs up *that* tree!" said Dolly, pointing to the other..

The squirrel was in no hurry to run anywhere. It looked quizzically at John and Dolly for a moment, but seemed to find them of no particular interest. It went down on all fours, and looked around at the ground in front of it. Dolly sat forward, rapt in concentration on the gray furry rodent, her hands in little fists with the thumbs tucked inside.

The squirrel took a couple of tentative hops in the direction of John's tree.

"Come *on*, squirrel!" John breathed.

"No!" said Dolly, squealing with excitement. "Turn around, Mr. Squirrel! Mr. Squirrel, *pleeeze* turn around. Look at all the nice big nuts in my tree. *Pleeeeeze* . . . oh, look!" She punched John's arm excitedly. "He's doing it! He's heading for my tree! Come on, Mr. Squirrel. I won! I won!"

The squirrel twitched its tail as it ran along the branch of Dolly's tree.

"He's waving at you," John said.

Dolly waved back. "Thank you, Mr. Squirrel! Oh, let's play again, Uncle John. There's another squirrel."

"All right," John chuckled. "But before we do, there's something I wanted to tell you about. You know, grownups like to play games like that, too. They don't do it with squirrels very often. They do it with a little ball which rolls on a big wheel, or with a deck of cards, or things like that. But they do it a little differently."

"How differently?"

"Well, the way they do it, if that squirrel went up your

tree, I'd have to give you some money. And if it went up my tree, you'd have to give me some money. And that's what they call grambling, or gambling, as some people say.''

"Oh." Dolly thought about it for a minute. "That would take all the fun out of it."

"For you, yes. But some grownups think it's fun to do it that way. It makes it more exciting for them. And that's what your mama does. She has a beautiful big house in New York where people can come and get food and drinks served to them, and meet each other, and play gambling games.''

"That doesn't seem wicked to me. Why didn't mama ever tell me about it?''

"Well, remember what I told you about things always seem worse when you don't talk about them? I think that's what happened to your mama. She didn't tell you about it at first, and then it got harder and harder for her.''

"But why?''

"I guess she wanted to protect you from people like Miss Wilcox, and their ideas of what's wicked.''

"She didn't do a very good job of it, did she?''

John burst out laughing again, and this time Dolly laughed with him; and the sound of her merry, musical little laugh almost made John cry. He stood up, and swung her up into his arms.

"Come on, let's go. We're going to have luncheon at the Wild West show with some of the performers. I'll introduce you to some real cowboys and Indians.''

They sat at a table with some of the strangest and most marvelous people Dolly had ever seen. There were Indians with copper skin and long, black, braided hair. There was a beautiful lady with wavy brown hair and a friendly smile, who wore a buckskin jacket covered with medals and blue ribbons on the left side of her chest. Her name was Annie Oakley, and Uncle John told Dolly that she was the best person in the world at shooting a gun, better than

Buffalo Bill himself. Dolly sat next to her at the table. Annie Oakley talked to her about dolls, and the zoo, and wanted to hear about all the special things that Dolly had in her room in her house in Bronxville.

"You know who Dolly's mother is?" John asked Annie Oakley. "Fannie Divine, of Divine's."

"Really?" Annie beamed, and Dolly felt a warm flood of pride. "That's wonderful. Your mama's a very famous woman, and I hear tell she runs the most honest game in town. Oh, I think that's so exciting. Good for you, honey! Does that mean that Fannie Divine is your sister, John?"

"That's right—my long-lost sister. I only just found out when I got to New York last week."

"Were you and my Uncle John cowboys together, Miss Oakley?" Dolly asked.

"No, not exactly," laughed John. "I was stage manager of a theater that the Wild West Show played at for a while."

"We tried to get him to join the show, but he wasn't interested. He just wanted to play Shakespeare, the big galoot. And call me Annie, honey."

While Dolly went on talking to Annie, John was involved in a conversation with her husband, Frank Butler. The topic was the same topic that was on everyone's mind—Eugene Debs and the strike.

"It could happen in New York," John said. "It's close. I don't think the railroad bosses realize how close it is. And if we get the other unions behind us, it could really happen. A nationwide general strike. The workingman of America is finally in a position to demand some respect."

"God, I envy you in a lot of ways, Whitmarsh," Butler said. "You're living in the present, and working toward the future, instead of endlessly playing out a make-believe past, the way we're doing. Oh, I'm not saying it's not a good life—I sure as hell never expected to be playing in front of the crowned heads of Europe, and I'm not sure I'm ready to see them overthrown just yet—not till they've finished wining and dining Annie and me, at any rate. But still, I think a lot about people who've changed with the times. Like you.''

''I don't know how much I've changed,'' said John. ''I was pretty much moving away from it when you knew me, but my uncles were union organizers. And my father published the *Independence*.''

''Maybe so. But I'll tell you someone who really has changed with the times,'' said Butler. ''I cut this out of the St. Louis paper when we played there a couple of weeks ago.'' He took a clipping out of his wallet, and read: '' 'If there is ever another war in this country, it will be between capital and labor. I mean between greed and manhood. And I'm as ready now to march in defense of American manhood as I was when I was a boy in defense of the South.' Know who said that?''

''No, but I like it. Who?''

''Frank James, that's who.''

Whitmarsh let out a low whistle. ''Frank James. Jesse's big brother Frank. Holy shit.''

''Watch your tongue in front of the child, John Whitmarsh,'' said Annie.

Annie was Dolly's favorite. She came on second, and performed her amazing feats of marksmanship, including shooting the ash off a lighted cigarette in her husband's mouth. But the rest of the show was exciting, too—the Indians, the recreation of Custer's Last Stand and a stagecoach robbery, and the amazing precision drill of the Aurora Zouaves, who wore North African army costumes and climaxed their act by scaling a high wall, forming human pyramids and helping the last man to the top using their rifles and rifle slings.

As they left the huge entertainment palace on Madison Square, Dolly asked her uncle: ''Where is my mother's gambling place?''

''It's not far from here, as a matter of fact,'' John replied.

''Could we go there?''

John hesitated for only an instant. "Yes, I think we can. I'll take you right now."

Robinson opened the door for them, and if he was surprised to see a seven-year-old girl with John Whitmarsh, he did not show it.

"Robinson, this is Miss Divine's daughter, Dolly."

"Hello, Robinson," said Dolly, shyly.

"It's an honor to meet you, Miss," said Robinson in his sonorous voice, bowing from the waist. "Will you be wanting to see Miss Divine?"

"Not right away, Robinson," said John. "I want to show Dolly around a little bit, first."

"Very good, sir." Robinson bowed again, and retired.

Dolly gasped at the high-ceilinged, crystal-chandeliered hallway, with its ornate oriental carpets on the floor, and huge, beautiful paintings in gilt frames on the walls. At the end of the hallway, she stopped before a full-length portrait.

"That's mama, isn't it?"

"Yes. It was painted by a very famous painter named James McNeill Whistler."

"It's beautiful."

He showed her the dining room, which the servants were setting up for the evening meal. It was in the front parlor. The tablecloths were damask linen, the plate silver and gold or the costliest and most exquisite of china, the glassware heavy, finely cut glass. He showed her the gaming room, in the center of the house, a room in which there were no windows, but where a lovely diffused light came in through a domed skylight. And he took her into the kitchen for their supper, which was served to them by an immaculately dressed Negro waiter who was silently attentive to Dolly's every demand.

As they were finishing supper, Dolly turned to John and said thoughtfully: "This is a very pretty place. Mama must be very proud of it."

"She is," John said. "And she has a right to be. She supervised all the decorating herself, and bought all the paintings and draperies and silverware and art objects herself.''

"I don't think I'd want a place like this, though.''

"Oh?''

"No. I'd rather be a cowboy like Annie . . . or like you, Uncle John.''

John averted his eyes, and rubbed them hard to try and force back the tears that were forming in the corners.

"I'm sure your mama will be very proud of you whatever you do, as long as you're happy, sweetheart,'' he said. "Would you like to go and visit her in her office now?''

"Oh, yes!''

Fannie answered the knock on her door in a beautiful brocaded velvet gown. Her hair was done in an upsweep, and she had a diamond brooch in an old gold setting around her neck.

"Mama!'' Dolly cried, and ran to her.

"Dolly!'' Fannie dropped to her knees, and gathered her daughter into her arms.

John left the casino shortly thereafter, and walked down Thirty-third Street. He was met at the corner by two policemen with John L. Sullivan mustaches.

"John Fowler?'' said one.

"What do you want?''

"I have a warrant here for your arrest on the charge that you, using the alias of John North, did wilfully murder a Pinkerton Agency detective named Jack Murphy at Homestead, Pennsylvania, on July 6, 1892.''

"You have what?''

"A warrant for your arrest. Charging that John Fowler, alias John North, did wilfully—''

"Hmm. If you know that much about me, then you must know my real name, too. Why does it say 'Fowler' on the warrant?''

"I don't know about that. Will you come with us peaceably?''

"It's all right. I know. Someone planned this little venture who didn't want my real name used. Sure, I'll come peaceably. What else would I do?"

And as John walked away between the bulky bodies of the two policemen, he heard a newsboy across the street shouting, "Extra! Read all about it! Eugene Debs arrested in Chicago!"

Chapter Thirty-nine

"I'm here to bail out John Fowler."

The desk sergeant took his time checking the records, and finally looked up.

"Hasn't been set yet, ma'am."

Fannie controlled her anger. She had not gotten where she was by losing her temper with cops. "When will it be set?"

" 'Fraid I can't tell ye. Reckon they'll let me know when they get to it, and not before."

"Come on, Sergeant." Fannie made her voice husky, and leaned forward so he could smell her perfume. "You can do better than that for me."

"Not even for you, Miss Divine," the sergeant said. "This one's sewed up tighter'n a crooked roulette wheel. Ain't nobody springin' that bird. He's up for murder in the first."

"But he didn't murder anyone."

"Well, now, Miss Divine." The sergeant leaned toward her, and his voice sank to a conspiratorial croak. "If that's the case, then you *know* you don't have a prayer of springin' him.''

Images flooded Fannie's mind, memories that had not haunted her in years. A little girl, standing at the door of a big house, watching the color drain from her mother's face. Outside the door, a huge, broad-shouldered miner with his cheeks stained with tears . . . *found dead in his cell, mum. They said it were suicide . . . but it were Gowen's thugs as done him in.*

Her father had gone to jail, and she had never seen him again. *If that's the case, Miss Divine, then you know you don't have a prayer of springin' him . . . found dead in his cell, mum . . . they said it were suicide . . .* but that was seventeen years ago. A wild, uncivilized time and place. And that was Franklin Gowen, ruthless, driven by hatred. This was New York. This was . . .

Jamie.

"And who should I say is calling?"

"Fannie Wh . . ." She stopped, stammered, lost her voice. What was her name?

"Yes?" The receptionist was brusque and impatient.

"Er . . . ah . . . Divine. Fannie Divine." One of the most famous names in New York, but she had forgotten it. One of the most powerful names in New York, but in this oak-paneled office it sounded silly and tawdry.

"I'm sorry, Miss Divine, Mr. Whitmarsh is in a very important meeting right now and cannot be disturbed for any reason. If you wish to leave a message for him . . .''

Fannie walked back onto the street. She was reeling, disoriented. She did not know where to go. She felt as helpless and confused as she had felt on the day her mother died, and she had taken little Jamie down to sleep on the barges of the Hudson River.

Little Jamie. He had needed her then, even though he did not know it. He had thought that he was self-sufficient, running with a gang, living in abandoned buildings, sporting the cocksure attitude of a cheap crook, until she had found him, and gotten him into school . . .

She smiled. Then she cried.

She cried right in the street, in full view of anyone passing by who might want to turn around and recognize the notorious Fannie Divine, the toughest woman in New York. She cried, and she was Fannie Whitmarsh, weeping for her mother who had no strength, who had only wanted a little pleasure in life and a man to take care of her; for her little baby brother Jamie, who needed so much love because he had none to give; for her dead father, and Johnny driven away from home.

Fannie would have taken care of all of them, if she could. She would have built a home for them, where they could all be safe and warm and sheltered from the world, the way she had done for Dolly.

But Dolly was no longer sheltered from the world. And Jamie and Johnny hated each other.

Yes, it was true. Her Jamie, and her Johnny. Each could destroy the other, given the chance. But Johnny had not taken his chance, and now it was Jamie's turn. He had the power.

But even as she wept, Fannie Whitmarsh was conscious of another part of her that held back, waiting its turn. She did not want to acknowledge that part. Fannie Whitmarsh was helpless, as she had always been helpless, against the manipulation of the little brother she loved so desperately.

She could no longer afford to be helpless. She could no longer afford to be Fannie Whitmarsh, even with her family. Jamie thought he had power and influence, did he? The bright young man on Wall Street, the boy wonder of the corporate boardrooms, the social lion of Newport? Let him try to match his power against the back rooms of the police department, and City Hall, and the Tammany clubhouses throughout the city of New York. Let him try to match his power against Fannie Divine. He didn't begin to know how overmatched he was.

Chapter Forty

Samuel Gompers, president of the A.F.L., came to Chicago for a conference with twenty-four other trade union leaders on the question of whether the A.F.L. would throw its support to the idea of a general strike. What came out of the conference was official A.F.L. opposition to sympathy strikes in general, industrial unionism as put forth by Debs and the A.R.U., and the idea of a head-on struggle between labor and capitalism. As a sop to the workers of the A.R.U., they voted to contribute $1,000 to Debs's legal defense fund. The *Chicago Tribune* vindictively, but accurately, headlined the story:

DEBS STRIKE DEAD
It Is Dealt Mortal Blows By Labor

John Whitmarsh was ushered into a small room at the end of the Centre Street police station. Waiting for him behind a table was a huge man, immaculately dressed in the handiwork of a Saville Row tailor, but with the flat nose and bearlike frame of an aging prizefighter.

"I didn't realize I was so important," John said. "Have they found out about the plot to overthrow the government and make the ghost of Karl Marx president?"

"You're free to go, Fowler," said the other. "It turns out it was a case of mistaken identity. And I suggest that you get out of town on the first train that leaves Grand

Central Station. You could even hop a freight. They're all running, you know.''

"Thanks for the advice. But I've got some business to attend to before I leave town."

"It's been done."

"Not all of it."

"Fowler, do you know who I am?"

"I've seen your picture."

The huge man spoke slowly and deliberately, looking straight into John's eyes. "I don't mean that. Look at me, Whitmarsh. Do you recognize me? Do you know who I am?"

Startled by the sound of his real name, and caught by the intense, hypnotic gaze of the other man, John looked hard at him. He felt something eerie, along the back of his neck. He did recognize the man. There was something uncannily familiar about his features. He had seen them before . . . but not on this face, not on Mayor Big Bill Henderson of the city of New York . . . somewhere else. *Where?*

Finally, John nodded, and his voice was hoarse and garbled when he tried to speak. He had to stop, cough hard, and start again.

"Yes, I know who you are. I've been wanting to meet you."

"Then you know why I'm here. And you understand what I'm saying."

"She doesn't want me to go after Jamie."

"Precisely. If it were me, I'd say go ahead. I don't know you, and perhaps I should care what happens to you, but I don't. I'd just as soon sacrifice you to get that little snot out of her life once and for all. But things being the way they are, I'm just telling you to take the advice I'm giving you."

John shook his head. "There's too much at stake."

"There's nothing at stake, you damn fool! It's done. It's all over. The strike is finished in Chicago, and there's not going to be a strike in New York."

"The hell there isn't! This is no game, Henderson! The wage cuts, the union busting—"

"I tell you it's been done. The New York & New England Railroad has rescinded its last wage cut, and they've made an agreement with the union that there'll be no more cuts for the next two years. That is, they've made a pledge to the workers. They won't recognize the union officially, though they've made separate agreements with the old brotherhoods. It's the best you're going to do."

"Jamie agreed to that?"

"He wouldn't have, if she hadn't put a gun to his head."

"What do you mean?"

"She threatened to tell the world about you. *And* about her. I guess he knew she would never even hint at that, unless she were serious. And Tammany played its part in the deal, too. A man who wants to do business in this town still has to make damn sure he doesn't get on our shit list, and your kid brother got the message in words of one syllable."

"It's not enough."

"It's all there is. Don't worry, that little prick's going to have his share of explaining when this gets back to the other members of the Railroad Managers Association. They'll think he sold them out."

"And the railroad workers?"

"They'll think *you* sold them out. That's how it goes, kid. It's all over. And if you're thinking there's a personal score left to settle, forget about that, too. She won't allow it. And she's holding the cards. If you want my advice, she's doing you a big favor. If you try and go after Jamie, nobody'll see it as a personal thing. It'll be like that crazy anarchist, what's-his-name, Berkman, taking a shot at Frick. It'll set your cause back so far that they won't even be able to organize sheep dogs in Montana. Just go, kid. Get out of town. It's all over."

John sat in silence for a few moments. Then he stood up.

"I can pick up my belongings at the desk?"

"Yes. And one more thing, kid . . . Whitmarsh . . . John . . ."

"What's that?"

"Well, I wouldn't want to see anything happen to you. I know . . . I know how you feel about her, and what you've done for her. And she told me what you did for Dolly."

"Yes . . . well . . ." John began, but he could think of nothing else to say.

Bill Henderson stood up, and stuck out his hand. John took it, and they gripped hard. A few moments later, John was out on the street in the blinding sunlight of a New York summer morning.

He walked across the square, blinking his eyes, stretching to work the kinks out of his muscles. New York seemed small, suddenly. He wanted to get out of its constricting streets and buildings, and back to the West. In his mind, he was already heading for the switching yards, picking out a rattler and riding it until he came to a place where the air was so clean that not even the railroad smoke could foul it.

He came out of his reverie. Not yet. He could not leave without saying good-bye to Dolly.

And as his mind grounded itself in New York once again, he looked around to discover where he had taken himself, in his aimless wandering, and realized he was in front of the offices of the *New York Sun*. He walked in, and walked back to the editorial offices. He recognized the man he was looking for instantly. Tall, courtly, handsome, white-haired and white-mustached, still lean and erect in his mid-sixties. Eyes that were clear and kind. John strode over to his desk. "Mr. Swinton?"

"Yes, I'm John Swinton. What can I do for you?"

"My name is John Fowler."

"I've heard of you, of course. But your face is very familiar, although I don't believe we've met before."

"My real name is John Whitmarsh."

Chapter Forty-one

John spent the afternoon in conversation with his father's old mentor. He found himself telling Swinton the story of his life, of the social unrest he had seen, and the battles he had taken part in.

"Sometimes I wonder if it's all worth it," John confided. "It takes so much out of you. And in the end—what? I hear the workers in New York are saying I made a deal and sold them out."

"That's what I've heard," Swinton agreed. "They'll do that. They've done it to me, they did it to Gene Debs, they'll do it to anyone who stands up and shoulders the responsibility. There is so much need, so much need, that no man can fill it. All I can tell you is what I told Debs: "They'll break your heart."

"And what did he say?"

" 'I'll not let 'em,' were his words. 'I swear that in this labor struggle my heart can only be broken by myself, and that can happen only if I prove less than true to myself. I can stand anything for labor, and I desire neither office nor honors nor rewards, only justice for the American working-man.' "

"Bravo!" said John.

"That is just what I said," Swinton told him.

"I don't know if I could say the same," John said. "I think maybe they have broken my heart. Or worn me out. So many losing battles."

"I'm not so sure," Swinton said. "With every battle, labor draws closer together. Could there have been such a strong industrial union as the A.R.U., if not for the model you showed them at Homestead when you organized the skilled and unskilled workers alike into one great strike? Workingmen all over America took notice of that. If you keep up the fight, you'll build on what you have done before. And if you leave it, and that is your right—it's the hardest struggle there is, and it does wear a man down—then others will build on what you, and others who fought with you, have done. It cannot be taken away from you, or from the story of labor's progress."

Dolly took the news that John was leaving again better than he thought she would. "I know . . . you're going to help people so they won't have to work so hard and suffer, like my grandpa did," she said.

"I don't know what I'm going to do, sweetheart."

"Then maybe you'll go back to the West and be a cowboy again. But you won't forget me, will you?"

"Never."

"And someday I'll come out and find you. And we'll be cowboys together. Or else we'll help people together."

It was harder for Fannie. She cried.

"I'll see you again," John said. "You won't lose me this time."

"I hope so, Johnny."

"I want to thank you for . . ."

"Don't, Johnny. I did what I had to."

"And thank Henderson for me. He's all right, Fannie. I liked him. And I can tell that he loves you. He'll stand by you. And you'll stand by him."

"And you, Johnny?"

And him? What could he say? He knew no more than the next day, maybe not even that. He wanted to go back to Texas, to see his wife and son. Would he stay? He wished he could think that he would. But he doubted it. He would still be moving—less and less sure, as he grew older, of what he was searching for.

Bestselling Books for Today's Reader — From Jove!

____ **THE AMERICANS (#8)** 05432-1/$2.95
John Jakes

____ **CHASING RAINBOWS** 05849-1/$2.95
Esther Sager

____ **GRAVE MISTAKE** 05369-4/$1.95
Ngaio Marsh

____ **LONGARM ON THE SANTE FE** 05591-3/$1.95
Tabor Evans

____ **MASADA** 05443-7/$2.95
Ernest K. Gann

____ **SHIKE: TIME OF THE DRAGON (Book 1)** 04874-7/$2.95
Robert Shea

____ **SHIKE: LAST OF THE ZINJA (Book 2)** 05944-7/$2.95
Robert Shea

____ **THE WOMEN'S ROOM** 05933-1/$3.50
Marilyn French
